TOY GUN

Other books by Dennis E. Bolen

Stupid Crimes
Krekshuns
Stand In Hell
Gas Tank & Other Stories

When you got a good friend
that will stay right by your side
Give her all of your spare time
love and treat her right

—Robert Johnson

[1]

THE BUILDING WEPT RAINWATER down vertical hectares of fresh concrete. It blocked the skyline, a raw minaret uncompleted; windowless, cluttered with mud-stained plywood; its gray head, storeys upward, indistinct against the sodden sky.

At mid-block Barry Delta drew into its private dusk. He stopped walking and gazed high, catching the wet-newspaper smell, strongly earthen, even from across the breezy thoroughfare. As he jogged to it on rain-shined pavement, his man leaned from a window of the overhead construction shack and called: 'You work Saturdays?'

Barry looked up. He could see that his man's jacket bore the shoulder-flashes of a private security firm. A lull in the traffic allowed him to answer: 'Only for special cases.'

'Is there any way I can be less special?'

'I might consider it if you let me into this place.' Barry glanced down the street at a phalanx of approaching cars. 'I'm going to get splashed.'

'Push on that big piece of fibreboard with the holes in it.'

'This one here?'

'Yup.'

A wide entranceway gaped. Barry stepped quickly through, almost overshooting the catwalk alongside the works. Below him was a floors-deep mud-darkness where cars would soon park. With his long coat billowing on an updraft, he found a wooden footbridge into what he saw would be the apartment house lobby. As he stood among rubble and idle tools his man emerged from the shack, now wearing an official-looking hard-hat and holding out another in his hand.

'You have to wear one of these.'

'Am I going to get hit with anything?'

'You never know.'

Barry took the hat and positioned it to a sporting angle on his head.

'When you said random visits . . . ' The guard gestured around him. 'I guess I didn't realize to what extent.'

'You do now.'

'On a weekend, yet. A federal civil servant sacrificing a Saturday afternoon. You get overtime?'

'Don't sweat it . . . ' Barry twirled, sweeping his eyes about the surroundings.

'My last parole officer handled everything by phone.'

'I like to get my hands dirty.' Barry grinned and looked downward. 'Or in this case, my feet.'

'I can sort of see that.' The man glanced at Barry's clothes. 'Is that a riot stick in your pocket?'

'Umbrella.'

'You're walking?'

'Yup.'

'No car at all?'

'Sometimes. When I need one.'

'I thought you guys always rode.'

'There's nothing wrong with public transit.'

'If you say so.'

'I take it you're driving?'

'Oh yeah.'

'Well I hope you don't mind spending all your money just to keep it on the road.'

'Nope.'

'It's way more expensive than people think.'

'I don't care.'

'It's not just gas and oil and tune-ups . . .'

'You don't have to tell me.'

'Taxes. License. Insurance. It's impossible to park in this town . . . '

'Yeah yeah, but I don't care.'

Barry noted by the man's tone that a pre-anger boundary had been crossed. He lightened. 'Motor enthusiast, are you?'

'You bet.'

Barry smiled. 'Well at least you're excited about something.'

They stood quiet for a moment and Barry noticed that aside from the traffic noise, muffled behind the high plywood barrier, the site held a tomblike hush.

'I take it we're alone here?'

'Yup.'

'So . . . ' Barry looked around again. 'I know we covered this at the office, and I have read the file, but hold my hand through this again. On jobs where they don't work weekends they get a private security firm to watch the place?'

'Yup.'

'Just you?'

'Sometimes there's a couple of other guys patrolling. Somewhere. They come and go.'

'What's the name of your outfit again?'

'Big Dog.'

'Big Dog Industrial Security Incorporated.' Barry spoke the full company name with his eyes half-closed and skyward, thanking his memory for just one more fortunate moment of uncharacteristic recall. 'How long's the shift?'

'Twelve hours.'

'Make a lot of money?'

'Hah!'

'You get by, though.'

'Depends what you mean by getting by.'

'Rent paid. Food. Smokes. One movie a week.'

'I sort of get by. It helps not to smoke.'

'Good man.'

'But I'm not getting rich, that's for sure.'

'That's okay.' Barry looked around them, further into the gloom. 'Is there anything fun to do here?'

The man gestured upward. 'Wanna go to the top?'

Barry stepped to the side of the building. To look sufficiently upward he had to tilt his head to the point of imbalance. He touched a few fingers to the clammy wall beside him. 'Way up there?' His sight-line straight-edged into a murk that never ended.

'Yup.' The security man peered at Barry. 'You're not afraid of heights are you?'

Barry looked firm into cold eyes. 'Not yet.'

'Okay then.' The guard turned and strode along the side of the works, past carpenter tables and cutting machines.

Barry followed close. The occasional naked lightbulb hanging from makeshift electrical works was the only source of illumination as they strode through the core of the building. Barry tried to calculate how many floors there were. 'Is the elevator in yet?'

'Not the inside one.' Barry's escort pulled a strap and a metal mesh panel slid upward, revealing a cage. 'But this one is.'

The construction elevator was attached to the side of the building with what looked like too-flimsy brackets and too-slender guideways. On the way up, the various rattles and bangs gave Barry more shivers than he expected. He was wishing he'd stopped at the bar for a quick one, booze-breath be damned. Near the top he actually began to tremble and turned his head away from the increasingly vertiginous view. 'I used to value my life . . .' Barry found that the simple act of speaking helped fight the apprehension.

'What do you mean, Mr. Delta?'

'This far up in the sky you can call me Barry.'

'Oh okay . . . This thing is pretty safe.'

'You know, I felt exactly that. In the common-sense kind of way.' Barry forced himself to peer through the grate below his shoes. In the general grayness they were too far up to clearly discern the ground. 'I mean, I guess it wouldn't pay to have workers routinely killed trying to get to the jobsite. But in my gut I know I'm closer to death than I was ten minutes ago.'

'Yeah, well. I suppose you never know.'

'That's not what I want to hear from the guy operating the lift.' Barry tried to chuckle but couldn't quite muster it. 'But you're right. I guess you never do know for sure. But I'm in the business of trying.'

'Trying to do what?'

'To know.'

'Oh.'

'I mean of course you're right, one never knows. But I'm trying to go against the natural rhythm of never knowing for sure, even though I know it's useless.' Barry tossed his hands around, glad to be distracting himself. 'The criminal justice system doesn't accept the kind of maxim that says you never know but I happen to be convinced it's practically an absolute. The system tries to defy this natural law with manipulations of what is applicable and calculations based on some kind of criminogenic actuarial probability. They think that if their agents, such as me, fulfill certain bureaucratic and surveillance-oriented procedures, the likelihood of someone like you re-offending is minimized to the point of an acceptable risk. Get it?'

'Of course I do.' The man spoke without looking at Barry. 'In the joint we got all that kind of attention for quite a while. I'd be stupid not to understand some of the philosophy behind it. But thanks, I think, for your version of the explanation. Nobody ever gave it to me like that before.'

'You're welcome.' Barry had barely listened to what had been said, even by himself. 'When do we get to the top? My knees are near to buckling.'

'Oh . . . So that's why the big yak-yak. You're talking away like a sociology prof just to keep your mind off this carnival ride, eh?'

Barry was able to smirk. 'Over-perceptive people can be annoying.'

'I bet you get told that yourself.'

'Never.'

The cage lurched, halted and settled for a second. Barry had a solid instant of trepidation and was more than glad to skip from the carriage and follow his guide close across the rooftop, stepping amid rubble and cast-off lumber.

A stack of metal-framed windows dominated one side of the platform. 'When do they put those in?' Barry asked, pointing, glad for any prop to support conversation.

'Already got a few floors done.'

'I didn't notice.'

'They're all open. Letting the tile grout dry. One of my jobs next week is to close 'em all.'

'Big responsibility.' Barry's remark came out sounding a little too wry. He regretted it immediately.

'It actually is.' The man spoke with a tilt of resentment.

Barry purposefully brightened. 'Well I'll tell you one thing. It's one of those better-you-than-me situations. I wouldn't want this job.'

'It's not so bad.'

'How many floors up are we?'

'Forty-two.'

'Jeesh. How many metres is that?'

'I don't know. A hundred and fifty or so. It's almost four hundred fifty feet, I know that.'

'Higher than I'd ever consent to live. In an apartment. Waiting for the elevator. Up in the sky.'

'Some people seem to like it.'

Barry stepped carefully toward a massive flapping tarpaulin. 'Nice tent.'

'It's a shelter for the workforce.' Barry's escort came and stood beside him. 'And it covers the elevator shaft. There's stuff there they don't want to get wet.'

Barry looked at the sky around them, feeling oddly joined with it at this elevated vantage point. The rain had ceased for the moment, but black storm-heads were dominant. In the hard breeze he could smell a coming downpour. 'It'll be doing its job a few minutes from now.'

'Is it gonna rain again?'

'I'd say that's highly likely.'

'Not just any PO, huh? Weatherman too.'

'This is Vancouver, friend. In the middle of March.'

'Point taken.'

Barry felt a fat raindrop hit his face. He put his hands in his pockets and made for the tarpaulin. His guide came with him and the two stood for a few moments and watched heavy droplets splash upon the bare concrete, plywood and the plastic-wrapped windows. Barry said: 'Why'd we come up here again?'

'Beats me. Wanna make a run for it?'

'Down, you mean?'

'Yeah.'

Barry turned up his collar. 'Does that thing have an emergency speed?'

'Going down it feels like it's going faster.'

'I'm not sure I like the sound of that.'

The rain knocked loudly as they bolted for the cage. There was a modicum of shelter at one end of the box but Barry didn't go for it because it would have meant standing too close to his car-mate. He needed to look the man over. He tried to note any changes from the first time he'd seen him in the office. That day he'd been dressed in black leather and jeans. He thought there had been tattoos at the wrists. He tried to remember. In the semi-light Barry could see no body art that the uniform didn't cover.

'Where's your tattoos?'

'Huh?'

'I thought you had tattoos.'

'You must have me mixed up with somebody else.'

'Could be. I sure see enough jailhouse tatties.' Barry decided not to think too hard about it that far off the ground.

A minute and a half later they bumped to stillness at the bottom of the shaft and darted for the interior of the building, shaking off the wet. A corner of the future lobby had a couple of folding chairs and a desk.

'So let's talk awhile.' Barry picked up a chair, flipped its back to the desk, and straddled it. 'You've got time, right?'

'I guess so.'

'I mean, do you have rounds or anything? Reports to make? Stuff like that?'

'Yeah, but not now and when I get around to it.' The security guard took a seat. 'It's you who shouldn't have the time. It's Saturday for chrissakes. You got no life?'

'Work, life . . . .' Barry spoke with deliberately comical hand gestures. 'Life, work . . . lots of guys have no identity other than their jobs.'

'You don't seem that type.'

'Yeah, well. Maybe. I don't know. In a world-weary way, if you know what I mean.'

'I don't know what the hell you're talking about.' A smirk. 'I wouldn't be surprised if you don't either.'

'Perceptive.' Barry grimaced slightly. 'Good for you. But you can relax a bit, please, and don't worry about my leisure situation. I have plans for later. Saturday-type plans. The sooner we do a polite conversation together the sooner it can be the weekend for me.'

'Conversation about what?'

'Sit tight and you'll see.

'Okay.'

'I don't mean this to be punishment.'

'No?'

'It can be a pleasant interlude.'

'Okay.'

'You don't believe me?'

'We'll see.'

'We're not getting off to a good start.'

'Let's just get it over with.'

'As you wish.' Barry shuddered under his raincoat at a gust of moist wind. 'How did you get this job again?'

'My cousin. He's good friends with the owner.'

'And the owner's name is . . . ?'

'Al something.'

'That's not enough of a name.'

'I thought this wasn't supposed to be punishment.'

'Not for either of us. I'm trying to do this job with the greatest possible dispatch. You may or may not understand that, but given your demonstrated perceptive powers I'd think you would. So I'm having trouble comprehending your attitude, here.' Barry let a tense silence set in for a second. 'Now do I have to explain why I need complete names?'

'I just don't have it right now.'

'I suspected that and it's something that is quite all right when couched in more respectful terms. I would therefore politely request that you get the name to me by Monday. Or even Sunday. Or even this afternoon. Put it on my voicemail. You have the number?'

'I think I still got your card.'

'I'll give you another if you don't.' Barry sat straight. 'Roll up your sleeves, will you.'

'What?'

'I could have sworn you had tattoos.'

'I told you. You got me mixed up with somebody else.'

'I have you mixed up with everybody else. Everybody's got at least a couple of jailhouse masterpieces.'

'Not me . . . ' He pulled his uniform sleeves to the elbows.

Barry looked carefully at the clean arms, noting no suspicious scabbing or bruises near visible veins.

'Satisfied?'

'Yes, but I think I'm losing my mind.'

'Honest enough mistake.' The guard rebuttoned his cuffs. 'You must see a lot of guys.'

'Lots and lots. So many I can't remember.'

'Remembering must be a big part of your job.'

'Yeah but there's forgetting, too. That's quite a necessary skill.'

'Huh?'

'So many faces, so many life stories. You guys. You come and go, it's like the old Johnny Cash song . . . I've seen 'em come and go and I've seen 'em die . . . over and over. It gets to be like your brain is an overcluttered hard drive. You have to erase some of the data banks so you can let other information be stored.'

'I've never had the problem.'

'Good for you.' Barry head-gestured at the surroundings. 'So I guess your boss Al something knows you're on parole and all the rest of it, right?'

'He knows some.'

'How much is some?'

'He knows I was in the joint.'

'And how is it that a security guard business can afford to hire a freshly minted ex-con?'

'My cousin talked me up quite a bit.'

'Thank heaven for family loyalties. Nevertheless, don't you guys have to be insured or bonded or something like that? Don't they do a criminal record check?'

'Sure. I guess. But it's not a problem.'

'How did you get bonded? Does this Big Dog outfit have a blanket insurance policy? Sometimes that's how you can get around it. Every employee is covered by virtue of their employment kind of thing. Is that what's going on?'

'Must be. They said there was no problem.'

'No problem until there is a problem.'

'Well, I try not to go around looking for trouble.'

'There's no need.' Barry sniffed. 'In my sad experience it comes looking for you.'

'I guess in your business that's more like a rule than any kind of exception.'

'Well said, but I don't believe for a minute you're uncertain about it. You've been around long enough to know what the score is. Refresh my memory. How old are you?'

'We went over this at the office.'

'My memory isn't the best. Let's take it from the top one more time. I think you're about thirty-two . . . '

'Thirty-four.'

'And a relatively fresh-faced, vital version of that age you are. I wish I could say the same for myself.'

'You don't look so wrecked. For a burnout.'

'It shows, huh?'

'Do pen time. You get good at spotting them.'

'Yeah well . . . For your information, I burned out several times already and always came back.'

'You say that like you're proud of it.'

'Damn right I'm proud. Every time I come back I'm better. Even if I'm worse.'

The man ignored the quip.

Barry hardened his expression. 'You don't like talking, do you?'

'I wouldn't go that far.'

'You seem not to readily respond to lightness.'

'What are you talking about?'

'During this conversation I've made several funnies. Light ones, admittedly, but good enough cracks nonetheless, throwaway *bon mots* if you will, that anybody normal might at least smile at. You just ignore it all.'

'Humour is a subjective thing. Don't I get any choice?'

'Well you should ask. Your choice seems to be to try to be in control at all times.'

'Is that bad?'

'It is when you're talking to your parole officer. It indicates things.'

'Like what?'

'Like you're not listening, for one. That you're dumb enough to think you can do it, for another. That you've got your mind made up, for still another.'

'I'm not getting you.'

'Just listen. I'll tell you a little more about supervision theory. The fact you don't laugh at a joke is a serious indication of possible wrongness.'

The security guard scoffed, averted his eyes.

'It says to me that you are resisting any and all exterior influences. If you were hanging with a bunch of scuzz-bags I would be impressed, but you're a loner, right?'

'Yeah.'

'And presently you are in the presence of someone who might be the only person on the planet who even vaguely knows you. A person in a position of trust, who you have no reason to think isn't interested in the common, the general and the individual good. Are you with me on this?'

'I guess.'

'Put simply, I can't help derive, from your lack of humorous affect, that you're up to something.'

'Man, that's quite a leap.'

'I know it sounds bent, but I've been around a few decades.'

'I'd like to hear you put that argument to a parole board.'

'I have in the past and I will again.'

'I'd like to see it.'

'No you wouldn't.'

'Oh yeah. I guess I'd have to be in the joint to get a ticket to that particular show.'

'Right you are.'

The men paused, each breathing deeply.

The security guard took off his hardhat. 'You can lose me real easy, the way you talk.'

'That's not what I heard. I heard you took a lot of courses in prison. University, et cetera. Read lots of books and all that kind of stuff. Did I hear wrong?'

'I spent my time as best I could. Got most of a BA in poli-sci.'

'Very good.'

'It's no big deal.'

'I heard you were some kind of near genius in some ways.'

'Well I know what's what, for chrissakes.'

'Okay . . .' Barry could not help his bemused derision to show on his face. 'What is what, then?'

The security guard shook his head. 'I don't think I understand about half of what we've been talking about for the last ten minutes.'

'Well, never mind all that stuff. I kind of get sidetracked with bullshit, I'm sure you might have noticed. I'm more interested in inspiration, the kind that improves life, that keeps a guy alive.' He paused again. 'You mentioned you like cars.'

'Right.'

'So what else keeps you alive?'

'I don't know.'

'I'm actually talking about insight, here. Or intuition. Something I sense you understand full well.'

'I really don't know what you're looking for . . . Intuition?'

'You know what I'm talking about.'

'Sorry.'

'Well okay, I'll go first. At this exact moment my intuition is working full steam. Know what that means?'

'Nope. Can't say I do. Do you know something special or something?'

The rain had increased, splashing loudly near the exposed concrete around them. A thickening vapour misted from the empty elevator shaft nearby. Barry flipped up his coat collar against the sopping breeze and hardened his face. 'I know you're up to something.'

'Huh?'

Barry caught himself being pleased at the alarm in the man's face. It was only there for an instant but he saw and duly recorded it.

'What do you mean 'Huh?'' Barry raised his voice above the weather sounds. 'You know what I'm talking about.'

'I've understood goddamn little of what you've been saying since you got here.'

'No need to get testy.'

'I don't know what else to do.'

'I explained community release forensic management to you. You said you understood.'

'Yeah but . . . What do you mean by "up to something"?'

'What has it meant to you when others said it?'

'Quit playing games.'

'Right you are.' Barry sat back in his chair. 'Straight out. No games. I like that approach. Please forgive me if that is what this feels like. I sense that you personally, despite whatever other intrigues might be up, would not play games under any circumstances. Let me be the same kind of guy to you. We'll start from the beginning. Precisely what was the offense you're doing time for?'

'Don't you know?'

'Of course I do but just play along. Please.'

The guard shoved his hands in his pockets, looked at Barry and sighed. 'Robbery.'

'What kind again? Armed, wasn't it?'

'I faked a weapon, never carried one. I was a junky in those days. Lay off.'

'Forgive me again but I must tell you that there is a palpable sense of blockage between us at this moment and I cannot help but see it like a brick wall down the centre of the room. It is just that real to me. Don't be greatly alarmed by all this talk of intuitive certainty et cetera, it's something I've developed over the years like an extra arm or something and it counts for exactly piss-all in terms of your continued liberty. I mean, the parole board needs better proof than my gut feelings in order to re-incarcerate.'

'Thank christ for that.'

'It may surprise you to know that I agree. But that is still another complicated philosophical argument for which we haven't the time right now. Suffice it to say that my instincts, nevertheless, are not to be ignored. I display all this to you openly in the hope that you'll take warning and desist.' Barry paused. 'Any chance of that?'

'You're fucking crazy.'

Barry rolled his eyes and threw up his hands. 'So many guys have said that over the years. People from all points on the criminal continuum.' He sobered. 'When was the last time you did a piss test?'

'What?'

'You heard. Urinalysis.'

'Talk about changing gears . . . '

'You said yourself what a pity it is to work on a Saturday . . . ' Barry spoke rapidly and without humour. 'Answer my question so I can get out of here.'

'What was my last urinalysis?'

'Yeah.'

'You should know.'

'I do know but I want to know if you know. It's important to me that you keep personal track of these things.'

'I tried when I got out.'

'In what sense do you use the word 'tried'?'

'I went there and that clinic you sent me to was closed.'

'I recall being quite careful in giving you the correct hours of operation. They're set up to offer a full range of convenient attendance times and urinalysis services for the most discriminating conditional releasee.'

'You don't have to try to be funny about it. I'll go on Monday.'

'You must go on Monday. I cannot over-stress the importance. You were a junky once . . . '

'Yeah. You know that already.'

'Of course, but I'm getting old and mentally frail. I need to hear it again.'

'Sheesh . . . '

'And besides, you'd be damn surprised how these stories change with the tellings. It's amazing. Just about the only story that doesn't change for most people is the actual truth. Lies warp, truth stays true. You see my method here?'

'Yeah yeah.'

'All right. What other types of drugs?'

'Some.' The man rolled his eyes. 'But junk mostly.'

'Cocaine?'

'Oh yeah, I guess. Once in a while. Not lots.'

'Now you see? That's not what you said last week.'

'You didn't ask me.'

'I did too.'

'Well, I forgot.'

'Forgot you did other drugs? Or forgot to tell the truth?'

'About the drugs.'

'All right then. So it's true, you have glimpsed the ugly countenance of poli-addiction.'

'That's a nice way of putting it.'

'I try to be delicate in everything I do.'

'You're not doing very good at it today.'

'Oh come on.' Barry made an effort not to smile too wide. 'You can take it.'

'I don't like going for piss-tests.'

'Nobody does. And I dislike sending you. For my money it is an offensive part of the job, mandated by fools who themselves don't understand the parole officer's job and so assume nobody else does either. In my book a good social worker knows the caseload well enough to sense the presence of mood-altering agents and takes the appropriate action in some more dignity-saving manner.'

'You're a strange one.'

'I'll take that as a compliment. But you still have to go for urinalysis.'

'Thanks a lot.'

'Just consider the clinic a giant urinal.' Barry smiled for the first time in many minutes. 'Think of going there not as a punishment but as an opportunity. Consider it a justice-system desecration ritual wherein you ride the bus uptown to deliberately piss against the great wall of authority. Get it? I order you to go for a u/a, you go and piss on the government. Nice, huh?'

'Fuck!'

'You drink water and coffee and then take the longest, foulest, most retributive whiz you can think of while a qualified lab-tech looks on.' Barry grimaced. 'Yech. Supervising piss samples. Could you do that job?'

'They get what they deserve.'

'That's a funny comment.'

'Anybody who takes a paycheque for watching people piss must have something wrong with them.'

'People say that about my job and the people I work with, i.e. yourself.'

'They don't know what they're talking about.'

'Ergo?'

'Ergo, I guess it all goes around in circles and I guess I might understand what you're saying. But I do know what I'm talking about when I'm talking about urinalysis. I pissed in lots of bottles.'

'You have, huh? What other stuff have you been addicted to?'

'Chocolate bars.'

'We don't have a test for that but I can usually tell by the complexion. You've kicked, I take it.'

'This is stupid.'

'Oh heck no. If I've learned anything it is that everybody has some kind of habit. It's what's kept me employed for more than two decades.'

'What's yours?'

'I asked you first and I don't buy the bit about the chocolate.'

'I already told you. Drugs. Junk. Simple as that.'

'I need you to think a little harder about it. A lot of people, everyone, can get hooked on even just the kind of behaviour you develop after awhile. Bad behaviour. Guys get to love it, all the knocking around, never mind the drugs. I'm sure you've taken all the programs . . . '

'Programs up the whazoo . . . '

'Programs up the ying-yang, of course. And they told you about addictive behaviour, crime cycles, impulsivity, blah blah?'

'Till my head spun.'

'Good. Then you know what I'm talking about.'

'No I don't.'

'Yes you do.'

'We can go on like this all day.'

'How did you look during those robberies?'

'How did I look?'

'You heard the question.'

'I wore clothes.'

'Same ones all the time?'

'No. Well . . . sometimes.'

'Were they just clothes, defining the casual you or the at-work you, or were they a disguise, the Bozo-the-Clown you?'

'They were my real clothes.'

'So you the ordinary citizen were the same in visual appearance as the junky and as the robbery suspect. You were everyone and all of yourselves sticking up those banks.'

'I guess you could say that. I didn't think about it at the time.'

'Did you ever think about it?'

'I thought lots, once I was in the joint.'

'Only then? Or did you plan these jobs thinking that if you just went as you were, people would think you were actually someone else? I mean, who would rob a bank dressed as themselves?'

'I didn't think about it. I didn't plan. I just did.'

'A man of action. Admirable in a way.'

'I got caught. That was the worst action of all.'

'Thank you for your candour. You don't see the idea of taking what does not belong to you as wrong in and of itself?'

'They had insurance.'

'What exactly was your procedure when you did these "I just did" robberies?'

'Procedure? I told you, I faked a weapon and got the cash.'

'What words did you use to indicate your intention?'

'I guess I said "Hand it over", or "Gimme the cash", or something like that.'

'Were all your victims employees of banks and retail places?'

'Yeah.'

'What was the proportion male to female?'

'They were almost always female.'

'You'd say "Gimme the cash" to a female?'

'I'd add a little extra. You'd always try to pick the one that looked the weakest. I'd say "Listen bitch . . ." I'd bully her a bit and tell her to gimme the cash.'

'Would your technique vary if you'd been having a particularly good or bad day?'

'These are pretty funny questions.'

'We're getting to know each other. Especially me you.'

'Why don't you just go through the motions, like your pals in the jails?' The man scoffed. 'Just phone it in. Nobody I ever saw in the system worked so hard. They didn't take the time to learn shit.'

Barry shrugged. 'I've always striven to be different. So bear with me. I want to justify my comment to you earlier about your likelihood to re-offend.'

'When did you talk about that?'

'When I mentioned that you were up to something.'

'Aw c'mon. You were just shooting in the dark.'

'Blind firing is nearly all we do in this work, my friend. If it was simple, if it was all written down somewhere in a manual, they'd have sent an accountant to supervise you. As it is, you might find me obnoxious in the way I seek to know every detail.'

'If you want it, you got it.'

'Please listen.' Barry changed his tone and he noted with satisfaction that the man had adjusted his own demeanor alongside. 'I know too much about you already. You and a host of other offenders past and present. I can think like you, for chrissakes, sometimes I have to consciously stop myself from doing it. When I imagine what you're up to I do it in your voice, practically. It's like living a live nightmare half the time, but that's my talent. I'm not much for paperwork, by the way, but I can get inside a guy's mind like Houdini.'

'That's just weird.'

'Nevertheless, if things go well for you, if you make it, you might just find you don't mind my company in that head of yours.'

'You were going to tell me why I'm up to something?'

'Of course. Now in the business we know that with an addictive type like yourself there are determinate characteristics. Ritual, habit, a certain joy in the predictability of it all. Criminal acts can become addictive in and of themselves, particularly when a scared little boy inside a grown human gets to frighten little girls out of their panties with his big bad threatening behaviour. I see it all the time. A guy turned on by violence or the threat of it or the effect of it on otherwise innocent folks can be just as ruthless pursuing that kick as a drug addict in search of a fix. And there are things that go along with this type of behaviour which deeply concern community correctional types like me. Like the fact that the mood-altering result of these acts is like a drug itself, causing a distortion of perception. The feeling of well being inside an otherwise dangerous, out-of-control situation. A failure to recognize that there are better ways of relating to people and getting your thrills, et cetera. And all this adds up to a guy who might not have complete control of himself. A guy like you.'

During his monologue Barry watched his man carefully. There had been wipes of the mouth, averting of eyes, blinks and shiftings of position. 'Do you follow any of this?'

'I guess.' The watchman steadied slightly when he spoke. 'You're pretty well-versed in this stuff, aren't you?'

'You may never know how much.'

There was another quiet patch.

'So you want me to go for a piss test.'

'And supply the full name of your supervisor.'

'And you want it done fast and for sure. Is that right?'

'You've been listening. Good.'

'And that will keep me out of jail. Right?'

'For now. In the long run we can never know.'

The beating of the rain continued. The mist from the elevator shaft had become fog. The prospect of a strong drink at the Yale beckoned Barry now in a serious way.

Barry's companion turned toward the inside of the building and gestured at the moisture-issuing gap. 'That's never happened before. Must be a way heavy downpour.'

'I should think about leaving before I'm even wetter than I'm going to get out on that street.' Barry stood and handed his hard-hat to the security guard. 'Is there anything more I can say to you or explain before I go that would make things more clear?'

'No.'

'Sure?'

'I'm sure.'

The reply was nearly lost in the increasing rain-roar.

The regular job of British Columbia's temperate eco-system is to create the planet's greatest softwood production. This requires all-season watering. On otherwise clear spring days, fluid-heavy clouds typically cruise the treed hillsides, dumping their loads in a virtual target-specific pattern to best slake the thirst of the earth's most lush evergreen grove. When the clouds blunder into the city, the skyscrapers trap them as great weeping zeppelins above the street, causing block-long flash floods that exceed the storm drains and send office workers fleeing with wilted newspapers over their heads.

In the sky above Barry's conversation, a concentrated, purposeful precipitation enfolded the building. The upper floors became obscured from street view. Vapour penetrated the open stages and anointed even the ceilings and especially the pipes and conduits and angles, dripping downward and collecting in ten thousand puddles. The process created water bodies of dimension, coursing toward the slightly canted centre, the major hole of the elevator shaft.

On the roof, the wind no longer had much effect on the tarpaulin, now holding hundreds of litres of water. Tufted ripples of collected rain swished about the surface, creating ever more expanding ponds and then conjoining in a Jacuzzi-sized blister near the centre, the bulge bellying heavy upon the sawhorses and two-by-four workbenches with their superimposed tools sharp against the plastic skin. A final weight of weather howled down from the blackest cloud and the jostling perforated the membrane and then a rip tore quick and issued water to the elevator hole and down, sloshing out a sucking exit loud like a monster tub drain, downward to the lobby.

Barry was making for the outside when the rushing sound developed. 'What's that?' He and the security guard looked up and around as the main bulk passed the lobby opening on its fuming way downward to the parking levels.

The bulk of the water struck the works at the bottom and spewed back up and out the doorway in a misting jet toward the men. It shot above the floor in a knee-high fanning arc, wetting the security man and seeking the fleeing Barry, who now stepped finely along the catwalk to the wooden door. As he reached the portal and wrenched it open the rush hit, flinging the wood wide and away from him in as much of an automatic convenience as Barry could imagine away from a supermarket. There was serious damp at his calves. He ignored this enough to make a show of turning to bid goodbye. The security man stood in ten centimetres of water and in an oddity of reflected light the stream appeared to writhe a shiny path from the dark figure directly to Barry's own feet. Disallowing the image to stay with him too long, Barry further ignored his wet Doc Martens and turned back to his escape. The door swung gurgling closed behind him.

The street was momentarily clear of traffic. Barry turned up his collar to the wind and strode across the way in the direction of the bar. In the time it took to walk the block the rain had stopped.

[2]

IN THAT YEAR Barry owned one of the high stools under the blacked-out blinded windows along the far wall behind the soundboard. From here he had an unimpeded view of the stage where the bands flowed out their R&B, but was far enough back not to have his eardrums blasted in. Here too was a direct sightline to the jumbo TV. Scotch, ale, hockey, the ball sports; all to the ubiquitous blues. This was Barry Delta's Saturday.

The Yale's heavy warmth and enfolding guitar sounds embraced him on this particular Saturday as he slid in from the damp. Barry stopped as he usually did to face toward the bar until acknowledged by his favourite server, Rikki, and only when she returned a smile did he slide off his coat and take his place. Then Rikki came with her serving tray—a big glass and a little glass—and then a version of "Sweet Home Chicago" to dissipate the cerebral aftermath of this afternoon's work session. Soon Barry thought no more about the security guard.

He finished his drinks and waved for more.

Rikki.

She conveyed the glasses down to the terry-covered table with liquid dexterity. 'There you go, sweetie.'

Barry drew money and held it out.

She took more than was needed and did not give back change. They smiled together.

Barry sipped at the little glass, watching as she went away. He allowed himself his usual silly desire. He drank to get rid of it but there it was: a teasing, testy, annoying conversion in the muscles of his stomach and the hairs on his skull. A visceral awakening when all he wanted was mental sleep. He scowled inside, unsure at what.

But if it was anything, Barry thought, it was his vicious knowledge of the folly of ever thinking to strike up with a skilled bar waitress. Half the parolees had made that mistake. Barry had known about Rikki over a boozy few years. In all that time, as fond as Barry had become of her and as generous as his tips became, their conversations had seldom exceeded the tens of words.

So in his forgetting, there were drinks and more drinks and drinks more. Barry's favourite beer was the local bitter if they had it. A good pint was a fine thing but most times a side whisky was the only way to complete comfort. Beer and scotch. Boilermaker heaven. He knuckled a shot glass and play-grimaced with each slug, enjoying the sting. He sipped the beer. The whisky felt particularly good today; the smoke of it in his nostrils, slight bite in his mouth, velvet burn spreading lovely from his centre.

From Barry's seat he could peer through the slit of light showing between the window blinds and their casings. He gazed to the darkening street and beyond, stared hard the two blocks to the top of the inky hulk he had just been washed out of. Even at a distance it dominated the view. Open floors and the mostly glassless windows sucked gloom from the clearing sky. The wet concrete had a singular black-hole quality, drawing light from the ambiance. He shuddered, mystified as to why.

Then there were familiar people around for book-and-movie chat, general gab and gossip. Rikki returned many times. Through the alcohol, Barry began to sense query in her mind about him. The looks she gave. Maybe it was vapour, imagination, wishful yearning, he couldn't be sure, but the cognition of her interest would not leave his mind. On one of her trips he said: 'You're the only honest person I know.'

Rikki giggled and Barry saw that his comment had been taken as goofy drunk-talk. He was lucid enough to appreciate her wisdom. He smiled cooperatively and went back to himself.

After four-and-a-half hours Barry drank back his last, clambered on his raincoat, saluted farewell to Rikki and glided happily to the door. Outside, full darkness had come. Home beckoned and would doubtless be the better choice. Barry laughed to himself and barked aloud—

'Of course it would!'—at this consideration. He raised a hand at a passing cab.

The trip was short. At his destination Barry strode up the walk and pushed the intercom button.

'Yes?'

'Me.'

'Come in.'

Barry pulled the door on the buzz and disappeared from the street.

He stepped into her as soon as the door swung wide and enclosed she and himself into a swaying knot. Her mouth was too warm after the rain-freshened air outside but they kissed away any sense of difference until all was their temperature and all was their friction together.

She worked her hands to his head and rubbed his ears. 'It's getting cold out and you've been drinking.'

'My little Champion of The Obvious.'

'Some women would be offended.'

'You're not some women.' Barry ran hands inside her robe and brushed naked breast, running fingers over snugness and around lovely curves where he could draw her against him and receive the heat-charge through his clothes. 'I am lucky.' He spoke into her hair.

On the bed Barry held her like captured prey, kneeling overtop, heads touching.

He wavered.

Needing to grasp the moment and enjoy, in a grappling mind-fog Barry fiercely re-regretted his blood-alcohol level.

Little happened for them.

He apologized and then mistakenly dozed.

Through a chatty buzz, awakening, Barry knew she was speaking and had been for some time. Though neither his conscious nor his unconscious mind could help him out, he sensed she would not know he had not been listening. He was helped by detecting the particular tone she used when talking about themselves, she and Barry. But now she had asked him a specific question which he had not heard and was staring at him, awaiting a reply. He groaned faintly and shifted.

She repeated the question: 'Is this the real Barry or the purported Barry?

'Aw . . . ' He tried not to sound too rumbly. 'I couldn't answer you the hundred times before. Why do you think I can now?'

'When we make love, when we actually do, I know you're actually here. Completely. It's a turn-on.'

'I'm glad for that, at least.'

'But who is it who is glad for that at least?'

'I don't know what you mean.'

'You know what I mean.'

'No I don't.'

'Come on. Your fervour. Passion. A weird horny eagerness when you want to be inside me. It's really you. But now this blasé irony you exude. You're almost repulsive. Which one is you?'

'My dear. We've had this conversation before.'

'Yes. So?'

And he would get around to saying something like: 'Most women I know at some time or other say they'd like their men to be open. To feel more. And share those feelings. Well, be it known that I've done that. I've shared my feelings. And what happened I should have seen coming and kept my mouth shut. I shared them, sure I did, but they didn't want to hear it. It scared them and they realized they liked their men hard and inscrutable like always and keeping their icky emotions to themselves.

'I mean, I can tell you stuff that should singe your mind. A nice person like you. Horrible. Stuff you'll know right away I should never share with anybody . . . '

This night she made progress with: 'There's beauty in you. You can't hide it. You express it physically, at least.'

'I'm a lapsed cutie. No question about it.'

'Don't be silly. You're a loving man. I can feel it. Sometimes when you're ignoring me and I don't see you for awhile I get it clearer. I don't love you for your flabby body or your alcoholic wit. I love your love. All these misfits you've known and cared about and worked hard for. You didn't just do it for the money. You do it because that's what you are.' She placed a hand flat against his chest. 'It's all screwed up in there, I don't know why but, admit it, Barry, you're a peach.'

'More like a lemon.'

'Stop it.'

'I'm rotten.'

'You are not.'

'Putrid fruit.'

'Don't be silly.'

'You wouldn't be trying to artificially make yourself feel better about us, would you? Forgive me, but you sometimes have the sound of a woman trying to convince herself of something she might not think is true.'

'I was convinced a long time ago.'

'You're sure?'

'Yes.'

He smiled. 'Cross your heart?'

'Stop it Barry.'

'I just don't want you to delude yourself.'

'See, there you go being sweet again. You know you're sweet, don't you?'

'Oh maybe.'

'Admit it! You know you're sweet and kind and caring.'

'Okay, okay.'

'I wish you'd be serious.'

He touched fingers to her cheek. For a moment he nearly palpitated with gratitude, feeling so thoroughly her worth, such loveliness at hand.

On the journey down her hallway he wondered if his unsteadiness was a lasting effect of the liquor or the consequence of being psychically emptied. On the sidewalk past her side of the building, sidestepping a foursome of pedestrians he had an impulse, fought it off, then, striding, turned up to her dark window, he said softly into the thick night: 'I love you, Diane.' Barry was confident no one would hear.

The expedience of a cab was tempting, despite the cost, but it wasn't raining. The nearest clock, on the back wall of a Korean grocery, indicated scant minutes until midnight. Barry fingered the coins in his pocket and knew without looking that there were no bills in his wallet. The cold approach of the wee hours made him think: The money he'd spent! Queasy, Barry pledged a stop to the madness there and then. He trudged for the bus stop, hoping the wait would not be too long and the ride not too trying, looking forward to deep slumber and an inactive Sunday, fighting the idea of going to the automatic teller machine inside the convenience store. He placed one foot in front of the other. He waited ten minutes. When the bus came he spoke to himself of the wisdom of knowing when it was time to go home.

Barry's preferred riding place was by the window on the double-seat side just ahead of the rear exit. If there was need of air this was usually the area that got it. One could well survey the street, yet get a pretty good look dead ahead. Barry had spent many a blessed semi-drunk ride in this seat. Sharing or not, he didn't care. This night, though, there were no vacancies at first and so he stood and then he was able to squeeze himself into the opposing sidelong racks at the rear, looking across at his bus-mates.

Among the usual students, shift workers, drunks, a guy murmuring to himself, readers, and over-scented clubsters, there were a pair of close-cropped starvation personalities. A couple, he could see, gaunt of face and uniformed in black tatters, so startlingly imagistic of concentration camp survivors he could not stop staring. Nor could he banish—through the fatigue and booze-fog—pictures throbbing within his mind from innumerable documentary war films. Forcing himself to turn away, Barry self-philosophized, and could not determine whether he was more intrigued than offended, the other way around, a mixture of both, or why.

He and she looked so much alike, pale and hairless, that Barry had trouble with gender identification at first. Then when reasonably satisfied that one was female he automatically tried to determine if she was at all attractive. After a while he forgot what he was doing and drifted off, enjoying as much as possible his liquor and sex buzz and the bus-rocking of the trip through the watery streets.

He presently caught himself giggling at some random thought, realized he'd been snoozing, and knew then with certainty that the effects of the day's boozing were far from worn off. He looked up and noticed that the bus crowd had thinned and that the head-shaved woman was staring at him darkly. He looked away and closed his eyes, hoping he hadn't snorted anything offensive in his drowsing. The ride continued.

At a stop just before the long run over the Granville Bridge, Barry opened his eyes to watch a woman with red hair get on. To Barry she was dismayingly beautiful. As she approached Barry caught himself staring, reclosed his eyes and scowled at himself. When he opened them again the bald woman was once more glowering at him. She was joined with not as much vehemence by her wan partner.

'You're disgusting!' She spoke with boulder-hard eyes on Barry.

'Huh?' In the ambient noise Barry wasn't sure what she had said, but he could not mistake the tenor of it.

The woman said nothing more, just glared at him and then at her male doppelganger. Barry did not know for a moment what would be best, to continue returning her intrusive look, turn away, or try to ascertain her problem.

Then it flashed on him what her problem was and in the reactionary tradition of over-fatigued drinkers Barry was absurdly angry at himself for even trying to consider her point of view. He sniffed hard and flexed his hands, resisting the urge to bluster. He accepted that because of certain factors at that moment he was not necessarily a right man. But in his mind he was sure, despite the alcohol-exhaustion and his Diane-dallying, that he would never be too far wrong, manners-wise. And there was no way in hell he'd ever apologize for well and dutifully admiring a lovely-looking woman. He made a point of not looking at the couple again. He studied the lights of the marinas below the bridge and then the bus was in a hard turn onto the beach route and he was glad he'd be getting off in a half-dozen uncomfortable stops.

But before anger could make him sizzle too much more, he decided to remove himself from the discomfort. Barry struggled upright and made for the exit, planning in his mind to be careful not to come any closer to his severe examiners than he had to.

Approaching, with a hand at the overhead bar, Barry had a thought about what might happen if the bus lurched at that moment. Even as he considered it, something or someone in the road caused the driver to deke sharply. Barry's sliding grip was easily broken as he stumbled, fingers clutching at the metal and gripping only air. His motor brain reacted, retracting his elevated arm in a hurtful snap. He nearly yelped in the effort to avoid falling, his mind a mélange of desperation and disgust at the silliness of how he must look. But what was worse—in this state of physical and metaphysical non-equilibrium—was where he was headed.

Barry backed heavily upon the indignant couple. The unnecessary misfortune of the moment assailed his drink-soused feelings near to weeping. He tried not to think of the abundant bad karma. The rest of the bus occupants wavered in their seats as the driver corrected, swerving. Barry stumbled aright but fumbled again upon the bristly heads.

Also, the umbrella had tumbled from his pocket. Barry spasmed aside to catch it, and did, but the clutching instinct did not serve him well in avoiding further full body contact. The effort made him twist and elbow solidly the man's head against the window. Surprisingly, however, Barry found the impact provided enough counter-force to finally steady himself.

'Arno . . . !' The woman's voice scored Barry's eardrums.

Barry knew he was in bad. 'Hey, I'm sorry . . . '

The looks in their eyes showed that there was no getting out of this with a simple apology. Barry straightened, leaning with great extension backward to get as far distant as possible. He super-carefully clutched an upright bar and stepped to the exit.

'Don't just walk away! You hit Arno.'

Barry looked back at them. The woman had risen and was pointing toward her companion with a spider-thin finger. Arno was rubbing his head and looking mystified.

'Look, ah . . . Arno.' Barry spoke directly to him. 'I think you could see I didn't mean it. Purely accidental.'

'You're a violent sexist!' the woman nearly shrieked.

The bus had stopped and was loading more passengers. Barry fought an impulse to just get out of there, four stops from home, and walk the rest of the way. Even in his groggy condition, which made him blink his eyes heavily in the effort of thinking, he knew this situation was ridiculous. Then anger took over and he knew he would ride as far as he wished.

'Get a grip. These things happen.'

'Don't try to justify yourself.'

Barry considered for a second. He nearly had a good reply ready when he involuntarily belched a beer burp into the space between himself and them and tried to squelch it, making things worse. He despaired that the gesture must have looked like a giggle or a stifled laugh. He had wanted to say something in reference to the woman's 'justify' comment, but the situation had now gained far too much tragi-comedic weight. Even worse, in his straining attempt to select the proper rejoinder to end this silly interlude Barry had actually begun to giggle.

'You think this is funny?' The woman sputtered. 'You're so disgusting.'

'Look, lady . . . ' Barry struggled for something actually humorous to say but could only manage: 'I've got just one thing to say to you . . . '

'What is that?'

'Uhhh . . . ' He looked hard at the dire pair, drilling away at him from dark, sunken eye-sockets. 'How was the Holocaust, anyway?'

They gasped deep and their eyes got wider. Barry knew now it was time to go. Though the bus was still moving he moved to the exit and put a foot down on the lower step to trigger the door. Then the woman screamed: 'Driver, this man assaulted us!'

The driver was pulling into a stop and had to call over his shoulder: 'What?'

Barry faced the front. 'Never mind.'

When the vehicle was halted the exit door did not open. Barry stepped up from and then back down on the electric runner to operate the door. It still did not open. He hopped up and down a few times but then saw that the driver had unbuckled and was making for the back of the bus. Barry and his would-be apprehenders and about a half-dozen cognizant fellow passengers waited tensely for him to arrive.

'What's up?' Here was the affable-voiced but visibly tired young transit man.

'Absolutely nothing.' Barry was careful to sound moderate.

'What's this about an assault?'

'He attacked my friend.'

'He did?' The driver looked to Arno.

'Tell him what happened Arno.'

Arno was still rubbing the back of his head. He finally spoke: 'It was likely just an accident . . . '

'It was not, Arno, I saw him attack you.'

'Atta boy, pal.' Barry was enlivened at Arno's evenhandedness. 'Just an unfortunate incident among gentlemen, eh?'

The woman stared at the driver. 'I insist you call the police.'

Barry scoffed. 'Aw, come on . . . '

'Actually . . . ' The driver turned to Barry and raised his eyebrows apologetically. 'Policy is that we always call the cops in a situation like this.'

'For crying out loud. They'll take an hour to get here.'

'There's some!' The woman was pointing out the window to where a marked unit sat in the centre of a near-empty supermarket parking lot.

'Okay . . . ' The driver started to speak.

Barry began to understand in his criminal justice-oriented mind that he had to leave the vehicle immediately. Even drunk he could see that the circumstances warranted it, the hazards of the prevailing attitude of excessive political correctitude mandated it, and for the next few seconds the logistics of the situation allowed it. His mind flitted for an instant over the potential images: Police questioning, histrionic wailing from severe-woman, the whining compliance of Arno to his girlfriend's wishes, the bus driver's tired urgency to see this sticky situation come to a close. Barry knew that even if no charges arose from this crazy incident, even if the cops laughed it off, even if he personally knew the officers and they sympathized with his plight, he would be in a spot. The parole service was a paranoid place to be these days. He'd get suspended for sure, pending investigation. Aside from the embarrassment—he prided himself at being immune to that kind of bullshit—the paperwork alone would be a bastard.

Barry shifted his weight and felt a puff of cool air issue from a crack between the flaps of the electric door. He had seen these folding sliders forced by any number of drunks, belligerents and farebeaters. Their flimsiness induced him to try a good push. They gave significantly.

'Stop that, mister!' The driver's voice was no longer affable or weary. Barry stuck all his fingers through the opening and separated the flexible parts with both hands. A hefty push through saw him down to the sidewalk.

He briskly strode at first, but then as the driver and the woman emerged from the bus and hollered to the police car he bolted, jogging in a crouch past the front of the bus and across four lanes of night traffic. He was surprised at his speed and clarity of mind now that the freshening night air patted his face. A few drops of rain tapped at his raincoat. He was down the street and around the corner before he heard the police unit start up.

From where he now was Barry heard a chirping of tires and assumed it was the police car exiting the parking lot at speed. This made him jump, darting across the street and into an alley. As he ran down the pothole-spotted lane he took deliberate pains to brainstorm his position.

It was hard to think. Home was four-and-a-half blocks away. If he could get there without being seen they would never know who they were looking for. There were alleys, back yards and driveways past small outbuildings, gardens, fences, gates and the other little characteristics of a neighbourhood Barry knew well. He went to work thinking of the best route out of this jam. The cops had likely been told he was some drunken rummy type with behavioural deficits. Little would they suspect that the wanted man was a local property owner, not to mention a federal parole officer stagnating on the job for about ten times longer than the average city cop ever had to serve on street patrol.

A glare of headlights knocked these musings from Barry's head and prompted an impulsive leap over a low fence. Before he quite knew he'd reacted he was running through a back yard and along the narrow aisle between houses. Without pausing he stepped between parked cars, bounded across the street to the far sidewalk and high-jumped over another fence.

His breathing was getting heavy. He laboured down through the dark walkway beside a house and into another alley, hoping his luck of access through these properties would hold, and thanking his uncommon luck for having bought a house in a pit-bull-free zone of the city. He jogged as lightly as he could down the alley and skidded stationary at the mouth to search for cars on the side street. He was alarmed at the depth of his gasping, the pain in his throat and lungs. It had been years since he'd run more than half a block.

Barry listened, struggling to discern sounds above his own wheezing. There was silence behind and the street before him was dark and calm. He crossed and continued his alley-run. A few doors down he swerved to deke into an open carport to look back and again listen for pursuit. A blinking police unit flashed past the end of the alley. As it receded Barry noted the blinking red and blue emergency lights glinting off the quiet houses and parked cars.

Gulping deep, Barry resumed his dash to the end of the alley and paused again in order to survey the street, blood pounding loud in his head.

Nothing.

Figuring they might circle back for another run, Barry gathered what energy he had left and sprinted, turning into the street to see if he could make it to the end of the next block. He reached it without the sound of a motor at his back and stepped to the sidewalk and changed course toward home. He sped, but slowed as he approached and passed a couple of pedestrians. Then sped up again to reach the corner and turned sharp into his street. Only three doors to go and a quick sprint into the shrubs and this whole bizarre interlude would be drinking conversation for all time.

Barry heard accelerating tires not far off. He trotted, knowing they would be on him in seconds if they were actually heading in his direction. In four seconds he was at the hedge and through the bad trim-job and into the walkway crossing the courtyard. To get to the door he had to turn behind an overgrown shrub. This made him invisible from the street. By the time the patrol unit rolled by, Barry's key was in the door. Then he was inside, gently closing, locking.

He stood still for a few seconds, looking around him in the dark entry, panting, wavering on his feet, understanding that to hear his heart throb like this was what it was to be so out of shape, drunk and stupid. If they got the dogs after him, he reasoned, the trail to his door would be damn suspicious. He shuddered slightly, standing silent in the dark, but only until he recognized that he didn't care. He understood that this was likely the last vestige of booze-courage left in him. Let 'em come, was his thought, stubbing off shoes and shucking his coverings. His breath came back. He noted the umbrella stand and checking his raincoat was amazed to find his was still there.

Almost but not quite had it become another public transit donation.

Or a piece of evidence in an assault case.

Barry slumped down upon a carpeted stair and cradled his head for a moment. Slowly he found and donned his slippers. By the time all this was finished Barry had begun to forget his crazy flight. He treaded up the stairs and into the kitchen for a drink of cold water. He drank long and then refilled the glass by the light of the refrigerator. The time on the microwave read 1:07. He wondered if he'd missed anything homebound he was supposed to do today. The refrigerator held reassuring quantities of milk, eggs, coffee.

Up the next flight of stairs was the silent bedroom. Barry entered on tiptoe and felt in the dark for the place to put his water glass.

He removed his clothes and left them in a heap before the closet with the dirty-clothes hamper within. Too risky to open the squeaky door at this time of night. He made it into the bathroom without noise.

Barry showered enthusiastically, feeling the symbolism of laving away the residue of his work, the bar-sitting, the Diane-scent, the bus grime, the fleeing panic. These all washed down the tub drain and out of Barry's mind. Teeth brushed, hair towelled, mind cleared, he turned off the light, opened the door and stepped from the bathroom.

'Barry?'

His wife's voice was too ardent to have just emerged from sleep. He was mildly irritated that she was awake and waiting for him.

'It's me. Go back to sleep.'

'What time is it?'

'Does it matter?'

He waited a second for an answer. He doffed his slippers and assumed she had gone back to sleep, stepping to the far side of the bed and sweeping the covers aside.

'Ahem . . . '

It was the private signal he never mistook. The order for a foot rub. In nine years together it had devolved into a simple sound for him in her throat. Tanya loved to have her feet rubbed.

He sought with his clean hands a delicate foot. 'You're awake way past your sleeptime.'

'You owe me for staying out late.' Her voice was pillow-muffled.

'Is it late?'

'Barry!'

'It's not late.'

'Maybe not for you.'

'Not for a lot of people.'

'Ummmm . . . ' She was lapsing.

He worked with his hands. 'Go to sleep, my sweetie.'

'Oooh, Barry. You're such a good foot-rubber.'

'I love your feet.'

'What have you been up to all day?' Her query was half-hearted, though laden with such fatal possibility that Barry nearly lost his breath. He did not answer. Soon his ministrations had their effect. There were no further questions. After a while he felt he could breathe again. His chest eased its pounding. Then his mind took a few mental swings at his heart and there began a savage brawl inside him. It took his soul a good while to break it up. In the past, Barry's women had loved him in their effusive ways and he had returned their tributes with whatever it was he exuded when amorous: He romanced, caressed, coupled, lied. Over time his efforts to change had consistently failed. In a particular swoon of credibility some years ago he'd let himself get married, thinking this might fix things.

Careful not to interrupt the steady pressure on his wife's feet, Barry dipped head-to-shoulder and intercepted a tear burning its way down the side of his face.

He stopped the massage only when he heard faint snoring.

'What have I been up to all day?' Though he knew she was far away from hearing, Barry determined that in answering his wife's last query he would at least not tell a lie to end the night. 'The usual, sweetheart.'

Then again to himself softly as he entered bed: 'The usual.'

[3]

THE SECURITY GUARD had seen the Crime Stoppers ads.

None of them mentioned tattoos or much of anything else. Could be a trick or something. Cops couldn't be that stupid. Could be he was playing a trick on himself by thinking too much. Could be that nobody knows. He stopped himself thinking and coldly selected this day's disguise. Accentuate the positive: why not?

There was the debate he'd been having with himself about the uniform. While a security guard image was an excellent introduction to almost any value-laden venue, he knew that the scam could be played once, maybe twice, but then it was out and dangerous. The media, the police, they'd spread it all around. Everybody'd be laying for a phony cop type. It could even get him busted by such mentally baffled types as his parole officer.

His PO.

Why had he even thought of Delta just now? Was there anything beyond mumbled confusion in that man's inane conversation yesterday? Fuck knows.

But there were more important considerations right now. It was important at this moment to put fire under a few crystals of this most excellent refinement of cocaine. He arranged the configuration and employed the foil and the butane lighter. Then a pregnant chemical pause. Sharpness returned from out the mental effluvia. Thoughts of Delta now were irrelevant.

And on the subject of weather, he looked out the window to see what was happening. Any kind of precipitation would abort the action.

He stepped past the kitchen table and spread half the curtains. Bright sky, light unchained. He craned for a solid view west. No significant clouds.

Okay.

He pulled the box from under the sink and shuffled among the cleansers for lint-remover. When he had it in his hand he removed the paper-roll cylinder and shook it vigorously, slamming it against the table to empty what was in there. The curled papers eventually showed themselves and he reconsidered the butterfly gimmick.

He examined the collection. So many cool designs: Harleys with skeletons; exploding zeppelins; swastikas; charging stallions. Plenty of others. These skulls with dead flowers hanging out of them were so freaky. The best press-on temporary body-art money could buy. A special Internet-ordered purchase all the way from Mexico by courier.

Yes, Mexico. Today in honour of that fact he would parade like a festive artifact from the Day of the Dead. Let the bitches ignore or forget or wet their panties and tell the cops that there were no distinguishing marks but . . . wait. There was something, officer. What was that, Ma'am? He had tattoos. Even though his sleeves were rolled down I saw a row of ugly death heads on his wrists. Or were they butterflies? Well, butterflies or skulls, they were brightly coloured.

He chuckled to himself, washing the skin and wiping the papers with their solution and dabbing his wrists. He was amazed anew at how real they looked. Having seen many tattoos—some professionally done, some crude jailhouse marrings, and every kind of mutilation in between—he was thrilled by the versatility of it all. Instant freak. Instant biker. Instant doper. Instant white-supremacist geek. Instant stockbroker with a tiny rose on the dark side of the wrist. Here he was, instant armed robber, with a disguise that could hardly fail to confuse.

He selected the evening's outfit, fighting the temptation once again to use the security togs. But a good headshaking and an eye-rubbing and another whipping toss-about of his noggin and a sensible choice prevailed; jeans, ratty black jersey, denim jacket with the cuffs unsnapped, extra-long-billed baseball cap. He went to the overflowing saucer he kept for coins and supplied himself with a pocketful of parking change.

Now for one further necessity. He whipped open a kitchen drawer and swept aside the drifting cutlery. Somewhere amid this cluster of chromed metal knives, forks, and spoons and scored plastic egg-flippers was a replica Smith and Wesson .357 Magnum. A thing of dark-blue lethal-looking beauty that, when wielded properly, scared the living shit out of anyone sensible. With a practiced toss of the wrist he flung open the works, spun the cylinder, tossed the piece back together and wedged it into his waistband. There was a mirror above the sink. He drew and aimed at himself in the glass. Even playing, in his touchy narcotic-fired state of mind, he was fleetingly alarmed. The look was that deadly. Especially if the gun was pointed at you by a creep in crappy clothes with nasty tattoos at the ends of sleeves not-quite-covering his arms.

Now to wedge the toy gun into his pants, button the jacket to hide it, grab his special valise with essential items, turn the lights out, lock the door and get to the car.

Now the car, there was something again; a cherry-condition near-antique 1965 Ford Falcon.

Like the gun, the very touch of the painted steel door, the upholstered welcome, rumble-comfort motor-cradle beneath, vibrating metal heart, the hundred joints of rigid body, struts and welds and bolts, steering column and the hard plastic wheel in his hands as he affectionately drove—let him be something he liked immensely. The streets flowed below like magic carpeting. He headed across town. It was always now, on the way, that he thought most about this car and what he was up to and why. This baby needed the choicest gas, designer oil, loving tune-ups, a touch of bodywork to remove rust peeking from around the license plate light, and he needed that blessed product, that refinement of coke. Crack and gas. Drugs and polish, car and driver under the influence of sixties-era Detroit steel and the purest distillations of South American vegetation.

There you had it.

He laughed, wagging himself and machine to and fro along the street.

His mind was a mental pit stop, he regalled. A mechanized oasis of crystalline clarity.

It never lasted though. Too bad you couldn't marshal this kind of essence on a minute-to-minute, as-needed basis.

He drove along, regretting. Then the motor missed a firing as he turned sharp into the downtown stream along Main and there was no more pleasure at all.

Shit!

He'd struggled with this problem for years but the car still hesitated on a sharp right turn. Years. Ultimately, the best efforts of mechanic and owner could not overcome what must be some kind of diabolical design flaw that the makers did not anticipate and never corrected and which always gave him irritation.

Goddamit!

He caught himself swerving, nearly swiped the side off a minivan.

Goddamn the irritation, the drug-wooziness, the loss of fucking control.

It took some blocks, air flowing over his face, cooling, to bring things back.

Funny that. Such big shots like car engineers and they couldn't properly configure as damn good a vehicle as this. Here it was, object of his primary affection, its steering wheel held firmly in his two hands. And not quite all there. The most perfect thing in his life and not in fact perfect at all. He wondered if he shouldn't run the car and himself into a cement wall at one hundred and fifty clicks and finish the whole conflict right there, he so hated the skank logic of it all.

Before he could completely dissipate into nihilism—a state, he was proud to say he did not fear, quite respected in fact, and enjoyed residing in for as much time as he could afford—his destination was in sight and he had to make the decision as to where Baby might be parked. Then he knew he had not completely decided on this day's target. There was a jewellery place he'd had in mind for years and he spun the car around the block a few times amid traffic to survey the situation.

It looked typical. Worthy. And nearby was the perfect parkade to put Baby in. Far enough away so he would not be associated with the car. And not too massive, well attended, no cameras, a stand-alone ticket-machine that would leave no paper trail, a place for possibly a several-day stay, depending on events. He swerved into the gate and proceeded to the top level where he readily found a three-in-a-row gap to park in so there was an open stall on either side. At least for now anyways. It was the best he could do under the circumstances. He went to the machine and pulled a few days' worth of tickets. From the valise he pulled a pipe and a vial. In seconds he had the flame going and a hit was on the way. He freshened. The job for the day and all exigencies possible organized themselves on the digital display of his mind. He saw with exhilarating clarity that he could handle it. Entirely doable. Easy. Hah!

He threw his gear into the valise and threw that into the trunk, the car's interior now free of paraphernalia. In a side mirror he adjusted the baseball cap to a casual-athletic attitude upon his head. The reassuring ritual of it sent through him an enticement toward adventure, action, and probable violence.

There was always the possibility that something wild might take place. Yeah! His audible pronouncement echoed from the concrete walls. He'd been oblivious to anyone observing him. He glanced around to reassure himself that he was alone but for a second he wavered, fear touched his innards and he made the usual mental movements to pretend this was just a silly smash-and-grab, a permanent borrowing of some little thing—Robbery Lite—to obtain a small sustenance for the week. The whole holdup thing, he reasoned, was just a component of his overall physical/psychological self-sufficiency in a wild world full of gainful struggle. Bounding down urine-smelling stairwells onto clean sidewalk he was confident in this mental reduction of things. It all made sense. He felt with his hand where the blue-metal piece was riding secure in his waistband and with walking the movement kissed the barrel perfectly down into his crotch.

The walk from the parkade to the target was four blocks. Maybe a five-minute trek. After such a pleasant drive the foot trip was arduous, taking too long. His feet felt like raw stumps hitting the sidewalk. But he thought for a moment and then things shifted and he decided to make it last. Slow down and let the feet firm up and allow time to focus the mind. Let closing time gracefully approach. Anticipate the set-up. Characterize the bodies. Let the clock tick down gracefully. As was his custom, he strode past the place and looked casually in, not interrupting stride, and continued down the street and around the block to reconnoiter again and remember what he'd seen and compare notes with what he'd see again in a minute.

Then came the most important phase and the one that maintained success for him and had yet to fail. He entered the store as a customer. A doofus-looking one, certainly, a semi-slovenly type not typical of the average jewellery shopper, but it always worked. He did the whole show, gawked at the gems, scratched his head, expressed ignorance at what a carat was, explained his circumstances—'This is for my mom's birthday . . . ' or 'I'm getting married and she has expensive tastes . . . ' —he would chat the charade all the way up to and including the production from his pocket of a credit card. In this case a long-stolen VISA to serve solely as a prop so that they became ripe for surprise, sure in their little minds that this was a sale, not a frivolity, a time-waste or a crime. He kept the card firmly in hand but slightly visible while surveying. And he'd keep looking at a downward pitch, the baseball visor over most of his face, and flash his interesting wrists, getting the sales staff too to look downward a lot. This way they were much less likely to notice him moving his head continually, in a little twitchy circular consistency as if he had a nervous disorder, a generally effective way to thwart those pesky security cameras in case they were actually loaded and working properly.

This day he chose the usual entrance style, stood at the door for a second looking uncertain, then a slow sidle to the wedding rings. The clerks did their usual routine. Though he looked grubby, though he gave no sign of true prosperity, they always thought they were doing a sales hook by feigning interest and romantic rapture at the prospective betrothal of some be-jeaned white-trash geek in from the street. He had reasoned some time ago that it must stem from some type of corporate jewellery-store sales maxim that dictated eager treatment even for those who didn't look like they had money. It was a fact, he knew, that some rich people preferred not to look their part.

Whatever, the sales jerks didn't fool him. He fooled them. He smiled and schmoozed and sleazed as much as they did and felt good by the absolute knowledge he would soon victimize these cretins. Systematically rape them in their heads and/or their bodies. Leaning close onto a stomach-high glass counter he flexed his abdominals against the unyielding presence of the concealed 'peacemaker'.

He sussed the layout, using the corners of his eyes, head low and moving, noting where he'd have to keep the cap-bill to avoid the cameras getting a clear shot. Then he turned to the personnel situation. There was one guy, a kind of thick type and not the standard limp-wrist these places usually had. He might be a problem, due for extra care once the action started. The girl, though, was a pleasing sight. She made him want to lick his chops in anticipation. It was all he could will up from his disciplined memory not to, she was that sweet, plain, open. Not great, though, but just right for him and maybe nobody else. Her smile a little lopsided. Tits too big. A suggestion of moustache. Clothes not fitting right. Over-eager. Kind of sloppy. Sloppy gorgeous. To him, as she spoke and smiled with crooked teeth, just gorgeous.

'Now this one is lovely . . . '

She raised a glittering object to the light, let him admire it for a second, then slipped it onto her marriage finger. As he duly regarded the ring an ambient illumination in the shop consorted into a tiny sharp blast of diamond fire at his eyes.

'Gee, I dunno . . . ' He enjoyed the competent flatness of his own voice at times like these. 'But you've got good taste.'

Then he performed another of his patented anti-apprehension maneuvers. He varied. Before the sales process got too far along he put the VISA back in his pocket and left the place. His leave-taking was as abrupt as possible short of being rude. He did this after perfunctory apologies for a certain state of indecision and not before noting for as much certainty as possible that there was no one in the back. No bosses, jewellery carvers, stockpersons, special customers, deliverymen or couriers or any goddamnbody. Typical Sunday afternoon robbing conditions. And now a varied modus operandi to flummox the cops.

This was important.

It was good to keep the authorities guessing, spread the crimes around so different jurisdictions were always started fresh on them, get different cops from different districts working together or at odds with each other. And ensure the place was undermanned. His style demanded overt control of the resident population, including customers if he was unlucky enough to have some around so close to the end of the business day, but he had no plan for the contingent surprise of someone coming out from the back. You just never knew who you were dealing with, how much they were aware of, what they were prepared to do about it and with what. Flight was the only option and it was conceivable, given the configurations of some of these shops, that there might not even be that. He shuddered at the thought, scaring himself. Then, angry, shaking his head. He felt an encroaching stiffness of the mind. He hurried around the block, ordering himself to do a further fifty seconds of deep breathing before he glanced hard through the window, yanked the jewellery store door open again and forcefully again entered, knowing his reappearance would signal to the staff that he had changed his mind and that a sale was now likely imminent. He scanned for any customers he might have missed: Just one, speaking with the guy at the silverware section. He strode with purpose to the watch counter.

This was another departure from routine. He'd always been a ring thief. He usually went straight for the rings and made the move. He knew he would eventually get around to this today, but due to the tasty sight of the girl he'd separated from his entrenched, tried-and-true procedure. She had in his absence switched from working rings and now stood behind the watch counter. There was just a little something else flitting about in his brain that swerved him, not seriously, he knew, but just enough to want to inject a little variety into the operation. Her face met him with ambivalent greeting; a sickly smile, some quivering of the lower lip. He lurched inside to see this. She was so average, he knew, so not exceptional. And it was just this middling quality that made him know his way into her. Poor thing.

As he thought this, and the drug-power let him absolutely know this, he understood with alarm in the charged anticipation of a job and in the presence of a luscious victim that there had been some other transgression in his mind. An interruption of the machine-solid logic, pushing him from the usual focus he brought to his work. He wondered where this suspicious reprogramming had come from. His attempt at thought now came to nothing; he could not get the wild potential of the next few minutes out of his mind and into a comfortable range of clarity. He knew that despite his best reasoning he would nevertheless go through with this business and maybe he'd regret it. Regret, despite his mental training not to allow the concept of regret into his life at all. At last a clear thought; no regrets about this one, whatever the outcome. He had definitely not regretted the previous four.

Four rip-offs in just over a week. He'd performed well since his release from jail and from the traditional peer method of smash and prance. He felt such liberation in the understanding that the good way to rob was not to gallop down the street, arms laden with crusty stones and gold sand, getting caught because your hands are too full to push the buttons on an elevator or the bag leaks or your shoes are untied or some other such stupidity.

And he had contempt too for the Asian teens and their twelve-year-old compadres who invaded these places, blowing out windows with shotguns and the little kids with their hammers and heavy gloves collecting the stuff into their smart cotton bags and running off to finish homework and wonder what Mom's cooking for supper. They were a freak bunch and ought to be sent back to their own country, wherever that was. The way they did it, somebody could get killed. The way he did it, as rough as it got, nobody was going to get killed. Except him, if he got careless. And in that case who gave a fuck?

He was proud of his style. If only he could get the calamitous thoughts—this girl, this store—out of his head. The day, maybe. Phase of the moon. He couldn't divine it. A function perhaps of his oddness of mind inside an otherwise spiffy armed robbery approach. Prudence would have him turning away. But looking into the eyes of this selection he was bugged anew by the irresistibility of it all.

It was the drugs, maybe.

Whatever.

Time to get underway.

'I'd like to try a Rolex, even though I haven't got the money to buy one because I'm getting married next month.'

'Welcome back. But you better not spend all your money on yourself. You'll need a nice ring for her.'

'Oh don't you worry. I aim to sleaze . . . I mean to please!'

She took the correct second to process the pun, then smiled kindly. 'I'll tell you . . .' She unlocked the watch window and removed the tray. 'You're a cheerer-upper at this time of the day.'

'What a compliment. You're going to make me forget what I came in here for.'

'I don't want to do that!'

'Almost too late!' He smiled at her, thinking of the hot irony she'd single-handedly created in the air between them. His crotch tightened and the tip of his dick poked at the faux weapon in his pants.

She looked at him. 'What kind would you like to see?'

'Huh?'

'Watch. Rolex manufactures an extensive line . . .'

'Oh, I'm sorry. I don't think I'd better. I just came over here to look at them and dream I guess.'

'Can I help you with a ring?'

'You can help me a whole bunch if that's okay.'

'I certainly will if you step this way.'

On the trip to the ring display case he had a further moment of perplexing ethical encumbrance. Then anger intruded and he decided that things would be worse than usual. As she stooped to the key clasp, he glanced into the mirror behind her. The male clerk was just finishing with his customer, bidding adieu. With his back to this action he drew the piece out, levelling it at about the place where her face would be when she came up from behind the counter. She rose. His estimate was perfect, the barrel ended at her nose. She yelped, her eyes expanded impossibly, making her downright ugly as far as he was concerned.

'Never mind the animal imitations, bitch. You know what this is.'

'A . . .' She gagged. 'A . . . gun.'

'No no no . . . a robbery, clueless. A robbery.'

She gulped. 'I'm sorry.'

'Shut your face and fill this with scrap metal, baby.' With one hand he whipped a plastic grocery bag from a pocket and handed it to her. She took it immediately, then hesitated.

'Get to it. Anything goes wrong I plug you and your friend.'

'No!'

He focussed on the mirror behind her. Across the store the other clerk was staring downward, looking like he was writing something on a pad of paper. Either he had not seen anything or was pretending he hadn't. No matter, he'd know all about it soon enough. The girl had stooped and begun picking off the rings from their display trays. She poked each gold circlet into the bag with special care.

'Hurry up!'

'Sorry.'

'Excuse me, Angie . . .' The call came from across the store. 'Sorry to interrupt, but . . .' In the mirror reflection the man was looking square at his back but apparently could not see at this angle what he was holding in his hand. 'Whereabouts are the new inventory forms?'

The girl stayed stooped. 'Um . . .'

He lowered the gun slightly. 'What's his name?'

'Francis . . .'

He swivelled, showing the gun. 'Say, Francis . . .' With both hands he straight-armed his aim direct to the man's face. 'Your girlfriend here has quite a workload. She needs you.'

'Holy shit!'

'No need for profanity, Francis. Just do as I tell you.'

'What do you think you're doing?'

'You start listening to what I tell you Francis or you won't want to know what I'm going to do. If you catch my continental drift, so to speak.'

'Huh?'

'I won't repeat myself again, Francis. You got keys?'

The man looked down as if making a major effort to think.

'Francis!'

'Yeah.' The clerk put his hand in a pocket, pulled it out with a ring of keys. 'You won't shoot me, will you?'

'Not if you do as you're told.'

Francis made a tentative move, then hesitated, staring.

'Lookit you people!' He leaned backward to yank a handful of Angie's hair. She wailed and then held herself silent, eyes clenched closed and leaking tears. With one hand busy and without taking his eyes off Francis he kept aim with his free arm. With a practiced thumb movement pulled back the heavy shining hammer. The click sounded to him positively theatrical. 'I'm not fuckin' around.'

'Okay, okay.'

'Now take those keys and lock that door.' He tossed a nod toward the front.

Francis stepped around the counter toward the glass doors.

He let Angie's hair loose and she fell to her task once more.

'Leave the keys in the lock, thatta boy.' Francis turned the lock and left the keys swinging.

'Now come over here.'

Francis slowly moved across the three metres of floor separating them. A blow over the ear felled him to his knees, eyes popping. He fainted over backward, easing to the floor in a near-viscous motion.

'Hah, hah. Francis you dumb prick.' He grinned at the metal in his hand. 'I said I wouldn't shoot you. I didn't say I wouldn't bash your minimal brains out.'

'Eeeee!' Angie noted the blood developing around Francis' head. She dropped the bag and put hands to her face.

'Stupid cow. Load that bag!'

He rammed the bludgeon into his pants, jumped over the counter and kicked her. She crumpled and screamed into the floor on hands and knees. He grabbed the bag, made sure there was at least something in it, and stuffed it into his jacket. He checked the doorway for any sign of someone in the back. No sound and no movement. No big deal, either. Things were at a point now where if anyone appeared they could just join the party. In the meantime, somebody was going to be touched.

Angie was still on her knees, shaking her head. He selected in his mind the perfect grip and made it so: From behind, a wide-fingered clutch of forehead and hair, with fingers pressing on eyelids and the thumb grinding in at one spot on the top of the skull. She whimpered as he wrenched her head as far back as the top vertebrae would allow.

'Do I need to tell you to shut up?'

The very sound of his words, the doom-sounding resonance of his low tone, made him giddy. He dropped to his knees and laid the knob of his solidified crotch into the crack of her buttocks, getting heated in his mind and in his hair until sweat began, crouched below the level of the counter, out of sight of everyone, wild and close.

'Feel that?'

'Aeeeiii! No, no, no . . .'

'Shut up and relax. I'm not going to fuck you.'

'Please don't . . .'

'What did you say?'

'Don't . . .'

'Whaddya mean don't?'

'Please . . .'

'You want it, dontcha?'

'No no!'

'Say you want it.'

'Please leave me alone.'

'I'm going to. But there's something you have to do first.'

'No, no, please I told you . . .'

He wrenched her anew. 'You're not gettin' the point, are you bitch?'

Her sobs were so deep he could not understand what she was trying to say.

'The point is right here, bitch.' He rammed himself into her. 'Now come to your senses and say you want it, baby. You know what I mean. Say you want me.'

'I want you.'

'With feeling.'

'For goodness sakes . . .' In her pause he noted a change. 'I want you.'

'You sure?' He tried to ignore the strength she was drawing upon in her anger. Time began to stretch. He was becoming aware of its passage.

'Yes yes yes yes I want you okay?'

'Well, okay, if you're sure.'

'I'm sure, now please leave me alone.'

He had hoped for more sobbing, but now she wasn't saying anything. He plowed her from behind again. She shook, repulsed, but did not cry out. He yanked her head in his hand. 'Uh, Angie, let's not lose attention here, I'm not quite finished with you.'

'Oh, fuck off you sick little pri—'

Before she could finish he had hauled out the piece and struck the back of her head, chopping a hammer-style blow straight downward. She stiffened, then went slack. He stood slowly up, letting her hair run through his fingers as she soundlessly fell. Putting the iron back in his pants, he noticed his hands shaking and was glad he'd stopped her from finishing the sentence. Her resistance had softened him in the crotch and made him sad. And now the day was spoiled. He was sickened. Without a backward glance he stepped between the counters, over the silent Francis, unlocked the door and was gone from the place in five seconds.

The sidewalk was normal, refreshing. He cheerily knew not to hurry. It occurred to him that the action with the girl was appropriate given her spirit, her willingness to be defiant in the face of violent odds. If not unconscious upon the floor of her place of employment at this moment, she might actually be chasing him, forcing a showdown from which there could emerge only one winner and one grievously injured or deceased. He took succour from this reasoning and cheered himself back up with the knowing that he had handled things well. In the history of his crimes he had not had to kill anyone. Not that he knew of, anyway. Though this one had involved two head injuries, he was sure he had not gone too far. He couldn't be responsible for people who came apart under the shock, got changed by the tension and were never the same. Some of them might commit suicide sometime, but that wasn't his fault. He pulsed prideful again at his non-lethal robbery methods.

With the bag of jagged objects clunking in his jacket and the chunk working a dent in his gut, he sauntered the street and considered his next move. His mouth was dry. It was another six hours until he had to don his security guard disguise. Time for a beer in a place where he could sneak into the alley or in the can and smoke sufficient rock. He turned a corner and slipped inside a pub, three-and-a-half blocks away from what he considered to be just another job well done.

[4]

BARRY DELTA REMEMBERS owning a car and swerving into an underground parking lot beneath a humming complex with clerks bolting about, bosses and bureaucrats and organizers with meetings on their minds and ubiquitous coffee pots at the ready. This was in the days of centralization, before computers and dependable electronic monitoring.

Nowadays he hops off the bus in the middle of downtown and walks to a near-empty office building. He nods to the elderly commissionaire at his desk in the lobby, then takes an elevator to the fifth floor and opens a locked door that leads to an empty hallway and another locked door. It is the small office space he sometimes shares with another parole officer, but which for the past three months because of reorganization has been his solitary domain. In his little chamber he puts down his briefcase and flicks the power switch on the computer. He pulls the pager and cell phone out of the briefcase or his pockets and plugs them into their chargers. He generally wonders then if he should have gathered coffee in a paper cup from a shop nearby or should he plan to go out during the morning for a break? He hangs his jacket beside the ever-present overcoat on an old-fashioned coat tree by his desk and carefully places keys in his pants pockets so as not to be denied passage through the doorways and checkpoints and controlled entrances he has to negotiate just to go to the men's room in this place.

This Monday morning the telephone rang before he could enter his computer password.

'Barry Delta here.'

'It's Myra, Barry. How are you?'

'Reasonable.'

'That's what you always say.'

'That's what I always am.'

'It makes it hard for a person to tell what's going on with you.'

'You're not a person, Myra.' Barry spoke while typing. 'You're a supervisor.'

'Have you done the March RA's?'

'Thanks for getting right to the point. They're coming.'

'Coming? It's almost May.'

'Yes, it's chaos out there, crime in the streets. And sorry, no, I haven't quite finished last month's risk assessment criminogenic statistical compendiums.'

'You have to finish those reports.'

'Of course. I'm typing right now, can't you hear?'

'Good. Fine. And I have to tell you, I've assigned you a new case.'

'You what?'

'Don't go crazy.'

'Crazy would only be a mild reaction, Myra. Now what the hell did you just say?'

'C'mon Barry. You heard me.'

'We've been through this before. I can barely maintain minimum frequency of contact with the ones I have now. I even have to work Saturdays.'

'Saturdays?'

'It puts a serious crimp into my drinking time.'

'You can't get paid for it. It isn't approved.'

'I don't give a fuck whether it's approved or not. The simple fact is that I'm doing this job as fast as I can and I still get more cases. Who is it this time?'

'Just a young kid.'

'Come on, Myra. You never give me just a young kid. What family did he murder?'

'Relax, he's just an assaulter so far. He's coming out Thursday. It's a touchy case, the board wants extra supervision.'

'The board can take a flying leap. I'll decide what he gets when I see him.'

'Suit yourself. Just get those risk assessments done.'

'Okay, okay . . .'

'You know how it goes in this business, Barry.'

'No. How does it go?'

'No matter what you do, if you don't write it down you never did it.'

'Aw man, what a psychology.'

'Nevertheless. We all have responsibilities.'

'Yeah, yeah . . .'

And I'm sending you the Stickner file today. You'll have it by Wednesday . . .'

'Who?'

'Your new case.'

'Say that name again.'

'Stickner, Wayne Sydney.'

'That's familiar for some reason . . .'

'Hmmm. We don't have any other case by that name. I don't remember one, anyway.'

'Well you were only in the business for what, a year?

'Sixteen months.'

'. . . Before they kicked you upstairs, so I'm not surprised you don't remember. But now we talk about it, I do. A long time ago.'

'How long?'

'Oh, ten years, maybe more.'

'This kid is only twenty. He couldn't be the same one.'

'You're right about that. The one I remember is dead.'

'Not one you arranged, is it?'

'Don't kid around. Rumours are hurtful.'

'Sorry, Barry. It's just that you've got this reputation.'

'Yeah.'

Her quiet told Barry that the invitation was open for him to expand. He remained mute.

She cleared her throat. 'Do you understand your assignments today?'

'Yes.'

'Okay, then . . .'

Barry hung up and turned to his email. Nothing important or interesting. He began a reply to one but found after several scratchy words that he wasn't right in the head. His mind had turned sour at his conversation with Myra. She was young, eager and competent. And he'd been a jerk toward her. He rubbed his eyes and stared out the window. Three more years to retirement. Still a reasonably young man. But the pace of things around here, the paper, the rules, the electronics. They were making him old. No use pushing things. Not in this environment. The idea was to avoid insanity.

He pondered.

Reputation, huh?

The phone rang again.

'Barry Delta here.'

'You have such a sexy telephone voice.'

'Oh hi, Jill. Not half as hot as yours.'

'You say that to all the women. Beth says you said it to her last week on her late shift. And it's rumoured you've said it to Elaine lots of times but she won't tell.'

'Forgive me for saying so, or at least hold off an harassment suit, but your whole crew over there is blessed with voices from sensual heaven. What can I do, lie?'

'You've kind of got this reputation . . .'

'Yeah, I know.'

'But a nice reputation. Nice. Nothing negative from what I hear.'

'Why don't you just base your attitude on what you yourself have personally experienced. How do I come out then?'

'A gentleman.'

'All right.'

'You have an amazingly good name for an alley-cat type.'

'I haven't heard that one since the forties.'

'You're not that old.'

'I'm older than you.'

'Yeah, but you're not that old.'

'How do you know?'

'You're only about a third older than me, that would put you in your mid forties. So you were only born in, like, the late fifties.'

'Right, so I got used to people saying things like golly, swell and gee whiz before I heard all the stiffer terms we use today and once, honest to god, one day in the schoolyard actually did hear a little girl describe a guy as an alley-cat.'

'A fountain of ancient historical information!'

'History is hardly ancient when you've lived through it yourself.' Barry paused to give her an opportunity to comment, but there was only silence. 'Now, what can I help you with?'

'Chantal is looking for you.'

'If she's looking for me why can't she pick up the phone herself instead of having you do it?'

'Two reasons: She's stoned to the eyeballs . . .' In her drawing-in of breath and knowing her as he did, Barry could visualize Jill's transformation to uber-sarcasm. 'And I wanted to hear your sexy voice.'

'Fair enough.' Barry made a performance of ignoring her dig. 'Guess I should get over there.'

He hung up.

It meant a trip.

And the paperwork would again have to wait.

Oh well, it was time to get coffee anyway.

Barry stepped off the bus in an area close to the beaches. He strolled for a block and a half past fine old houses, some immense. On one of them a sign by the door said: Ring For Entry. Without a pause Barry whipped the door open and strode on in. From the hallway a set of glass doors opened on the sitting room. Several inmates lounged there, some new ones he had not seen before. Barry noted their visual inspections of him, the half-averted, half-stoned, half-caring, half-hostile looks. He tried not to notice that a couple of them might be pretty.

Jill was on the phone when he got to the office. Jill was pretty, and for Barry had become an object of discomfiture. He took a seat and tried not to look like he felt, suffering, bothered. To him she'd become a good-bad distraction, heavy but encouraging, like pockets full of power tools. She finger-twirled the phone cord and her hair, looking away from him. He squirmed, taking only slight enjoyment that in his middle age he could still get naturally Viagra-ized, like a teenager. He almost didn't notice when she hung up and spoke to him.

'Thanks for getting here so quick. She's at least awake now.'

Barry wasn't thinking. 'Chantal?'

'Who else?'

'Was she asleep before?'

'I'm sure I mentioned she was under the influence.'

'Of what substance?'

'Unknown.'

'Where has she been?'

'Claims a job search.'

'Do we know this to be true?'

'No. And she's evasive about who, where and what.'

'Anybody seen her hooking?'

'Nobody who would tell us.'

'But if she's high it's the only possible scenario. She's not exactly employable.'

'Well, she's high. That's all we really know.'

'For my part that's enough to get going and doing something.'

'That's why we called you.'

'Was she high last night?'

'Of course she wasn't.' Jill rolled her eyes. 'Otherwise we'd have called the overnight duty officer. She was cool as a zucchini last night as far as we know and the six o'clock bed checker didn't report anything.'

Barry rubbed his temples and tried to compute what was of most concern in the room while doing his best to slough off his annoying attraction to Jill. 'What are you telling me?'

'You know what I'm telling you.'

'Yes, I know what you're telling me but I don't want to know.' He nodded toward the room full of housemates. 'Do you think she got it from one of the lounge lizards?'

'Maybe, but that's beside the point. Rules are rules.'

'Okay, but I have to piss-test her.'

'Of course.'

'It's taking four days or more to get results.'

'What?'

'That's right.'

'What happened to twenty-four hours?'

'Some kind of legal ruling. They have to revamp the whole system.'

'That makes it tough.'

'I'll say. And they're giving us heat about frequency. Too many urinalyses and we blow the budget. I have to get extra clearance, be absolutely sure, do collateral contact interviews, et cetera. In a case like Chantal's, where her offence involves the slaughter of innocents, or at least the murder of her tricks if they don't behave, I can sometimes make an exception and get it sooner. Not always, though.'

'I'll have to alert the executive director.'

'She likes me.'

'Hah, that's funny. What did you do to her, anyway?'

'I've never been anything but professional and courteous to her. And the one before her. And the one after, I'll testify right now.'

'She gets mad if somebody even mentions your name.'

'I have that effect on women. Especially ones my own age.'

'Aha . . .' Jill's expression was genuinely uplifted. Barry could see that something made solid sense to her. 'I finally see.'

'Glad I could clear this up for you.'

'You sort-of have.'

They sat for a moment, smiling at each other. 'Meanwhile, rules are rules.' Barry spoiled the silence. 'What are we going to do with our beloved Chantal?'

'Rules are rules.'

Jill stood up. 'Let me clear the way.'

'Absolutely.'

'Give me three minutes.'

Barry waited in the office with the door open while Jill ran up the stairs. He heard her steps above him for a few seconds, then her footfalls on the second flight of stairs and then they faded in the general hum of the house. Then she called down to him and he proceeded up the stairs.

Jill motioned to him from a doorway. In the room a housecoat-clad young woman lay facedown on an unmade bed.

Barry stood close by the bed and spoke downward to the back of her head. 'Chantal, do you realize what you've done?'

'I didn't mean to.' Her voice was muffled and blasé. 'I just got a bit stoned.'

'That's not all you did. You got us kicked out of this place.'

Chantal turned over and stared blearily at Jill and Barry. 'Why?'

'You know why.'

'No I don't.'

'Yes you do.'

'Quit playing with me.'

'But it's a good way for me to find out how far-gone you are.'

'I'm not far-gone. I took something to sleep better.'

'Something that you maybe had on you last night?'

'Maybe, I don't know. Something I had from before.'

'This is getting worse,' Barry sighed, looking around. 'Isn't it Jill?'

'It certainly is, Mr. Delta.'

'The evidence is piling up that our friend here has violated the cardinal rule of any good community resource facility.'

'One of our stiffest rules.'

'Yes. Thou shalt not bring drugs into the domicile.'

Chantal moaned. 'They searched me when I got here and didn't find it so it doesn't count.'

'Hmmmm . . .' Barry looked at Jill, bemused.

'Okay, Chantal.' Jill smirked back at Barry. 'This isn't some kind of game show, here. You can take your choice. Be guilty of bringing in drugs or guilty of hiding them. Same thing. Immediate discharge.'

'Not so immediate . . .' Barry interjected as subtly as he could. 'We have to wait for the test results.'

'The book says forty-eight hours.'

'I think I mentioned it might take longer.'

'Anything longer will have to be approved by the house manager.'

'Whatever, we need some time. We've gotta get some kind of interim arrangement in place. Tell it all to your manager. If there's trouble, let me know. The only alternative is city lockup.'

Chantal moaned again and sat slowly up. Barry tried to remember if she'd been this thin the last time he saw her.

'Losing weight, dear?'

'No way. I feel like a cow.'

'Oh, that's right.' Jill turned to Barry. 'Chantal has something to tell you.'

'Oh?'

'Yeah!' Chantal spoke more a whine than a word. 'I'm pregnant.'

'What?'

'You have to get me an abortion.'

'I do?'

'You're my PO aren't you?'

'That I am. I just don't know where it says I'm supposed to get you something like an abortion just because you tell me to.'

'You have to do something.'

'I would agree with that. I have to do something.'

'And fast. I'm in the eighth week or something . . .'

A resident passed slowly by the open door. Jill and Barry suspended their conversation for the time it took for her footfalls to fade down the stairs.

Jill turned to Barry. 'Maybe we should take Chantal down to the office and discuss this.'

'Good idea.' Barry stepped toward the door.

'I don't wanna go anywhere.'

'Then stay right here, Chantal.' Barry spoke quietly. 'I'll let you know what we come up with.' He let the statement settle for a moment. 'I guess I should ask, though, officially. What do you want to do?'

'With the baby?'

'Yes.'

'I can't get stuck with a baby.'

'You're sure?'

'Look at me.'

'I am . . .' He looked at her small body on the bed. He'd ignored the bruises on her arms and a nasty scratch on her knee. He swallowed and said: 'I see a woman capable of caring for a child if that was what she really wanted to do.'

'You do not.' Chantal sniffled into a sleeve of her robe, as if she had a cold. 'Get me an operation.'

'I'll have to talk to your doctor. I'll have to get you to approve in writing.'

'Show me where to sign.'

'It's not just that, it's the whole thing of it.'

'What are you talking about?'

'Sometimes people need therapy after an experience like this.'

'Experience? Barry, you know my experience.'

He stood dumb for a moment. 'I do?'

Jill chuckled.

Back in the office Barry slumped into the couch and Jill took her chair at the desk. She ignored the ringing telephone, closed the door with her foot and said: 'So why was it you got into this business?'

'It's so long ago I forget.'

'Oh don't be a baby.'

'Please don't mention children.'

'This happens all the time.'

'Funnily enough, this is the first time for me.'

'What are you going to do?'

'Why is it just me who's got to do something?'

'You can't just wallow in despair.'

'Excuse me for wallowing here on your couch. I'll try not to get anything on it. Just gimme a minute and let me think.'

'There's still the other thing to deal with.'

'I know, I know. Can you help me with that?'

'I can't get to the manager about it until the end of my shift. That'll give you a little time.'

'Hmmm. She likely won't bother us overnight. That means it'll be morning or even tomorrow afternoon before she checks on what's going on.'

'Plus, she's busy with some kind of accreditation exercise so you can pretty well count on a day's grace before she tracks you down on the phone and lets go the decree. So from there you have another two days. That runs into the weekend.'

'Perfect . . .'

'Though difficult for the staff. Chantal's been irritable, a veritable bitch if you want to know the truth. Maybe it's the pregnancy.'

'She was bad before, don't worry. I've had her in two other places.'

'A real challenge, huh?'

'So much so that I'd recommend additional verification if possible. Can we fit her for some electric jewellery?'

'Hmmm . . . monitoring program's going through staff shake-ups.'

'They were never that good anyway.'

'Minimal help at best, but . . .'

'Better than dick.'

'Better than dick.'

'So what do you say?'

'I'll have to get a hold of the EMP coordinator to see if they have a bracelet available and whether or not they'll have sufficient staff. It's a bit of bother. Not my job, but the sort of thing I'd do for a friend.'

'Such as me?'

She regarded him wryly. 'You think you are . . . ?'

'Yup.' Barry smiled.

Jill's hair splayed luscious past her shoulders like in a shampoo commercial. 'I can see in your eyes.'

'What can you see in my eyes?'

Jill laughed. 'You're thinking of asking me out.'

'I couldn't do that.' Barry paused, unsmiling. 'I'm married.'

'Right answer.'

This was a day of the month when Barry got himself down to the harbour district for a nosh of good fish. He stepped off the bus and made for the best eatery he knew, a place cluttered and busy and the air ocean-steamy with many decades' redolence of seafood cooking.

He slid into the last available seat, in a booth across from a casually dressed man in his fifties.

The man looked up from a menu and furrowed his forehead at Barry. 'You keep being late you'll have to sit out on the street.'

'Gimme a break. I'm looking for an abortion.'

'What do you call that job of yours?'

'Thanks for the charity . . .' Barry grabbed a menu and opened it, burying his face between thick plastic covers. 'Of mind and spirit.'

'Charity's for social-worky types.'

Barry looked at the man. 'I've seen you get soft for the right kind of rummy.'

'Only my father.' The man looked back at his menu. 'Now what are you gonna have, so I can order something different.'

Barry didn't have to look long at the menu. 'Cod.'

'Go for the good stuff. Halibut.'

'Too expensive. Might as well have prawns.'

'Now you're talking.'

'Well if you go for that, why not go crazy and get the Alaska crab?'

'I heard that stuff has aluminum or phosphorous in it. Or something.'

'Mercury. All fish has mercury. Twentieth-century industrial pollution. A known fact.'

'I thought that was just fresh-water fish.'

'Everything, is what I heard.'

'Yeah, well . . .' The man put aside his menu. 'I'll just have the chowder.'

'Oh I'm sure that's low on base metals. Maybe I'll have that too.'

'We both can't have the same thing.'

'Who made up that rule?'

'Nobody. It just makes good sense.'

'You're getting a distinctly It-Doesn't-Have-To-Make-Sense-It's-Just-Our-Policy flavour to you.'

'Speaking of flavours I see they got that oolican grease potion on the menu. That's that fish-gut supergoo the natives cook up in a hollow log on some godforsaken beach up north and they let it rot real good and fester away and then they sell it. Ever had a taste of that?'

'Can't say I have.'

'It'll put hair on your eyeballs if you survive.'

'I like fish, but . . .'

'You'll never know for sure until you sniff this stuff. You'll feel like a dead salmon just swam up your ass. You burp ocean currents for days afterward. The time I had it I sweat herring juice so bad we had to change the bed sheets. Cats followed me everywhere. My wife almost left me. It was glorious.'

'I'll just bet.'

A distracted waiter made it to their table, bringing tea and water. Both men ordered.

Barry sipped his tea. 'Where's your suit?'

'They got me on Attack Force this week.'

'With all the young guys?'

'Yeah, they need a mature type for this job we're doing. I'm the oldest by like twenty years.'

'It's starting to happen to me all the time. 'Specially when I meet my supervisor.'

'How young could he be?'

'She.'

'Oh no, they got a girl telling you what to do?'

Barry hoisted his tea in a toast. 'Three years to retirement.'

'Don't start talking like that. There's no way a punk like you should be on a pension.'

'Nevertheless, there I'll be. Fifty and gone.'

'Well, don't gloat about it or this fine example of inter-departmental law enforcement info-sharing will coming to an abrupt fucking end.'

'Have it your way.'

The food came. The place was so loud they nearly had to shout to talk.

'You guys particularly busy?' Barry spoke with his mouth full of fries.

'Pretty much, but not as bad as usual. Why? Need us?'

'Maybe.'

'Somebody on the rampage?'

'I got a guy with a history of holdups. I'm pretty sure he's faking tattoos. Anything like that showing up on the cameras?'

'What do you mean, faking?'

'He's one of these guys with the attitude that us simple servants are a bunch of decerebrated drones. Thinks I didn't notice he had tattoos one time I saw him and none the next. Sleeves. Probably rolls his shirts up a little so you can see some but not all, and gives the impression of some big brawny body-illustrated exhibitionist biker. You know the type.'

'Oh, you mean the scared-little-boy-psycho-momma's-boy-dick-head-fuckface-haywire-ridiculous-heatbag-with-childhood-issues kind of offender. I gettcha.'

'Whew!' Barry raised his eyebrows. 'Anyhoo, if you see anything like that . . .'

'I'll skip over to the general investigation floor and look up their security photos.'

'Thanks.'

'Think nothing of it. Might be reasonable information, even if it does come from you, my friend.'

Barry beamed. 'Nice to be thought of that way.'

[5]

THEY LOLLED, BARRY sealing their moisture with a knee clamped in the join of her legs.

He closed his eyes, noting daytime sounds through the cracked bedroom window: cars rumbling at slow speed, distant idling delivery trucks, footfalls and fragments of conversation. The whisper of a bicycle pedalling past. When he opened his eyes, Diane was looking into him with an expression he'd seen before.

He saw love in there, but it was a thing he knew to be no good to him. It was almost embarrassing. He fought the nervous impulse to giggle, and kept silent out of respect for Diane, who at times nearly smothered him with the vigour of her affection. She was a warm and giving and smart woman who through charming circumstance—an art opening, Barry in attendance because a parolee had gotten himself a show at a gallery interested in helping street people—had come to be his lover. Diane, he later learned, was the accountant for the place. They'd observed on colours and the validity of folk art and quickly found out they shared an interest in sex. Months had turned to two years. For Diane he knew that as their comfort together had grown the situation was as undesirable for her as she could ever contemplate. And because he was terminally blocked, limited in the extent he could give, at a loss as to what to do, he was certain of the doom coming up fast on their horizon.

Diane kissed his wrist. 'I've been having baby thoughts again.'

'I guessed.'

Barry kissed Diane's forehead, hoping she might forget what she was thinking.

'I just want to talk about it.' She drew back slightly. 'You don't have to participate.'

'Your feelings are important.'

'Thank you. Now listen. I told you before. Tony wants to have one.'

'Yes.' Barry let her feel the tensing of his body at the mention of another man. 'Tony's a good enough guy.'

'How do you know? You've never met him.'

'Any guy with a taste in you has to be okay.'

'*Okay* may not be all I look for in a man.'

'What are you talking about, specifically?'

'I fear boredom. I fear it maybe more than you do.'

'Your dalliance with me would make that evident.'

'We're more sound than you think we are.'

'Oh yeah.' Barry sniffed. 'We're real square.'

'Come on, Barry. I want to talk seriously.'

'The subject is serious enough.'

'I just want you to know one thing. You have no responsibility here unless you want it.'

'What does Tony think of the responsibility?'

'He's willing. He loves me, or so he says.'

'Love?'

'C'mon, Barry. We both know you don't know where you're at about love. That's fine, but don't go thinking everybody has the same problem.'

'Have you been seeing a counsellor or something?'

Diane drew slightly away. 'In a minute I'm going to be angry.'

'I know and I'm sorry, but a child makes things so deadly grave I can barely breathe talking about it. I've covered this ground before. I'm older than you. In relationships, for some reason, I never make it past a short-term intensive or long-term part-time arrangement. I've never come close to success in the permanent long-term.'

'What about your wife?'

'She's special but the poor thing is suffering for it. I mean, would you want to be married to me?'

Diane slackened. 'If I were her I'd hate me.'

'I'm ashamed to say, but you'd have to hate a lot of women.'

'I think I'm getting jealous.'

'You can't do that. You're the other woman, remember?'

'I sometimes forget.'

'I'm sorry.'

'You're not sorry. You want it this way.'

He knew that in the next thirty seconds Diane would be rising up and going away from him. When she did, he was fatally uncertain as to what he would say. Instead, he found he could do little more than enjoy these last moments of her heat with him in the bed.

Then she was sliding from under the sheets. 'I feel sorry for you.' She slipped into her robe.

'Aw, Diane. Don't start that. You know I've heard it before.'

She scowled. 'You don't like being a good man, do you?'

'Don't be silly.'

'You wish you were more like your criminals. Their behaviour fits more with your personal philosophy, doesn't it?' She struck her feet into slippers. 'You should be so real.'

'What do you mean?'

'They're more honest about themselves than you could ever be. That's the difference.'

'At the risk of inflaming you further, I've heard that one several times before too.'

'I'll bet you've even thought of it yourself, you're so brilliant.'

'Aw c'mon . . .'

Diane left the room. Barry sighed and pictured himself in a movie, knowing that about now, the rough anti-hero would roll up in the bed and root through his jeans to get a cigarette. He got out of bed and began to dress.

When he got to the kitchen she was doing dishes and did not look up.

'Oh come on.' He approached and spoke to her back. 'We can be civil, can't we?'

'Is that what life is to you? One long civility session?'

'Well no, but . . . come to think of it, it's not a bad aspiration, though. There are worse ways to try to live.'

'All I know is Barry . . .' She stopped her work and turned to him. 'This is no life. This one I've got. It's no life. The one you've got, trust me, it's no life either. We're both grownups here. We've got to decide something, either together or separately or both, and then get on with it.'

'And having a baby, that's your proposal for a new start?'

'It's as good as any. It's not a bad thing to want. There are worse ways to try to live.'

'Yeah yeah, touché.' Barry stepped back from her, looked away and then directly at her again. 'And you'd want to have it with me?'

Diane sighed—a long, tumbling, droopy shouldered effort that left her visibly diminished. She absently wiped her hands on a tea towel. Barry thought she never looked more beautiful, standing morose in her robe in the middle of her kitchen.

'Yes.' She paused as if to let him be sure of what she had said. 'I've thought about you and I love you deeply and I think you'd be the father I'd want for my baby.'

Barry shifted from one foot to another and looked past her out the window. 'This is surprising.' He looked to the floor. 'I don't know what to say.'

'Don't say anything. In fact, just shut the hell up.' Diane stepped to him and wrapped him in her arms. 'Seriously. You're making me angry when you talk today.'

'I wish I could change that.'

'Don't try.'

'I can't understand it.' Barry reverted by lilt of voice to an attempted humour. 'Must be the atmospheric conditions.'

'Stop it.'

'The tides.'

'Forget it.'

'Must be the moon and stars.'

She sighed again. 'Must be.' She poked his chest with a forefinger. 'If lame humour is what makes it safe for you, it must be.'

'It's okay. I can handle it.' Barry tried to sound somber. 'I'm touched, I really am.'

'Good. At least you recognize your own condition.'

'No, I mean I'm emotionally affected. I feel closer to you.'

'Well then at least something vaguely good has come of this.'

'That's better.' Barry rubbed her back with both hands.

Diane warmed against him and snuggled her head into his chest.

They were quiet for a long while. It occurred to Barry that this was clearly crunch-time. Never had there been a more obviously appropriate moment to declare his commitment either way. He knew the silence was becoming weightier every second but—in view of his morbid indecision—could think of nothing to say that was safe.

She disengaged herself and locked him in a stare. 'I guess I'll just have to keep looking.'

'Not necessarily.' He knew his face was darkening. 'We can keep talking about it can't we?'

'Time marches on.'

'Uh huh, but let's not rush into this.'

'Fine.'

'Although . . . I'm aware of the competition with Tony.'

'Don't let that bother you.'

'I can't help it. Also, I'm wondering, what's the big attraction to sharing offspring with me?'

'Your eyes for one thing. Beautiful blue.'

'You're not serious.'

'I am.' She spoke while looking deeply into them.

[6]

ON A NIGHT when he was short of cash after an emergency rock purchase he had the fake piece with him and the convenience store was just sitting there, in the middle of a strip-mall, the usual brown immigrant tending the till.

Perfect.

It's important to be versatile, he was thinking.

Up the street there was the exactly right place to park.

He trimmed his walk on approach so that the only customer he could see was walking out of the place just before he stepped into the light. The only description would be a shadowy man, no details. Leave that for the surveillance camera. He checked his cap bill for perfect position, then wrenched the door open and strode to the counter.

No small talk this time around. 'Fuckin' grease ball . . .' No point.

While oathing, he lunged, pulling the phony weapon out of his pants, and swatted the inundated clerk at ear-level. The man, who was about sixty, went down.

'How's that, Carlos? Okay?'

He looked out the store windows. No one was in sight as far as the lights accommodated. Head down, he vaulted the counter and stood partially upon the sputtering man. He was bleeding from a scalp wound and it wasn't much to just stomp the head back down to the floor and cause further blood. He checked the till for the fifteen dollars he expected to find, pocketed this, then stooped to check the clerk's clothing. He found a wallet and took forty dollars from there. There were a couple of dollar coins in a front pocket. A total take of fifty-seven dollars. Not so good, but it nonetheless equalled three extra hours of necessary high. It negated the probability of an angry, dangerous evening. He jumped back over the counter and walked out of the store and into the darkness.

Three nights later, just off work, he drove by the same store. It was payday and there was plenty of crack and he didn't feel especially like drinking or doing anything at all but the look of the place inspired in him a desire for just one special thing. Like a court order of the soul, as soon as the idea was served on him he knew there'd have to be execution. He circled the block a few times, taking note of persons and vehicles, their movements and/or lack of. Then a close look at the clerk from the darkness of the parking lot across the street. There was again only one. He inspected the heads bobbing about the magazine rack and those striding to the back for the milk and eggs. Then he lit up a few stones and thought how he was being so good not cranking like he used to. He worked in his head, trying to feel perfect about right now, this night, this deal. It took significant smoke.

He sat too long, waiting for the store to clear, shaking his head and cursing aloud into the night for no particular reason. For some reason—fatigue, excitement, drugs—he could not make the weird and persistent intrusion of irrelevant facts and arguments go away. His mind reeled out and selected his stored-away random political readings like a library microfiche machine. He forced himself to think about an article he'd read in a business journal. He tried to think about when he'd hit another jewellery store. The jumble of mental threads distracted him. He stepped out of the car and walked a block and then returned, no less cluttered. Then he was somehow able to dismiss his discomfort as irrelevant. There was only one surefire cure for such mental distraction.

It got late and the store cleared out. He stood for a time at the opened car trunk and changed his outfit there in the parking lot, invisible in the shadows, standing still when headlights played at him. He reminded himself that because he had just hit the place a few days ago, extra care was required.

He was aware of a visceral yearning for the score. It was there both reassuring and unnerving, so strong it flexed his jaw involuntarily. He literally felt himself champ for the sweet palm-full of cash and another thing he could not label. He stashed the uniform in the trunk and the phony gun in his jeans. He pondered the aspects of cocaine distillate.

When he walked across the street, over the curb and through the landscaping of the store front he was confident, once again timing his appearance to the last exiting customer. He was at the door before it fully closed and the clerk barely got a chance to look up before things were in full confrontation. Damned if from under the cap of the convenience store clerical army uniform the bandaged face of his earlier victim didn't peer out. The security man chuckled. The clerk recoiled and began a move for something under the counter.

With speed and without thought the assault was taken behind the counter. Tussling, he resisted the impulse to use the gun as a club. All he wanted to do was make sure the alarm didn't get punched before their conversation could take place.

Yes, conversation.

'Hey Jose or Fernando or whatever. How do you like this?' He held the clerk firm, gripping handfuls of polyester shirt, burning his scariest drug-stare into the older man's dark eyes.

No answer.

'No really, you can talk to me.'

The clerk stared back.

He slammed a fist into the man's mouth. There was sputtering and blood-spray, but he could see by the way the clerk resumed his composure that the blow had not greatly fazed him. He was slightly surprised at the man's resiliency and sensed now a power-laden rectitude.

'Now look Hernandez or Jorge or Lopez or whatever the Hispanic hell your fucking name is, you're gonna have to talk to me.'

A look passed the clerk's eyes, a recognition of something. He said a word: 'Yehhs . . .'

'Okay. What I want is, I want to understand something. I must figure out what you're doing here, I mean, I know what your job is, it's to give change and get shit-kicked by any gunslinger who cares to stride in here and assert himself in any minimal way. It's to subjugate yourself to any kid with a nickel for candy. It's to supply designer water to arrogant and distracted urbanites who don't even switch off their Volvos when they dash in here for their Perrier and ice cream and condoms, et cetera. I mean, you're a dog, mister. A pet. But they don't even pat you on the head and say good boy. I mean, there's a sociopolitical aspect to all this that I hope you're sensitive to because I'd hate to think I brutalized a poor sucker like you twice in one week and you still didn't get the significance of it all. I mean, fuck me man, you're exploited, do you understand?'

He shook the clerk.

Still more recognition registered on the man's bruised face and now he returned an almost knowing stare. 'Please continue . . .' The clerk sputtered slightly but expended noticeable effort at clear, accented enunciation. '. . . with your examination of my status.'

'Thank you, I will. Do you know that despite whatever personal merits you might possess you are nevertheless a virtual asshole of society? You actually serve two purposes. You pass the shit on to other people who want the shit. They in turn fuck you up the ass by their demands for convenience and cheap labour.'

The clerk's eyes conveyed no attitude about this information either way.

'Are you a religious man?'

This brought a slight flaring of the nostrils.

'I can see that you might be, likely being from a Catholic country and all. But you're not exactly in a holy place now, are you? Do you know that this society that buys gas and chocolate bars from you routinely accepts people living in fornicatory unions as legitimate citizens? Do you know that a favourite summertime romp for your average customer is to travel twenty blocks west of here and take their clothes off and advertise their non-piety on one of North America's most notorious nude beaches? Do you know that your customers, co-workers, armed-robbers, passers-by and/or bosses don't give a devout fuck for any high-held principles you may have? The consortium of dentists and accountants who own this and fifty thousand other dumps like it across the continent give it to you repeatedly in every orifice by their act of employing you to do their dreary, underpaid and, may I add, dangerous work for them . . .'

He paused for breath. 'How much do you get paid?'

'Seven dollars per hour, sir.'

'There you go. Risking your life for peanuts. You have a terrible situation here Señor . . .'

'Fernand.'

'Fernand. May I call you Ferdy?'

The clerk closed his eyes.

'Okay, look. What I was saying is, I got a job.' He unclamped a hand from the clerk's vest to pull the false weapon out and point it to the ceiling. 'The work I'm doing here as a matter of fact . . .' He waved the pistol around to include the store and environs. 'These are not big scores, but I get paid about twice what you do, maybe a little less, but I could work about fifteen minutes per month for what you make all month. Get me?'

The clerk had opened and closed his eyes several times during the monologue. He silently nodded at the security guard's insistence.

'So Ferd . . . why don't you rip this shit-spot off yourself? I mean, the crime has already been committed against you and all your little brown buddies who come up here and take these dead-end meaningless shit-hole jobs away from us lazy white people. You've got my permission, for one. How much have you got on you?'

'Pardon?'

'How much cash have you got on you right now? You had forty the other night. What have you got now?'

The clerk slipped a hand into his pants pocket. He pulled out a number of small bills and a few coins. They spilled onto the floor.

'Whattayou got there . . .' He let the man go, levelling the gun. The clerk went quickly to the task of counting.

'Seventeen dollars and seventy-three cents.' The clerk's voice was a quietly cooperative monotone.

'Not even twenty bucks. Cautious this time, huh? No more getting ripped off for a week's pocket money by some freak with a gun the size of a hard-on, huh?' The security man smiled widely and nudged the clerk on the bicep with his free hand. 'Good going, guy. But you should have carried more, you should have been more trusting. You know why?'

The clerk looked away.

'Answer me, boy.' The clerk turned back to face him. 'You know why you should have carried more money?'

'I do not know, sir.'

'Well I'll tell ya . . .' He gestured to the till. 'Open that.'

In a second the clerk had sprung the till open and stepped back. The security man leaned over and dug a hand into the cash. 'Hmmm . . . Not much here, either.' He roughly palmed up the bills, counted the take and was about to say something to the clerk when the front door swung open and a man stepped toward the newspaper rack, not looking at the counter. The clerk stared with wide eyes.

'Excuse me, sir . . .' The security guard turned away from the clerk, put the money on the counter and stepped fully into the customer's view.

'Yes?' The man looked up and stared with unfocussed eyes.

'Please stay where you are.'

'Holy shit!' The customer lurched back at the sight of the gun. The security guard sprang. 'My god!' The man was struck as he spoke and dropped as if turned to water. He stared up at his assailant with more surprise than fear.

'Do you have a family?' He stood looking down, hands and gun at his side.

'What?'

'Is there a group of kids and a wife waiting for you out in the car, or are you by yourself?'

'Don't hit me anymore . . .'

'I asked you a question asshole and I want an answer. Is there anybody outside?'

'I don't know what you mean.'

'Yes you do.'

'No I don't.'

'Where are they?'

'Where are who?'

'All right you've had it.' He planted his feet firmly apart on the floor and with a two-handed grip trained the big piece at the man's head.

'Please don't . . .'

Silence. The man whimpered and stared at the large hole in the barrel that was pointed at him and began to blurt, sobbing, and spoke. 'I'm alone. Okay? There's nobody out there. At this hour of the night I don't take my family anywhere. Now don't shoot me okay? Don't shoot.'

'That's better. I'm proud of you, man. Families should be tucked safely in their beds at this time of night.'

'Fine.'

'So what do I look like to you?'

'Huh?'

'What is your opinion of who and what I am. I'm curious.'

'I . . . I don't know what you mean.'

'It's not that complicated.'

'What are you?'

'Yes. Keep your answer to one sentence, please.'

'You're a . . . a crook.'

'I thought you'd say something like that.'

'I'm sorry, I . . .'

'No no no, don't apologize. You haven't had much to work with. Your conclusion is valid as far as it goes. But let me ask you. Might I be anything else?'

'Anything else?'

'I'm getting a little impatient with your lack of comprehension here, friend.'

'I guess you could be something else.'

'Right. Thank you. That's exactly what I was getting at. As in: Could I possibly be a nice guy in another life?'

'Uh. I guess so.'

'Thanks again. Right answer. I mean, if you think about it, it might be hard on a guy's feelings to be considered just a crook, present circumstances notwithstanding. So I'm glad we got to this juncture without my having to brain you with this nasty piece here. In fact, I was just having a deep conversation with our friend Fernand here.' He gestured with the gun. 'Now just lie there, okay?'

'Okay.'

He lowered the gun and glanced out the store windows. Then he swung casually back toward the clerk, waisting the piece. 'Ferdy, my man. What was it? Seventeen?'

'I do not understand.'

'In your pocket, man! It was seventeen bucks, wasn't it?'

'Yes.'

'Okay. Here.' He fingered the bills on the counter. 'It's what I call a matching program. You carry seventeen bucks, I steal that much from your employer and give it to you. Okay?'

The clerk just stared.

'It's the least I can do, Fernand. Kind of brings us closer, doesn't it. We're kind of in this together now, no?' He paused, enjoying the proceedings but aware that time had passed, the limit for safety at this kind of thing was long past. 'And after all that hot air . . .'

More silence. He looked at Fernand closely, knowing this night's entertainment was about five seconds from finished. The clerk avoided his gaze.

'You pushed that button, didn't you Ferdy?'

'No.'

'It's okay, I understand. Just doing your job. Don't worry about it.' He chuckled, scooped out the few loose bills in the open till and pocketed them. On the way out he spoke to the customer: 'Good night now. Take care,' but did not pause to hear a reply.

Driving away, playing it over in his mind, he understood that he was again using too much cocaine. Dicking around with convenience stores is fine for thrills, but jewellery awaits. Time for another executive action, the finery score, the major movement toward glitter acquisition. The Mynah Bird of Crime, that's me.

At home, he guffawed aloud in the empty room. He laughed and laughed. When he finished he let the silence return. He listened close to the quiet, sobered. In minutes it offended him and he shuffled to the kitchen and ruffled his paraphernalia. He thought for a moment and then knew he had a clean fit somewhere among the drawers and counter space. The needle, fuck the smoke. It would kill the last of his supply but he tried not to think about that.

After the hit his mind cleared itself of the mental residue. There was energy, then sleep. By the gray light of next day he was able to concentrate on the matter at hand.

A score.

Where?

He went to the living room and rooted in the magazine rack under the TV and found the city map he was looking for. He unfolded it on the coffee table. Over the past three weeks he'd hit here, here, here . . . Where was that convenience place? Should the jewellery hits be mixed in as the same status as the convenience store? Maybe he should be hitting more late night smash-and-grab immigrant-run milk-stops for the quick fifty they were worth and to hell with the high-profile risk of the rock candy stores. Naw. His mind did quick math and the numbers were nowhere near where they had to be. Despite the hassles, the risk, the ten-cent-on-the-dollar fence money, et cetera. Big scores it would have to be.

He felt under the couch cushions for a felt marker. He found one he was sure had been there from when he'd tried to keep himself occupied doing that Doodle-Art poster as part of his rehab program. It was bright pink. The gem stores made a cute constellation in the general area of downtown.

Hmmm. Looks like a pattern. Better get out of town for this one. He looked again for where the convenience store might be and considered giving it a double pink marking but stopped.

If the cops ever found this piece of evidence there would be the distressing fact of having helped them close the files on all these wonderful mysterious hits. Not a chance.

He gathered up the map, crumpling and ripping randomly. Then the pieces went into the bag with his wet garbage. Biodegradation. The perfect Exhibit-A destroyer.

Then there was the awareness of the passage of time and the perfect state of stone he was in and the realization there was a stale date on that and then more of the plan travelled into his head. He gathered the patented Mynah Bird of Crime operational paraphernalia into the sports bag and looked at his wrists. The last job had been skulls. Butterflies were not his mood today. He muddled about for a few minutes to seek further choices. Anchors and chain attracted him. So did silhouettes of the girl with big boobs. But neither thrilled him at this particular moment.

He realized that no decision was a decision. Besides, in keeping with the interesting configuration of his evasion tactics, no tattoos, this time around, would be consistent with the desired inconsistency. That was it. Bare sleeves. He adjusted the ball cap, checking for facial visibility in the hall mirror, then left the place.

Today, the sight of the car, usually as close to an aphrodisiac as he wanted to get to, gave him a mental start. Same thing as the tatties, too used. Sooner or later some good citizen was going to mention the presence of a collector-car in the vicinity of all these robberies. Two and two might get put together.

He waited until near evening, fixed again, guzzled miscellaneous pills he hoped would extend the stone, and set out on foot to the subway. On the ride out he let the drug-honey sweep him and make a pleasure cruise of the rumbling elevated tour through the eastern part of the city and across the suburbs, past parks, broad mountain vistas, kids playing in back yards, office buildings, streets of houses and apartment buildings. On a street of stores he noticed a boarded up shop-front with a faded sign. He had a deep regret at not looking up the address of the place he had in mind before launching himself all this way for possibly nothing. He knew where the place was but had not actually seen it for three years. Since before his last jail bit. It could have moved by now. Or gone out of business. This was bad planning. His elation evaporated. He filled up with fear. In the occasional instant of clarity he cursed his drug predilection. Just thinking this way stiffened him. He found himself staring like an owl. He swallowed hard, but there was nothing to swallow. He tried to flex his hands but couldn't be sure he wasn't blinking his eyelids instead. By the time the train was where he wanted to go he was virtually catatonic and missed his stop.

He watched helpless as the line took him soaring over the Fraser River on a bridge so thin it seemed to disappear under the train car. The sensation made him feel he could take a flying fall at any moment and plunge a hundred metres into the water and keep going into solid mud.

Dread scrabbled like a trapped rat through the shell of his body. He crawled in his seat, willing that he achieve unconsciousness, and in fleeting clarity understood that he was useless as an armed robber for today.

Angry, he mourned the taking of his nerve and sanity. In the moment when the train slowed into the end-of-the-line station he determined his recovery. He tried again to flex his hands, trained an eye upon them, saw the faintest of movement.

Okay, that's it. Not a single light-up until my mentality comes back. And even then not too much, just enough to calm down and get eating something and then sleeping. Tomorrow will be another day.

These resolves brought him back slightly, enough to maneuver out of his seat and forward. Even then he could not elude the terrors of the subterranean imagery he'd been tripping on for the last three kilometres of aerial track, tumbling helpless in paranoia and anger. He was near seething meltdown. He felt like taking out the next person who spoke to him. He could have easily wiped out this whole car-full of citizens. As he stepped from the train to the platform and walked the breezeway and the escalator and below the track and waited for a return train, he fantasized the pleasure of terminating some of these stooges waiting here with him. The whole place was his hunting ground. With all his proud heart he wished that this play-act piece of metal at his belly was the real article so he could go about some well-deserved selective culling around these parts. The cripples first, he especially despised them. If you're too gimped to walk and open doors for yourself then to hell with ya. The Chinks and Hindus next, what the fuck are they doin' here anyway? Reload and finish off anybody else still standing, fuck 'em all . . .

When a train came and he boarded, this small action changed his mood still again and he saw himself as he truly was and would always be: Their Savior. Yes, little did they know how close to terminal violence they'd all come. He was their man, their protector. With one transaction in a downtown bar, a two-hundred-dollar deal at most, he could have the real ordinance and then there'd have been shit to pay. If only they knew. They'd be shitting themselves. With gratitude. He'd have people coming up and kissing his feet, lifting him in the air, adoring to extremes. He might even have women fondling him, sending him into new worlds.

Fondling. He'd fondle them all right, he'd grab their tits and force them down on the floor and rip their clothes and stick his hands into their wet cracks, deep. If he met resistance he'd rip them apart, literally. The notion put velocity to his thoughts. Put both hands into them and dissever. Just rend them without a thought for how it would feel or what it would do or who might care if there were women laying around in various states of gory disassemblage inside this otherwise antiseptic transit car which now was rocketing across the urban-side and he remembered with acid in his mouth that he'd forgotten to gaze down to Eighth Avenue when they were going back through New Westminster to see if that godforsaken gemologist was still there.

Dammit!

DAMMIT!

Fucking narcotics anyway!

Fucking mung-head-confused-mental-blitz-disorder think-deficits.

He didn't know what to do. Then a phrase entered: 'Remember your relapse prevention skills.' He mouthed the words to himself. Laughter entered. The thought of it! Correctional programming swerving his thinking at a juicy time like this. He could almost see himself. Then, against his will, he actually could see himself. Sitting there broiling in his assigned place in the penitentiary classroom. Bent thoughts. He pictured the massive hard-on he often got watching the teacher. The twisted speculations about her. Imagining her cunt. The hilarious irrelevance of drug abuse programming amid high male horniness and pussy deprivation.

Pussy *depra-vation . . .*

The laughter started in a serious way and then there was no stifling it. He clutched himself, rocking. People cringed and avoided looking if they hadn't already done so during his eagle-frown stage or his leering stages. Impulse control hell! Cognitive thinking errors up your ass! And then everything was funny. The colours of the plastic seats, the cheerful manic bonging before the station announcements, the inane poetry on the overhead panels. The looks on people's faces. He was almost off his seat, in a seizure, suffering hilarity, trying to get steady himself as the car braked into an inner city station.

He staggered off and down the escalator stepping two at a time to get out of there and away from the too-bright lights and into the comforting gloom. Not laughing. Knowing now that though he was a short walk home, he wasn't sure his feet were up to it. He stumbled, recovered, had trouble lifting his knees. Standing planted on the sidewalk, he forced one in front of the other and nearly fell. He tried again. Great concentration. He did not care that people stared at him. At the crosswalk he sidled aside a teenaged girl holding a bicycle. When the light changed he gripped the rear fender and staggered along with her.

'Hey!' She twirled but did not stop, instead, quickened her gait. 'Let go.'

He could only geek a slanted smile at her and grip harder, trotting along. By the time embarrassment stopped him they were across six lanes of street. He gladly let go the bike. She was gone instantly.

Fine. One small offence for today. No complaints, no cops. He appreciated this small perfection.

Making his knees agree with his feet and getting his body to follow along was a major chore. He'd never been this stoned. Halfway home, trekking somber through alleys of light industry and half-built artist live-work studio buildings, he caught a spasm deep in his gut. He stood, wavering, gripping himself. Something in his intestines wanted out with the most expressed urgency. This confounded him, as it was present in his mind, despite the addlement, that he had not eaten anything for nearly three days. It passed in a second and he thought he might continue but then there was another deep pang and he wondered if the foul water of his intestines and the silly coke psychosis he was shaking off with every step would let him get home and take a dignified shit in the privacy of his own bathroom. He semi-ran down a dim street and turned a corner one block from home but doubled over at another mangling stab. He tried to move and folded again, stumbled, staggered to a ruined carport where he fell, ripped inside, clutching as best he could but failing reekishly. Leaking at first and then splashing, spraying, his exploding excretion running so strong into his pants that the jets created a drag at his cuffs.

He was aware of his face resting on an oil-smelling piece of plywood.

When next his eyes were open he knew major pain. Cold and stress. The stink that was himself at least said he was alive.

Fucking narcotics.

Orange-rayed streetlights across sticky eyeballs. Broken glass winking like forgotten diamonds.

[7]

DESPITE THEIR WIDENING chasm, dinner at home on a Friday night with his wife was something Barry looked forward to.

They were amiable, sipping wine: he washing and seasoning the fish, and she perched on a high stool chopping vegetables. Barry liked to cook things she enjoyed. Tanya was demonstrably appreciative of this. Barry knew in a sad way that cooking and eating was lately their most viable aspect of communion. And even now amid the heaviness of his heart there were in these mechanics of food preparation certain wisps of sheer emotional enjoyment. Sentiment, he decided, refusing to die.

He girded himself in the determination that this night's conversation was the one in which something would happen. He was determined to tell and tell all. He was prepared to spend the night on the street, in a cheap hotel. In his mind he prepared a small carrying bag, picturing the essentials: tooth care, hairbrush, underwear. While he potato-peeled and salted and set the water to boil he prepared.

Early in the relationship Tanya had voiced admiration and surprise at his culinary skills.

'Years of bachelorhood!' He had spoken flippantly; not wanting to admit, for some reason, that he honest-to-god liked cooking.

'With meals like these I'm surprised you stayed single so long.'

Surprised? He pondered now.

He had wondered, in those early days, if she'd been as surprised as he had been that they were together at all, let alone married, given the circumstances of their first date. The thought made him drift, sautéing on auto-pilot, tuning her chat away, ignoring the music on the kitchen CD player just enough to recall: He remembered himself running, running.

One minute he'd been making charm with this new delight, Tanya, the next he was vomiting across the restaurant and shambling into the night, mad for air. It was the aftermath of a work memory—something lying coiled in his brain—that caused it. It was a year in which a parolee had killed himself with drugs and lay undetected for some weeks. Barry had discovered the body.

Flies. Putrefaction.

Barry resisted an image of eyeballs in a maggoty mess.

He thought, because of the placid passage of some weeks, that the incident may not have cost him. Then the Greek restaurant and the pressure of enticing this new woman. The effects of retsina on an empty stomach. Too-pungent hummus. The waft of roasting lamb, its body displayed in full rigour by the foyer, rotisserating over sizzling electrical coils. Barry had started at the convulsions in his middle, then stared dumbfounded as his body rejected all it could in a perpendicular stream from his mouth.

He ran the four blocks to the beach and flung himself in, clothes and all, tasting salt, connecting back with his life through the core-reaching chill of the water. But still sick as death, mentally suppurating, melting in dread. Tanya had stood by on the shore, bundled him and drove him home. He thought he would never stop shivering. He simmered for an hour in the bathtub, quaking, blubbering. The memory of it frosted the back of his neck even now, twelve years on. He looked up to his wife as she finished telling of her day.

' . . . And then if that wasn't bad enough they came through with another slide that has to be in court Monday morning. Bastards. There's no regard for pathology staff nowadays. It's all rush rush rush . . .'

'Yeah, I find that too.'

'Don't be silly. You just cruise around all day.'

'I beg your pardon?' He turned to her.

She stopped chopping a carrot and examined him. 'What?'

'I just cruise around all day?'

'Well that's what it looks like to us workers stuck inside.'

'That's not fair.'

Tanya frowned and went back to her knife-work. 'Don't overreact, Barry.'

'But . . .' He breathed deep and forced himself to ungrimace. 'Aside from being hurt at your summary dismissal of my work I'm remembering you on the shore of Barry Delta Beach.'

'Oh don't be silly. I know you work hard.'

'And you know there's a psychological price to pay. And I pay it.'

'Okay okay . . .'

'You might not think that kind of stuff stings but it does.'

'Stop it! I'm sorry, okay?' Tanya put down her knife. 'God. Barry Delta Beach.'

'I was suffering from the mother of all post-traumatic stress reactions.'

'Well at least you didn't try to get me to do your laundry afterward. That was a big plus in your favour.'

'What are you talking about? After you took me home and cleaned me up I actually pulled myself together enough the next day to cook you dinner. Don't you remember?'

'How could I forget? I almost ate a shard of glass from when you blew up the broccoli.'

'Now don't try to characterize that episode as anything other than the comedic turn I meant it to be.' Barry smiled, but he had never enjoyed Tanya's tendency to be harsh when recalling travails which in the span of years should normally have morphed into hilarity. 'You laughed at the time.'

'What else could I do? A guy barfs over half the customers in a Greek restaurant, not to mention me. Then he runs into the ocean and splashes around in his office clothes for a while. Then he invites me up to his place and tries to cook broccoli over a gas flame in a glass casserole dish with an iron steamer rack inside it.' She rolled her eyes without humour.

Her tone left him empty. 'And then disaster struck . . .' He gagged, gathering breath. 'And struck again. And again. And it just kept on striking and still does today . . .' He looked away from her.

'Barry . . .'

He felt her slide off her perch and move to him, touching his shoulder. 'What's wrong?'

In the second it had taken for her to get to him he had managed to recompose and keep the water from his eyes and hoped the redness wasn't too bad or that she might think it was from the post-work beers and the wine they were drinking now and maybe the onions she had been cutting. Turning to her, he knew that these thoughts were misguided, that it would be better if she detected something. Then he hoped outright that she would see his trouble and make him admit to it and elaborate and then maybe he would be relieved and perhaps on his way out the door and on the way to being Barry Delta again instead of some arch-immoral phantom. 'What's right?' He turned away, adjusting the heat under the potatoes.

'You're upset.' Her tone was loving.

He accepted the gift of it, even though he was grimly aware that nowadays she only used this voice when he was demonstrably down.

'Look . . .' He lifted the lid and looked at the potatoes, then put it back down and looked away again, out the window at their pleasant street and the easy fading light to the west. 'Look.' He turned to her. 'It doesn't matter what's wrong or whether I say what's wrong, it's just wrong and that's all there is to it. There's nothing that can be done.' He paused to watch her face. 'You know everything that's going on and there's nothing that can be done about it . . .'

She said nothing, but sighed.

Barry waited for an examining question—'What do you mean I know everything that's going on?'—fearing how he would answer. He visualized her facial expression at the ugly knowledge she would acquire by reading between the lines of what he said. He noted her expulsion of breath and then she reached about and enfolded him and nuzzled her face into his chest. 'That stupid job.' Her voice held a preclusive all-knowingness that never failed to bait Barry.

'I'll give you a clue.' Barry fought an impulse to flex his arms and fling her away. 'It's not the goddamn job.'

'You say that but I see what it does to you.'

'I've told you before. It's not the job. It's been a fun job . . .'

'Fun. You just finished complaining about PTSD. How could you say it was a fun job?'

'You don't understand.'

She shook her head, also in an annoyingly knowing way. 'Oh, but I do.'

'What crap.' He nudged her out of the embrace. 'If you can't figure it out I can't explain it.' He picked up a dishtowel and began wiping the counter. 'Just never mind.'

'Well give me a chance. What's bugging you?'

'I don't exactly know. I was hoping you might help me figure it out.'

Barry stopped wiping and looked up.

A darkness now tinted Tanya's face. 'You're being nasty just for effect now, aren't you?

'What?'

'Why can't we spend a nice night together without you turning cruel?'

'Cruel?' Barry was incredulous. 'Cruel? I haven't even got to unpleasant yet. There's abrasive and belligerent to come first. Sweetheart. You know I'm not being cruel. I just need you to think hard about things.'

'Think about what?'

Barry sighed and considered letting himself blaze up into rage. 'Can't you just think?' He sighed again and looked downward. 'Can't you just figure out why we're having this discussion?'

'I still don't know what you're talking about. In fact, you're not making any sense at all, Barry.'

He could not suppress a bitter laugh. 'What would you know about sense? You're married to me, aren't you?'

Her hurt then came true in the wrinkles near her eyes and her downcast tilt. The look disappointed him because he knew it was meant to shut him down, back him off.

Barry scowled. 'Oh smarten up.'

'I hate it when you drink.'

'That's a dumb statement. I always drink. I've drank since you've known me. I was drinking when I first barfed on you. What the hell are you complaining about?'

'Barry!' She turned as dramatically as he knew she would and darted from the kitchen.

He didn't watch her go, but resumed his cooking, adjusting the music upward to cover his own dark thoughts and try to dissipate the negative emotional effluvia left in the room. His hands shook a little but he steadied them. He had gone too far but he knew he needed to. He ired anew at her shortcomings of intuition and his doubts about her naiveté and his lack of courage to just come out and confess. He stopped working and wrung his hands. He was tempted to open more wine but didn't.

Later, with dinner prepared and on hold, he climbed the stairs, lurching slightly, feeling the wine, and encountered her facedown on the bed. He had their glasses in hand and placed Tanya's near her head on the night table.

'Here I am.' He sat on the bed and put a hand on her leg, tilting his wine with the other for a deep drink.

No answer.

Barry was prepared for this response.

'Tickle . . ?' He made motions to her ribs and was careful not to spill his drink while teasing.

'Stop it.' She spoke through the pillow.

'Come on . . .' With his hand he probed tenderly, careful, knowing fully how dangerous this was, how illegitimate, and how much in his emotional exile he sorely desired it to work.

'Barry!' Tanya rolled away and settled on the far side of the bed, glaring. 'Why does it end like this more and more?'

'What?'

'Don't pretend you haven't noticed. You're too smart for that. You're too tuned into yourself.'

'What are you talking about, specifically?'

'Don't use that tone with me.'

'What tone?'

'I can't believe you talk to me like that when you're supposed to love me. I just can't.'

'Like what? Let me know what it is and I'll try to change it.'

'It fills me with fear that you say you don't know.'

'Why be fearful? You're in the company of someone who wants only the best for you. As best as possible.'

'You know your best isn't very good these days. I know it too. But it doesn't have to be that way. The truth is you don't have to be anything with me but honest.'

'I'm honest. Honest as I can be.' He chose his next words carefully, despising himself. 'In my way.'

She spoke instantly. 'You don't know the meaning of the word.'

'Well who deified you when I wasn't looking?' He drank his wine. 'I don't have to listen to this.'

'No you don't and I don't like to be the one saying it. But it's real Barry. I don't know when you're going to honestly face it.' She coiled into a kneeling crouch on the bed, fists balled at her sides. 'We've come apart.' She hollered into his face. 'Face it. Face it!'

This was hotter than things had ever gotten, at least in Barry's memory. In fact, Tanya's voice and motion suggested approaching violence. Barry was confounded by this revelation. Despite working in corrections all his adult life he had seldom encountered physical conflict. He wondered how he would deal with it. Then too was the awful revelation that she was now mouthing words that he himself had intended to use. While ruminating around this, he was startled at the onset of her tears.

'Barry . . .' She attempted to say something but he did not hear it, issued as it was amid sobbing.

His heart sat dead in his chest, useless as rotten cheese, and he was chagrined to be still holding a wineglass in his hand. He placed it cautiously beside hers, knowing the drinking for the night was ended. He was regretful at his state of inebriation. It made his thinking muddy, his spirit too stale for combat. He tried to think of the next thing to say. He was weary now, and sought to alleviate, assuage, even placate if it would get him a recess. He rued this strain of marital virus they were suffering. They had caught it, they were suffering, and there did not appear to be any remedy. In an effort to medicate himself, he had inflicted wrong upon her, whether she knew it or not, and he gravely disliked himself for it.

'Tanya . . .' He began but did not have the content to follow through. 'Tanya.' It ended up a simple statement.

Her crying stopped and she lay down and was still for a time, breathing deep. The silence, like the guilt, got to be a near-tangible presence in the room. Barry girded himself, madly searching for the right thing to say, doubting he would survive.

Finally she said: 'You're a bastard, Barry, and I love you.'

'I love you too.'

'As sick as it is, I know you do. I know you do.'

There were more tears. Barry hoped it didn't matter that he wasn't fully clear on what she had meant. He supposed that she loved him, but that was his specific problem area, defining love. He wracked his brain and his rancid heart. For a moment the intimacy of their struggle moved Barry, brought him closer to Tanya, yet then the iniquitous presence of others in the room—known by him, hidden from Tanya—scorched him like acid. Sitting with them there were all his female friends: Diane especially; unsuspecting Rikki from the bar; maybe even Jill, whom though he hadn't touched nonetheless pleasured him in the realm of fantasy. He imagined them as distracted goddesses, perched on his shoulders like gaudy puppets, and wished to whatever god might listen that they not be there.

He shifted on the bed, trying to refocus a caring for his grieving wife. But the crowd with him interrupted the psychic flow; too many inputs, conflicting energy. Guilt rose in him like sewage, stinking all around and solely a product of him. His goddesses departed. He was nauseated and wallowing, a swimmer in refuse with no chance of rescue and years gone by without a clean breath.

No life at all.

'Aw christ I can't stand this!'

His statement dangled for longer than he thought it should if Tanya had understood him. Then she said: 'We'll have dinner in a minute.'

'What?'

She remained face-away. He met then a terrible fact that he had known was extant in his married life and was a ubiquitous flavour of his overall life, but which was a thing that hurt him more than exposure, even more than vulnerability. Barry shivered. It was solitude that slapped him here. He could not counter the anti-empirical fact of the coldness in the room.

Barry had been alone all his life and it looked like that state was going to get more intense before it eased, if ever it did. Trying as he was to position his heart and mind to give care to Tanya, whose suffering he thoroughly lamented, the effort only made him more barren and bereft. Regret took over, more with every second, and then he was nearly in tears himself amid his wife's own sobbing.

'Tanya . . .' He tried speaking again, more for him than for her. 'We gotta get a grip, here.'

She turned to him without words and he reluctantly knew to collect her then in his arms. Sure enough, there were kisses and then they were making love like it might have been in the early days if Barry could only remember what it was like then. When that was over they lay upon the bed entwined, listening to the wavy sounds of the kitchen music lilting from below. Barry was glad to have met at least one of Tanya's wishes and the culmination he had had inside her was what he wanted at the moment it had happened. But in the denouement he'd been fleetingly uncertain as to who it was he was actually with—his goddesses asserting their franchise on his libido-soul, or his needy, oblivious wife—and the aftermath was yet a deeper despair. He noted that with every love session the effect was becoming less recreative and more vacant. And, given his distractions, perverse.

At the same instant Barry paradoxically knew Tanya would be fretting that his semen might be going for naught inside her body as once again she did not conceive.

Yes, it's true, Barry reminded himself—horror of horrors, decrepitude of spiritual decrepitude—despite their fading connection, despite Barry's multiplicitious philanderings and outer darkness of soul, they'd been trying to have a child for years.

'Barry, I love you so much.'

'I know.'

'It's such a curse.'

'I know.'

'I want so much. I want so little.'

'I know.'

'I want a baby.'

'I know.'

'Do you?'

'Uh huh.'

'Really?'

'I think I do.'

'You come along with me to the appointments. That's loving. Those are the times I'm happiest about us.'

'I'm glad.'

'What are we going to do?'

'I don't know. Have dinner, I guess. Beyond that, beats me.'

'Barry . . .'

He was tired now to the point of folly, sinking under wine and the sex, and smirked when he should not have. 'Tanya . . .' His retort was a too-insolent-to-be-funny echo.

'Don't be flip. You know how I feel.'

'I know and I'm not trying to be flip. I'm just trying to be. I don't know what to say, I guess.'

'Mister Mouth at a loss, huh?'

'You could say that.'

'There have been times I have loved your mouth. When it's on me.'

'I love my mouth when it's on you.'

'How can lovers be so different-planet? It mystifies me. Then it kills me.'

'Don't let anything kill you.'

'Easy for you to say. You dodge bullets all the time.'

'I thought I just cruised around all day?'

'You know I didn't mean that.'

'Thank you. But you were right, sort of, about the job. It was fun for a lot of years, but I've outgrown it. Or it's outgrown me.'

'Let's work on you going somewhere else.'

'Easier said than actualized. Other than what I do, I'm kind of unemployable.'

'I'm luckier. I hide in a safe laboratory and get a paycheque.'

'Oh you get a paycheque do you?' Barry shifted position to half-sitting. 'Hate to change the subject but, before it all goes to clothes and facials and cosmetics, et cetera, I need your contribution for this month's expenses.'

'Barry, how could you talk about money at a time like this? I mean, our relationship needs serious work and you think about finances?'

'I couldn't help it.' Barry kept eyes on his wife. 'Somebody has to.'

'Oh for crying out loud.' Tanya turned away and rolled slightly. 'I don't know . . .' She shifted further and spoke into the wall. 'We need a vacation.'

'What?'

'We've got to get away.'

'Are you kidding?'

'We always used to go to San Francisco.'

'We can't afford it.'

'We can't afford not to afford it.'

'Tanya, we're broke.'

'No we're not.'

'Actually you're right. We're not broke. We're less than broke. We're so deep in the hole we can hardly see light. I wish we were just broke. Then we could wait for next payday and we'd have money.'

'You're being dramatic.'

'Dramatic. Solemn. Hysterical. Take your pick.'

'I just got paid.'

'And if we didn't spend a cent of it and lived in a tent and begged on the street, all your money and all our money for the next three year's worth of yours and my paycheques would barely get us out of debt. I mean, I haven't even got any leave time at work because I cashed it all in.'

'I know, I know . . .' She waved her hand dismissively.

Barry waited for a moment, considering. 'You're not listening to me, are you?'

'Sure I am.' She turned and sat up. 'But do you really want to get into this? I mean, we've been over it before. I've got to stop spending. We've got to budget. But wouldn't we be better off if you didn't spend every Saturday, and I do mean every Saturday, all Saturday, boozing like an idiot at that bar of yours?'

Barry let this sit for a moment. He acknowledged to himself Tanya's skilled skewering, but wondered if she knew how close she was to uncovering so much more than just his liquoring. He let silence intervene and perhaps leaven her attitude. He could see that indeed this made her reconsider.

Eventually she spoke again. 'Whatever.' She shrugged. 'Let's eat dinner, okay?'

Her emotional energy was clearly sapped for the night. He had been past endurance long ago. Though still fearful and dreading, Barry lost his will to kick over their comfortable lie. It was just so much easier to relax and sup. It was so much easier to enjoy the music and be silent.

They opened another bottle of wine.

[8]

BARRY REQUISITIONED A CAR and drove to the halfway house.

When Jill met him at the door he was surprised. 'You're on shift?'

'Shouldn't I be?' She led him to the office and left the door open.

'You worked the weekend and now you're working all week.'

'I need the money, okay?'

'The age-old requirement.'

'Who doesn't have the problem?'

'I dated a rich-bitch from the west side once. She considered money irrelevant.'

'I'd like to try that.'

'What? Money or irrelevancy?'

'Bitchiness.' Jill sat down at her desk. 'And it wouldn't be too much of an effort, Barry. I haven't had my coffee yet, so keep the repartee to yourself this early on a Monday morning.'

'Roger-Dodger. Is our patient ready?'

'If you mean Ms. Crabby International, the answer is yes. No matter what she might tell you, the answer is yes. Please get her out of here.'

'That bad, huh?'

'Worse. We're pretty sure she supplied a couple of crazy ladies in here. They ended up in the hospital. We found a dirty syringe under a carpet. There was a wad of money stolen from somebody's room. We don't know who did that but for sure somebody will end up hurt for it. Around four this morning somebody put a match to a newspaper on the third-floor fire escape. Good thing we're handy with the extinguishers. And somebody snuck a boyfriend into their room and had to be hauled out of here by the cops.'

'Whoa. How much of all this might be Chantal's doing?'

'A lot, but we don't care as long as she's out of here now. You're taking her for the procedure, right?'

Barry nodded.

Jill's brow furrowed. 'Where is she going afterward?'

'Questions, questions.'

'The Director is giving me heat. Chantal has to go. She has to go now. No post-operation sympathy or anything like that. You can't entertain any thoughts of keeping her here.' Jill's words were jokey but her tone was serious. 'You know that don't you? I don't have to remind you, do I?'

'Oh lighten up. I'd prefer it if she were going to a shelter maybe somewhere in the Salvation Army archipelago but I haven't got it fixed yet. And I don't know if I want her to know that, because unless I get a call in the next two hours she's likely going to end up in semi-custody with a transmitter clamped on her ankle.'

Jill nodded. 'You're right. Better not tell her until she's out of here.'

'Or she may never be out of here.'

'She'd make a heck of a scene.'

'It's too bad. This is the best place for her but I guess eviction is part of the treatment.'

'Yeah, and she earned it.'

'I know.'

Jill bent to the desk. 'What clinic are you using?'

'Such curiosity . . .'

'I'm sorry, Barry, no time to flirt.' She kept her eyes on a printed form and held a pen at the ready. 'Now where is she going. I've got to record it.'

Barry sighed. 'I got her into the Jones-Rutherford Centre. They have some kind of sophisticated funding. I had to call around for a place that didn't mind taking a short notice case who can't pay right away.'

Jill scribbled on the form. 'This is kind of beyond the call of regular duty for you, isn't it?'

'Sort of.' Barry tried to darken appropriately. 'Sure could use a coffee.'

'Caffeine won't do any good in a stressful situation like this. It'll make you feel funny.'

'I don't know that funny is quite the adjective I'd use here.' It came to Barry that if their conversation was going to turn poignant he would rather be speaking to Jill in a more enfolding circumstance, like a quiet cocktail lounge or on a blanket at the beach. In the moment, Barry lost a judgment fight against impulse: 'I'd prefer to see you in nicer surroundings.'

'Ditto.' Her voice was dismissive, as if she had missed the pass Barry had thrown. 'But meanwhile . . .'

Barry and Jill looked up in unison as Chantal appeared at the doorway, frowning. 'Don't stop flirting just because of me.' She stepped inside the office, lugging a lumpy kit bag.

'We haven't anything interesting to talk about except you, my dear.' Barry regarded her carefully. 'How are you feeling?'

'I'm not your dear.'

Jill sniffed. 'That's an understatement . . .'

'Fuck you.'

'I apologize.' Barry spoke overtop Chantal's sneer.

'You don't have to.' Chantal pointed. 'She said it.'

'But you were right about the 'dear' comment. I try to be a gentleman.' Barry spoke to Chantal but gestured toward Jill. 'Even amid the non-civility, I try to be a gentleman.'

'Oh, how civil.' Jill countenanced her sarcasm.

Barry winced.

'Civility . . .' Chantal cast her eyes skyward and put a school-girlish finger to her lips. 'My Gramma always told us kids to be civil.' She dropped the mime. 'When she wasn't drunk out of her skull.'

Barry brightened. 'Well, I guess it was good she had a head on her shoulders at least some of the time.' He remained smiling.

'Don't try to cheer me up.' Chantal re-darkened. 'She was a bitch. My mother was a bitch. My father and brothers and cousins were son-of-bitches. And I'm a bitch.'

Jill shrugged. 'Have it your way.'

'Don't say stuff like that.' Barry spoke to both women. They awarded him with synchronized sidelong eye-rolls.

Then both spoke:

'You don't know what it's like living with this . . .'

'You don't know what it's like staying in this . . .'

Barry raised his hands and kept his cheeriness. 'Let me assist you charming things out of your misery.' He stooped and gripped Chantal's kitbag. 'Let's get the hell out of here.'

Chantal turned and began to stride. 'A-fucking-men.'

'Don't let the door hit your mid-priced butt on the way out, Chantal.' Jill turned to her desk without bidding Barry goodbye.

Driving the car, stinging over Jill, Barry hoped not to have to talk. He had to exert himself to hide his dismay when as soon as the facility was a block behind them Chantal said: 'I think that bitch likes you.'

'I hope she does and she's not a bitch . . .' He wanted to stop there but considering their most recent exchange, could not help but add: 'At least not always.'

'I bet she'd like to fuck you right there in the office, with us girls outside listening. That would be just her kind of power trip.'

'Whoa! What's been going through your head?'

'I just told you.'

'Quite the scenario.'

'It's true, though. You're a guy, you don't see the stuff women do.'

'You mean intuition?'

'Whatever you call it. Some guys practically have to have their dick sucked before they know a girl likes them.'

'Hmmm. I'll ponder that.'

They drove quietly for a moment. Barry resigned himself to getting done at least a little bit of the necessary case management that was due in the situation.

'Meanwhile . . .' He cleared his throat. 'There's the problem of where to put you.'

'Well not back there, that's for sure.'

'I thought it was a good place for you to be. Better than the street.'

'No place is good if it's not your own.'

'Yeah, but. For now it's where I wish you were still staying. It's the least restrictive option and at least I'd know you weren't hitting the streets again.'

'I'm always going to be on the streets.'

Barry let this one go, mostly because of the irreducible truth in the statement and the unpleasant official things he would have to do when the occasion arose. In all the years of meting out penalties for bad behaviour, Barry had never let the parolees be aware of how much it pained him to finally throw up his hands and send them back to jail. The notion of incarceration personally appalled him. Just walking inside a prison was still anxiety-producing after all these years, and he always drew a relieved breath when past the final gate on the way out. In any case, bruised as he was at the chill he had felt from Jill just now, with Chantal he was in no mood to debate or discuss.

Instead, he decided on a fresh approach to assess her current state. 'Anyway, never mind what might or might not happen. What could possibly have you talking about power trips among resource facility staff like that?' He regretted how high-handed this must have sounded, but forged ahead nevertheless. 'Gimme an example, something concrete and recent.'

Chantal said nothing.

He turned to her. 'You don't want to help me out here?'

She stared at him and then looked away.

'Look. If you think making my job harder is a kick, you're not unique.'

'I don't need to be unique.'

'Bullshit. Purest lie anybody ever tells: 'I don't need to be unique.''

'That's a weird way to talk.'

'Not about you.'

'Fuck off.'

'Fuck off, yourself.'

'You're unprofessional.'

'What would you know from "unprofessional"?'

'You're a fucked-up PO.'

'That's not very nice, considering all I've done for you.'

'You're obviously burned out.'

'When did you become a personnel analyst?'

'You should do everybody a favour and quit.'

'C'mon, don't get me pissed off.'

'And Jill's a cunt.'

'Whoa . . .' Barry almost swerved the car into another lane. 'That's enough of that, young lady.'

'Fuck you.'

'No.' Barry gripped the steering wheel. 'Fuck you.'

'I'm gonna put in a grievance.' Chantal spoke with arms crossed. 'You're abusing me.'

'I'll tell you all about abuse if you have three hours someday.' Barry fought the feeling he had, the feeling that it would be great to fire off a tirade at this nasty person, just for the pleasure of a steam release. But he caught himself, reminded internally of who he was, how close to retirement he might be if only he could arrive at that date without a serious ethics complaint lodged against him.

Chantal sat glowering out her window at the city flashing by.

Barry glanced at her while merging the car into a major thoroughfare and gauging the remainder of their trip at about five minutes. 'Do you want to know where you're going after this?'

No answer.

He let a block go by.

'It's comfortable. I did the best I could. But I couldn't get around the bracelet business.'

'What's the difference?' He noted a quaver of vulnerability in Chantal's retort. 'Who cares?'

'Well I do and you're going to too because you'll be electronically surveyed and every time you go in or out a door you have to have clearance. It's crappy, I know, but the best I can do for now.' Her quiet softened him. 'It's no way to live.'

'That's for fuckin' sure.'

They approached their destination. Barry visually swept the curb on either side for a parking spot.

Chantal raised a pink-enamelled finger and pointed. 'Who's all those people?'

Barry saw a bundle of citizens but nothing else of particular interest. It occurred to him that he didn't know the exact address of the clinic he was seeking. He pulled the car into a bus stop to look at the piece of paper in his pocket. Then he looked up the street for the building, eventually picking out the numbers above the single solid door of a plain-sided building with no windows. The people on the sidewalk—maybe twenty in number—were arranged in a wide perimeter around the door. Then he noticed the placards.

'Damn . . .' He shoved the paper back in his pocket. 'Protesters.'

'What the fuck do they want?'

'Shouldn't be a problem.' Barry drove past the throng. 'I think they're supposed to keep their distance. Court order or something.'

'I'll shit-kick 'em if I have to. Nothing's keeping me from getting this over with.'

'Atta girl.' Barry was relieved to find even the slightest common cause with Chantal, as piteous as this common cause might be. 'Just lemme park this beast.'

Barry found a space in the next block and they walked quickly back toward the clinic. The voices and commotion of the protest group became prominent as they approached.

'Motherfuckers,' Chantal muttered.

'I'm with you on that.'

There were uncontrolled crosswalks at either end of the block. To cross the street they had to wait for a gap in traffic. Halfway over, attracting attention with their approach, Barry judged it might have been better to try walking down the side of the street the clinic was on and just duck into the doorway. This way the gaggle of sign-carrying demonstrators had less prior indication of their intent. He cursed himself for the lack of planning. As it became definite that they were heading to the blockaded doorway they were surrounded forthwith.

'Young woman, we would dearly like to speak with you.' It was a middle-aged man holding a baby.

A youngish woman stepped up. 'This does not have to be.'

Chantal jutted her chin. 'Fuck you, assholes.'

A fiery-eyed elderly lady fixated on Barry and lunged, whipping her stick-mounted sign into his path. Barry recoiled, realizing that he was staring at a life-size picture of a freshly aborted fetus: Bloody, fractured and grotesque in a plastic bucket. 'Shit!' He jumped, unable to maintain the cool he would have preferred. 'Get that out of my face!'

'Please don't let this girl kill your baby!' The lady pleaded to him. 'Children are our future!'

'Get real, you stupid bitch!' Chantal moved close to Barry and elbowed a path toward the door. 'Do you think I'd fuck him?' She pointed to Barry, speaking out of the side of her mouth. 'This kid is a Brand X. Nobody knows who it belongs to and I sure as hell don't care . . .'

There was a general cry from the demonstrators. 'Shame on you . . .' They appeared intent on closing ranks to form a barrier, but Chantal attacked like a cornered beast. With bear-like fist-and-forearm chopping movements she ground her way through the stationary bodies, thumping a woman to one side, kneeing a man into the sidewalk and stabbing downward with a stiletto pump. Thusly she cleared a path for her and Barry to the door and powered the palm of one hand loudly against a large red button.

Someone moved near Barry and spoke: 'What's happening here, sir?' He snapped to, gaping dumbly into the lens of a video camera. A young woman stood staring at him with microphone in hand.

'Whaaa . . .' Incoherence was all Barry could manage.

Then there was cursing and he realized it was Chantal, holding open the door of the clinic and kicking at a thickly-spectacled young man wielding a satchel full of pamphlets. She managed a vicious field-goal-style boot at the satchel. Reading material fluttered about them like dead leaves in a windstorm.

Chantal screamed to Barry. 'Get in here, you clown!'

Barry stepped to the door. The TV interviewer pursued him but in another second he was enclosed in the startling calm of the clinic. A lab-coated woman was locking the heavy steel door. A sign directed them to a waiting area. Faded magazines on overburdened racks. There was a reassuringly medical feeling to the place. A woman at a desk asked him about insurance.

'Yeah . . .' Barry flashed his ID. 'We have that covered.'

'You better.' Chantal chipped in. 'I sure can't pay for it.'

Her sharpness reminded him of something. 'Hey, did you call me a name back there?'

'No, dickhead, I did not. Now give the lady some money so we can get this crazy shit over with.'

'Shit?' Barry was finally yielding to exasperation. 'Is that what this is to you?'

'Oh don't get drippy.'

'Sir, are you responsible for the young lady?'

Barry turned to the blue-smocked clerk at the desk. 'I'm her parole officer.'

'Dammit!' Chantal spat. 'So much for confidentiality.'

Barry rolled his eyes. 'Your life is as public as the phone book. I thought you'd be used to it by now.'

The clerk spoke up. 'Is this Ms. DeAlbrecht?'

'Uh, yes it is. And as I said, I'm her PO. Barry Delta.'

'Well Mr. Delta, if possible, could you please afford Ms. DeAlbrecht a decent level of respect.' The woman, who was calm and middle-aged, furrowed her forehead at him. 'This is undoubtedly a difficult time for her.'

'Yeah . . .' Chantal spoke at Barry. 'Listen to her. It's a difficult time for me, stupid.'

'Look, you want this operation or not?' Barry could not stop the heat rising in his face. 'You can pop this kid in maximum security for all I care.'

'Fuck you.'

'One more endearment like that and it's over, my dear. I hope you hear what I'm saying.'

'Mr. Delta . . .' The seated woman arose. 'Ms. DeAlbrecht is obviously upset!'

'Damn right I'm upset.' Chantal pursed an exaggerated pout. 'Get me a doctor!'

'Oh for chrissakes . . .'

'Please stop it.' The woman was out from behind the desk and took Chantal's arm. 'Come with me and I'll introduce you to the surgical team.' She led Chantal down a hall. It was clear to Barry that he was not invited. They were soon out of his sight and hearing. He stood for a minute in the deserted waiting area and looked around. After a few minutes he guessed he was indefinitely alone and took a seat, leafing though the magazines.

Ten minutes later the woman returned and silently re-took her seat. 'Mr. Delta.' She held up a handful of papers. 'There's administrative work to do.'

'Okay.' He stood up. 'How's she doing? Is she co-operative?'

'Yes, but . . .' The woman hesitated. 'Though the procedure is not particularly painful, she's asking for quite a lot of sedative.'

'I'm not surprised. Chantal's been a multi-narcotic and substance abuser since she was a child.'

'Oh. I know these things are common . . .' The woman looked pained. 'But I'm still a little shocked to hear them.'

'Yeah well. Walk around in my shoes sometime.' Barry stood up and shrugged.

At the desk he looked at the numerous forms. He pulled up a chair and whipped out a pen. After ten minutes of filling in blanks he handed the papers back. 'Guess this gets to be some kinda zoo.'

'Whatever would you mean by that?'

'Well that crowd out there, for one thing. Must be quite a stress to go to work every day through that.'

'I suppose. But everyone is entitled to their opinion.'

'I guess. They get pretty rough, though.'

'Not often. Today they're reacting to the latest bubble-zone decision. The courts have knocked it down. It has them all encouraged.'

'Encouraged? I'd hate to see when they get flat-out enthusiastic.'

The woman sighed. 'You get used to it, Mr. Delta.'

'Just like in my world . . .'

'As you say.'

'. . . I been around that professional block a few times.'

'It was hard to tell, what with your . . . irritation.'

'Sorry. Guess that was quite a display earlier, eh?' Barry hung his head. 'I must be slipping.'

She smiled. 'That's permissible.'

Barry realized that the clerk's was the first smile he'd seen today. He happily went back to his seat and resumed his magazine reading. For nearly an hour he took in *National Geographic* and then began to wonder how long the thing would take.

A woman wrapped in pale green approached. 'Are you Mr. Delta?'

'Yup.'

'Ms. DeAlbrecht will be getting ready to leave soon. The doctor would like to speak with you.'

'Uh, okay but . . . I'm not her husband or boyfriend or anything.'

'Nevertheless, you seem to be responsible. She'll need some care for the next few days.'

'Okay.'

She led him down a corridor and into a room.

'There you are!' Chantal was under a thick strata of blankets and had a loose, dreamy look on her face. Her manner at seeing him was outrageously pleasant.

'Yes indeed.' Barry looked around. 'How are you?'

'I'm great . . .'

A woman in a lab coat entered the room. 'She'll be woozy for a while.'

'Woozy . . .' Chantal slurred. 'Woozy.' She smiled slightly and then slackened into semi-consciousness.

The woman took Chantal's wrist and consulted her watch for a few seconds. Then she looked at Barry. 'Are you the husband?'

'No. I'm the parole officer.'

'Oh my.' She replaced Chantal's wrist and held out a hand. 'I'm Doctor Hearn.'

'Hi. Barry Delta's the name.'

'Chantal will require close supervision for the rest of the day, Mr. Delta.'

'She's going to a secure place. They know where she's been.'

'We need to know that she will receive counselling and birth control information.'

'I guess I could arrange that.'

'We have material here for that purpose.'

'Great. Though I guess I have to say, it seems kind of late for that.'

'Not for next time.'

'I guess you've got to think in those terms. Though you'd think she might be at least a little slowed down by the experience.'

'Thinking has little to do with anything when it comes to certain things.'

Chantal opened her eyes and moaned.

'What kind of care does she require, specifically?'

'Just watch her. We had to give her quite a dose of anesthetic. She seems to have a tolerance.'

'That's not surprising.'

Dr. Hearn gestured toward the front of the building. 'And be careful when you leave, there are crazies out there.'

'We saw. Even got our faces on the evening news if they use it.'

'Was there violence? They're not supposed to try to stop you from getting in here. We have a court order.'

'There was a bit of a tussle, but we handed out more than we got. Chantal saw to that.'

The doctor issued a tiny chuckle. 'I don't know why I find that slightly funny.'

'I don't either but I slightly do too.'

'Must be the work. You find humour and lightness wherever you can.'

Barry was taken. 'That's for sure.' Before he could think of anything more to say Dr. Hearn turned to her patient and put a hand on her forehead.

'How are you Chantal?'

'I'm okay . . .' The doctor checked her heart rate again. Then she worked with a stethoscope.

Chantal moaned. 'Aw man . . . Can you get me something for the pain?'

'There shouldn't be any, Chantal. You weren't more than five weeks along and the procedure went fine. You'll have spotting for a few days and you might feel unsteady for the rest of the day. Other than that you're fine.'

'I need something. I don't feel good yet.'

'You will.'

'I need something right now.'

'And yet you are actually okay, Chantal.' The doctor's voice was firm. 'In my opinion you require no further pain meds.'

Chantal rose on her elbows, not taking her eyes off the doctor. 'Not gonna give in, huh?' The women faced each other squarely.

'Nope.'

'You're a hard one.' Chantal's eyes narrowed. 'You're a smart one.'

Dr. Hearn maintained half a smile. 'That's what they say.'

'I'd second that.' Barry was glad to pipe in, standing off, enjoying the show.

'That'll be enough out of you.' Chantal flared him a bloodshot look.

'What happened to your pleasant mood?' Barry clowned. 'What happened to: "There you are." I would have liked to get used to that.'

'What pleasant mood? I feel the shits.'

Dr. Hearn smiled wider. 'Take an aspirin and go right to bed when you get home.'

'I'm not going home.'

'Oh?'

'Yeah.' Chantal swung out off the cot and stood wavering in her hospital gown. 'Thanks a fuck of a lot.' She lurched for her clothing on a chair, snatched them up, and made for a small adjoining bathroom.

'She's not herself.' Barry spoke to Dr. Hearn as the door slammed. 'I'm sure she's actually grateful. Thanks for everything.'

'It was relatively nothing.'

'No it wasn't.'

'You're right, but now you have to do your part.'

'Yeah. The birth control stuff. When her mind is clear I'll be sure to give her the lecture.'

'Make it light and entertaining.'

'Gee, that's the only way I know how to be . . .'

Chantal reappeared, struggling into her jacket. 'Ewww!' She bleared them a jaundiced glare. 'You guys are sickening. Want me to leave?'

Dr. Hearn chuckled.

'Sweetie, watch out.' Chantal spoke intently to the doctor. 'I've seen cunt-hounds before, but this guy takes the fuckin' cake.'

'Goodness.'

'Chantal . . .' Barry was at least pleased that he was able to modulate his voice. He turned to Dr. Hearn. 'We'll be going now.'

'I'll get you an escort.'

'We'd appreciate it.'

With the advantage of surprise and what seemed like real trepidation on the part of the demonstrators at encountering Chantal again, everyone kept their distance.

Barry drove slowly. 'That was some performance back there.'

'Aww I was . . . just kidding around . . .' Chantal spoke in a garble. Then she was coughing heavily.

'You okay?'

'Smoker's lungs. I'll get better when we get there and I can have a good hork.'

'Uh huh . . . probably more info than I needed, but . . . okay.'

They rode quiet for a while until Chantal emitted an audible sigh.

'What was that for?'

'That stuff they gave me. Strong and fast. Good shit . . .'

'Hospital clean. They didn't buy it off some sweaty rock dealer downtown.'

'You got that fuckin' A. But there was extra. They gave me something really cool on top of it.'

'How do you know?'

'By the shitty way I feel now.'

'I'd guess that's a fairly sure sign . . .'

They rode some more and Chantal drew a cigarette out of her bag. Barry watched sidelong as she put it in her mouth and fumbled for matches.

'Don't you dare light that thing.'

'Oh come off it.' She spoke with the cigarette between tight lips. 'I just had a goddamn abortion for fuck sakes.'

'No reason to stink up my life. Just chew on it or something. Eat it even, that would be a good way to get a nicotine hit.'

Chantal pulled the butt from her mouth.

'Wouldn't it?' Barry glanced aside at her.

'Look . . .' She tucked the smoke back into the pack. 'I don't wanna fight with you anymore.'

'Good instinct . . .'

Barry went on driving. When they pulled into the facility she turned to him. 'Are you gonna make me wear a bracelet?'

'Damn right.'

'Why?'

Barry parked the car and turned off the ignition. 'I don't have to run it all down for you, do I? You know the story.'

'I just lost my kid for chrissakes.'

'Oh please.' Barry scowled, looked away, then back again. 'What are you doing time for again?'

'You know already.'

'Tell me again.'

'Murder, okay?'

'You're a lifer, Chantal. At the grand old age of thirty . . .'

'Twenty-nine . . .'

'You killed a john when you were zonked on drugs, and for what reason? Insulting you? Did seven years in the prison for women. Took all the drugs you could get your hands on. Didn't put the time to good use and get an education or anything, yet you luck into a parole because you were so young they felt sorry for you. You get out and get wired all over again and start hooking. I pull you off the streets and find you a women's resource centre to stay in. You burn that place by dealing and using drugs. The only place that'll take you now is a semi-secure electronic monitoring centre with bars on the windows. You get knocked up. You have an abortion. Nobody steps up for you, no family, no friends. The only person in the world who even knows about you is your parole officer. All that . . .' Barry realized he was caught up in his rant and had forgotten where he was going. '. . . all that and earlier today you have the nerve, the gall, the unmitigated cheek to call me names.'

'I said I was only kidding.' Chantal smiled. 'That doctor looked like she kind of liked you.'

'Never mind that.'

'You saw it too.'

'Stop.'

'You're kind of incurable, aren't you?'

'That's up for speculation.'

'Kinda like me.'

This stopped him. 'Will you just go along here, Chantal?'

Silence. Then:

'Okay.'

'Be a good girl.' Moving to open his door, Barry tried to sound suitably sepulchral. 'And please don't kill anyone.'

[9]

MYRA CALLED THE minute Barry had his computer up.

'You don't answer email.'

'Sure I do.' Barry mouse-clicked while he spoke. 'When I get around to it.'

'It just means I have to waste time getting you on the phone. I notice you seldom return voicemail either.'

'Yeah well, you know . . .' Barry noted with slight alarm that he had seventeen messages unopened. 'The older you get the tougher it becomes, blah blah. What's on your mind?'

'That new case gets out today. We're late getting a hard file to you so pull the profile off correctional management service.'

'I don't need a file. I told you. I had this guy's father on my caseload. I can intuit this one.'

'We're not funded for ESP.'

'Oh, hey! That reminds me. Can I get an abortion funded?'

'What?'

'It just occurred to me. We were in a hurry and I didn't actually get clearance. I figured there was a budget somewhere.'

'Back up, Barry. Abortion? For whom?'

'DeAlbrecht, Chantal. We just went and did it.'

'Who told you it would be covered?'

'I just assumed.'

'You know better than that.'

'Sometimes I do. Then sometimes I just go with what's in my heart, Myra. Don't you ever do that?'

'Don't patronize me, Mr. Delta.'

'Oh, you don't have to be like that . . .'

'Have you lost it or something? Should I be recommending an occupational health referral?'

'I'm perfectly occupational. Don't worry.'

'Barry, will you be serious?'

'How can I be? I'm in need of a frivolous bit of stress-release and, even if I do say so myself, fun conversation. Of course I know I have to get medical officer clearance before something like a pregnancy termination, and of course I know enough to pull the profiles off CMS before a new client comes in. Especially for an esteemed client like the living-breathing offspring of the infamous Wayne Stickner. Now, what the hell did you call me for?'

'I received your latest risk assessments. By the looks of my preliminary look-over, you haven't been doing a good job lately.'

'Big news.'

'Your frequency of contact is off. Collateral consultations are near non-existent. You seem to spend most of your time consulting community resource facility staff.'

'Well jeez . . . how do you write about pushing back demonstrators at an abortion clinic and almost getting yourself donged on the head with a placard? By the way, I'd recommend Chantal DeAlbrecht for bodyguard service if you ever need it.'

'You were in a physical altercation?'

'I think you'd call it that. It was scary like one, anyway.'

'You'll have to do a Special Incident report. Right away. Did anyone get hurt?'

'Hey look, Myra. I told you about it just to get a laugh. It wasn't that serious. And I don't want any more work.'

'Barry, you have to record things. It's the only way they officially exist.'

'Man, that sounds existential.'

'Seriously. You could get in trouble if someone makes a complaint as a result of a physical incident.'

'Yeah yeah . . .'

'And you have to start working to standards.'

'Yeah yeah . . .'

'And it all has to be reflected in your RA's.'

'Look, no matter how you dice it, those things don't tell the whole story. 'Specially the way I write 'em.'

'That's exactly what I don't need to hear.'

'Whoops!'

'Never mind the clowning. When are you going to improve on all this?'

'I'm too busy . . .' A buzzer sounded close to Barry's desk. 'Oops, gotta go.'

'That might be your new case.'

'Yes it might. I'll go see.'

'Procedure says you can't see anybody until you've reviewed the proper documentation.'

'Oh for crying out loud. Do you think I can't eyeball a guy like Wayne Stickner's kid without looking at a file? Where do you think I've been all your life, lady?'

'You're lucky I appreciate your connection to the good old days, Barry. There's such a thing as insubordination you know.'

'Lady, I was insubordinating when you were putting up a fuss about nap-time.'

'You might be good at this business, Barry, a lot of people would agree. But you don't do yourself many favours, do you?'

'I have legions of adoring parolees to do favours for me. I get my respect from them . . .' Barry knew he'd gone far enough but couldn't resist the coup de grace. 'By earning it.'

Myra sighed. 'I'm going to do a full review of your files. Let's hope this unprofessionalism only refers to your attitude toward me and not to your whole caseload.'

'Be my guest.'

'I'll be in touch.'

'I know you will.'

'Do you understand your assignments for today?'

'To the letter.' Barry was prepared for the click of Myra's vigorous hang-up, pulling the receiver away from his ear just in time.

He pressed the intercom button and called: 'Be with you in a minute', then went to the CMS site and in seconds had punched up the records for Wayne Stickner Junior, scanning psych reports and criminal history. Despite years in the business, reading all manner of fascinating work-ups from the great festival of dysfunction which was his professional—if not his personal—life, Barry was nonetheless riveted by the sheer scope of young Stickner's outlaw familial history. Nevertheless, it did not take more than two minutes to see that though the bloodline did tend to do federal penitentiary time, father and son were importantly different. Then the visitor buzzer sounded again and he picked up his wall-receiver and asked who it was. The voice asking for him on the other end was an echo down the years. He pressed the catch to spring the outer door and went into a hallway and down a corridor and opened an inner door and there stood what he expected—Wayne Stickner Jr.—a youthful resonance in human form of one of his most notorious past parolees, dead now almost ten years. Dead, Barry sighed to himself, of prison and drugs and fighting and theft and argument and stupidity and all the endless idiocies. Without saying a word he extended his hand.

Barry could see that young Wayne felt hesitation for a second, then tentatively raised his hand to the invitation.

They shook solidly.

Barry paused, thinking for a second. Wayne Senior had died in prison for reasons some of which Barry was aware of but others he was not. The only thing he was quite sure of was that Wayne was dead and that he, Barry, was responsible for it in some limited way. He felt a tingle of guilt in the presence of this person. Then, in a strange revelation, even though Barry Delta was frazzled to the core by the correctional dance he'd been bobbing to for most of his life and sorry for so much of it, the look on this twenty-two-year-old lad's face rendered him oddly cheered.

'Come on in, old chip.' Barry surprised himself with his airy manner. 'Back here.' He began to lead the way.

'Chip?' The voice was a more clear aural version of what Barry remembered of his father's whisky-and-cigarette rasp.

'I knew your dad.'

'I know.'

They came to the office and sat down. Barry regarded the younger man. Though Wayne was fresh in years, there were scars in evidence, old cuts and a rent upon the forehead. Nothing unusual for penitentiary experience. Barry noted again his solid physical resonance of a memory-borne phantom.

'So you know I knew Wayne Senior?'

'Yup.'

'How much do you know I know?'

'I know that Dad was a complete fuck-up and my mother spent her life trying to compensate for the fact that in a weak moment she'd coupled with a rummy who couldn't provide, wouldn't support, and took advantage at every cheap opportunity.'

Barry was taken aback by an intelligence that gleamed from the eyes and resonated in young Wayne's evenly delivered words. 'That's quite an encapsulation.'

'I've got more to tell if you're interested. I've been waiting to meet you most of my life.'

'Holy hell, that's not much of an ambition.' Barry sat back smiling in his chair. 'But we have met before. Do you remember?'

'When I was nine. You came to see Mom.'

'That's right. I vaguely remember a young guy heading to school. Hen-pecked by his mother.'

'She did a lot of hectoring at the men in her life.'

'I haven't got fully into your file yet. I prefer not to, actually, and let guys tell me themselves.'

'Sounds fair.'

'So why are you doing time?'

'It involves Mom.'

'Oh?'

'Not in a criminal sense. I did something because of her, not for her or to her or under her influence. She was never as bad as the men she was with.'

'Forgive me for saying, but in the case of your father that was for sure.'

'You can say whatever you like about my father. I saw him a hot three times.'

'That's all?'

'For a total of maybe fifty days. Most of that was when I was a baby. Mom says he was drunk and or stoned most of the time. I didn't know him.'

'Want my impressions?'

'Maybe someday.'

'Okay. You were going to tell me why you got in trouble.'

'That's easy. I was Mom's pimp.'

'Oh?'

'I'm sure you can see it. She was desperate to make a living and she didn't have an education or work experience.'

'But by the sound of it you do. You're remarkably well-spoken.'

'I put my pen time to good use. I did most of a BA in anthropology.'

'The best of them hit the books.'

'Thank you. It's too bad some of us have to be committed to bitter experience before enlightenment falls.'

'Some of us never achieve that fall. Not in a million prison terms and a billion text books.'

'That's been my observation. I guess you've been around a long time.'

'Yes . . . but that's no substitute for actual wisdom. Go on, tell me about your life with Mom.'

'I loved her. So much. She was my everything, but she seemed to have doom in her head one night when I was ten or eleven. She came home from some debacle my father had sent her on. Just before he got killed. It was a strange time. She had apparently been trying to get some money for him to bribe his way out of not being shanked in the joint and she was as depressed as I'd ever seen her. She sat up late that night and cursed to herself in the kitchen. I couldn't get to sleep. I never knew what happened but a few days later my dad was dead and mom made this decision to get onto the streets and be a hooker again. She made the effort to lose weight, firm up and get some clothes to go working in.

'It was sick. I watched it all. I watched it and spat on the floor and cried and carried on. I made her life hell. I went up and kicked her. She didn't hit me back. She cried. I cry every night thinking of what it must have been like having your kid kick you like that. I wailed away for nights at a time because even at that age I knew what she was doing. But she went out anyway. I watched her. And I stopped crying about it for a while but now I cry about it again because I realized something recently that was even worse than kicking her. Even worse than hurting her and making her miserable. I cry nowadays because I got to expect her to dress up and go out for the night and come back with enough money to buy food and send me to school and get me a yearly pair of designer basketball shoes.

'I started being okay with the fact my mother was a prostitute. The routine of it became part of our lives. As I got more and more attuned to it she started having third and fourth thoughts about it. She wanted to quit. We used to talk about it late at night when I should have been asleep.

'She wanted to quit when she saw that I was used to it. It freaked her. I had been opposed to it so long and then I had to swallow my feelings and keep quiet and it surprised me that when I finally started to talk about it again I was completely on the other side of the debate. I wanted her to keep going. She was in her early thirties. I was fifteen. She'd been keeping us going for almost three years in relative comfort. I was old enough to understand the jam she was in, to know she didn't have skills enough to get a job and support us in a style to which I'd become turned on to. I ended up forbidding her from quitting. She cried and we fought. Physically. I even kicked her again. She was strong but I got the better of it. I'll never forget this. I punched her when she had me down on the floor. She thought she could just sit on me and I'd be under control. But I punched her and she toppled and I got on top of her and grabbed her neck and throttled her. I didn't know what was doing this to me. But I abused my own mother who I loved more than anyone in the universe and yelled at her and forbid her to stop hooking. I can barely believe this even as I tell you. I forbid my mother to stop hooking and I made her dress up and go out that night and I became, guess what, her pimp. It's as plain as that.'

Wayne paused. Both men shifted position in their chairs. Then Barry said: 'And she's dead now?'

'Of course she's dead.'

It came out as a snap, but Barry knew by the pain on Wayne's face that he had not meant to be harsh.

'I mean, how could she be anything else but dead?'

'You're right. I don't know the details, but I get a sense.'

'Officially she was killed by a couple of drunken bastards who treated her like I was setting her up to be treated. I'm to blame. I should be doing life.'

Barry let further silence leaven the heavy air. He said: 'Maybe you are anyway.'

Wayne nodded. 'What did you think of my mother?'

'I'm sorry, but not much. I only met her the once, years before your dad died. When I came to your house.'

'I remember a guy wearing tweed.'

'That was me.'

'There were lots of visitors in those days. Social workers. The police. You were the only one with a Harris Tweed on. You looked like you were uncomfortable sitting on the furniture.'

'I stopped wearing tweed years ago.'

'You're still the same though. I thought about you a lot when I was doing all the stuff I'm telling you about.'

'Really? I would have thought you'd try to forget.'

'I wanted to be like you. I figured you'd have to be tough but fair.'

'We'd all like to be tough but fair.' Barry laughed. 'But anyway. Did you ever get in trouble as a kid?'

'Never. Mom was good with me. She kept me straight and I liked it that she did. I don't know how it happened, living like that, but, aside from the terrible events I've related here, things were reasonably calm when she was around. Until I took over, then things slid.'

'So tell me the rest of the tale.'

'We were living up north. From mill town to mill town. Smoke pumping into the sky all day. Kids on drugs, everybody drinking.'

'Guys in pickups with permanent ball-caps grafted to their heads.'

'You got it exactly. These two sawmill guys took her to a party. I knew them slightly. Steady customers. They drove her out to a place in the woods and had their party. For some reason she took a drink.

She rarely drank when she was working. I figure they must have made her do it. She normally wouldn't unless she was home. I used to administer the whisky. She liked her drink. Anyway, they stayed overnight and as near as anybody knows they drove her back into town early in the morning. It was winter and dark out, twenty-five below. She was near to blacking out. They let her off downtown when they should have driven her somewhere, to a hotel or a coffee shop. They should have just taken her home or something. She had on these light clothes. Even if they'd let her off at the bus station or something. She staggered into an alley and went to sleep beside a dumpster. The garbage men found her and took her to the hospital.

'She lasted a day and a night. I was with her the whole time. For a few hours in the afternoon she almost came out of it and started yakking in her coma. Everything she ever thought she babbled about. The guys she'd been with, a lot about me. About Dad. A lot of crazy stuff. At one point I was sure she was confessing to a murder in an underground parking lot somewhere years ago and carrying on about buried treasure and taking cars apart and on and on. It seemed like she was off-loading all the garbage that had cluttered her mind over the years. She mentioned your name. Either that or it was the name of the town. She once lived there. I couldn't tell. But hearing your name got me thinking about everything that had happened. I listened close to everything she said. I wish I'd had a tape recorder. I felt like she was giving me all the stuff she hadn't covered yet. The thought of crying over her or anything emotional like that wasn't possible; I was too busy trying to listen to what she said. She talked about her life as a little girl. Or at least I think she was talking about herself. There was a lot of material I didn't know about. She talked about being pregnant with me. There was a moment where she was in such pure joy. I thought, I hoped it was over me but I couldn't be sure.

'They left us alone in the hospital. The doctors had done all they said they could do. They were constantly trying to raise her core temperature and get her organs going. There were machines everywhere. I ignored everything, just listened. She talked until the middle of the night and then just lay there and breathed. She breathed heavier and heavier and her face went slacker. I saw her as a little baby and then there were times she looked unbelievably old, wasted and horrible. I started having hallucinations, drifting to sleep and jerking awake when I thought she'd said something. I woke up and she was breathing like through a scuba snorkel, thick and gurgling. I listened for a long time. The hospital was quiet. It was about six in the morning. She'd been dying for twenty-four hours. It felt like she'd been this way all her life. It was all I could remember of her. Weird. I started feeling strange, coming awake like that and then I realized her breathing was disgusting. I knew I'd never be able to take another ten seconds of it. I jumped up, almost nauseous. I closed my hands over my ears and turned to her and tried to apologize but I was just going to have to leave because I couldn't stand it anymore. I felt so ashamed. I tried not to think of how horrible I'd been to her and how responsible I was for her dying and I must have been crying and carrying on like crazy for a good few minutes. Then I took my hands away from my ears and it was silent in the room.

'I knew what that meant. She was peaceful, but I was filled with terror. I took one last look at her. Then I turned around and ran out before I could break into little pieces. I kept going. Out of the ward, out of the hospital, across the parking lot. I'd forgot my coat but the cold didn't do a thing to me. I just kept going. I got to the main street and went into a diner and ordered a coffee and sat sideways at the counter looking out at the traffic, barely seeing anything. I wanted my head to go blank for a while. I'd been thinking too hard and trying to remember everything she'd been saying. And to tell the truth maybe I just wanted to forget her for a while, you know? I was ashamed of the feeling but there it was. I just stared out the window and drank the coffee and tried to feel the steam of it on my face as a starting point to feeling something other than grief and numbness and overload. I was trying not to feel too alone. I knew I'd have to face it eventually. Sooner than later, in fact. The idea scared me more than death. I was so alone it felt like I was frozen solid. I envied my mom. I envied my dad.

'Here I was and the closest thing to me was a half-gone cup of coffee. And then while I was staring blankly ahead of me I saw a car go by outside that twigged something and I realized that it was the car of one of the guys who had picked her up. I watched it go down the street and right away felt life rush back into me. Something took hold in my head. I could live again if I just did one thing. The thing was clear and plain to me. I had to get justice somehow, it was only natural. The idea warmed me. It felt so real and pure and right, like a river running downhill.

'I jumped up and ran out of there and down the street. The car was gone but I knew where they worked and ran like hell through some backyards and down a dead-end street and climbed the fence by the mill and ran across the parking lot where I knew they'd be. They were getting out of the car when I got there. Without a thought I ran at the guy on the passenger side and rammed his head against the door and grabbed his throat and shook him hard and kept slamming his head against the car and the car door. There was blood immediately everywhere and the other guy came around and tried to pull me off. I hit him good and started back at the other guy, kicking him on the ground. There were other guys getting out of their cars and we attracted a crowd. The driver went to the trunk and came back with a tire-iron. I'd finished with the guy on the ground so I just turned to him and stood there and stared. He hesitated, so I lunged. He took a swing and missed. I stepped in close and made some moves. He aimed high and hit me sort of on the side of my forehead. You can still see the dent. I didn't lose consciousness, didn't even fall down.

'The people watching started yelling at the guy to hold off, I was bleeding. Just standing there stunned. He didn't know what to do. Then the crowd parted and the RCMP walked in. A female constable. New, I could see it on her face. Just learning the job. She told us to break it up and tell her what was going on. I looked at the gun in her holster and realized I wanted to die. Right then. Join my mom and dad. It felt as natural as it had felt to need justice. I grabbed the iron away from the guy. I went at the cop as fast and scary as I could so she'd have to shoot me. I came at her, feeling good about not being around anymore. I went right into it, into death, and it felt cool and alive and all my problems and all my pain were postponed indefinitely. I fell in love with the feeling. I still do now, thinking about it.

'But anyway she didn't go for her gun and I slammed against her and she tripped backward. Then some logger-types in the crowd grabbed me and flipped me over and took the tire-iron away.'

Wayne stopped talking and sighed. 'And that's the story.'

Barry sat straight in his chair. As the narrative progressed he'd had a palpable sense of aging, sinking, and feeling heavier and heavier. He knew anything he would say would be insufficient, so simply quipped: 'And it is illegal to try to kill yourself in this country.'

'Yeah there was a lot of talk in court about attempted officer-assisted suicide.'

'Good. It should have mitigated sentence. Your mental state. Everything.'

'Yeah, but I got convicted anyway. On the assault peace officer charge. And assault causing bodily harm. The guy I beat was pretty badly hurt. They gave me four years. My lawyer was legal aid, his first criminal case. My mom never even got mentioned.'

Barry just shook his head slowly.

Wayne shifted in his chair. 'I was relatively okay until I fell on the cop.'

'You were never okay.' Barry tried not to look too affected. 'But if you want to stay clear of all that stuff, listen to me a little, do what you're told for a while, then you're okay now.'

'Then I'm okay now.' Wayne was exuberant. 'Yeah. Okay.'

[10]

IN THE AFTERNOON of this heavy day Barry drove his wife down to the fertility clinic and parked the car in an expensive underground stall.

In the office, as was their routine, Tanya went to report in and Barry tried to figure out where they should best sit in the crowded waiting room. Women were everywhere, mostly by themselves. Barry had to stand up for a while beside where he'd marshalled a chair for Tanya. Eventually there was enough space and they sat together. He watched the big clock above the receptionist. On some occasions they had waited as much as two hours past the appointed time. They had been five minutes early on this day. Now it was twenty minutes past and there was little movement in the waiting room. The doctor was busy. She was perhaps the busiest female obstetrician/gynecologist in the city.

Busy.

Barry fixated on what that meant: Busy. Yes, he knew what busy meant. It meant driving across town with insanity at the beginning and end of your journey. Criminals in crisis; bureaucracies in paroxysms; paperwork sheeting out from computer printers in a malevolent flurry. Things to do, people to see, places to go, shit to pay. Yeah, yeah. Time. Reports. Time. Contacts and reports. Time.

Barry relaxed, thinking. He knew that this sojourn, this particular set of minutes and hours sitting here in the waiting room of his wife's fertility doctor, would at least be stuff he could let pass by in justified limbo, a caught moment or two wherein he could mentally kick back and not be responsible. There would be no talking, the silence and close company of the waiting room allowed no privacy. All this added up to a challenge for Barry not to think of what a sham it was for him to be here, a joke, a pity; stupid, sick, dishonest and nugatory. He shuddered and gazed aside to Tanya.

She was busy too. Tickling her laptop now, trying to keep up to her big-time career in the forensic lab. She was conscientious, a thing Barry much admired, and it was after all still officially work time. She'd blossomed and bloomed, burgeoned in her job these past years. Barry was proud of her. She made good money, more than he.

Fine.

At least there was that.

He leafed through magazines, read about movies. He checked the clock. Almost an hour past their appointed time. The waiting room had shifted but not become appreciably less crowded. The notion of anger entered his thinking.

Anger.

Appropriate?

Probably. For some people, possibly even for him. He had always set himself apart as a person in a profession where anger might naturally be an hourly occurrence, but where the saintly mental constitution of its better practitioners allowed the maintenance of a Zen-like attitudinal repose. He prided his possession of this quality, worried when he lost it, as this morning with Chantal, and held it as a point of social-worker pride that most of the time he was even-tempered. But now amid the arid pointlessness of the waiting, at least for him, Barry considered the possible effects of an angry outburst. Disruption and drama. Upset for the receptionist. Perturbation for Tanya. Fear and trembling for at least some of the waiting patients. Probability of positive outcome? Next to zero. For all the manly assertion points that might be credited to him, he knew that the accumulated minuses of being a cranky man among women would wipe him out. Barry waited awhile longer and then tried to see what Tanya was working on. Some kind of scales and data fed into a graph. He couldn't get a mental grip on it, the view he had. But he knew that there was so much more he could not get a mental/emotional handle on that he willingly gave up, sighed, looked around and then back to Tanya and leaned over and quietly said: 'I guess this isn't a good time to bring up my total frustration with life in general and this process in particular, is it?'

Tanya stopped her data entry but did not look up.

'I mean, does this appeal to you?'

'We have to do it, Barry.'

'We haven't asked ourselves the question of what we have to do for some time now.'

'Are you having reservations?'

Her question brought up the prospect of the big subject, the one he had let burn an acidic hole in his brain for some time. He felt around in his soul to see if there was strength. After a day of jostling abortion foes, fencing with his boss, mentally communing with his latest parolee, Barry knew that what was there was insufficient. 'Forget it.' He worked to keep his voice a whisper. 'Just ticked at this delay again, I guess.'

'It is cruel.'

He widened his eyes to her. 'I'd use that word, yeah.'

'But I want you to be sure, Barry.' Tanya folded the machine into itself and slipped it into her bag. 'I mean, this is no picnic.'

Barry saw on her face and in the depths of her eyes that these words were of critical importance to her. He exerted madly to say something reassuring to her and not lie at the same time. 'I . . . I think we're doing an important thing.'

'You're having second thoughts now?' Her lightning conversion to the interrogative gave him alarm. 'We had this conversation three years ago.'

'Second thoughts? I've had third and fourth thoughts.' Barry looked around and knew that though the other patients were not looking in their direction most of what they were saying was public. 'I've had fifteenth and twentieth and hundred-and-forty-ninth thoughts.'

Tanya looked away, then back at him. 'That's natural.' She spoke quietly, aware also that their talk was not private. She stared Barry square in the eyes. 'Do you still want to do it?'

'It's what you want, isn't it?'

'That's not the question.'

'I just wonder if we've gotten caught up.'

'Caught up?'

'Yeah. In the momentum of it.'

'Momentum?'

'We've been coming here for years.' Barry looked about them and lowered his voice even further. 'We've done all the tests. We've jumped through all the goofy hoops. It's cost plenty of money. It's been such a long slow slog I can't even exactly remember the initial idea. As time goes by I don't feel like I'm getting any more thrilled with the idea. And this seems all too familiar . . .' He waved his arms about them. 'Penned up here two hours past our appointment with a bunch of desperate people who are looking back at us and thinking the same thing.'

Tanya had darkened while Barry spoke and now turned to him, eyes half-closed with what he took to be some kind of disgust. 'Your point being?'

'My point is, do we really know why we've been coming here the last few times?'

'Barry . . .' Tanya's voice lowered as her intensity rose. 'We're trying to have a child.'

'I don't know about you . . .' Barry strove on despite the knot growing in his chest. 'But I get the feeling it's hopeless. I get the feeling the doctor just doesn't have the heart to tell us.'

'That's ridiculous.'

'Is it?'

'Barry, I'm getting very pissed at you.'

They stopped talking as one of the patients, nose in her year-old issue of *People*, cleared her throat.

In a whisper, Barry said: 'I wish just once in a while you'd listen to what I'm trying to say.'

'Barry . . .'

'Fine. We'll go through this charade one more time.'

Tanya looked at him with the beginning of tears in her eyes. 'I've got to find out what's wrong.'

'Maybe there's nothing wrong. Physically, anyway.'

'That's why I'm here. I've got to find out either way.'

Barry sat for a moment, uncomfortable with the closeness of the room, letting their flurry of words dispel. 'Okay, but let's have like a mental re-exam of this whole thing, okay?'

'Of course. But here and now isn't the time and place.'

'I agree.'

'Tonight. We sit down and talk.'

Barry hesitated. 'I don't know what time I'll be home, but yeah. Tonight.'

'I'm doing my stuff for next week tonight, but . . .' Tanya opened her day-timer and flipped a page. 'I'll be home working on this.' She tapped her laptop inside its cover. 'Come home and we'll talk.'

'I will. I may be late but I'll be there.'

They went back to an unfocussed time-using stare about the waiting room. There was movement, a couple emerged from the examining area and another two were called in. Barry and Tanya were almost unaccompanied for the next half hour. Barry read another magazine. Tanya did not unfold her laptop, but fidgeted with a key chain for a time and then pulled a pen out of her purse and attempted to balance her chequebook.

When they spoke to the doctor they sat apart in the cramped examination room. The gynecologist perched on the side of the table with the chrome attachments and regarded a document in her hand and others in a thin file folder. She looked up at them and smiled.

'My most loyal customers. How are you?'

'Fine.' Barry and Tanya answered in unison. The doctor went back to her reading.

'Well, we have the results of the new laparoscopy. And also the latest semen analysis. Mr. Delta you will be interested to know that you still have a motility count in the normal range.'

'Thank you.' Barry's manner was dry. 'Thank you very much.'

'It is a good indicator, isn't it?' Tanya spoke anxiously.

'It certainly is as far as that aspect goes.' The doctor put the file down and faced them. 'Though we knew early on that sperm count wasn't going to be a problem. If I recall we did the testing at the outset and there is little change from then. Which was . . .' she checked the chart, 'three-and-a-half years ago. Very little change from then until now. So swimmers are not the problem.'

The specialist rifled another page of the file. She set down the other papers and examined this new paper with frowning concentration. 'We did a test this time that we don't usually do at the outset in your type of unexplained infertility case. An antibody test.'

'Whose?' Barry had to know. 'Mine or Tanya's?'

'Well, both eventually. But for now we ran the maternal aspect.' A pause. Barry felt she might just be feeling awkward and not genuinely in need of further examination of evidence. 'We might have found the problem. Or a problem, at least.'

'It has to do with antibodies?'

'Yes sir, it does.'

The doctor turned the printed side of the paper toward Barry and almost proffered it as if this might make clearer to him what she was going to say. 'According to these indications, your wife's antibodies are specifically attacking your sperm. It is unclear why that is.'

'Hmmm . . .' Barry tried to lighten. 'What a battle it must be.'

'Can anything be done about it?' Tanya spoke as if Barry hadn't.

'Certain things can be done.'

'And they're expensive, right?' Even while heading irreversibly out of favour, Barry could not help risking further emotional banishment by raising a most relevant question.

'Well, sir, that's a relative consideration. What value do you put on a new life?'

Barry was silent.

'My husband understands the cost factor. What we both want to know is what we have to do.'

The doctor spoke for five minutes, explaining what had to be done. Barry and Tanya emerged from the examination room and moved through the emptied waiting room. Later on, Barry wondered how it was that even before they were out of the building he had already forgotten what the doctor had told them.

[11]

STILL ON THE job at seven that evening, Barry parked on an eastside street so iffy he wondered if he would ever see the government car again.

In this particular block he had once heard gunshots in the middle of the day. Down the street the stripped hulk of a not-so-old SUV rusted on bare rims. Hookers stood on opposing curbs. Pugilistic men with shaved heads patrolled in cars with blacked-out windows. Asian gangsters dined for free in terrified noodle houses. Shadow-eyed junkies paced their way down cluttered alleys. Kids stole umbrellas from cars and sold them for two dollars toward a pebble of crack. Cops cruised by wearing sunglasses in the evening, waiting to hear about critical incidents over the radio.

Otherwise, for the city's worst area—as the day's light receded, birds chirped, and a sweet breeze from the Gulf of Georgia perfumed the scene with cherry pollen—it wasn't too bad. Barry watched as an elderly gentleman caned his way along a sidewalk, struggling to make the bus. A tattooed street girl noticed and stood in the door, holding it open for the fifteen seconds it took for the duffer to make his ride. They acknowledged one another with warm words.

Barry smiled.

He locked the car and walked across the street to a grubby low-rise apartment building. Pressing the intercom button, he at once wondered if the thing would work in its battered condition and imagined palpably the smell of the place within, his destination; the rising filth of the carpets, the grime of its hallways and broken elevator. An unintelligible buzz emitted from the electronic panel and the door lock clicked. He pulled quickly and was in. The smell was as he imagined but the elevator worked.

As was his instinct, Barry stood to one side of the door and knocked. Though Vancouver was not a major gun city, what with the proximity of gun-crazy America he knew this fortunate phenomenon could break at any time. He stood even further aside as the locks clicked, the chains slid back, and the security guard swung open the door to let him in. Barry observed his mufti. 'You're out of uniform.'

'I didn't go in today.' The voice was flatter than Barry was used to. A quick take on the eyes was in order, but the place was dark as could be. There was also the expected malodorous funk, making him believe that the murk was at least partially caused by smoke of some kind.

Without further words Barry proceeded to the outer rooms of the apartment, which was the standard L-shaped one-bedroom-kitchenette-living room-hallway set-up. Holding his breath, he went straight for the sliding glass windows of the living room, parted the greasy curtains and found a handle. He pulled open the window and leaned half out of the apartment, gasping. He turned back to his parolee, who had followed him closely through the apartment. 'I need air to work.'

'Sorry. I been sick.'

'Oh?' In the limited light Barry noticed redness in the eyes, nothing much more.

'Here.' The security guard made for the side of the room. 'I'll pull these curtains.' He yarded the full expanse aside, allowing twilight through the filmy glass.

Barry pulled the window to its widest. In the new light he regarded the room. A kitchen chair and a love seat with a back leg missing. A crumbled coffee table with numerous burns and stains.

'Contemporary junky central.'

The man gestured around. 'I always lived like this, using or otherwise.'

'I guess you go with what you know.'

'That's what I'd say.'

'Yup.' Barry pulled the chair near the window and perched on it. 'Sick?'

'Flu or something.' The security guard stepped over to the love seat and sprawled on it, balancing with a foot on the floor, swaying to and fro in a practiced motion. Barry tried not to be distracted by it.

'Or something.'

The statement hung for a moment while both men exchanged sombre looks.

'I know what it looks like.' The man looked away. 'I'm okay.'

'I'll need you to prove it.'

'The usual way, I suppose.'

'Yup. But there's even more disturbing news.'

'What's that?'

'The results aren't back from your last test. That was what? Two weeks ago.'

'That was when you told me to go, yeah.'

'Okay, that's interesting.'

'Huh?'

'When I told you to go.'

'Yeah, so?'

'Why do you make a distinction about when I told you to go?'

'I'm not gettin' ya.'

'Is there a difference between when I told you to go and when you actually went?'

'I can't keep track of all the times I go.'

'I instructed you to go two Mondays ago. Has there been a problem since?'

'I went.'

'When?'

'Around the time you told me to go.'

'Around the time?'

'Yeah, pretty close.'

'I know you're more or less an alert kind of guy. Why do you think I'm chewing on this issue so much?'

'Because. I guess it's no good to tell a guy to go and then have him wait three days or something to get his system washed out before he takes the test.'

'Good boy. Now how do you fit into that scenario?'

'I went as soon as you told me. Maybe the next day, no later.'

'I'll have to leave that there for now. I haven't had a chance to check on it. All I do know is that the result is not in yet, and that's bad news either way. It means you either went much later than you say, didn't go at all, or that in fact you did go and they found a positive result for something and are having to retest to be sure. In any case, there is warning in the air for me here.'

'I don't know what you mean.'

'I think you do. Anyway, we were talking about your drug testing. Assuming you did go when instructed, I apologize for the time it's taking.'

'How much time?'

'Too much time. Something we're radically short of. We could circumvent this sticky process if you'd simply say what's up with you. Maybe ask for some help. Now I know that's quite a concept, asking for help. But I have every feeling right now that we're up against it, you and me. I mean, I appeal to you as a rational man, as I am sure in your lucid moments you are, to consider things. If you cop to a problem at this point, before you're charged with anything, before the legal fireworks get touched off, I can send you back for a few weeks, get you dried out, put you through a relapse prevention workshop, and boom. You're back here and starting fresh again.'

'I would do that if I felt I needed it.'

'Why do I feel like you need it?'

'Search me. I mean, you have to be sharp to keep a job as a security guard. Did you ever think about that?'

'Oh, stranger and more desperate people than you or I have worked in the private policing area. That's a definite non-starter. Do they do drug-testing at the jobsite?'

'Not as yet, but I would expect so.'

'So you don't know that for sure either?'

'No. Sorry.'

'Don't be sorry, be safe. Think hard about what I said. If you come forward, things are manageable. If the cops come forward, things are fucked.'

'I get you.'

Both men looked away.

Barry examined again the state of the room and the shadows upon his parolee's face. 'And what are you sick of again?'

'I told you. Flu.'

'Or something.'

'I don't know for sure. Maybe it's food poisoning.'

'What are the symptoms?'

'Are you a doctor as well as a parole officer?'

'Don't be touchy.' Barry smirked. 'I'm just asking as a friend.'

They both chuckled.

'So.' Barry sobered quickly. 'What are the symptoms?'

'I barfed.'

'This place smells like shit, not barf.'

'Yeah, well. That too.'

'Uh huh. Tell me more.'

'Not much more to tell.'

'I'm absolutely sure there is.'

'What the hell do you want?' The security guard swung his feet to the floor. 'You know about my barfing and shitting. You wanna know about my burping and farting too?'

'Not necessarily. I was hoping we could talk about your pissing.'

'I pissed in the bottle like you told me to.'

Barry reached into a jacket pocket and pulled his cell phone. 'Have you got their card? It's got their phone number on it.'

'Yeah. It's in my stuff.' The security guard rose from his tilting seat and stumbled toward the hallway. Before he was gone he stopped and said: 'Uhh . . . no. I think I cleaned out my loose papers and all that crap.'

'Never mind.' Barry touched a speed-dial key, then looked up. 'What's the time?'

The standing man looked at his watch. 'A few minutes after seven.'

'Might catch 'em.' Barry listened to the ring tone for several turns. After thirty seconds it was clear the office hours at the lab had passed. He jabbed dead the phone. 'Missed 'em. But I gotta know what's going on. Feel like going back to the joint?'

'What kind of question is that?'

'A pointed, direct, clean and accurate one, I'd say. How's about an answer?'

'You're not getting anything out of me.'

'I noticed that.'

'I mean you're out of line. For a simple servant you like to throw your weight around way too much. I've got rights here. If you suspect me of something you have to have more proof of it than a hunch and a sloppy checking job at the lab to do something about it. You try sending me back on this flimsy shit you'll hear about it from my lawyer.'

'I know I will. Nevertheless, what am I going to do with you?'

'Nothing. I'm working and minding my own business.'

'But you didn't go to work today.'

'I told you I was sick.'

'I work the evenings without benefit of overtime or other such perks because I want to accommodate my boys and girls in their work schedules. I sacrifice, in other words. If you have certain daytimes free when I can see you during business hours I need a call from you.'

'I'm sorry. I didn't realize.'

'Okay, you know for next time.'

'Assuming there is a next time.'

'Good observation.' Barry rose. 'Sit tight, lay low, and call me first thing tomorrow. Don't forget.'

'I won't.'

'Are you working tomorrow?'

'I don't know.'

'Call me in any case.'

'Okay . . .'

Barry walked out of the room, expecting not to be afforded the courtesy of being seen to the door.

Driving away, Barry pulled out his phone, hit another speed-dial key and listened for the various ring tones and shift clicks and buzzes to get through to the ultimate after-hours non-emergency telephone service at the police department. When someone answered he asked for the Attack Force Duty NCO. Presently a voice interceded:

'Detective Jones.'

'Bill. Glad you're on shift. It's Barry.'

'I thought you retired, boy.'

'Me? Quite the contrary my man, I'm working overtime. Just cooking along. Try to stop me.'

'I haven't got time. Easy as that might be to do. Anyhow, how might we help you this evening?'

'You know that character I was speaking about who uses the suspected phony tatties? I saw some leftovers on his wrists tonight. He had a long shirt on but I saw them when he went for the time. I think he's your man somewhere. What have you had done to you recently?'

'Convenience store rip-offs. Gas-bar knockovers. Carjackings. Park muggings, though they might be your gay-bashing situations that turn into robberies. Jewellery store jobs. Home invasions. Et cetera. You're talking a one-guy approach here?'

'Pretty sure he works alone. Kind of a cantankerous bastard. I don't think anybody could co-operate with him, and vice versa.'

'Okay, well scratch the home invasions and the gas-bar thing.'

'Convenience stores don't seem to me his kind of gig. What's the story on the jewellery stores?'

'There's a sex angle. He gets the staff down on the floor and plays goofy games. Does a frottage number on the women, humiliates and batters the men. Not afraid to use violence. Carries a big pistol. Hasn't fired it yet, only swings it. How's that sound?'

'Close.' Barry thought hard. 'Come to think of it, close.'

'Well, that's about it for the crime roundup lately.'

'Any sightings on tattoos?'

'Nobody even mentioned any.'

'How about the surveillance tapes?'

'They're poor. Two of the jobs there was no film in the camera. The rest are blurry and the guy wears a wide-brimmed cap, seems to be hip about keeping his head in shadow, moving around, et cetera.'

'Experienced, eh?'

'At least a little, anyway.'

'Well, that just makes me even more suspicious.'

A pause. 'Aw, that's torture.' Detective Bill's smirk was audible. 'Bein' suspicious.'

'Certainly is. Death to any relationship.'

'Spoken like a veteran.'

'Thanks man, for giving me that much.'

'Don't mention it.'

Barry drove for half a block trying to come to a solid decision whether or not to try to bring the full power of the special police into his business.

The detective interrupted his pondering. 'So where is this fella?'

Even with the crackling phone Barry caught the change of tone in Bill's voice. Police action was like that. In the transition from intuitive social work to the grind of street justice, the seriousness of it, the gravity of hitting the pavement with hard info that might terminate crime, was tangible. It still surprised Barry after all the years; a charged sense of impending action, positive, precise and potentially deadly, like a gun in the hand.

'In his crib.' Barry gave the address from his head while braking for a light.

'Well it's not a slow night. We got some other stuff happening.' Detective Bill paused. 'But this sounds pretty acute.'

'I think so.'

'So what's got you riffing on this guy? Specifically.'

'Oh a cluster of things. The phantom tatties I mentioned. The is-he-or-isn't-he drug question. I just had a good talk with him, gave him every chance to cop, social-worked him good, did a phone-dialling pantomime, opened the door to making rehab an okay option, even humoured him some. Nothing worked. Tight like a clam. A real anti-authority snob. It's the attitude mostly, I guess. There seems to be a psychology aspect. Some kind of they're-not-smart-enough-to-get-me complex too, I imagine.'

'Does he have a car?'

'Yup.'

'Damn, that'll take more resources.'

'Do what you can.'

'We can get on him by tomorrow.'

'Sooner the better.'

'How are we covered, legally, if it turns out he's not John Dillinger after all?'

'Not too bad. I've got a beef on a missed urinalysis appointment that he wasn't willing to own up to. He looks an awful lot like junk-sick or some such. I won't know until I actually do get piss-test results. He's lying around. Maybe lost his job. All reviewable stuff, violations of conditions, et cetera. I could pop him for a two-week cool-off at least.'

'We'll get back to you.'

A click, Barry jabbed the power button. Then he killed his pager too, and that was all for duty this night.

[12]

CHANTAL NEEDED SOMETHING to cover the appliance on her ankle.

She went next door and took some essential items, heavy leggings and a shiny plastic raincoat she'd seen her roommate wearing. They covered what they had to cover and in combination with the hot pants looked at least slightly sexy.

Now for her midriff. She hoped the spandex didn't show too much of her bloating. She felt terrible; her abdomen throbbed like a giant toothache. Then a quick search of her pack for essentials. Pills. She gulped several and chugged them down with water. She sat for a moment on her bunk, breathing deep, then stuffed as many things as possible into a clutch purse and hid that in the bigger bag she had lifted from her other roommate.

The staff looked up as she approached. Chantal held an unlit cigarette in her hand.

'Just gotta get a smoke, huh Chantal?'

'Just gotta.'

'It's almost lights-out.'

'I know.'

'Borrowed Candi's coat, huh.'

'Yup. She said I could use it.'

'That Candi. Generous to a fault.'

'I guess.'

Chantal pushed on the door. It held fast.

'Remember. No further than the sidewalk.'

'I know.'

'That thing will rat on you for sure.'

'I got it.'

'Okay. You've got ten minutes. Have a good smoke.'

'Thanks.'

'Remember. Don't butt it on the building.'

'I remember.'

'Thank you.'

The door buzzed open and Chantal strolled into darkness to join a coterie of anonymous puffers, their positions marked by glowing orange dots in the shadows. She stopped in the midst of the group and lit up. Someone moved close and almost said something before she dodged away, expectorating a viscous clot. She further hacked artificially to discourage conversation. In seconds she was on the far edge of the smoke bunch.

'Hey, isn't that Candi's jacket?' Someone held up a lighter.

'She said I could wear it.' Chantal scanned the wide and busy avenue beyond the parking lot. 'Anybody need smokes?'

Silence.

'I gotta go to the store.' She spoke this to no one, moving away.

Then she was running and she knew that immediate recognition of what was going on would rifle through the group and any instinct to make a fuss would be covered firmly by the imperative not to rat. The Candi thing had made more trouble than she thought it would. In the universal con-code, which sanctioned capital punishment for the offence of ratting, a time-honoured further clause also mandated a similar punishment for theft.

She sprinted to the corner, glad for the pair of shiny new trainers she'd shoplifted the week before. She crossed the wide avenue and flagged a cab. Here again the running shoes helped. The driver made a quick scan and though she kept the coat closed around her she could see he was skeptical until his eyes hit the housewife footwear. That got her in.

'Evening.' The driver flipped on the dome light and gazed at her in the rear-view mirror. 'Nice coat. Don't look like rain, though.'

'Oh I kinda like to be prepared for anything, y'know?'

'Good idea. So where to?'

Chantal waited the maximum allowable seconds before responding: 'Downtown, okay?'

The driver had already had a close enough look at Chantal, but then noticed the facility across the way. 'You got money?' He did not wait for an answer. 'I don't take blowjobs. I gotta have cash.'

'I can pay, but . . .'

'Fuckin' who-ers!'

'Look . . . why don't you just drop me at the bus.'

'Fuck off. Now.'

'I'll be nice to you.'

The driver reached with an expertise that could only have been borne by experience and unlatched her door.

On the sidewalk, trudging aside the roar of six-lane night traffic, Chantal tried to shake off the deep insult the cabby had inflicted. She'd heard it a thousand times.

Whore.

A thousand times.

She gritted. What did he fucking know? She fought the need to scream into the night and then screamed anyway, arcing and aiming into the sullen sky, shrieking even, wailing and blazing herself into the airspace above the city. She willed that she would generate a fatal echo within the din of the traffic. She knew a single rolling tear from an eye would ruin what was the last of her cosmetic supplies so she curtly finished being emotional and reverted back to the more serviceable coldness that was her acquired skill.

When she reached the bus stop, she perched on the bench and fished in her bag for the pumps. She flung the workout shoes into some shrubs. The tightness at her right ankle made her peevish. The seconds ticked on. She tried to ignore the dead space of the bus not coming. Every moment spent sitting out here was dicey. Who knew? Someone at the electronic monitoring program might actually be doing their job. Even without her little beeping bracelet, a random police cruiser would be sure to slow down and give her a look. With effort she held herself from panic and looked for the bus. It was not there. Every pair of headlights could be the end of her little adventure. After five long minutes she saw the trolley round a corner and trundle her way. She paid the fare with the last coins she had, most of which she'd also stolen from Candi.

At a stop downtown, she disembarked and strode delicately toward her old spot. The night was chilly without being too cold, clear and calm, and the way she felt it had better be the best night of her career if there was any way she was going to feel better at the end of it. There was a gnaw, a tangible sharp chewing going on down in her stomach. She'd been careful to eat something back at the facility, even though she wasn't hungry, to try to avoid just this kind of feeling. It got in the way of the easy expression she had to have. The easy, sleazy, fucky kind of look all the dickheads wanted. She caught herself, shoving negative thoughts back into her skull and trying to clear her mind, eyes and face of the trouble, all the trouble. Trouble, trouble, trouble and hurt. My name is trouble. My brain is trouble. My body is trouble. My insides hurt. My crotch is trouble. Who wants to pay for some trouble?

She was on the corner she'd worked while on the run a few months ago. There was one other girl there she did not recognize. She got the look.

'Don't sweat it, honey.' Chantal waved. 'I'm cool here.' She undid the borrowed coat and dropped it into a trash can as she sidled over.

'I never seen you.'

'I'm cool. I been away for a while, but I'm cool.'

'You better be.'

'I am.'

Chantal preened a little, combing hair and flexing shoulders. Down the block she saw three figures approaching, all women, their gait and sway the patented visual signature of streetwalkers.

As they approached one of them brightened. 'Hey, Chantal!'

'Marci!'

'You killer bitch, you. What the fuck happened?'

'I been in a halfway house full of dykes. How 'bout you?'

'Not much fun. I been hanging out at the safe injection site.'

'Where?'

'You haven't heard? They let you shoot up in a warm place now.'

'My dickhead PO never told me.'

'Bummer. Hey, did you hear about Alfie?'

'No. What happened to Alfie?'

'Dead. Somebody offed him in an underground parking lot. Bullet in the back of the head.'

'That fucker. I told him to stick to girls and not go dealing with those dope dicks.'

'He never listened.'

'So who's the big boss now?'

'Everybody's working for Stu.'

'Little Stu?'

'Big Stu now. He took over Alfie's barn. It's kinda good now, actually. Better than when Alfie was here.'

Chantal sighed and looked around. The woman she'd spoken to earlier was still glaring at her. 'This is fucked.' She took Marci aside. 'What do I have to do to get back on?'

'Stu's cool. Just remind him how good you were for Alfie.'

'He hardly knew me.'

A car drew to the curb so quietly Chantal did not notice until she saw that Marci and the other women were not listening to her anymore. She looked where they were looking. The car windows were blackened as usual. The driver's side rolled electronically down and a young man with a clean-shaven head and a solid case of acne leaned outward. He saw Chantal. 'I know you.' He looked closer. 'I think I'm glad to see you.'

'You're Stu. I used to work for Alfie.'

'Alfie's dead a mile. Where you been?'

'In a halfway house for dykes.' This from Marci, standing off a ways. There was laughter among the group on the sidewalk.

'Halfway house?' Stu's expression changed and he looked slowly up and down at Chantal.

'I'm on parole.' She lifted her laden ankle and tapped the device through the thick legging. 'It's cool as long as I wear this . . .'

'What!' Stu did not bother to look.

' . . . It's just 'lectric jewellery.'

'Heatbag bitch! Get the fuck off the corner.'

'Stu, come on. They're slack as hell at that joint. Nobody's hassled me yet.'

'You're from this curb and out this street and away this town and off this planet before I come back. Or fuck will reign, understand?'

'Come on Stu. It's okay . . .'

'And if the cops or your PO or a social worker or a street ministry type or any other such bitch, dyke, fag, pig, asshole or concerned citizen shows up here because of you it's going to happen anyway. The off-planet part. Get it?'

The others had orbitted away from Chantal. She swallowed hard and looked long into the face of baldheaded Stu. 'Pizza-faced dick. Alfie did you a favour just to piss on you.'

Stu drew back his head and smiled, staring cold into the dark street beyond Chantal. Then the electric window rose and sealed, and the car left the space it had occupied. Chantal rummaged for the coat in the trash bin, put it on, and looked about her at the receding corps of streetwalkers.

'Marci!' Chantal sprinted. 'Gimme just a minute, okay?'

Marci turned and broke from the squad. Her face was not the friendly port Chantal had hoped for, yet she did stand still in the streetlight and wait until Chantal approached.

Chantal was careful to get the first word in: 'I'm hurtin'.'

'I'm not that fixed myself.'

'Anything at all you might have . . .'

'It'll have to get you gone, Chantal. Sorry, but you should know better than to bring radar into the jobsite like this. What's the matter with you?'

'I just lost a kid this afternoon.' A pause to let it sink in. 'I got damage. Help, willya?'

Marci's face changed. 'I got codeine. I might have some valium left . . .'

'On you?'

Marci took Chantal's arm and led her to a doorway, out of the light. She produced a Ziploc bag of pills and poured a dozen or so into Chantal's waiting palm. Then she turned the tight waistband of her hot pants over and pulled the seam apart and picked three blue pills out like a bear pulling grubs out of its own fur. Chantal took these directly to her mouth, dry-swallowing hard.

'Marci, you're a babe.'

'Yeah. Get lost, eh? Hope you do okay.'

'I'll get this fuckin' thing pulled off me.'

'That'd be good.'

Marci back-drifted into the darkness. Chantal stood with her handful of Tylenol-3s, thinking of ways and means of doing these small delights to their greatest power. For seconds she stood, stymied by the limited capacity of her mind in organizing the various options available. Then she remembered Rick's, the main hooker hangout. A coffee shop. Perfect for now. Without consciously making a decision her feet were moving to take her there. All she needed was a few minutes in the washroom. She could manage that.

Half of Stu's flock were taking coffee and preening in the fluorescent glare of the diner. They did not have to look at Chantal to make her know they knew she was there and that she shouldn't be. Finding a certain curious comfort with excommunication, she made immediately for the washroom in a silent beeline, buoyed that her friendlessness meant she would not have to share her pills. Inside, she turned on the cold water and cupped a hand under the stream to sample the water. Before it ran completely cold she had gulped a couple of the white pills. More water in her hand, she gulped again. Repeat, repeat, breathe, panting, then repeat again and the pills were gone. She straightened at the sink, not turning off the water, and sighed. Then she grabbed her bag and strode to the door, imagining and executing in her mind the direct route to the outside and the hell away from these catty bitches. The fresh air would feel prime and it did. A gust of car-driven breeze ruffled her coif and washed over her hot face. Lovely. At last, lovely. The pills had barely begun to work but she felt fine.

Across the street a couple of twenty-somethings came out of a stripclub. A cab chirped to a stop aside them, blocking Chantal's view. 'Hey!' The call escaped her before she had time to think and she knew the old survival instincts were kicking in to help her. She kicked across the street. Cars screeched for her, she waved at them with both hands in the long coat, flashing her spandex. When she got to the cab the boys had climbed in and were watching her with grins. She was feeling attractive.

'Hey girlie . . . nice dodge.' She could see that one of them was at least impressed by her dicey prance across traffic.

'Sweetie . . .' She pouted as cutely as she knew how. 'You need me, don't you?'

'Need you?' The one who hadn't watched her so much sneered. 'That's a fuckin' good one.'

'Ooooh you're so hot too . . .' Chantal spoke through a half-open window, her rear hanging in traffic. She could feel the wind of the cars passing inches from her body. 'I like hot boys.'

'We're real hunkaroos.'

'You can't talk here.' The driver spoke over his shoulder to no one in particular.

'Do you do . . .' The intent one stumbled, blushing. 'Umm . . .'

'Sure I do "umm". I do everything you umm want me to. Umm, baby.'

'Wow!'

'Well let her in.' The less interested one took the initiative. 'Open the door, stupid, and let her in if you're gonna.'

The door opened and Chantal knew to spread herself across to the middle where she could have equal influence. She had to be quick to beat the nearest boy from sliding over. She half-sat on him. 'I like boys.' She cooed her finest. 'I like boys a lot.'

'Where to?' The driver still spoke generally.

'You guys got a room in town?'

'Yeah we do, Miss . . ?'

'Chantal is my name. What's yours?'

'Never mind that.' The driver turned around. 'Party if you feel like it but I gotta get out of this spot.'

'The Ramada.' The distant one had firmly redirected Chantal's fingertips when she was settling into the seat beside him. He exuded a peevish impatience. The tone of his voice made Chantal know the evening's score would take time and effort.

'I guess you can tell we're from out of town.' The friendly one hadn't moved his hands or body away from her like the other one. Chantal wormed into him and flapping her lashes as breezily as she could, peered close into his eyes.

'Where you from, sweetie?'

'Oh we're from a town called Revelstoke . . .'

'For fuck sakes, Terry! Don't tell her anything.'

'Why?'

'She's a fuckin' hooker for chrissakes.'

'I know that, stupid.'

'Boys! I'm your entertainment for the night.'

'Yeah, well . . .'

The cab was moving swiftly into mid-town. Chantal enjoyed the softness of the seat beneath her and the warmth of the car. Her stomach felt better. She rejoiced that the pills were starting to work.

'Jeez Don, loosen up, willya?'

'I got no money for this. Do you?'

Terry pushed a hand into his jeans. 'Think so. There's a bank machine in the lobby.'

'You think we're takin' this whore into the hotel?'

'Well . . .'

Chantal slid fingers under Don's thigh. It was worth a go, had worked before in similar circumstances, and she felt like she would die if she did not get the money and did not get a good rush before the night was over.

In this thought-train she realized her fingers were getting numb under the hard bulk of hostile Don but Terry was still cozy against her on the other side.

How to play this?

'I'm starting to like you guys . . .' She massaged Terry's thigh and went for excess, leaning into Don and opening her mouth to his face, wondering what might have the best effect, settling on a darting tongue-touch to his nose and a cheek rub and a ruffle of his profile with her hair.

'Ohhh, baby.' Terry moaned.

'Fuck!' Don spat, recoiling. 'She stinks like cigarettes.'

'Come on, Sugar. You can be nice, can't you?'

'Don't call me sugar or anything else you disgusting piece of trash. And for fuck sakes don't try to kiss me again or I'll smash your face in. If there's anything I can't stand it's a smoke-bitch.'

'Hey watch it, Don. These city girls carry little guns and knives and they're pretty tough I heard. Are you tough like I heard, Chantal?'

'Tough? No, baby, I'm gentle. I wouldn't hurt a fly.'

'There you go, Don.'

'This whole thing is starting to piss me off.'

'Don't talk like that. This is my holiday too you know.'

'I say it because I mean it.'

'Well just shut up, okay?'

For the second time tonight Chantal had to hold herself upright as the cab swerved violently to the curb and stopped. The driver turned and glared at her.

'Okay sister. Get out.'

'Gimme a break.'

'No.'

'I'll piece you off. Come on.'

'Hey driver. Don and me are just having a little argument. Nothin' heavy.'

'All three of you are going out in a minute.'

Don yanked his door handle and in one movement lurched from the cab, cruelly gripping Chantal's wrist. He wrenched her off the seat and sent her sprawling across the sidewalk. Passing tourists paused to watch the bit of TV-style action. In a slick movement Don whipped himself back into the cab and slammed the door. The cab moved instantly and Chantal was only able to stand up and make certain she still had her bag before they were completely gone.

She stood for a moment, wavering. The pills were working more. She did not especially suffer the coldness of the air upon her shoulders. After a minute she noticed a short man in front of her. One of the tourists. 'Ma'am.' He held something in his hand. 'I think you dropped this.'

Chantal looked at the object in his hand and then at her bag. It was partially open and she could see the last of her make-up and a couple of dimes glinting back at her. The man handed her the object and she looked at it. A shiny, lightweight, easily concealed straight razor. It had belonged to Candi. One of the essential items. She looked at the man who had helped her. He was walking away. She wondered if he knew what exactly it was he had handled in his soft pink hand. She zipped the bag tight and slid the razor into a pocket of the stolen coat.

She proceeded down the slight hill toward the old part of town. The direction did not matter to her. She did not care. Walking and walking, it was soon that she broke with full consciousness, forgetting, and walked on in a stupor.

At some point later she stood stupid in the middle of a pedestrian mall and met the eyes of an oncoming man in a business suit. She liked the way his tie was loose and his muff of curly hair fluttered in the breeze. 'Hey sweetie.' She spoke to him at their passing point. 'Want company?'

Though he was striding hard like someone who had somewhere to go the man broke pace slightly and turned to her.

'Baby . . .' His expression was instantly derisive. 'You should be so lucky.'

In the second it took she saw her ugliness, reflected in the man's face. Then he was striding away, hands in pockets, hair flying. A gust of air threw his tie up over a shoulder and waving in the currents and looking to Chantal like the mocking salute of a child facing rearward in a car going down a road toward good things. Things that she would never see or have and could never hope for in all her miserable life.

The pills. Energy. Madness and memory. Her ugliness and his smug perfection. Their fate together. The razor came naturally to hand as she sprinted. His neck was a target before he could sense the footfalls behind him and before time caught up with them they were alone on the sidewalk and a red shower was warming her face. The man stopped and teetered.

'Wha . . . ?'

She struck again, cutting deep as he turned, leading the blade across from the back of his head and down a cheek and as Chantal leaned forward, across his throat and then back again, jabbing and hacking, her free hand playing defense against his flailing. She cut with no mercy, feeling attractive, until he dropped to the dampening pavement, legs kicking useless at the night air.

Chantal stumbled on. A few steps away she slid in her shoes and tumbled and decided because the warmth of the pills was so snug and she had no more energy and the sidewalk was her home that she would just curl up and drift to an untroubled sleep.

[13]

WITH THE PHONE and beeper shut off and buried in his clothes, Barry drove downtown and swung the car into the government garage.

Walking the downtown, thinking about a bus, Barry knew he'd be debating about whether or not to dismount at the Yale for a well-earned brew and a shot before the trudge home. Ultimately he was wrong; there was no debate. Craving distraction, in minutes he was listening to the warm-up act.

The place was crowded but his regular seat was still available. He headed for it, hoping Rikki would be quick tonight, but before he could get there, he heard his name being called. There were several voices, female voices, so he stopped immediately and there it was again, women calling his name. He looked over the crowd and isolated a table below the jumbo TV. Looked like a girls'-night-out group. Most of them were looking his way. One of them was Jill. He recognized most of the others as workers he'd met once in a while at the women's facility.

They called to him in unison, as much as semi-drunk ladies on an innocent tear could be unified. He knew he was caught, and was surprised at himself, given that this was a table full of women, for being reluctant. But in the instant of recognizing his name across the buzzing crowd and through the silken vibes of the blues music he regretfully put aside the comfort of a snug and solitary drink. He winced mentally now at the imperative to talk and the mental-moral-visceral consequences of being attracted, which he was to at least three of the five women present. The shrug he gave then was intended to be visible. He waited for them to simply wave and go back to themselves. When they playfully did not he stepped a methodical path through the chairs and people and came upon their table.

'Evening, girls.'

'Women!' they shouted, some angrily.

'Yeah, yeah, I know.'

They made room for him. Unconscious or not, resistant to intrusion on his solitary state or not, he made sure to sit beside Jill.

The one over from Jill, a woman he could not recall having met, leaned toward him. 'So you're the notorious Barry Delta!'

Barry smiled wide. He noticed the near-empty glass of beer in front of Jill. 'Can I buy you a drink, Jill, or are you already pissed?'

'I can drink you under the bed anytime.'

The women hooted. Barry puzzled at Jill's curious choice of boast, with all its suggestion of grappling privacy, but put it down to the reputed fact that sexuality was apparently the permanent context of all female discussion.

Then Rikki came by and he was quietly tickled that he hadn't had to call to her. She plopped his boilermaker on the table and stood looking at him with her patented incendiary smile. He sipped quickly from the whisky and looked at her, then fired a twenty direct from his pocket into her hand, waving to dismiss the necessity of change. She took the bill and winked. He caught her private grimace at the gaggle of women he was with. He shrugged. She sauntered away. Barry gulped his beer and thanked providence for the easy alignment he naturally achieved with at least some women. He saw that Jill had watched the performance with glaring interest.

'How'd you get such a reputation?' This from a woman Barry had liked when he worked with her but whose name he had utterly forgotten.

'You're gonna have to help me out here. What are you talking about?'

'Well you know you're our favourite PO.'

'Gee really?'

'You know that.' Another of them, this one Barry had only met once or twice and had not been attracted to. 'You're the only one who takes the time to talk to us.'

'I don't see how the other POs can get around doing that. I mean, you guys are on the scene day and night. You know what's happening.'

'You've got some of the toughest assignments.'

'Well . . .' In mock-machismo Barry drew hard on his beer and picked up his shot glass and looked at the whisky. 'I've been around a while.'

'Exactly how long have you been around?'

'Oh, twenty-four years, off and on. In this service. Mostly on. I worked in the States for a few months one time. San Francisco. Loved the weather but I couldn't handle the gun thing. Down there guns are like opinions. Everybody's got one. So I came back.'

'Is it really true that you're married?'

This came again from the one he couldn't remember the name of but had liked. He noted she was at least semi-drunk, they all seemed to be. 'Yeah.' He looked around the table and realized he was bone-weary for some reason. 'Why would it not be true?'

Jill shrugged. 'It's just that you have this reputation.'

Barry tired to smile, but found he could only grimace. 'Smile when you say that.'

'You don't act married.'

'Well I am. So . . . there you go.' He drank, hoping the subject would change before he put his glass back down.

'I think it's pretty shitty.' Jill would not let go of what seemed to be the topic of final fascination to the whole table.

'Hey, aren't you guys supposed to be out for a good time?' Barry turned to her, unsmiling. 'What makes you so judgmental tonight?'

'Oh . . .' Jill caught herself. 'Sorry. We had some shit happen.'

'How bad?'

'Not very, but we're just tired, you know.'

'Naw . . .' Barry finally managed a smirk. 'Not energetic old me.'

'Oh right.'

'Anything you want to blame me for? I charge reasonable rates for punching-bag service.'

'No thanks. We're just blowing off hot air over the whole fucking social-service correctional gender-political bureaucratic structure.'

'Oh. Okay . . .' He took a drink, beginning to regret where he was and who he was with. 'I hope you get it worked out.'

'Forget it.' Jill's voice was flat. 'What did you do with Chantal?'

'She needed an abortion and a place to stay. I got her both.'

'Just like that.'

'Oh come on . . . what else do you want me to say?'

'Were you a friend to her?'

'Did you advocate for her?'

'I can't be a friend to the caseload. You all know that. You should be friendly but you can't be a friend.'

'That's cold!' This from the woman Barry did not know.

'How do you know what's cold?' The table went quiet. Barry gazed over toward his favourite sitting spot and wistfully yearned. 'I'm sorry, but I'm not sure I can listen to a lot of criticism right now. I had a bitch of a day, too.'

'You're gonna fail us . . . aren'tchoo Barry?' He hadn't clearly heard the slurring in Jill's voice before now. With near dismay, Barry observed this did not make her any less attractive. Despite the vague political danger of his staying in this company, her allure was an intoxication strong enough to make him stay seated. The situation improved when half the party got up to leave. Jill refused an invitation to go for something to eat, her eyes on Barry. She ordered water on Rikki's next go-round. The music got better and louder and they listened. Then the rest of the women said their goodnights and Barry and Jill were alone. Barry's drinks went down and worked their benevolence and his fingers and feet loosened.

At a break in the music she seemed to muster her conversation: 'Barry, there's something funny about you. It's something funny but it's not ha-ha funny.'

'Oh?'

'It's your attitude towards women.'

'Uh huh.'

'Didn't anybody ever tell you that?'

'Lots of times. But I haven't listened.'

'Well I've just got to say it.'

'So it's my attitude.'

'Yup.'

'Help me out here. Tell me what you think my attitude is. I honestly don't think I can put it into words myself. Tell me your version, then maybe I'll know better.'

'There you go. Mr. Flip.'

'Sorry if I sound that way. Seriously, tell me what's in your mind.'

'Well, it's women.' Jill leaned closer. 'You seem fascinated by them, engrossed, attracted to them. Yet I sense you don't understand them in the least.'

'What man can claim he does?'

'I don't know. I've met some who seemed to have a clue. At least on an elemental basis.'

'What element, specifically?'

'I don't know, I'm just making an observation about you.'

'Is it an observation or a criticism? It sounds like a slag.'

'You sexualize any and all contact with women.'

'Sexualize?'

'Yes. Take me for instance.'

Barry had stopped the scotch after the second round and was now on beer alone, trying to slow down. He shook his head slightly, thinking. Nevertheless, despite his determination to not let things go completely to hell, the state of his ineptitude this night caused him to answer with: 'I'd like to.'

Jill sighed.

'I take that back!' He laughed as he said it, he hoped she knew that it was at himself.

'I wasn't trying to be funny.'

'No no, I know you weren't. I mean . . .' Barry collected himself. 'I thoroughly didn't mean to cheapen your statement like that.'

'Accepted. But the way you're acting now just exemplifies the problem, doesn't it?' She paused, looking closely at Barry. 'How long have you been objectifying women?'

'I'm not sure I know what that means.'

'That's not surprising.'

'I'm sorry but the concept escapes me. Objectifying? I've thought about this kind of stuff more than you might think, and I've always had a block, an understanding cramp, that stops me. Simply put, I don't know what you're talking about and I thus don't know how to fix it. But I'm open to being taught.'

'You look on all women as potential bed partners, don't you? Above all. Before anything else.'

'I don't think so but I might understand why you feel that way. I mean, you've seen me with women and you've experienced for yourself what I'm like as a flirt. I admit it. But that's not all there is to me. I'm certainly not just a hunter-gatherer. It would be facile to conclude that of me. Sure I go for pretty women, but there's a lot of other stuff I like. Humour. Intelligence.'

'I find it difficult to see beyond your permanent bedroom leer.'

Barry drank and looked away. 'I have no excuse . . .'

Jill looked at him with what he feared was coiled sarcasm, ready to fling a stinger. He braced for the hit. Then she said: 'Yes, I see.' She spoke without looking at him. 'Are you separated from your wife?'

Barry opened his mouth, preparing for a lie. He started to speak. Caught himself. 'Shit!'

'What?'

'Oh . . .' Barry pushed his chair backward. 'I forgot something.'

Jill sat silent, rubbing a fingernail in the condensation of her water glass.

'I have to run down to the phone, okay?' Barry stood up.

'Of course.'

Eschewing the government cell in his pocket because of the likelihood of having to justify a personal call to Myra, Barry ran to the back of the bar and dropped a coin into the pay phone, praying Tanya would not be so furious as to not give him a chance to explain.

Explain.

Why had he not gone straight home?

Forgetfulness was not going to suffice as an explanation. She would not accept it, he was not sure he did either. It was the content of going home, the plan. Baby discussion, yuck. Some sort of denial-based amnesia. Barry scowled involuntarily.

By the third ring he began to scheme.

After fifteen rings he was concocting full speed what he would say to her, the defensive anger he would show when at last he returned home and demanded to know why she had not answered the phone.

More rings. He slammed the receiver down.

Back at the table Jill was seated as before, but with a fresh glass of club soda in front of her.

'Is everything okay?'

Barry wasn't prepared for the question.

'Huh?'

'You looked worried.'

'Naw naw . . .' He lifted his glass and drank the last of its beer.

A moment went by with Barry trying to think of what to say next.

Jill saved him the trouble. 'So?'

'So? Uh . . . oh yeah. You were asking me something.'

'Are you or are you not separated?'

Separated?

'The reason I ask . . .' Jill's voice was low but determined. 'You sure act like it.'

He pictured Tanya. Her face and her voice. Their interminable wait at the doctor's office. Their house. The phone ringing and ringing to the background sounds of weeping.

Then for some reason he could think only of his riding the bus every day, and work, and trouble. There was no more marriage information. He shook his head, turning away from Jill and struggling.

Nothing.

He turned back to her. He saw that she had been prepared to wait for an answer. Her face was perfect to him in that moment. Pure loveliness. He desired in that moment with all his essence to touch her, kiss her mouth, entwine fingers. Shut away the annoying bar noise and assuage the sway of the alcohol and banish the fatigue pervading him. But he knew himself, knew his failures. He understood in that moment that he was not up to living his life, not capable of full participation. The causes were many, he also knew, and the first one that popped into his mind was that of indecision. In that moment he decided to resolve something, to change. He tortured his heart about it. He winced inside. Swaying, he felt he might collapse altogether and fought his physical being back into alignment with the chair he was sitting on and the table he held onto with both hands and the woman he was speaking to. From this tempest the answer was almost easy.

'Yes.' Barry spoke, proudly, he realized, not lying.

'You're separated.'

'Yes.'

'You're sure?'

'Uh huh.'

'Okay. One more question.'

'Go ahead.'

'Can you change?

'Change?'

'Yes. Can you?'

Before Barry could respond Rikki was at the table pulling Barry's sleeve and pointing to the TV screen above them.

'Hey!' She pointed upward. 'You're on the news.'

'Wha . . . ?' Barry looked at her and then up to the screen. Though the large projection machine did not produce a sharp image, and the angle was acute, there was no denying that the huge silent speaker depicted was himself. For a second, bound up as he was in the torpor of the moment, he couldn't comprehend why this was.

Rikki had to shout. 'So you're a star, huh?'

His abortion clinic video-bite. The realization jolted Barry to near nausea.

'Hot stuff.' Jill sounded peevish again.

'Shit . . .'

Jill nodded to the fleeing Rikki who pranced away among the tables, tray balanced skillfully in hand. 'Your barmaid girlfriend seems to think it's a big kick.'

'She likes me.' Barry felt peevish too. 'Most real women like me.'

'What's that supposed to mean?'

'Just another of the wrong things I've been saying tonight.'

'Don't be too hard on yourself. You're a TV personality.'

They watched as the remainder of the news item flickered by. A shot of the protesters, the scuffle, himself, Chantal decimating the mob. Barry was thankful they didn't show Chantal's assault on the elderly woman. Beside him Jill yawned.

'What time is it?' She touched at her empty wrist.

'Well the local news, which we're watching, comes on at eleven-thirty.'

'That late!'

'If you think before-midnight is late, then yeah. It's late.'

'God, I've got to get going.'

Barry stood. Jill took his hand as he helped her up. She gathered her purse and sweater and they made for the door.

The sidewalk greeted them with a cool breeze from the fish wharf, the scent of salt and creosote snapping Barry to an acute consciousness. Jill let her sweater fly with the airflow. She seemed to be wondering whether or not to put it on. Barry spectated every movement, enjoying her fluidity and the fact he could think of no other thing or person at this moment. The clarity of his mood yielded boldness, and he decided once again to go for broke: 'I want to touch you right now.' Bold in his newly self-granted freedom, he felt it proper to reiterate: 'I'm sure of it.'

'Hmmm . . .' She seemed not to be listening, but trapped the sweater in folded arms and turned to him. 'Should I put this on?'

'That I'm not so sure about.'

Jill worked her hands into the sleeves and placed her head in the neck-hole. She looked at Barry and held up her arms. 'You can help me with this if you like.'

'Of course.' With both hands and all his fingers he agitated the sweater down her body. When it was in place he moved his arms to his sides. 'Can we do that again?' He grinned.

'Hmmm . . .' She dithered, not moving.

The street traffic churned on, unmindful of the couple standing by the entrance of the bar staring at each other. The combined effects of desire and alcohol began to make Barry suffer. He tried not to waver in the breeze.

Jill glanced down and pulled a plastic-clad bus pass out of her pocket. Then she moved dramatically closer to Barry and said: 'No.'

'No?'

'Yes. No.'

'Okay.'

'There's my bus!' Jill sprinted across the street against a DON'T WALK sign. Barry did not feel like running, even though it was also his bus. Jill made no attempt to see if he was following. In several seconds she had disappeared inside and the bus was grinding from the curb, beginning its up-hill labour across the Granville bridge. Barry watched it diminish in the massive distance and sink promptly out of sight beyond the horizon-like crest.

He looked at his hands. He'd located bus change in the awkward moments following the sweater maneuver. He forced himself to count the coins and saw that there was not enough for bus fare.

It hit him. Bus fare to where?

Nowhere at the moment, if what he had just said to Jill was to have any force at all. He willed it have total weight. There were things to consider here.

Living arrangements.

Homelessness.

With difficulty ahead, the want of further drink intervened. Barry listened vacantly to numerous far-off police sirens, knowing by their ubiquitous warble that things were normal, then pocketed the money and made for the door of the club.

[14]

THE MYNAH BIRD OF CRIME knew this might be a turning point. Whatever the deal, he was tired of fooling around. No wrist-art for this night.

He checked the street through the curtains: Nobody.

Nobody in the truest sense of the fucking word.

Nobody out there who gives a shit, I know it.

Nobody cares about me or what I am or what I've done. Or what I'm going to do.

This is as it should be.

There should be freedom in this society.

As long as you don't hurt anybody. As long as nobody gets killed. As long as you don't have any bullets in your gun. As long as you don't even have a gun that shoots. As long as your weapon is just your brain.

He armed up with jacket, gloves, jogging shoes, loose coinage. Of course, the mock piece. Its bulk in the waistband of his jeans was its usual comfort. Comfort was what he needed in these, the minutes and hours since Delta spewed his vile effluvia around these rooms.

Fuck.

He was out the door, cursing and striding to the bus stop. No car this time. No gas. No insurance. Barely bus fare. No money of any real consequence. No more shit. Fuck. Sitting at a bus stop in the fucking rain. Fuck. Delta. Fuck. No shit of any kind. Fuck. Nothing to take the edge off. Fuck. Nothing to build up an edge on. Fuck.

Holy suffering shit, man.

He held his head in his hands. There might be just enough logical matter left in there to organize something.

He cried out with the effort of thinking and knowing there were no narcotics in his world at the moment. A young girl at the bus stop took notice. He watched her and imagined what she might be thinking, how pathetic he looked. He flexed his fists and bit into one of them until there was the muddy taste of blood. He centered on the pain, gripping himself with it.

You've gotta do a knockover for chrissakes.

He flexed more and bore down harder. He quivered with the pain, doubled over on the bench. Then the girl and the other bodies around him arose in unison as the bus pulled to the stop. They stood around him and began to board. He was still clenching his fists. His brain committee held an emergency session. The message came through loud:

Unclench.

Get up.

Step into the vehicle.

Toss the fare.

Find a seat.

Await further instruction.

He stared out the window. The jouncing of the bus let him feel his body more correctly. As the bus got him across the bridge and into downtown he began to assume control. His mind freed itself and wandered slightly. He could not forget his two-hour-old conversation with Barry Delta. What was going on there?

On the evidence it was clear that he might have to accept that Delta was capable of ulterior thought. This was a frightening proposition. He yearned for the aid of blessed cocaine to clarify this important area of query. Clarifying coke, not rock, not that goofifying accelerant, not quite yet. Just coke for a few snorts. Good old brain-greaser. That would be the first acquisition, post-score.

Score.

The deal he was thinking of had materialized one evening when he still had the car. A drive through town with nothing particular to do. An image had stuck in his consciousness and he'd swerved to circle the block and look again. A small place near a rummy residence run by the Sally Ann, so frequented by scuzzrats he'd never considered this area before. But there it was, a small independent glitter store with a sweet virgin behind the counter. Nobody else.

He'd watched until it closed. Thin business. Nobody else in the store. Ripe.

Now he rode the bus with the solid metal at his belly. He closed his eyes slowly and let the pictures come to him. The place. The jewels. The babe with the frightened, respectful expression on her face. He'd watched her for enough time to know what she was like. Somebody's daughter. Her face pleased him. He let himself like her.

Riding the bus he came up with these facts and was sufficiently surprised to smile. He felt alive. Even without blow. He closed his eyes again to try to keep the feeling. It held. He tried opening slightly to see if it flew out from him. He re-closed. Still there. He opened and then closed. Still feeling alive. Still imagining her lovely collarbones.

Yes, he'd watched her a long time. Dark hair.

The bus slowed and a collective groan came up from the ridership. He opened his eyes to see a visual cacophony of police and ambulance lights firing up the streetscape like a movie scene. The bus pulled into the nearest stop and the driver spoke on the PA about a delay.

No matter. Almost there.

He swung from the rear door and strode, knowing by the way the air felt on his face this was a good thing. He decided to brave the police situation on his way to the score. He felt giddy.

Giddy?

With all that had happened, and his regretfully drug-free status at the moment, the realization gave him alarm. He wondered about a psychosis factor. He was not new to this kind of thing. In the present context he knew it for a disaster if you were trying to do something that took talent. He strode fast, thinking exertion might force out enough sickness to let him function.

Not breaking stride, he assessed the police action. The thing seemed to be playing down. They hauled a hooker into a paddy wagon, paramedics were closing their ambulance doors and somebody with a uniform was hosing blood off the pavement. The bitch looked supremely fucked up, too, he noticed. Yelling like a psycho. Babbleshit. Never get to that state, my man. Never let them see you so fucked.

He took in the assembled onlookers and the sight of them caused an instant acidic sizzle in his gut. They think they're looking at something but they're not. This is nothing. Mere aftermath of idiocy. He almost had an impulse to yell at them to come along and see a real crime happen. With no fuck-ups. That would be something. This was nothing.

He marched proudly on.

He tried to visually order things again. He had the piece. He knew the girl-profile behind the counter. He could picture the counter, glass. Sliding doors behind, easy to swish aside when the time came. The place was on an alley and close to the confluence of three transit routes. He swore out loud. He'd forgotten to get a bus transfer.

He tried not to let this major slip skew his mind.

Think, boy!

Abort?

Naw. His yen was too strong. He dug in his pockets for the remaining change. There might be enough. He didn't bother to count it, knowing he would do the score anyway.

He walked on, turned a corner and let out a word:

Fuck!

The place was dark. It was nighttime after all. He tried not to let himself think about how stupid he was. For a moment he was frozen to the sidewalk, struggling with panic. The stupidity. It chilled him hurtful like frozen rain. He wrung hands together and squeezed until the pain brought him back. He stepped forward just to do something with his body. He walked. He passed the front of the place as a cop car roared through a near intersection, lights urgent. He kept walking, eyeing the store with heat, until he was past and looking at the side of the building along the alley. His brain relayed a fascinating message almost before his eyes registered the information.

There was a side door, with light coming from a tiny window in the centre of it.

He stopped, alone in the semi-light. Another patrol car flashed by, then an ambulance. He waited for the sirens to abate, appreciative that on an otherwise active thoroughfare he was luckily alone. Across the street the Salvation Army shelter loomed mostly dark, the men behind their myriad windows mostly blinded, shuttered against the night outside and the noise. A thin figure stepped out the front door and stood. The face became lit like a Halloween mask as a cigarette got ignited.

He turned back to the alley and let his eyes find the light from the security window and the luminous slit at the bottom. He stepped closer, then closer again, then walked right up to it and examined the metal door as casual as he could without looking like a burglar.

There was the expected peephole.

Touching the wire-mesh window, running fingertips down the roughened, rusted jamb, he no longer felt the drug itch. No more whining. A plan formed itself so quickly in his consciousness it felt like it had been there all along. He stepped away from the place. Down the street he'd seen a bicycle locked to a storefront. He hoped he'd seen a helmet too. In ninety seconds he was there, standing in a protected entrance bay. The tattered bike and helmet were fastened by a piece of chain.

With an expertise borne of an apprenticeship in petty crime he wrenched the helmet away, the cracking of plastic timed to be swallowed by the noise of a tow truck rattling by. He held it up to the light. He enjoyed a welcome clarity of thought, placing the helmet upon his head and fastening the chinstrap. The damaged part was to one side. It fit reasonably well. If he kept his head turned no one would be able to tell him from a thousand typical bike couriers.

Rushing back in disguise, he was beginning to be nagged by the drug itch, but—in sight of the score—rebounded with the exhilaration that progress toward a goal always paid. He knew he could hang on. There was no one in the alley. He looked around. Down the way a few parked cars stood dark. He watched their interiors for a few moments, checking for movement. At the door he did not hesitate to knock hard and position his forehead at the peephole.

At first, silence. He strained to hear something above the dull inner-urban din. When enough seconds had passed he knocked again, this time pounding with a closed fist on the tough plate steel. He heard something like throat-clearing. A shadow darkened its way across the glass. The peephole clacked open.

'Who's there?'

A male voice, old and accented.

He yelled: 'Package!'

'A what?'

He rose on tiptoes and shoved the good side of his helmeted head close to the peephole. 'Courier. I've got a package for you.'

'Deliveries are in the day. What is it you have?'

'I dunno what it is but it's a package and it's for Ezra's Jewellers at this address and we're a twenty-four-hour-a-day delivery service so you make up your mind, okay?'

'This is out of usual . . .'

He could think of nothing more to say and then he knew there was nothing more to say. He stepped slightly back from the door and gently tapped his toe in a pantomime of the symbol of impatience. He knew this would be virtually invisible through the peephole but felt that for absolute authenticity the part must be played out in full. He began to hear machine sounds, metal on metal. Clicks. He knew the job had been done and tightened himself for action. As the light-cracks around the door widened he reared back and then slammed full weight on it, sending the thing and himself smashing inward and around.

He had barrelled past the man standing by the door. Wheeling, he faced a smallish fellow wearing a work-shined leather apron over a three-piece suit. With haste, he pushed the steel door loudly shut. They were in a cramped workspace with bench-mounted equipment, cutting and polishing tools, boxes and filing cabinets, an old desk. The man, who was older than the security guard's father would be, stood firmly upon his feet and appeared just slightly flummoxed at being forced sideways from the door.

He whipped the pistol out and levelled it belly-height. 'What the hell ya doing working so late, fella?' He pulled the hammer on the weapon.

'Good that you should have such an ugly instrument to show me the foolishness of letting someone in at this hour of the night.' The man's voice was much bigger than his stature and more than vaguely humorous in tone. 'Ach, such a lesson.' The man shrugged, rolled eyes and tossed up hands.

The security guard stood with the gun pointed, mind jammed.

'Whassamatter?' The old man opened his hand and posed grinning at the helmeted gunman. 'At first you are so fast but now you go slow.'

He realized with terror that before him stood nerves and guile. Too, he was choked beyond believing at the speed he had been rendered uncertain. The result was a terminal peevishness and absence of fun. The only way to take over would be through an escalation to pure violence. He lunged, swiping the barrel across the man's face. The metal made contact with bone and flung blood away to the near wall. The man staggered back but remained on his feet.

'What . . ?' The well-dressed jeweller wiped his face. 'You intend to beat me to sense with that thing?' The man spat blood and grimaced. 'Better a baseball bat you bring . . .'

'Shut up!'

'So original. Why don't you shoot and don't waste time with all the chatter?'

'Get back there . . .'

He stepped at the man, digging the barrel into his chest. To his bitter surprise it was like trying to chisel rock with a block of wood, the phony gun met solidity which did not yield. The struggle cost him far more poise than he wished to invest. He stepped back. This thing was going bad so quickly he almost lost his breath.

'I'll kill you mad fucker!'

'I should be called mad by such a person?' The old man spoke as if there were a third party in the room. While talking he had maneuvered and touched something under a countertop. 'There. I call some friends to join the party. Give you some playmates. Fun, eh?'

'Fuck!' He was shocked at the crazed pitch of his cursing, thinking incongruously of the apprehended hooker only half an hour ago.

'My, such advancement of higher conversation among armed robbery people. Used to be you just wanted money. Now you want to yak yak all night about nothing.'

'Shut up!' He raised the piece and tried to pull back the hammer.

The realization he had already used that threat vast moments ago immobilized him.

'I was robbed by the best.' The old man continued, crossing his arms, ignoring his assailant's gun-struggle. 'You think you're better than Hitler?'

'You're fuckin' crazy old man!'

'Crazy. I should be crazy after the number of times I get robbed.'

'Where's the stuff? I mean it.'

'Stuff, he calls it!'

Once again the stunning non-intimidation of his victim—hands tossed ceiling-ward, eyes to the heavens in exasperation—transfixed the armed robber. In his near-delirium he fought against looking aside to assure himself there was no one else in the room, listening.

'Some of us give our lives to this . . . stuff, you call it. Beauty. It means nothing to you?'

Maybe later he could figure the next logical move. For now there was only this powerful man drawing him places he did not want to go. He had forgotten what he had come to collect. He could not think at all for several seconds. He was momentarily nostalgic for the convenience store smash-and-grab. He nearly wept. The man kept speaking. A logical thought finally entered: Time. Time.

He wondered how long he'd been there and if the man had actually tripped an alarm. He knew he had no means of finding out, but processed further the irrefutable fact that this crudity of a job was over. The despair of it surprised him in its depth. He again fought tears. It was wholly beyond him to deal with this person, a mental black hole. The more he tried to reason the less he could comprehend. Then the man stepped to one side and snatched a thin, shiny hammer from a bench.

This image shook and distilled from his addled state the last fully lucid comprehension he would have.

Fear.

He turned and fled.

On the street, running through rain, it was a block before he knew to slow to an inconspicuous stride, wrench away the bicycle helmet and tuck the gun out of sight. The gun. No authority at all. He didn't know what he could do with it. No authority, no fear inducement. A useless piece of scrap. He wanted to toss it away. There was a trash bin at the end of the block.

But footfalls rearward, a running pattern. He jumped into a jog and peeked behind him. In the streetlight shadows, two black-shouldered monsters trotted. He head-longed to a panic-run. Two blocks passed without thought. If there were orders to stop, he did not hear them. His navigation through the streets was random. A close miss with a taxi jolted him and he stood stationary for an instant, looking around.

He had the vague instinct to find a crowd. The one he could immediately think of was the night scene on Granville Mall. He galloped up the long hill past the major bus stops. The waiting passengers took no heed of a running man in this district but he knew they would snap to when puffing police officers rumbled behind. The exertion was clearing his head. He began to run, finally thinking, with as much velocity as he could accumulate among the strolling citizens, knowing he needed just a little more time to develop a plan.

The bundles of people in the street by the theatres, bookstores, arcades and booze clubs of the mall rose to sight. He wove into the shadows of some storefronts and then across the street into a throng and then down through another bus stop, lingering almost to a stop among the standing hordes and looked about him for a solution. The cops were coming; he knew that by the hush rushing down from the block he'd just sprinted. He looked across and about, begrudging the seconds, then gave up and sprang across to the fast food joint on the side of the street opposite to the cops. He would try to melt into the burger crowd and find a back door.

As soon as he was on the other side he knew the police had cottoned on. In fact, now he looked a bit, there were speedy bicycled shadows stalking him. Inside the restaurant he rushed into a dead-end of high counters, servers and the kitchen. Too much staff around, too many people. He turned and blasted up circular stairs, coming to a mezzanine with no egress except further up. He went. Then there was the top floor with only a few people and he ran down along a rank of tables, heading for the hallway he saw at the back, hopefully heading to a fire exit and clear alleyway beyond. He thanked building codes and the civilization he was living in for making it an imperative to offer escape to everybody in a public building, no matter the inconvenience to management or police enforcement. He rushed. Seeing possibility. Elated.

The shouts had been continuous since the beginning of the chase. He had been glad to ignore them. Now they were especially loud because of the close, hard-surfaced confines of the restaurant. For some reason they bothered him now. Coming close to the escape hatch, almost out of sight, he turned to see whose was this authoritative voice. A young officer stood on the stairs at the mezzanine, his weapon pointed upward, perfectly trained upon himself the target. He turned away and in that instant he saw the far exit burst open and another black-bristling monster enter, face crimson with effort or antipathy, he wondered which and then didn't care.

He stopped, relieved, and drew the piece, knowing what he was doing, hearing shouts and knowing what they were saying. In the second it took he raised the pistol in the classic, useful, two-handed combat grip and crouched, feet apart. He was in no need of drugs and it felt good that there was no possibility of his being shot in the back. The fire escape officer simply would not do that. There was time for a contact of eyes between himself and his adversary on the stairs, whose eyes, mouth and ears seemed to be full open in complete concentration of effort, sound and aiming. He deliberately aligned his front sight on the officer's face. The hands below the face then bucked and gases emerged from the 9mm Beretta, flushing well into the space between them. The projectile was amazingly visible to him out of the mini-cloud, as were others behind. His brain seemed capable at this fine moment of almost anything: The perception of objects; his superlative cellular state; the absence of want; the fluidity of thought. They are taught not to wound or wing, he knew. They are taught to hit the mass. Hit the mass repeatedly until you stop. That was the objective of police shooting, he knew, to stop. Not necessarily kill. That was for him to decide. He smiled in the impossibly little time left, at least enjoying from a crazy point of view the crystalline mental imagery of being shot.

But as he descended floorward the exultation escaped. He imagined it fizzling through the new holes in his torso. As a last thing to think he wished it could have been yearning for love or some familial remembrance, but it actually evolved into that familiar yen for drugs: a banal, one-dimensional point to die on. His last sensation a hot, disappointing pain.

[15]

BEFORE THE DOOR of the pub fully closed Barry somewhat forgot about Jill and his housing conundrum and wondered why there were so many sirens in town tonight.

Full moon? Welfare Week?

'Or is it my fucking caseload!'

His spoken-aloud thought was sucked into the din of what he guessed was the band's final set for the night. He ordered by winking at the surprised Rikki standing by the bar and then hunkered at his table, tuning to the music. The band was just finishing a solid delivery of "Hoochie Coochie Man". He was glad it was still busy enough so that Rikki did not get to him until it was over. In the lull between songs she slung his beer down and smiled at him.

'Where's your girlfriend?'

'She let me down.'

'How could she do that?'

'Dunno.'

'You're such a cutie.'

'Mystery to me.'

'Poor thing doesn't know what's good for her, I'd say.'

'You're so very kind.'

He pulled out his last twenty and tipped her well. On the next round he knew he should be going but when Rikki was there again he ordered another. This time he took back his change. 'Sorry, but I have to keep every cent so I can get the bus.'

Rikki paused. 'Oh?'

This single word was delivered with such significant change of tone that it made Barry look up at her.

Her forehead creased with a puzzling effort. 'Well, you know . . .' Barry realized she was choosing words with superlative care. 'If you want to hang around another half-hour you don't have to take the bus.'

'Oh?'

'I have a car.'

He was almost unsure of what he had heard. 'You do?'

'Yup.' She gave back the money he'd given her. 'This one's on me anyway.'

'Hey . . .' He took back the bill. 'You're the girl of my dreams.'

'Woman.'

'Right, sorry, the woman of my dreams.'

Barry watched her stride away. His hand on the beer glass was unsteady for a moment, and it was a while before he could drink.

He looked across the emptying bar and tried to get his mind off women. It was useless, now the floodgates had been breeched. The memories swept in. The cop, whom he'd betrayed so cravenly. He re-grieved the loss of her. It was all so fucked. Then the psychologist, Jenna. She'd been sweet and supportive and entirely too sincere and he'd left her in dust and anger. And Janis, worst of all. Looking for love, thinking she had found it. Little did she know she had stumbled across the infamously Teflon-emotioned Barry Delta.

His disgust was such that he decided to find a mirror to see if he could dare look himself in the face. He stumbled through the tables and chairs, head high to carefully pick his route. In the men's room his mind had changed and he purposefully averted his face from the mirrors above the sinks. He locked himself in a stall, sat down on the toilet lid and thought about weeping. He closed his eyes and cradled his face in his hands. In the blankness more women formed: Georgina, a receptionist, disappointed in some way or another, he couldn't remember how, but dead of sadness, lying in her blood on a cold bathroom floor. Diane, pining for the future she deserved. And Tanya, Barry tried forlornly not to let himself think of her. In what had transpired this single night he knew he could never see her again. Certainly never look her in the eyes. Absolutely never be with her again in any meaningful way. When he opened his eyes, his vision was warped and the room was spinning.

He lurched up and wrenched the stall door open. With one hand he made a cup and drank deep of the water from a sink faucet. He drank more than he wanted and kept drinking. It involved a lot of catching and slurping. He was aware of others in the room, going about their business. He drank still, needing to banish drunkenness with water. When he paused he needed to urinate, did so, then resumed a moderate pace of water consumption until he had passed a point where he knew he could not force any more down. His gut was an uncomfortable mass only slightly less tight-feeling than his skull—his eyes bulged and puffy—but at least now in the function of overcoming drunkenness he was coming free of sentiment.

On the way back to his table he was surprised how quickly the place had emptied. He seldom stayed until closing. He watched Rikki serve the remaining customers, wait for last call, clean up, encourage drinkers to finish, and finally head to his table. Presently she led him through the empty bar and out the back door to the parking lot.

Her car was a battered Honda Civic.

Though he'd drunk a carboy full of beer that night, the sight of the car quaked for him such a nostalgia-wave that Barry nearly fell over. It was the exact kind of car he had kept for decades. And now there was the thrill of being in the company of a woman he had never entertained having a chance with, who swung in her fingers the keys to this sentimental favourite of his.

'I think I'm in love.'

'I hope you're talking about your mother.' She selected a key and trained it to the passenger door.

'Your car. I love your car.'

'Oh.' Rikki opened his door and stepped back. 'Okay.'

'I spent my life in these things.'

They got in.

She started the engine and flipped on the lights. They buckled up and were driving so quick through the darkened city that Barry hardly noticed that they'd started to move. 'Whoa . . .' He tried to follow their route but his head began to spin again.

'What's the matter?'

'It's okay. Forgive me. I'm kinda confused.'

'You're certainly drunk.'

'No thanks to you.'

'Hey, you paid for all of 'em except one.'

'Let's get some coffee.' He could barely remember getting into the car.

'Excellent idea.'

They stopped at a Denny's on Broadway, where coffee and menus were instantly conferred. Barry was glad to be drinking something non-alcoholic. As the intoxicants gradually left him he was further gladdened to be sitting across from Rikki. It seemed unreal. And on the very night he had impulsively self-declared his independence. The karma of it nearly spooked him. It even made him contemplative, and that made the melancholy rear up and interior darkness encroach. Then for some reason he was elated again. Damn. These haphazard surges of up-and-down emotions were beginning to annoy him. He determined inside to curb his drinking from now on. Thinking about sobriety brought on raw lustiness at the sight of her across the table, pretty in the three o'clock morning ethereality. He tried not to giggle at the tightness in his crotch and all the crazy thoughts.

When the server came, Rikki ordered a grilled cheese sandwich and offered to buy Barry something.

'Oh man, I'm glad you're so thoughtful . . .' He tried desperately not to sound too doddering, realizing he had not eaten since lunch. No wonder he'd gotten so drunk. He glanced at the menu and ordered a grilled cheese sandwich too.

Before they could start talking Rikki looked downward and scowled. 'Shit.' She side-longed a look across the restaurant.

Barry followed her gaze and located a clutch of tired-looking business types.

'What?'

'Don't look. I think one of them's a friend of my husband.'

'Husband . . . ?'

'We're separated. He can't get used to it.'

'Oh?' Barry hadn't noticed them when they came in, so now he looked over purposefully. After-work company men, he could see—jackets off, ties loose—out for jocular good backslapping times. They all smiled confidently. He could hear just enough drink-loosened companionship to be wary of their potential for some kind of group-bravado dynamic. He turned back to Rikki. 'My least-favourite category of social cohort.'

'Glad to hear it.'

'What kind of feeling should I have about this?'

'A fine feeling.' She looked briefly again at the group. 'False alarm.' She looked back at Barry. 'And even if it wasn't, we'd be okay anyway. I mean, you're a nice guy and I'm taking you home or wherever you want to go. I'm a sober driver, you certainly wouldn't be. I can do whatever I want. Can't I?'

'No argument from me. But business-types, all that control bullshit. What does your husband do?'

'Ex.'

'Divorced? I thought you said you were . . .'

'Separated. For a year now. We haven't got around to making it formal.'

'Okay.'

'He's in new car sales.'

'Oooh, all that gaga pressure. Occasional panic. Pecking-order jealousy. All that pack-animal anxiety . . .' Barry tried to think of something appropriate to sum up but his mind was still muddy. He decided to blurt something: 'My general experience is that with male group dynamics, decency is never far from suspension. Whatever the socio-economic background.'

Rikki sighed. 'They're mostly okay guys when you get to know them.'

'Except, I take it, this ex of yours.'

'He's okay when he's not on coke.'

'Oh man, a used car salesman and a coconut too?'

'*New* car sales.' Rikki's tone was neither warm nor harsh. 'He's just an ordinary person in most of the ways people are ordinary.'

In the slight pause Barry understood that he had better be more respectful. He sipped his coffee. 'I guess you could say a lot of people use cocaine and in some worlds that makes them ordinary. But a guy with a coke habit is bad news any way you read it, pressure sales or no.' As he heard himself speaking the words he was dismayed again how much his mood could darken without warning. 'Otherwise, I'm sure I don't know what you mean by *ordinary*.'

'Well I guess you're kind of drunk so I'll explain it carefully.' Her face was now as dark as Barry thought his mood was. 'Guys like my ex are some of the most honest people in the world.'

'The car salesmen I've met were near-psychos. I had one physically stalk me out of a showroom once, daring me to come back in and make a deal, calling me a coward.'

'I didn't say they weren't driven. You can be honest and offensive at the same time.'

Barry smiled in a way he hoped would not be patronizing. 'Let me hand you my spin on it. In my experience, guys like your ex are bright people but not deep. The women too. Men and women are the same on this these days. They're smart but not well read. Because they're sharp they're usually well off but have no taste. They're somewhat erudite at whatever they do but haven't got much perspective. The gap . . .' Barry set apart his hands to mime the chasm he hoped to convey. 'The space is the place where the cunning goes. The nastiness. Such a setup, intelligence and non-texture, inevitably accommodates intrigue, sabotage, secrecy and destruction. Mostly to those people who choose not be engaged in such opportunistic provocateur-ism.'

Rikki was drinking her coffee, smiling.

'It's the reason there are SUVs.'

Rikki laughed.

'You think I'm kidding.' Barry drank his coffee, nearly burning his lip. 'I don't mind.'

'No no, tell me. How does your theory of so-called *ordinary* people relate to their driving choices?'

'It's simple. The bright-but-shallow set are in a zone where their humanity is shelved in favour of vanity. I say they shelve it, they don't completely lose it. It's the reason you see them genuinely tearful on the evening news after they've run a stop sign in their Ford Exploder and smeared the heads off a family in a Honda Civic.'

Barry allowed no time to for Rikki's expression to turn grim. 'I mean, I've had the conversation. I've asked people I know who are reasonably smart and outwardly decent why they yield to faddism and drive a wasteful, clumsy, gas-greedy murder machine. The blank looks I get. I say "If you hit someone, you're likely to kill them." And they say, "Your point is what?" These types are the new amorality: Their interests first, no matter what. Might is right. No such thing as love thy neighbour. They are no one's brother's keepers. And church parking lots are full of these monstrous fuckers! So by their creed, if you end up beheaded by someone in a bigger vehicle, it's your own fault for not participating in the roadway arms race. In other words, accept my religion of self, or take the chance of dying on your drive to the mall. All you'll get is a few tears in prime time, until their humanity shuts off again. It's every dickhead for themselves. Basically fuck you. In my estimation . . .' he scowled, nearly carried away, 'crime pales by comparison.'

Barry found that he was nearly out of breath. 'But hey, I'm kind of mentally overheated right now, so just let me listen to your *ordinary* explanation and maybe I'll survive.'

'Whew! I don't know.' Rikki's smile had returned. 'My ex drove one of those. He did a lot of conspicuous consumerist things. But I don't think he meant for us to end up sixty thousand dollars in credit card debt.'

'What!'

'I mean, I should bear some of the responsibility, shouldn't I? I mean, I knew he was feeling the pressure.'

'This is sounding like something out of Court TV.' Barry sipped coffee again and a thought hit him. 'Not to mention my own life. He didn't learn financial mismanagement from my wife by any chance, did he?'

'Familiar story?'

'I'll say.'

Barry was gratified at how casually Rikki had taken the mention of his wife. The food arrived. They passed the time on less resonant topics.

When she finished her sandwich, Rikki settled back with another cup of coffee.

Barry eyed her fingers. 'I'm impressed you don't smoke.'

'I quit last year.' She hesitated, looking at him. 'Tobacco, anyway. Got rid of a shaky husband and cigarettes all at the same time. It had a kind of symmetry.'

'Good for you.'

'It wasn't that hard.'

'That's not what I've heard.'

'And I'm halfway through my degree in communications.'

'Excellent.'

'And I have an apartment with hardwood floors.'

'Better and better.' Barry put down his coffee cup. 'Can I see it?'

Rikki let an appropriate pause go by. 'Don't you have to go home?'

Her tone was casual but Barry knew gravity when it weighed upon him.

'Nope.' He beamed, confident. 'Believe it or not I do not have a home to go to right at this moment.'

'Don't be silly.'

'Silly is the last thing on my mind.'

'I think you're serious.'

Barry leaned closer and noticed that in the raw diner light Rikki looked younger than he had thought she was. Her eyes shone a genuine interest and he grasped a strong instinct to tell her the full truth and feel better for it.

'I've got a wife.'

'You mentioned.' She looked at him slyly. 'But I've always known it.'

'Hmmm . . .' Barry shifted his eyes back and forth in what he hoped would be a comic rendering of suspicion. 'I've never been one for jewellery. Never wore a wedding band.What gave me away?'

'Your headlong mode of drinking. Those lost looks when you're into the music. Your Saturday afternoons, as if it was the one day you're allowed out. They way you always seem not to want to go home. The way your eyes shift when you speak about anything more important than cars or criminals. All that talk tonight with that table full of girls.' She drank her coffee. 'You really gave it a shot with the pretty one.'

Barry felt nearly sober now. 'You're fairly well spot on. But there's a lot more to the story. Want to hear it?'

'I guess I can stay awake.'

'She's the nicest person in the world.'

'Don't ever describe a woman like that.'

'Why not?'

'Nice. It's such an insult.'

'How so?'

'Women like to think they might be talented or gracious or kind or humorous or intelligent or any of a hundred other actual things. The word *nice* has lost its meaning in our world. Any woman worth knowing is going to hear a put-down in being dismissed as *nice*.'

'I'll have to think about that for a while.'

'It's pretty simple.'

'Oh I don't disagree. I'm just trying to grab myself some perspective. Thinking up old conversations. I might have said something like that to the women in my life and maybe insulted them without knowing.'

'Well, that's a good exercise. A little late maybe, but nonetheless . . . .'

'I get what you're saying though, essentially.' Barry shook his head. 'I fear I know little else where women are concerned.'

'I was picking up that impression, Mr. Charming.'

'You've got it right.' He tried to smile. 'You're apparently a dead accurate estimator of people. Yet I sense that you won't judge me for what I say.'

'I'll do like anybody else. If you tell me something about you that's disgusting, I'll maybe reserve my opinion for a moment, think awhile, turn things over in my mind, then likely conclude that you're disgusting. Simple.'

'Fair enough.' Barry paid her off with a smile. 'But this really is sort of disgusting.' He took a breath, measuring his thoughts. 'And you're going to have to let me use the word *nice*. In its popular sense of okay, or pleasant, or sweet. Just this once.'

'If you insist.'

'Thank you.' Barry took a breath. 'She's the nicest person in the world. But it's a calculated, mechanized niceness. Like it was written in her day timer to be nice for a certain time each day.'

'Aside from your persistent use of that word, there are worse ways to be.'

'That's what's so disgusting about it. It's just about the only complaint I have. I know it's a picky beef but it's pushed me right away from her.'

'You're saying she's not real?'

'I guess.'

'Bullshit.' Rikki's tone was clinical. 'There's got to be lots of things that pushed you away and it couldn't just be your wife's flair for phoniness.'

'Well, yeah. She always seems to have to blame someone else for everything that happens. She cares too much what other people think of her, excluding me, of course. And she won't hear any divergent opinion. She's a scientist. Kind of naturally entrenched in rote thinking.'

'How did you two ever get together?'

'God, I don't know.'

'That's more bullshit.'

'Well sure but . . . I've never understood it. I mean how we got together. We met at a wild time in my life. She stood up to my weirdness and seemed not to mind. I truly loved that. But right away she started bugging me to get married. She was literally rude about it. She wouldn't get off the subject. It was never my style, I never saw the sense of it, but to shut her up I gave in. It was okay for a couple of years. But after awhile we were used to one another and then without knowing it we started to have contempt. I don't know when it started. It was the stuff I mentioned, her blaming, and spending and ignoring me. I found myself miserable with no handy way to fix it. We did counselling, but I hated it so much it didn't do any good. We were both so distracted, jobs, et cetera. For a quick out I started misbehaving. Old habits die hard. I was always notoriously multi-relationship. I just reverted to my old predilections, trying to make myself feel better. For a while it kept me going, gave me enough ego-strength to take the disappointment of my marriage. In the end, of course, it just made things worse . . .' Barry threw up his hands. 'What makes two people who don't like each other get married?'

Rikki rolled her eyes. 'I don't know. I'm not a therapist.'

'You can be mine right now.'

'Don't you have one already?'

'I'm that bad?'

'You're not bad at all. That's just it. I've seen you with people. In the bar. There's something about you . . . even only getting to talk to you a few seconds a few times per night, I could tell you were a good guy. You shine intelligence. Whenever there are people you know in the place they always want to talk to you. You're friendly and seem to know a lot of stuff, tell stories, buy people drinks, feel the music. I'm beginning to think you're worth saving.'

'That's kind of you.'

Rikki frowned for the first time. 'Sarcasm will get you nowhere.'

For Barry it was as if the diner's lights had gone out. 'No, no . . . it's true. I know it sounds dubious but . . .'

'You're not kidding.'

' . . . Maybe I shouldn't say I've never had anybody be kind to me. One of my girlfriends is constantly trying to get me to acknowledge my personal virtue.'

'Girlfriends?'

'Yeah. I've just got one right now.'

Rikki rolled her eyes for the second time in less than a minute. 'I guess I shouldn't be surprised.'

'No. It's classic with me. I can't remember when I've only been with one woman at a time.'

'Ho-kay . . .' She looked at her watch. 'Please go on.'

'Well . . .' Barry had lost his line of thought. 'I guess she's got some other problems for me, too. But . . .'

'This is your wife now?'

'Yeah. I'll tell you about Diane later if you want me to but for now this is about my wife.'

'Diane is the girlfriend?'

'Right.'

'And your wife's name?'

'Tanya.'

'Good. So we have Diane and Tanya. What was the name of the one in the bar tonight?'

'Jill. She's out of the picture. Never was in, actually.'

'Not for lack of trying on your part, though.'

He let that hang for a moment. 'Was it that obvious?'

Rikki ignored the question. 'Anybody else?'

'Not at this time. Though let me think . . .' Barry found he had to exert some effort. It wasn't just the drink still in him. There had been so many, and his emotions had run so fluid this night, he would have had difficulty remembering what day it was. 'No . . .' He paused, careful. 'There's only those two right now. And I don't know for sure about Diane.'

'Whew!' Rikki drank the last of her coffee. 'Well, if we've narrowed it down, I guess I've got time. Tell me about her.'

'Well, that's where the story gets kind of grotesquely funny. Their issues dovetail. They both want children.'

'Hah!' She leaned back in her seat. 'So you have to make a choice.'

'Right. If I want to stay with either of them I have to make a choice.'

'And that's ohhhh so hard . . .'

'You know it.' He gave her another smile. 'You know a lot of stuff.'

'Maybe. But I haven't found that it helps a heck of a lot. I still get fucked over.'

'Figuratively speaking, of course.'

'Both ways.'

'Wow, don't talk like that.' Barry grinned. 'It's like putting a bottle in front of an alcoholic.'

'I've done plenty of that, too.'

'Man. What a couple of burn-outs.'

'I was thinking that very thing.'

'A connection?'

'Maybe. But there's been a connection between us for a long time.'

Barry fought the compulsion to gulp. 'There has?'

'Hasn't there? Don't you know that I watch for you?'

'You do?'

'Of course.'

'Wow.' Barry enjoyed something warm spreading through his chest. 'I guess you get guys hitting on you all the time. I mean, bar work. Lovely girl like yourself. Occupational hazard if there ever was one.'

'Many times per shift. They're all eff-ing a-holes.'

'Every one?'

'Any guy who hits on a bar waitress is a jerk-off, exclusive. Their thinking is all wrong, they're idiots from the start and it just gets worse.'

'Man, what a reduction. Spoken from hard experience.'

'No comment.'

'Well that just makes this more of a special thing for me.'

'I'm glad you feel that way, but what do you mean by "this"?'

'This? I don't know. The talk. This place. The grilled cheese . . .'

Rikki smiled and reached to touch his hand. 'Like I said, I watch for you.'

'I do for you, too.' Barry put his hand over hers. 'But to tell you the truth, I considered it a routine thing for me. Habit. The drinker-seeking-solace kind of phenomenon.'

'It's that too.' Rikki drew back her hand. 'And that dumb statement further points up your shortcomings with women.'

'Huh?'

'You're so thick . . .' Though smiling, Rikki nearly yelled. 'I've had a thing for you for ages, stupid!'

'Oh.'

'Sure. The main thing is that you never hit on me. That's major. And I think you said once you have a good job . . .'

'I'm a federal parole officer.'

'No kidding! I knew somebody on parole once.'

Barry laughed.

'Kidding!'

'I got it.'

'Anyway . . .' She sat back. 'That makes you an attractive guy by my standards.'

'Well.' Barry chuckled. 'Intensive stroking. Whew. I don't know what to say.'

Rikki darkened comically. 'But your talk here tonight kind of put me off.' She lightened slightly. 'But just now your talk about yourself almost put me back on.' Her brow furrowed deep. 'Are you getting all this?'

'Kind of. Can we go to your place?'

'We'll go to my place soon enough. I just want you to understand something. I find you attractive.'

'Thank you. Likewise.'

'And I suspect that might be a weakness in me. Okay?'

'Uhh . . . I guess so.'

'Don't you see? I'm a rational woman here who isn't drunk. Yet I'm inviting a problem-plagued guy into my life, for at least one night anyway. But it's an impulse I've decided not to fight. That's weakness. Understand?'

'Don't be so rough on yourself.'

'Do you understand what I'm saying?'

'About asking for trouble? About searching for life in somebody and knowing you might have to take a lot of shit before you find it?'

'Exactly.'

'I get it.'

'Good boy. Now let's go.'

On the short drive to Rikki's place Barry rejoiced in his clearing mind. He was able to establish with some solidity the personal commitment that he must not take advantage of this woman, that he must resist getting involved solely because of his attraction.

It felt so good to be thus determined that he decided to blurt it out. 'I can't make love to you.'

'Well then . . .' Rikki pulled the car into a space in front of a prewar three-storey walk-up. 'I suppose we could just fuck.' She turned to Barry. 'But that wouldn't be too romantic.'

'That's just it. It's not sex that does it for me. It's romance. I crave the stuff.'

'I could kind of tell by the dripping enticements in your conversation tonight.'

'Hardee-har-har. You know, I could get to like your sarcasm. It's akin to my own.'

She turned and kissed him. He felt a brush of tongue and the accompanying surge of heart rate. She pulled back and turned off the engine. 'We're definitely akin.'

'I didn't finish the story about my life.' Barry tried not to let the pounding in his head affect his speech. 'I decided tonight not to go home. I'm separating.'

Rikki's expression gravened.

'The thing is . . .' He goaded himself to tell the truth. 'Aside from a few little plusses, like you right now, I live in a terrible world. A sewer-hole. A dark and bad world and the only thing light and good in it is me . . . ha-ha!' Barry began to crack himself up at the repetitive emptiness these words had gained over the course of the night. He remembered with chagrin that over the years he had used the same speech so many times he couldn't remember who had heard it and who had not. He struggled to finish, nevertheless. 'And right now I'm not enough, okay? I need something cool and giving sometimes, even if it has to be right out of the sky from nowhere. I need it right now. And I didn't tell you all this to get to bed with you. I told you that because I need a place to stay for the night. Honest.'

Rikki was smiling. 'Honest or not, that one sounds like a pretty hackneyed piece of speech. Have you tried it on anyone else in the last few years?'

'I'm not sure.' Barry was too embarrassed not to lie.

'Well phony speech or not, I'm offering you a place to stay for the night.'

'Thanks.'

'I'm glad we got that straight.'

Barry followed her up steps and into a neat, surprisingly elegant apartment with lots of space and original art on the walls. She threw off her coat and took Barry's. He wandered to the living room and sat in a large, comfortable well-worn armchair. Rikki appeared with a glass of water and flopped onto the couch. She picked up a small tin box and pried the lid. 'I'm going to smoke a joint. Join me?'

'Sure.'

'Head clearing a little?'

'That coffee did me good. So did the talk.'

She raised a hefty-looking joint to her face and fired up a lighter. He watched as she drew a lungful. She handed it over. It had been a while since Barry had done weed. He liked the smell more than any effect it had ever had on him. He noticed himself yearning for a shot of scotch as he pulled in smoke. He coughed and reached for the water.

She took back the joint. 'This isn't the best stuff.'

'It's okay.' Barry whacked a fist to his chest. 'I didn't need these lungs anyway . . .'

She giggled.

'Even though I'm dying and weed just makes me cough . . .' He mock-slid out of his chair, clutching his ribs. 'At least I find your laugh intoxicating.'

She looked at him, not laughing. 'I hope you don't mind using condoms.'

'Absolutely not.' Barry went to her on his knees.

After the happy occurrence of their evening Barry was not surprised at how natural it was to kiss. Then to bed and in the scant minutes before dawn finding comfort and forgetting.

But then the incident:

Barry dreamed.

Death and work.

Love and struggle.

Then he sits in a sandbox with a beautiful woman. He looks at his companion and does not recognize her but thinks this might be Tanya. But then it is clearly the newly amorous Rikki. He reaches.

Barry woke to a thing that had happened several times over the years. While asleep he was copulating with the woman he was in bed with. For a few seconds he did not know who she was, but with wakefulness remembered and enjoyed the ride, ramming her joyously, contacting the sculpting of her body and regaling in her velvet pull. Then he was coming, rich and trajectoried, sending full. Rikki tensed. Barry recognized his unsheathed state and tensed.

His thoughts were dark. He prayed she might go back to sleep without noticing, then slapped himself mentally for being so foolish.

[16]

THANKFULLY THERE WAS not much to say at leaving-time: Barry dressed while Rikki semi-slept. After further apologies he made it out and, by an unfamiliar bus route, got to work only an hour past due.

He felt lifeless, a carcass, dragging itself into the elevator and struggling to stand erect. His breath, clothes, eyes and hair spoke of late drinking, rootlessness, misbehaviour. He avoided glancing into the mirrored walls of the foyer. In his office he realized he'd forgotten to activate his cell phone and pager. He groaned aloud, then sat at his computer and flipped switches, entered passwords, grateful that his mind knew where to go and what to do, but dubious at what good he might effect today under the circumstances.

He ignored the predictable email plea from Myra. Today there were a couple of urgent flags. One notified him of Chantal's arrest on a charge of murder. Barry gulped, barely noticing himself clicking on the other flag, thinking it likely something trivial by comparison. But this one screamed at him even louder. The shooting death by city police of his most recent home-visit. Barry had to clamp his jaws to block a rise in his gut. He swallowed back down a load of bile-laden stomach. His head swirled, rebelling at the horrid drinking, the scant rest, the chancy sex, the lack of breakfast; and now the bilious terror from the computer screen. He closed his eyes and held his head in his hands. His stomach roiled. He needed the men's room.

After horking whatever was left in his stomach and cleaning his mouth five times, woozy and alarmed, Barry speed-dialled the number for Detective Bill. The ring signal chimed without end and kept chiming. He wondered who he could call before the showdown with Myra. There was no one. He knew the conversation with her would yield the phrase: 'There will have to be an inquiry . . .' and he craved at least a little inside advance intelligence to fend her off with.

The phone rang. With one hand on the mouse, he picked up with the other and could hear Myra's breathing quick and definite in the earpiece. He found he could say nothing.

'Barry . . . ?'

'Yeah. It's me.'

'Do you know?'

'I think so. There were two disasters, right? There wasn't another one I don't know about?'

'Two are enough. One is too many.'

'Myra, I know this is bad . . .' He entered codes while speaking, waited for files to come up. 'I have to deal with things quick, so could we get going here? Is this all you wanted to say to me?'

'There will have—'

'To be an inquiry.'

'Don't be snide. You're in enough trouble.'

'Trouble?' Here was where Barry knew he would have to fall back on platitudes. 'These were criminals. They did criminal things. We took what steps were necessary to minimize risk. We lost. We don't often lose this big, but we lost. What's the big deal?'

'A citizen is dead. A cop is in therapy trying to deal with shooting someone in the line of duty. The chief is talking to the media, handing the parole service over as incompetent slobs. Ottawa is hopping. The deputy minister personally called for an update two hours ago. We've been stalling him until you got in. Where the hell have you been, anyway? We called your house and your cell and your pager and there was no answer. Are you having some kind of personal problem? You've got some explaining to do. I mean, a guy who was apparently using a replica handgun and carrying pseudo security guard ID who was bombed to the eyeballs on who-knows-what? A lifer like Chantal, who already killed one john, on drugs and walking away from minimal security to kill someone else? And you're somewhere nobody can find you?'

'It's crappy alright.' Barry spoke with hand on mouse, scrolling. 'And it's going to look shitty on your CV.'

'This is no time for your impertinent repartee, Mr. Delta. It's time to be an adult.'

'Adult!'

'Just get your reports ready *tout suite*.' Myra ignored what Barry might have been ready to say. 'Work them up good. Try to explain what was going on. I mean, did you really think Chantal's risk was being managed at that place?'

'She had a goddamn bracelet around her ankle!'

'She did?' There was a pause, Barry sensed an encouraging uncertainty. 'It wasn't noted in your running record.'

'I haven't had time to update my running record, I was too busy visiting with our other disaster.'

'You saw him recently?'

'I left him last night around seven-thirty. I phoned attack force about him right after.'

'The police neglected to tell us that.'

'Stick around, they'll neglect a lot more before you grow up.'

He could almost see her deep sigh. 'Please don't insult me. I'm trying to help.'

'Okay then.'

'What was the story with this other one?'

'We had him cased from the beginning. I put attack force on his ass as of early last week. We'd been trading clues for the last month. The urinalysis delay stopped me from doing anything sooner. Otherwise I was on him like rain. If there were any screw-ups they weren't mine.'

'So it sounds like you were on this case.'

'Like I said . . .'

'There's no running record.'

'It just happened last night. I just got in this morning.'

'When and how exactly did you refer him to the police?'

'Last night about seven-thirty or eight. By cell phone. Five minutes after I last saw the creep.'

'Referrals to attack force usually take five days.'

'When you've got friends like I have on the police force, things happen.'

'Well. If this is all true we might get out of it without too much blood loss.'

'And your career is safe, dearie. Keep preening, there might yet be a deputy ministership somewhere in your future . . .'

Barry spoke these last few words into a dead phone. He was momentarily appreciative of Myra's appropriate pluck in shutting him down. He fought the encroachment of a grudging respect for her. But then his hangover was booming anew.

Coffee. Anything to distract. Maybe a doughnut too.

He thought of a muffin shop down the block. He'd look like a clown to the commissionaire, who would comment on his six-minute workday. But he'd have coffee. The mere thought of a good cup was numbing his work-mind into blank spots. He snatched his jacket, thought about setting the alarm but decided that he'd be right back. Simply a hassle. To hell with it. He almost ran to the elevator and was down on the street in no time.

He downed the first cup reading both daily papers' accounts of the overnight criminal catastrophes. No mention of names, and as usual the press had the legal status of the offenders all wrong. No matter, much the better for him and Myra if the reading public thought the crimes were committed by provincial probationers instead of federal parolees. He munched down a muffin, chugged another cup. Then there was distress in his gut again and he was reminded of the night, the way it wouldn't all just fade away. Barry stumbled for the washroom a second time.

Afterward, sleep was all he could think about. He felt so shaky he knew it would be no good going back to the office. He'd only had a few hours out of the last twenty-four. He trudged up the street and almost stepped aboard a bus before he remembered his decision last night not to go home. He turned and squeezed out of the bus queue, letting the current of people wash around him and staring ahead in distraction until all were gone and the bus pulled out and left him alone on the sidewalk. He resisted the urge to use his cell phone, knowing that Myra would check the numbers called, so he looked up and down the street for the nearest public telephone. He dialled Diane's number, then remembered the time of day and hung up before the answering machine took his quarter. He dialled her work number.

'Diane, it's me.'

'Oh . . . hello you.' He could barely hear her above the street noise. 'Where are you?'

'On the street. Sorry for the racket. I need a place to stay.' Barry waited through the expected pause. 'I'm in some trouble.'

'I guess you'll explain it to me when you can.'

'Right.'

'Of course I'll help, but we have to talk.'

'Sure.'

'It can't go on like this, Barry.'

'I know that.'

He had sensed she would be taken aback by his lack of resistance. 'I'm glad you're taking it so nobly.'

'You kind of pretty well handed it to me that last time we were together.' He paused, as much to give her respectful consideration as to allow a diesel bus to blast by. 'How's Tony?'

'He's fine. Better than you, it sounds like.'

Barry found himself bereft of anything to say. He waited with Diane, in silence.

'So what was the problem?' She was tentative. 'You need a place to stay?'

'Uh huh. Right now. I'm sick. Or something. I gotta crash for few hours and clean up and get my head together.'

'You still have your key?'

'Sure.'

'Okay but . . . I'll be home by five. Tony's coming over.'

'I'll be out by then. And I'll leave the key.'

'Where will you stay tonight?'

'I don't know.'

'Oh Barry . . .'

'Talk to you later, okay?'

'Of course.'

'Thank you, Diane.'

'I'm sorry. Whatever it is that's happening to you, I'm sorry.'

'You're a pal.'

Walking downtown, Barry had to turn off the phone and set the pager to silent alarm. Otherwise they kept beeping and tweeting their little electronic hearts out. It was a distraction Barry just couldn't face up to at the moment.

At the apartment he showered, hoping for a better outlook once the accretions of the last twenty-four hours were washed away. He felt marginally improved. The clock read 11:20 a.m. as Barry slid between the sheets. He thought of checking his voicemail but forgot about it in the act of getting comfortable. He hoped for a good two hours' slumber and then he'd consider his next move. Sleep would heal, or at least temporarily anaesthetize.

Sleep would not come. Barry willed his mind not to think. Then with a jolt he knew he had neglected to do something too important to put off. He was not surprised he had suppressed it. He reached for the bedside phone and dialled his home number, knowing and hoping Tanya would be out. The service clicked on after the third ring. For a second he panicked at what to say.

'Umm . . . sorry about last night. I'm okay. I'm not coming home today, either. I'm sorry. I've got trouble. I'll talk to you when I get my thoughts together. Don't worry. You'll just end up angry, and I'm sorry. I'll call you when I can. Bye.' He hung up the phone, knowing this wasn't good enough by light years. Knowing too that it was all he could do for the moment. Knowing he would have to do much more soon. He lay his head back on the pillow.

Barry's next thought took place at 3:31 p.m., according to the information his eyes took from the bedside clock. At first he thought this was part of his dreaming—a fragmented spectacle in which at one point he had been hunted by a wild animal—but realizing by the changed light on the walls of Diane's bedroom that the hour was actual he flung himself from the bed.

Feet on the floor, Barry ignored the dull crush of a sleep-headache and turned the beeper back to full-on to see who had called. The last number had registered an hour earlier from Myra. There were tons of others that he did not recognize. He pulled on his clothes. Outside, the spring day was ripely ending, with the beginnings of rush hour rumbling up on the quiet streets of the West End.

Barry found a bank machine and took out his last sixty dollars before payday. A cab came by as he made it to the curb and he was dropped outside the office in minutes. He punched elevator buttons and had to move aside from the swarm coming off the car full of people heading home. On the ride upward his stomach kicked and his brain almost booked off for a few seconds. It made him reach for the handrail and hold on, shaking his head. He realized that other than the muffin this morning he had not eaten a full meal for almost a whole day. He wondered about his blood sugar. The elevator door opened. He walked to his office and was startled to see the outside door propped open. The alarm system! In the strides it took to get there, Barry's problems with loss, failure, homelessness, poverty, fatigue, hangover and hunger melted. Mortal terror entered him now. The thought of his office, files and computer components, open to anyone with lock-picking ability, unalarmed and unmanned, made him sick anew. He almost pushed over a young woman coming from the direction of the washrooms.

'Barry!' Her voice was too familiar.

'Myra?' Barry looked at her. 'What are you doing here?'

'What am I doing here? I could laugh out loud at that question.'

'Could you please tell me what's going on.'

'What's going on is that you weren't here. We've been working for hours and the place was wide open.'

'Working . . ? We . . ?'

Myra stepped toward Barry's cubicle. 'I informed you that there would be an inquiry.'

Barry followed her into his workspace and saw a suited man rooting through his filing cabinet. 'My filing's not up to date.'

The man and Myra exchanged a look.

The man almost smiled. 'We noticed.'

'Who are you?'

'This is Mr. Seville.' Myra gestured. 'From audit branch.'

'Audit branch.'

'Yup.' Mr. Seville dropped a file into a cardboard box on the floor.

Barry stood while they resumed their work, ignoring him. 'You audit guys dress real well.'

'Uh, thank you.'

'Barry . . .' Myra nudged him out of the office. 'I think it would be best if you proceed for the rest of the day and let us finish up here.'

'Proceed?' For the first time Barry noticed a dolly loaded with two boxes of documents parked in the hallway ready to be wheeled out. 'What the hell is this? An inquiry or an inquisition?'

'Don't get defensive. You know the protocol.'

'I try to be good at ignoring it. You know that.'

'You won't have access to computer services for a while.'

'Oh yeah? How am I supposed to work?'

'Do community visits for a day or two. This won't take long.'

'It's already taking long. And why not let a guy know there's going to be a raid like this? It's not right.'

'What's right about leaving the office open and unalarmed for most of a day?'

'I can explain.'

'Get ready to explain a lot.' She stood with hands on hips.

'Man . . .' He slumped against the wall, shaking his head. 'I know I've been loose and wide lately and last night was utter fucking madness. But this is cold. Just cold.'

'Don't take it so hard. You said it yourself. This is a risky business.'

Barry looked her in the eye. 'I know I've said that but have I ever said it to you?'

'I think so. Or words to that effect.'

'Hmmm . . .' Barry looked away. 'Must have been a moment of weakness.'

'Well, it's best you get stronger and try to be accurate as possible about what's been happening.'

'I don't like the sound of that.'

Myra gestured toward the elevators. 'Get going. Before I say something you really don't like.'

'Don't worry. I was irate this morning. I mean, if I have to admit something, I was rattled. Really rattled.'

'I think I noticed.'

'Whatever. I should apologize for the things I said. I know I violate a lot of civil service law about respect for supervisors, et cetera. But I didn't mean to be abusive. I'm having a hard time.' Barry folded his arms across his chest and looked to the floor. 'Is there any sense in my telling you this?'

'It's the first useful thing you've said to me. Too bad it might be too late.'

'I don't like the sound of that either.'

'Like I said, you better get going.'

Barry turned and started toward the elevators. 'Thanks.'

'Oh!' Myra called after him. 'Your wife phoned.'

Barry turned. 'What did she say?'

'I just took the message. She sounded upset.'

'Sorry you had to tackle that. I'll speak to her.'

'Okay.' Myra watched him get on the elevator. 'Bye.' She stayed in the hall, just within his view, until the doors closed.

Barry had mysterious tears in his eyes by the time he got to the sidewalk. After a time he stopped and stood with clenched fists. Then he could not help but bark 'Fuck!' loudly to a storefront full of surprised shoppers. With his verbal out-letting and now painful tension mounting in his hands the anger dissipated, leaving him better. Certainly not well, but better. He opened his hands and let the pain go away.

He experienced an odd sensation. Hunger. Some raw tuna would taste good right now. He started walking again. He noticed a well-dressed young woman watching him and he was embarrassed that she might have been alarmed by his outburst. Barry smiled as best he could and said: 'Sorry, Ma'am.'

She gazed at him for a moment and then moved down the street. Barry continued on his way, wondering how many more women he would be apologizing to.

[17]

LATER ON, BARRY made a call that he'd been meaning to make for months. He stood in the street and stabbed out the number on his cell. An old man scratched a hello.

Barry checked the hour on the clock tower at Granville and Georgia. He saw it was just after nine. 'Jeez John, did I wake you?'

'Wake me? Far as you know I mighta turned into a corpse since the last time you seen me. What is it, five years?'

'Don't be silly. Last spring.'

'Yeah, well, in the life of a guy my age that kind of gap can be eternal. As in forever. Get it?'

'Yes yes, you're mortal. You told me. I don't believe it but you insist it's true.'

'Come on out and see for yourself.'

'As a matter of fact I need to.'

'Don't be too shocked at what you see.'

'John . . .' Barry had too-soon run out of gas to kibitz. 'I'm in a jam.'

'Why didn't you say so.' Barry was reassured to hear the automatic kick-in of John's social-worker voice. 'Got wheels?'

'No. I'll have to bus it. Can you stay up that late?'

'Sure. This time a-night you'll have to transfer twice.'

'I know the drill. I'm coming as fast as I can.'

'That's what your girlfriends used to complain to me about.'

'Very funny.'

Barry took a harbour ferry and transferred and waited and transferred again and made it to Deep Cove in just over an hour. The stop was on the small main street that led onto a dock. The inlet water at the end was black oil in the darkness, reflecting streetlight. The path to John's house took him through high shrubbery and quiet, almost overgrown roadways, up a slight incline past old houses originally built as summer cottages. With John's bungalow in sight, Barry stopped walking for a moment and experienced something he hadn't felt in months, maybe years. It had been easily a year since he had been on this walk and he didn't remember noticing it. He listened to the away-from-the-city silence. There was the calming sense of nearby water and the sounds of birds overhead. That was it. He let it touch him. He hoped that these seconds' worth might enter his ears and permeate his brain with just enough salve to see him through these coming days and weeks.

Barry knocked on the screen door and waited for a call from inside. He could hear a television. Nothing happened. He knocked again louder and heard a clearing of throat. Barry pulled the screen door open and turned a knob on the inner door and stepped into John's modest house. The fry-scent of ten thousand plates of bacon and eggs met his nostrils. Then there was the cigar smell, pitting its tropical perfume against the breakfast remnants and yielding a genuine personal odour that Barry unmistakably knew as John, his old friend and parole service mentor.

'Hey!' Barry called into a vacant front hall. 'Is there a cantankerous old pensioner living here?'

From the front room Barry heard movement. He prepared himself to see John and not react to the changes the year would have made. When the bulky man appeared seconds later Barry was elated at how good he looked, possibly better than the last time he'd seen him. He knew John would perceive his reaction.

John took the stub of a stogie from his mouth and bellowed. 'Confounded I'm alive, eh?'

'You've looked worse.'

'I just got out of the hospital that last time you saw me.'

'Oh yeah, right . . . no recurrences?'

'Nope. It's all or nothing these days I figure. It was pretty bad last time, though. Next time I have pneumonia I'll tell the ambulance not to bother with the hospital and just keep on going to the cemetery.' John smiled genuinely and brought his thick spectacles up to peer at Barry. 'How the hell are you?'

'Well, that's controversial.'

'You look the shits.'

'Thanks for not mincing words. I guess I am the shits.'

'I figured so.' John gestured with his cigar back toward where the sound of a television was audible. 'Was all that commotion in town that's all over the news anything to do with you?'

'Yeah. A lot to do with me.'

'Uh huh. The only reason you're out here.'

'John, lay off. Gimme a cup of tea or something.'

The older man headed through a doorway. Barry followed. He noticed now that though John looked fine, he moved slower. In the eating area just off the kitchen, John flopped into a chair and rested his arms on the table.

Barry stood, looking at him. 'So don't I get tea?'

'Kettle's on the stove.'

'Some host.'

'I want you to feel at home.'

'Okay.' Barry made a move to the sink.

'Besides, tell you the truth, I can barely do that kind of stuff anymore. I would if I could but I can't stand up that long. Kicks hell out of me.'

Barry grabbed the kettle and ran water, he spoke to John over his shoulder. 'It's that bad?'

'Don't get old, boy.'

'We all try the best we can, but I don't know, maybe we were asking for it. We used to eat a lot of high-fat, low-fibre, high-salt lunches.'

John grinned at Barry through cigar smoke. 'One thing about paying a polite visit out here. Try to keep your sanctimonious health diet gobbledygook out of the general conversation.'

Barry put the kettle on the stove. 'Right.'

They settled with hot cups in hand. John looked again at Barry. 'You do look like hell.'

'You mentioned that.'

'Well, you do.'

'It's been a bad day. In fact the whole week's been pretty shitty. For that matter, so's the month. And all things considered it's been a crappy year. The decade's been no hell either. Come to think of it, the whole last century and the first part of this one's a bugger if you take a hard look at it . . .'

'Oh quit whining. You didn't have a war to fight didya? You didn't have the depression to live through. You didn't get polio because you were born before they had a vaccine. You didn't go to Vietnam because you were Canadian. The government paid for most of your university. You were lucky. You and your crowd got jobs right away because there were plenty of 'em. You always had a car . . .'

'I don't know about that one. I'm bucking those demographics right at the moment.'

'What? No car?'

'Nope.'

'That's because you're not using your head.'

'Actually, it's kind of an environmental choice.'

'Bullshit. You're broke, aren't ya? The civil service is no place to work these days. You haven't had a raise in six years, they don't pay overtime anymore. You got that high livin' spouse of yours. Admit it, you can't afford a good car.'

'Sure I can.'

'You're supporting a wife who has expensive tastes. You got women friends, probably a steady girl. Still playing around with anything that gets within grabbing distance?'

'Aw John, lay off . . .'

'. . . You drink to beat hell. Eat out most nights. Taxes are higher than ever. You're financially screwed. Right?'

'Speaking of screwing, I need some advice.'

'Don't change the subject.' John stubbed out his cigar. 'Ya need money?'

'No.'

'Well you need something.'

'Just a place to stay. For a night at least. I left my wife.'

'That's no big surprise.' John looked down at this tea and his dead cigar. 'Sorry to hear it, though.'

'Thanks. It's no big deal.' Barry examined the floor. 'It's me. It's just me.'

'Oh it's her too but I hear you, boy. It's you, alright. For right now and right here it's gotta be you.' John sipped tea and fumbled for another smoke. 'What brought it on?'

'Oh a conglomeration of stuff. Not one thing and another. A lot of things that I thought were nothing but when you add them all up it's actually something. You know.'

'Uh huh.'

'I mean, I've done the thinking. We started out alright but it was under duress, you know. Remember that body we found that time and the rot and all that? Remember I dated her just after and I spewed up across a restaurant and she followed me as I ran away and stood by on the beach while I splashed around like a mental case? Well, I liked her an awful lot for that. Maybe too much. Lately I realize she might only like me when I'm in crisis. She only likes it when I'm crippled. She doesn't listen to me otherwise. She's kind of a law unto herself too, more than I can relate to. It's generally her way or no way. She broaches no criticism. It's like Nazi Germany. All the subtle and not-so-subtle control going on. I have to account for everything and then I'm made to feel guilty if I bridle at it. I can't live like that.'

John nodded gravely. 'So why tonight and not last week or next year or never?'

'I just got to the end, I guess. And when I got to the end I knew it was the end.'

'Good observation. It shows you're not that far gone.'

'I hope so.' Barry sipped his tea. 'So I need a place to stay for a night or so.'

'You can stay as long as you need to if you can stand the bachelor life.'

'That may be hard.'

'Welcome to the world of woman-less home life.'

'I've had plenty of that and you know it.'

'So is that what you wanted to know about screwing?'

'Huh?'

'You had a question a while back.'

'Oh yeah.'

'Well we got lots of time. All night. How's the caseload?'

'Oh fine except for the murderous hooker I apparently let loose on the john population last night. Got one dead body over that. Then there's the replica-handgun-toting psycho armed robbery guy who just committed officer-assisted suicide. Got himself perforated in the vital zones. That was last night too.'

'Pretty busy.'

'You could say that.'

'Glad I'm out of it.'

'Me too. You're too nice a guy.'

'Hmmm.' John pushed his tea away. 'We need a real drink. Whisky?'

'If you got some.'

'Better be careful . . .' John rose slowly and went to a sideboard. 'From what I hear of that jobsite of yours these days they'll make you do a piss test for booze.'

'You're not far from the truth. The good thing is that alcohol only lasts around twenty-four hours. You can make some kind of excuse. Smack lasts three days, generally. So does cocaine. THC runs you thirty days minimum under most circumstances . . .'

'How the hell do you know all that stuff?'

'That's parole work in the modern world, my man.'

John produced a bottle of scotch. 'Still take it neat?' He lined up two glasses.

'Always.'

'That's m'boy.' John poured.

Barry grinned at the drinks on the table. 'Like two piss samples in a row.'

'Cut it the hell out! You're more far-gone than I thought.'

'There were good times.'

'Thank christ for that.'

'You had good cases. I remember that native kid.'

'Which one?'

'The one we scared the shit out of and took him for a ride to the reserve.'

'Oh yeah. Charlie.'

'How'd he do?'

'Fine. Eventually. Far as I know.'

'That's great. So nice never to hear from them again.'

'It sure is.'

'I only had a few of them. Maybe only one.'

'Only one?'

'Only one that did his time, buggered off and never darkened the criminal justice doorway again. Steve something. Can't remember his full name.'

'He was the guy you hid after the Squeeg ruling.'

'That's right. That was a crazy time.'

'I'll say. There's probably guys still running after that one.'

'Steve did his time and stayed away forever. I heard from somebody years later he moved back east and started a business or something. I hope he's doing fine.'

'What do you think the secret to his success was?'

'I don't know.' Barry sipped whisky and thought. 'I got him to do something once. Something extra.'

'Rehab?'

'No no.' Barry looked away, unsure how much to tell. 'I eventually gave him my car.'

'Your car? Which one?'

'The first one. The white Civic. It was a thrapped-out mess.'

'Not as bad as your second one.'

'Hoo, that was a rattler now, wasn't it?'

'How'd you manage to get that thing stolen?'

'Or even weirder, why'd I ever go and reclaim it from the cops?'

The men smiled together.

'Anyway, this Steve. It was my all-time greatest success story. I traded him my car. He just took it and disappeared.'

'Maybe that was all he needed.' John drank and reflected. 'A car.'

'Hmmm . . .'

'There's a lesson in there somewhere.' John chuckled.

Barry looked at the older man and fought a tear. 'John.' He drank to cover his faltering voice. 'Seriously. You don't mind my leaning on you?'

'Didn't I ever tell you what the score was?'

'What do you mean?'

'Love.' John took a drink. 'I don't mean it in a mushy sense. It's what made it real, two guys on the road after our crooks. Doing them some kind of good when we could, tossing them in the can when there was nothing else. It was a tough go, morally. We had to keep the cops from railroading the boys whenever they had the chance. And yet we had to be their ultimate punishers. While being punished ourselves. We had to be men of love to understand both sides.'

'Men of love.'

'It might sound flaky. But it's what I've always felt.'

Barry shook his head, incredulous. 'I'm glad I came to see you.'

'It was the only thing you could do. Good boy.'

'You're pretty sure of yourself for a senile old semi-cripple.'

'You should have seen me in my prime.'

Barry smiled. 'I am.'

[18]

BEFORE JOHN WAS up, Barry showered and put on his three-day-used clothes. He could not find a hair-care product among the old man's toilet articles. He looked in the mirror for a longer time than usual and peered closely at this new look. The wet-down coiffure made him seem older, more concerned-looking. He was heartened slightly by the trace of authority it added. It almost made him laugh.

He smiled into the glass and saw how that looked. Lightweight. A frown was certainly more dramatic with slicked-back hair. Almost gangster-esque. Doing all this clowning he knew he was just putting off the inevitable.

Work. He moved sweatily in his rumpled outfit and gathered up his jacket in the living room. The clock over the mantel read 7:10. He wondered if he should rouse John enough to bid goodbye, decided against it, reconsidered, decided no again but resolved to call during the day. The door latched quietly shut behind him.

In town Barry walked toward the office, passing the big bus stop on theatre row. He was taken in by a flashing familiarity among the myriad scribbles, faded posters, lost children's faces and the hopeless glued-on detritus of the shelter walls. He ignored the twigging in his brain and hurried on, thinking about coffee. Down the street he passed another shelter and this time the image poking from the glossy framework could not be dismissed. He stopped, backed up and looked at a poster, not fully understanding for a few seconds exactly what it was.

There was a picture, a colour photocopy, fuzzy and distorted, of a man much like himself framed within a television screen. When he read the caption above—BUS ATTACK!—and then the one beneath: Wanted: for Assault and Unlawful Flight, still the clarity of the situation, what he needed and wanted to comprehend, did not arrive. Barry shook his head, trying to exorcise the still resonating scotch demons in his brain.

He read again the caption, and then the fine print below, and finally comprehended:

> This man is wanted for questioning after a vicious assault aboard a transit bus three weeks ago.
>
> Please contact Ms. Jennifer Mayhew-Smith.

Barry stopped reading. He reached at the paper, hit glass, scratched at it, found the glue to be so firm he had to use an office key to pry each corner and peel slowly. Then he took his whole key chain and scraped, scarring and marring until at least half the poster was fluff on the sidewalk. The remainder hung mauled past recognition.

He almost staggered, making for the office. At the building entrance, the commissionaire gave him the usual smile. Barry rejoiced that this cheerful official drove to work, parking beneath the building, and would not normally be exposed to street-art. The elevator ride was too slow. In the office he slammed the switch on his computer and checked for voicemail with the other hand. There were no phone messages. The computer didn't seem to be working. He was about to call tech support when he remembered he was cut off. No files, no access to the system, no email. He cursed.

Barry's mind writhed. Memory of the bus incident made him seethe. Anger overrode reason. He could barely concentrate. Assault my ass! He considered suing the bastards, whoever they were. No matter how odious he found court, he couldn't get the idea of a good preemptive lawsuit out of his mind.

Half an hour passed. He still couldn't think. The place was quiet as a mountain meadow. He regarded with palsied eyes the emptied file-cabinet. The phone wasn't ringing. Barry picked it up and checked for a dial tone. Working.

Had he actually assaulted anybody? The substantive facts of it all, the elements of the event, were fragmented in his recall. He'd stumbled, hadn't he? The bus lurched. He had been drinking. He had been weak with fatigue. He began to sidetrack with memories of Diane, then what was bothering him today, went back to it, then recalled that he was separated from his wife and hadn't actually spoken to her about it other than by voicemail. Then there was the investigation by audit branch and his current computer-deprived helplessness.

And there were Wanted posters up for him all over the city.

The phone rang. Barry girded his mind. He picked up.

'Barry Delta here . . .' The sound of his automatic telephone voice was self-reassuring. He could still make dignified sounds even when his world was dissolving.

'Mr. Delta. Wayne Stickner here.'

'Wha . . . ?' Barry's mind reeled. 'Oh . . . sorry. I was about to yell at you. I thought you were the ghost of your father.'

'I will be a ghost pretty soon if I don't get some work.'

'Yeah . . .' Barry fought to focus. 'Yeah, work. A tricky deal when you're just released . . . what're you looking for?'

'Anything. Literally anything.'

'Hmm . . . used to be we had a job-finding outfit that worked with the parole service and they were pretty good for situations like this. They could get a guy a construction or a ditch-digging gig on a day's notice and at least you'd have food money in your pocket for a couple of days.'

'That would be great.'

'Yeah but they cut the program a few years back. Restraint. The deficit. Conservative political agendas. Bankers in Brazil. Sun spots. Who the fuck knows why they cut it but they cut it and you're presently shit out of luck . . .' Barry caught himself and noted the silence on the other end of the line. 'Have you applied for welfare?'

'Yeah, but they could only give me a voucher for a smelly room downtown and a side of fries at the local roach diner.'

'That's rough.' Barry shuddered at how close he, too, was to the street.

'If there's anything you can think of. Even a lousy ten bucks would put a better face on things.'

'Face. Yeah . . .' Barry thought for a second, realizing he'd begun to daydream, his own issues taking precedence. Especially the issue of right now; his visage all over the city's bus shelters, just waiting for someone to recognize him and tip off these fanatical transit riders. But the mention of the word "face" . . .

The idea came. For about two seconds Barry kicked around the ethical question, but this day felt so desperate—this time felt so desperate—he resolved to be a drastic man and said: 'I might have something private. Confidential. Between you and me. There's fifty bucks in it.'

Silence on the line. Barry imagined it was a thinking silence. 'You still with me?'

'Sure I am. What do I have to do?'

'There's a bunch of posters around town. I want you to get rid of them.'

'Posters?'

'They have a picture on it that I find embarrassing.'

'Oh yeah?'

'When you see them you'll know what I mean.'

'Okay.' Barry had the impression Wayne was writing something down. 'And you want them torn down.'

'Yeah. All of them. As many as you can find.'

'How many are there?'

'I have no idea. These people are rabid. There's no reasoning with rabidity. They're likely in all the bus shelters but they might have broadcast the thing across the country for all I know.'

'I'll have to ride the bus all day.'

'Well there's the fifty in it for you. Plus expenses. Got bus fare?'

'I gotta go right now and get a pass from welfare. Then I'll get right on it.'

'Good man. Gimme a call in the afternoon. And thanks for not asking questions.'

'The only question I'll ask is: Where's the money?'

'And your answer will be forthcoming. Phone me and I'll take you for a snack someplace. Okay?'

'Gotcha.'

Hanging up, Barry marvelled at how much better he felt about things.

But then the phone rang again. All the fatal possibilities ran through his head about whom this might be. He caught it before the second ring.

'Barry Delta here.'

'It's Myra.'

'Of course it is.'

'How could you possibly know? We don't have caller ID, Barry.'

'Yeah, cheap government phones. I knew it was you anyway.'

'Why do you say that?'

'Because.'

'Why because?'

'Just because, okay. Could we stop talking like children and get down to your bad news?'

'How do you know I've got bad news?'

'A couple of blown cases. An audit review. How could it be anything good?'

'Barry, get a grip, okay?'

'I will. I definitely will.' Barry decided it was a promise to himself as much as to Myra. 'What's up?'

'Relatively good news, for your information. You're looking okay on the case management end. I got Mr. Seville to go easy.'

'I hope it didn't involve anything detrimental to your personal integrity.'

'Don't talk like that. I got him down to just one more standard. Then I think you'll be off the hook.'

'One more standard. What's that?'

'You have to take a drug test.'

'What?'

'It's been policy for over a year. Didn't you get the memo?'

'You're kidding.'

'It's right there in the departmental regulations. Everybody got a copy.'

'I don't have time to read those things. They stack up and I just chuck them in the recycling.'

'You're supposed to file them in your regs and directives binder. Do you even know where that is?'

'I think it's maybe one of the ones I threw out last year when I was rearranging. I needed the shelf space.'

He could hear Myra sigh. 'To a large extent you had this coming.'

'Seriously, though. You are kidding about the drugscreen.'

'I am not kidding. You have to report immediately.'

'Where? To the same place we send our caseload?'

'No. There's a corporate clinic downtown.'

'Corporate? Since when did this social service agency start fancying itself a corporation?'

'It's a technical term, Barry. Can't you have just a little respect? I mean, we've been a good living for you all these years.'

'There was a time I thought so too but now I'm told to go piss in a bottle.'

'Everyone has to live by standards.'

'This one stinks.'

'Nevertheless . . .'

Barry tried to think fast, near-panicked with the certainty of a THC reading from his pot-session with Rikki. 'I . . . I can't get downtown. For a couple of days at least.'

'Barry, you are downtown.'

'I'm leaving just as soon as I get off the phone. Home visit out in the 'burbs.'

'You have no caseload outside the city. The clinic is on Georgia Street, it's open until 1730 hours. Please get there before it closes.'

'Is that an order?'

'No. Despite what you might think of me, Barry, I'm not into authoritarianism. Defy all you like. Consider me a simple advisor.'

'But there will be shit to pay.'

'You've been around long enough to know who will pay and in what currency.'

'Well put, kiddo.'

'I'm not a kiddo, I'm your supervisor. I'm telling you for the last time. Don't speak to me in that manner.'

'Aye aye.'

'Just get going.'

'I will.'

Barry hunched over and found he had to knock his head with closed fists to get his brain moving toward logic. He'd been sent to a course some years back on the subject of administrative tribunals. If he had to testify about his blown-up cases it would greatly complicate things if he was to leave a hot piss sample for marijuana.

Complicated indeed. Barry nearly laughed aloud at the situation: A just-released con on his caseload was out somewhere working for him, tearing down wanted posters put up by people who considered him, Barry Delta, a law enforcement official for over two decades, a criminal; the social program he'd worked in all his life now called itself a corporation; he was being investigated bureaucratically for law enforcement actions he had taken intuitively; he was due at a clinic to urinate in a bottle and he had no intention of doing so; his best friend was a retiree who felt sorry for him and had to provide him shelter; he felt intense dread at leaving a wife who, as far as he knew, had not attempted to get in touch with him since the event; his mistress had dumped him to have a baby; he had gone out and had unprotected sex with a dope-smoking woman of child-bearing age he had only truly known for three drunken hours.

Barry laughed aloud but hated the sound. He shut himself up and swivelled to face the window.

What to do? A state of concentrated crapulence. For half an hour he released his mind of responsibility, hoping in its freedom it would circle back around and provide at least a little perspective. In the end he managed to step back at least enough to be slightly tickled at all the irony. Then something formed in his mind. He'd get going all right. Right out of here. In fact his flight response had never been stronger. But first a little interference.

He swivelled to face the phone, picked it up, flipped in the directory for a number, then dialled.

'Smith, Smith, Fordham, and Pithorn . . .' A legal-secretary voice sang in Barry's ear.

'Hi, can I speak to Lance Pithorn, please.'

'Mr. Pithorn is in conference. Can I take a message?'

Barry left his name and pager number.

When he hung up the phone rang again.

'Barry Delta here.'

'Not for long I don't imagine though, huh?'

'Detective Bill! I was wondering when you'd crawl into the sunlight.'

'Pretty dark out there today, boy, looks like rain. Anyway, what I hear, it's you should be looking for cover.'

'So how can you help me with that, Bill?' Barry laid as much sarcasm on this last word as he thought he could get away with. 'What happened on that thing I sent you on? Fuck it up real good, did ya?'

'If you'da been at work these last few days I coulda told you.'

'What? That I gave you directions to a robbery guy and you just go out and shoot him?'

'The hamburger stand shooting? We didn't do that thing. That was some of our regular guys answering a silent alarm.'

'That wasn't you guys?'

'Nope. We were too busy.'

'So I go to all the ass-saving trouble of keeping a relationship with you special cop-guys, have fish dinners with you, stand for all your endo-cop distrust and ill-ease, point out my dangerous cases to you as quick as possible and you don't even go after the tip when I give it to you!' Barry tried to sound jokey but realized he was for too angry for that. 'What kind of fucking cop are you?'

'The busy fucking kind. We were all set up on the Falcon Bandit but then we got swamped seeing to your other famous success story. The hooker-girl slash-up . . .'

'The which bandit?'

'Guy who drives around town in a '65 Ford doing convenience store jobs. Clerk in one of them saw him go to his car. We been looking for him a week now . . .'

'That's the guy I put you on!'

'What?'

'It's right here.' Barry shuffled a stack of yellowing offender profile printouts on his desk. 'He worked as a security guard. Owned a cherry '65 Falcon. There couldn't be more than ten of them left on the road in the whole country. That's the guy I put you on.'

'But the hamburger stand victim was on foot.'

'Well duh! Ever heard of a change-up? This was a pretty canny guy.

He's the one with the transferable tattoos, et cetera. I can't believe this.'

'Why didn't you tell us about the car?'

'I did when we had lunch the last time. At least that he had a ride anyway. I never actually saw the thing. And he said he'd sold it by the other night, anyway.'

'Whew. Well . . . that's a helluva screw up.'

Barry didn't know if he would laugh or cry.

'But, as I've been complaining . . .' Detective Bill's voice revealed discomfort. 'Not only did I have people staking out convenience stores, then we had to do the clean-up on your street-walker girl.' There was still silence from Barry's end of the phone. 'What's her affliction, anyway? You shoulda seen this poor guy.'

'If it was anything like the one she did ten years ago I can well imagine.' Barry sensed he should stop talking, but could not resist adding: 'Almost the same circumstances.' Though it felt good to get his blood up, Barry was struck now with a cold foreboding that echoed from his own words. 'Thus rolls my head into the sewer trough.'

Detective Bill took a moment and came back conciliatory. 'Couldn't you've locked 'er up?'

'I did. As much as I could. I was depending on other people, though. And there were varied aspects to it. She was the one I needed the abortion for. I guess I felt a bit sorry for her.'

'We took the bracelet off. Some guy from the monitoring program came and got it today.'

'Good. At least I don't have to handle it.'

'Not much good, those things.'

'Naw.'

'I guess she wasn't gonna go for voluntary lockup under the circumstances.'

'Naw. And we had essentially nothing on her. This was the tightest I could make it.'

'Well it's not gonna look good. This fella she carved up was some kind of citizen. His family's up in arms.'

'Yeah and it's going to be hard to explain that a girl like her, with a record like hers, when she gets a parole like she has, she has rights. She can't just be thrown in jail because she's in a bitchy mood. I mean, I had bad feelings about her but sometimes all you've got to go on is luck. I just needed her to get through one night without disaster, you know?'

'Better get a good lawyer.'

'I'm ahead of you on that by about forty-five seconds, Bill.'

'Ever occur to you you're in the wrong business?'

'Well it used to be kinda fun. Besides, I don't know what else I could do.'

'Yeah. Same with me.'

'Oh well.'

'I guess everything happens for a reason.'

'I'll tell them that at my trial.'

'I guess you're in a pretty pinch of shit.'

'Quaintly put.'

'Anything I can do?'

'Tell 'em I tried to stay on top of the jewellery guy.' Barry spoke seriously. 'When the time comes.'

'No problem.'

'Otherwise, wish me luck.'

'I can do that too . . .'

There followed a droning series of non-important exchanges and Barry wondered what else they would talk about. He was thoroughly tired now, even though it was only ten-thirty in the morning, and began to resent Detective Bill's continued presence on the phone. His energy drained away with every sentence and so did his concentration.

' . . . It's like you were a wanted man all of a sudden . . .'

Detective Bill kept talking but Barry did not catch it all. Then a certain word lurched his mind into foreword gear. 'Hold it! There is something you can do.'

'Name it.'

'I think somebody's harassing me with a nuisance complaint.'

'Oh yeah?'

'Have you seen a poster around town? I think they're mostly in bus shelters. Looks like me.'

'Nope. Strictly private transportation for me. Tell me about it.'

Barry told the history. It took some time. When he finished Detective Bill said: 'Better leave it with me.'

Barry hung up. He decided to go out and look at a newspaper, public exposure be damned. The thought of further phone work gave him a headache. He lurched from his chair and made for the hallway. He needed fresh air and a coffee.

[19]

LATE IN THE AFTERNOON, Barry Delta trudged his way through rapid rain, forcing one foot in front of the other. He did not want to go where he was going. His overcoat fluttered wildly, as if it too protested the trip.

He was doing something he had never done, always swore he would never do. He cut across a parking lot where the wind was extra discouraging, then along another street, walking faster than he normally would so as to be there sooner and not submit to the distaste coming up to him as he got closer. On a street in Gastown he found the address and walked up a two-storey flight of creaky wooden stairs. The office door had a frosted window in it, old-time private detective style. The door pinged softly as he closed it. The waiting room was of seasoned leather and panelling, but not opulent. Barry softened slightly. So far the place was as he would have it if, god forbid, he had ever become a lawyer.

Expecting a receptionist, Barry was surprised to see Lance Pithorn pop out from around a corner. He knew the man from numerous rancour-tainted court entanglements they'd had through the years.

'Mr. Delta.'

Lance extended his hand and Barry took it instantly, unexpectedly comforted to be in the presence of someone who likely understood trouble as well as he did.

'Mr. Pithorn. Call me Barry.'

'I'm fine with Lance, also. Come right in.'

Barry followed the lawyer into a cluttered site with paper and chairs littered about. He had to concentrate to see the desk Lance stepped behind. The best part of the place was an array of floor-to-ceiling windows with a street and harbour vista Barry imagined would be hard not to daydream through. He looked around him. 'I expected some staff.'

'They left for the day but I'm still here. As usual. Defense work takes a lot of nights.' Lance gestured at the clutter. 'Find a chair.'

'Your office is as messy as my life.'

'Then you do have difficulties.'

'Oh, I've got difficulties all right.'

Lance settled into a well-worn red leather wingback. 'And it's something you think I can help you with?'

'Yeah . . .' Barry lifted some files off the seat of a clerk's chair, removed his overcoat and laid it over the back, then sat himself down. 'But let's put this into perspective. I'm not in the kind of jam your usual client is in. The reason I'm here is to tell you a story and get your take on it and if you think I'm in trouble I invite you to suggest what I might do about it. I hope you don't mind operating that way. I should also say that I know you do not specialize in labour law or administrative matters but I think you'll see that the pickle I'm in has elements of the criminal cases you have handled.'

'I'm flattered you think I might be able to help.' Lance pushed hands into his pockets, a seated maneuver that Barry could see was borne of aged habit. 'I've watched you for years, Barry. You've always seemed most capable.'

'Thank you, Lance. I knew I needed to talk to a guy who I'd personally witnessed getting dead-to-rights murderers off on technicalities and obfuscations and creative legal arguments, et cetera.' Barry hoped he did not sound as cynical as he felt. 'Not that I need that kind of steam, but I just feel I might like to have the kind of guy on my side who sees the bigger darker picture. I'm inside the thing. I can barely make out my hand in front of my face. I need your perspective to get my bearings. I hope I'm not sounding melodramatic.'

'Well, tell me the story. And thank you, by the way, for your affirmation.'

'That's okay.' Though their exchange was scraping a little, a leftover of their adversarial roles, Barry felt by Lance's bemused smile that he was essentially with him. 'So should I tell it?'

'Please.'

Barry spoke for more than thirty minutes.

At the end of the story, Lance reached for a pair of reading glasses. 'You'll have to get me the statutes.' The lawyer spoke while looking down and writing. 'And the administrative regulations and departmental instructions and whatever else it is that authorizes and mandates your position and that of your immediate supervisor.'

'Of course.'

'If I put myself in the position of prosecutor for a moment, Barry, could you answer some questions?'

'The best I can.'

'Good. Why did you not check the employment of the security guard fellow?'

'I did. I visited the jobsite. But you're right. They will allege I didn't fully check out the employer. That was a thing on my list but there was no real imperative to go right out and do it. It would have been nice, but my workload wouldn't allow time.'

'That may not look good as an explanation.'

'I checked his work out on my own time. On a Saturday. If there's any question of my rigour in supervising the case that's got to count for something.'

'Perhaps. But why when you later perceived him to be not working and living a questionable lifestyle and acting strangely did you not immediately suspend his release?'

'I took the least restrictive option. When you read the regs you'll see that that's what's indicated in the directives. As an alternative measure I had a special police unit follow him.'

'Is your contact with this special unit logged?'

'If not at the police station, then by my cell phone records.'

'Excellent.' The lawyer smiled. 'Of course the police will take no responsibility.'

'They plead the same as me. Too busy. I've already found that out for sure.'

'But we can argue the point at least to a draw.'

'I was hoping you'd say something like that.'

'Now then, about the prostitute. How dangerous was she?'

'Hmmm . . . that's a tough term to work with, dangerous. I mean, given a certain set of circumstances she could go from zero to murder in under five seconds. But just sitting there normally she wouldn't be what you would call dangerous.'

'These "circumstances", what specifically would they be?'

'Her triggers are anger and men. She's disinhibited by drugs. If she's availed to that combination she's definitely dangerous. I put her in a place where I reasonably thought all those factors were controlled.'

'And your arrangements were somehow . . . violated?'

'That might be one way to put it. Screwed up, generally.'

Lance scribbled for some minutes before he spoke again. 'Were you informed by the monitoring agency that she'd left her designated area?'

'Only by pager. And that was turned off.'

'Were the police informed?'

'They got the call, logged it, and put it with all the other emergencies they had to contend with.'

Lance was busy writing again.

Barry glanced out the windows at the yellowing skyline. 'Does this mean you'll take the case?'

'I can't say for sure until I see the documents.' The lawyer shifted in his chair. 'It'll cost.' He named a figure.

Barry exhaled. 'Man, that takes a bite. I might not be able to afford it.'

'Can you afford to lose?'

'I don't know. I haven't done the math. I'm eighteen months from retirement.'

'Please do the math and let me know.'

Barry thought for a moment. 'If somebody gets blamed, it's likely there'll be a lawsuit, right?'

'A good possibility.'

'If anybody is to blame, it's likely going to be me, right?'

'Inescapably.'

'Hmm.'

'If what you've told me is correct you'd at least be a party, if not the primary defendant.'

'Well I sure as hell couldn't afford that.'

'It's something to consider.'

'And I can likely get some help with legal bills through the parole officer's association. They're kind of a stunned outfit generally but once in a while they do something creative.'

'I'm glad to hear it. I sense money is an issue for you.'

'Absolutely.' Barry thought of something else. 'But there's the pride thing too. If I'm going out I don't want it to be over a lame-ass incompetence charge.'

'This is entirely up to you.'

'I guess.'

They sat for a few moments without talking. It occurred to Barry that despite the deadliness of the subject matter he was actually beginning to relax. The early evening quiet, embodied out the window by a spectacular crimson-gold sunset, permeated the room and was doing a good job of calming him. He was surprised that a consultation with a lawyer could be so soothing. The composure in Lance Pithorn's voice—his casual concision in discerning the issues—held Barry like a giant pair of hands. Then he thought further about what they had spoken of and he remembered something else.

'There's another thing. Two things, actually.'

'Please tell them.'

'There's a kind of vigilante Wanted poster for me on bus shelters all over the city. Some kind of bogus assault allegation.'

'Are the police involved?'

'I'm trying to find out.'

'Until you do there is no point in addressing it.' Lance paused. 'What else?'

'They want me to submit to urinalysis.'

'I was expecting that.'

'Is it legal?'

'Probably not, at least in an absolute sense. But that's immaterial.' Barry met Lance's analytical stare. 'I take it you do not wish to submit to the test.'

'Right.'

'Fine. Don't.'

'Just don't?'

'Right. The authority on that is muddy at best. The law is controversial and has never been universally accepted. Many cases in the United States have been successfully contested against comparable legislation. In Canada we're still struggling with Charter issues relating to the integrity of the person, et cetera. It'll be years if not forever before there is anything you can take to the bank on it. So ignore the order for now. Besides, you signed onto the service long before there were such requirements?'

'Oh yeah. Long before.'

'That factor alone is dominant. There is other law about this. I'll work on it. In the meantime, you must understand me perfectly . . .' Lance took off his glasses. 'Do not, under any circumstance, submit to the test.'

'I won't.'

'No matter what anyone in any capacity tells you.'

'Fine with me.'

'Of course there is a downside.'

'I can imagine.'

'As illegal or otherwise inappropriate and inadmissible as it might be, your refusal to submit will be a red flag. They'll know something in the case hitherto only suspected might be more aggressively developed. They'll come at us and try to unearth anything they can find to see if there is fire beneath the smoke. This is what I would do if the positions were reversed. That is, of course, if they're going to come at us at all.'

'You're right to speculate whether or not they will actually proceed. Even though it's the federal government we're dealing with here, there's a major chicken factor. Particularly once they learn that you're involved. Plus, if we're going to be co-defendants in a suit, they don't want to crumble my credibility all that much, at least not right away.'

'You're thinking like a lawyer, Barry.'

'Thanks, I think.'

'You've got things fairly well configured into a combat perspective. That's good. We must be prepared for the worst.'

'Absolutely. But if the scenarios you've outlined are all there is to it, from what I know of these people and their legal department, the issue of my refusal of urinalysis will at least get lost in the confusion. The other stuff, we'll have to see.'

'Fine.' Lance leaned back in his chair.

[20]

BARRY STRODE FROM the law office and under a sky inked dark with evening. The intermittent downpours had stopped.

He enjoyed the shimmering tableau; every neon storefront shone transmogrified images in the rain-wash about him. His transit to downtown in the laundered air was a tonic and put him in a good mood. Lance Pithorn, a lawyer of all things, had reassured him. It felt so good to have independent power on his side.

At his destination coffee shop Barry wheeled in and swept past a sorority of office women sipping their day's-end lattes. He stood to the counter, ordered a macchiato and looked around. The place was full and he had to spy carefully to see everyone and identify them as not the person he was looking for. The women, all gorgeous, gave him a cursory regard. He ignored them willfully, shuddering. He could not let such distraction take away from the current business. He turned back to the barista, paid for his coffee and found a place at the rail looking out on the street. Before he took a second sip, Wayne Stickner was at his elbow.

'Hey hey . . .' Barry pushed over to make room for the man and the large garbage bag he was toting. 'Laundry?'

Wayne smiled. 'No.' He swung the bulk below the counter and out of sight. 'Yours.'

Wayne opened a hand and unravelled a knurled paper.

Barry examined the image. 'Fuck me!'

Wayne grinned. 'It's a good thing I'm not a private detective. I'd have had to ask you some pointy questions.'

'Just hold your curiosity for a while. I'll comp you a ticket to my trial.'

'Fine.' Wayne took a seat.

'Coffee?'

'Excellent idea. What can I buy it with?'

'I've got it if you want it . . .' Barry put a hand in his pocket. 'And here's for the other.' He pulled the hand out and passed it under the counter, touching Wayne's sleeve.

Wayne palmed the money and disappeared it smoothly into his jeans. 'Thanks for the work.'

'Thanks for being available on a moment's notice.' Barry smiled, drank his coffee. 'Where are you staying tonight?'

'I dunno. I just got through doing your chore. I had to do every stop out to the university, east to Boundary, south to the river, north to the harbour. There were scads of them. Who did you offend?'

'I thought you weren't a private detective?'

'Sorry.'

'Naw, it's okay.' Barry looked around. 'I guess I sort of pushed somebody on a bus once. I was drunk and hardly remember.'

Wayne emitted suitable mirth. 'How the mighty will fall.'

'Who the hell ever said I was mighty?'

'I thought you were way up there.' Wayne turned sombre. 'But come to think of it nobody could be working with sludge like my dad and not be sludged up themselves in some way.'

Barry twinged. 'Don't speak about your father that way.'

'You know what I'm talking about.'

'I know what you're talking about and more about what you're talking about than you do but nobody—and I mean absolutely nobody—should talk about their own father like that. Whether they're in prison or dead or more-dead-than-alive or whatever. You have to not disrespect him, as irrational as that sounds in your case.'

Barry saw that Wayne was taken aback at his near-vehemence on the subject. 'It's just something that's fundamental.'

'Okay.'

'It's linked to a theory of mine, having seen how guys get warped by what happens to them as children. You see a guy who got whipped by his dad. Maybe even raped. As bad an experience as you can imagine. When they get older they just hate the guy purely. There's nothing else to them. It encompasses and permeates. They can't think about anything else and all their behaviours are defective because they don't do any thinking, they just walk around with this cocked-at-all-times weapon of hate inside them.

'So then the problem is so interwoven, so hard-wired into their systems that it's tough to get them to behave in any other way than angry. What they have to do, if they have the intellectual capacity—and it does take brains, dumb guys just about never change—is identify this hatred they carry as the problem. Not the fact their fathers were assholes. That's past. That's common. There's nothing you can do about that. What they have to do is get in touch with humanity again by finding love.'

Wayne was paying somber attention.

'Now love is a tricky deal.' Barry was caught in his own momentum. 'I know it sounds sappy but I'm not talking about romantic face-sucking stuff. What I'm talking about is the everyday, cellular-level state of existence that we all get granted as a virtue of the fact we were created by the processes of two people who may or may not have known each other very well but nevertheless then got you to a point where you stand today more or less by your own bi-pedal suspension. All that took a lot of effort. Even if you were abused on the way, this progression still involved a basic and powerful expression of love. It just wouldn't have happened otherwise. It's the kind of elemental earth-wind-and-fire affirmatory juice that weights us down and stops us from flicking off the surface of the planet into outer space. It's that basic.' Barry knocked back what was left in his demitasse. 'Am I making sense here?'

'Absolutely.'

'You lie slightly. But good, because this is purely where I come from as a PO. I have no other attributes, really, except this kind of reduction of observation into recommendation. I mean, the kind of intrinsic love we carry is a value beyond quantification. It literally keeps us alive. Babies who are not nurtured—you can feed them all you want but if you don't nurture them emotionally—will die, we know this. So as you walk the earth thinking you don't like your parents—some guys say they hate them, some delight in ignoring them, others steal from them, I've had guys on my caseload who killed one or other or both of them—as you go along this way you are ironically only here because of them. If you claim to hate or disrespect them, you actually direct negative energy toward the root of your own existence. This is unwitting suicide. It'll destroy you, sure as shit, and you won't even know why. If you disrespect your father you shoot yourself in the emotional foot, cut yourself off at your spiritual ankles. Betray yourself in every possible way.

'I mean, it's no wonder guys get in so much trouble. If you don't get this concept completely under control you'll just never get a line on living. It's not that simple, granted, but you've got to do it. We all do.'

'I think I get it.'

'Damn, I hope so. I think your mom did as best she could. Your dad, I know he was a blank at best. I mean, I know. He was less than zero. I'm pretty sure he even tried to have me offed one time, but it doesn't matter. To you he was a man whose existence was essential. To my mind the best thing for you to do if you want my advice is either try to find out, or at least imagine, one good thing he did. Just one thing. And never forget it. And honour him in your mind for it throughout the rest of your life. It's the secret to psycho-social self-containment, I swear. Simple as that. Difficult as that, too.' Barry paused, aware of heat under his clothes. 'I don't know how many more ways to Sunday I can express this. I know it all sounds a whole hell of a lot like first commandment dogma, but I hope it helps . . .'

'You should write a book.'

'Hah!' Barry snapped out of his stern countenance. 'I can barely get my reports done.'

Wayne eyed Barry's empty cup. 'Are you ready for another one of those?'

'Hey, let me get you one.' Barry slid off the stool. 'Keep that fifty whole for a bit.'

A few minutes later Barry placed a steaming double cappuccino in front of Wayne. 'Hope you like this stuff.'

'I was into it back a ways before I went into the joint. I found the only spot up north that did it. An old Italian guy.'

'It's the real stuff.'

'Ever been to Europe?'

'Once, just out of university.'

'I wanna go real bad. I wanna finish those three courses short of my degree, then I want to go over there and maybe never come back.'

'These things will be available to you in the not-too-distant-future, my friend. Keep clean, get a job, save some cash. You can apply for a passport just as your sentence expires. They'll call me up and I'll give the okay. It only takes ten days. Then you can be gone.'

'Just about exactly seventeen months from now.'

'Got it all planned out, eh?'

'You betcha.'

'In my happier experience in this business, guys with solid plans are the ones most likely to succeed.'

'That's good to know.' Wayne tentatively sipped his tiny drink.

Barry smiled. 'So you studied hard in the joint did you?'

'You told me to.'

'I did?'

'Yeah. I'll always remember.'

'Hmm . . .' Barry tossed back most of his espresso. He wracked his laboured synapses to recall what young Wayne was talking about. 'Well anyway, I'm glad I said it.'

'It must have happened to you before. The smallest thing you might drop in the course of conversation comes back years later in a big way. Beyond anything you'd ever expect.'

'Yeah, all the time. But usually in a bad way.'

'I guess it works that way too.'

'It sure as hell does.'

They watched shoppers pace outside the window. Barry began to think about getting going. He looked downward. 'Can you dump the bag?'

'No problem.' Wayne pulled at the bulky sack. 'There's still a few stops I didn't get to downtown here. I'll do those and wander over to that flop they sent me to last night. There's a dumpster in the alley behind.'

'So you don't know for sure where you're going to land tonight?'

'No.'

'I'll make a call. The Sally Ann is a better situation than any social services referral flop. Okay with you?'

'Fine. They charge?'

'Only if you have money. Keep that cash in your pants. You're broke, I'll tell 'em.'

'Good.'

Barry pulled his cell phone and spoke low. It was late in the day and the shelter was full but he managed a favour from the keeper. It incurred a debt but he was glad he could do it. He sent Wayne off with free accommodations for a week.

Sitting by himself in the emptying coffee shop, Barry remembered he was homeless too, and wondered who else he could call.

[21]

BARRY PUSHED OFF from the café stool, gathered his overcoat around him and walked into the night. Where to, he wasn't particularly concerned for the moment. He strode briskly and the exercise cleared his mind. He wondered who he might call.

He did not feel like riding transit enough to go back to John's place.

Any ideas he had about crashing at Diane's were swept aside at the thought of her new boyfriend and their procreative agenda.

For a second he considered Rikki. Sooner or later he would be speaking to her. Despite the fact they had only known each other in a meaningful way for a total of six hours, they'd gotten on well, even in the awkward aftermath. But there was too great a bundle of issues to deal with. Something from his murky emotional depths kept him from calling her.

As the evening lengthened, Barry moved with stiff strides though the districts. He brushed past the expensive hookers in front of the clubs downtown and toward the grunge of the east side. He wandered through the closing-down rabble of Chinatown, saw the street-walking budget girls, mused at his orientation to the city by way of prostitution prices. The thought made him smile but then the smile made him uneasy. He'd known so many hookers in his working life. Most now jailed. Some missing. The rest dead.

He gravitated toward the office part of town. A half-block from his own he decided to go up and rest awhile to consider his next move. He flashed his badge, told the night commissionaire he was working and might not be down all night. In his office he sat in the dark with his feet up on the computer credenza and his swivel chair adjusted back as far as it could go. He thought about sleep, doubting it would come.

An annoying luminescence through slatted window blinds nudged Barry conscious in the gray dawn. His dream, about a lumber mill job on the greenchain one summer—two-by-fours parading on an endless conveyor belt—melded weirdly with the stripe-image poking at him through sleep-sticky eyes. He swung legs to the floor in an impulse to move, but his knees buckled instantly and he slid from his chair, a numb hump hitting the carpet. He groaned aloud at the general deadness in his lower body. He massaged his lower limbs, grimacing in advance for the pain of recirculation and, picturing the image of his floor-bound distress, laughing at his predicament. He writhed and quaked there for a good five minutes. When finally back to health he was weirdly elated at surviving another night of homelessness and gathered up his coat to head out for some coffee. He marvelled at himself, formerly a shower-a-day man, that he didn't care how smelly his clothes were.

Down the street he got a newspaper from a box, whipped out his last viable credit card to get ten dollars from a convenience store ATM, and headed to a cheap breakfast place he knew. Over coffee and eggs the paper fell open at the classifieds, apartments for rent section.

It had been years since Barry had lived on his own. He pulled a pen and gamely started marking prospects. He calculated how long it was until another payday, how with the combined pull of a cluster of credit cards he might scrape together enough cash for a damage deposit. His bachelor memories—the steady train of women, thrown-together meals, all-night boozing with impunity, late-night TV viewing without harassment—while at any other time might have warmed him with nostalgia, all oozed into irrelevancy now.

Back at the office, he began the telephone work and by noon had a list of likely places to be checked before the end of the day. He found that his computer was back online. He got busy and actually accomplished a significant amount of paperwork before quitting time.

Nobody bothered him. It was one of those unlikely golden days. His boss did not call. His wife did not call. His former mistress did not call. His latest girlfriend did not call. He did not desire to call them. After the soul-wracking past few days he had little emotion to spend today. Only a sense of passing. An unsettling sense of passing, but there it was. Renewal, he knew. Renewal somewhere in all that scary vacancy. Once in a while he felt like collapsing. His heart felt like it might simply stall. He ignored these panic-tugs. Barry determined to himself that he would hold on for the renewal part.

By sundown he had an apartment in the basement of an old brick heap near Granville and Broadway. It was small, subterranean; two windows, dingy, cheap, somewhat dusty, walking distance to three major transit lines. Perfect. Best of all, the place was available immediately.

He took a cab to the Salvation Army thrift store and picked out a battered futon frame, a sleeping bag and a couple of nightstands. At a bedding discount warehouse he bought a new futon with still another weighty credit card. He trucked it all home in a cab and set up shop. By midnight he was having dinner and a beer in a local bistro, a friendly, snug place with a bar out front. The neighbourhood felt exactly right. Barry could hardly believe his good mood. He curled up in the sleeping bag and willed himself to dream of better times.

Next morning he eagerly got to the office and attacked anew the monster paperwork. By ten o'clock the phone rang.

'Barry Delta here.'

'I have to say that in view of the circumstances I'm surprised you reported for work.'

'Myra. How nice to hear from you.'

'Mr. Seville tried to get me to formally suspend you but I told him you probably wouldn't show up anyhow. You made a liar out of me.'

'I did nothing of the sort. Mr. Seville did. How can you stand to hang out with such a ghoul anyway?'

'Don't forget that according to you I'm a suck. A big suck.'

'Oh don't take that kind of crap seriously. You're only a suck if you're pissing me off personally.'

'Speaking of urine . . . .'

'Did I go for my test.'

'Yes. I meant to ask you that.'

'I bet you did.'

'Yes. Did you?'

'No.'

Stilted silence on the line. Barry enjoyed the dead air. 'What's your next move, Ms. Management Junior-Genius?' There was further quietness, then the sound of throat-clearing. Barry jumped in: 'Don't take it so hard. There's bound to be a section in the personnel manual about this kind of thing.'

'You think this is just a stepping-stone job for me. You think it's just getting ahead.'

'What else could it be?' Barry was struck by the familiarity of Myra's peevish girlfriend-like tone. 'You're not a true social worker. You're not an altruistic activist trying to undermine something unjust or corrupt. You appear to be simply following along with some set of middle-class expectations. With that kind of ambition, why didn't you become an accountant? Pathetic, if you want to know my opinion.'

'What makes you think I want your opinion?'

'Because I'm older than you and by definition wiser.' Barry pressed a jokey tone, but knew he was going for broke. 'Of course you want my opinion. My approval, even.'

'What are you? Delusional?'

'Listen . . .' Barry forgot to mask the angry reflection in his voice. 'I'm not pissing in any bottle. You can forget about that right fucking now.'

'No need to be abusive about it.'

'I'd say the abuse was flowing pretty thick in the other direction.'

'You think you know everything . . .' Barry detected true lamentation in Myra's tone. Her voice put him in mind of his wife in her more plaintive moments. 'You don't.'

'Aw now, don't go getting all choked up on me. I need you to be strong and be a leader. Tell me how to get through this day and what to do while I'm doing it. Buck up, girl.'

'They said you were a handful. They didn't know the half.'

'Now come on, no whining. Just smarten up and tell me what this call's all about because I've got real work to do on the streets of this great city. I'd like to get to it if you don't mind.'

'Despite your jaundiced view of everything, Mr. Delta, there is more to me than just a management toady. If you took the time to get properly acquainted you might think differently.'

'Well now you're talking like an adult. Why don't we do lunch sometime soon?'

'Not until this matter is resolved.'

'Fair enough.'

'So . . . you won't do the test?'

'I won't do the test.'

'Okay. I'll have to advise Mr. Seville.'

'You advise Mr. Seville.'

'You leave me no choice.'

'I suppose not.'

'Alright then . . .'

'Oh by the way. Who does my lawyer talk to? You or Mr. Seville?'

'Your lawyer?'

'You heard me. A guy named Lance Pithorn.'

'Oh . . .' Barry heard her ear rub against the receiver. Then: 'You must feel quite badly about all this.'

'Myra, what fucking planet have you been living on? My livelihood is being threatened here and my reputation impugned. Of course I feel badly. Badly doesn't do it justice, I'm right peeved. Try having a geek like your Mr. Seville come snooping around. Try being told to piss in a bottle.'

'We had to submit to urinalysis at staff college as part of the intake process.'

'You kids these days will do anything to please your masters, won't you? Does it never occur to you guys to question authority?'

'It wasn't like that.'

'Well it's like that for me . . .' Barry had a moment of inexplicable despair, a deep futility, that any further talk to Myra was useless. 'So unless we have anything more to talk about this conversation is beginning to waste our time.'

'Okay. You can go.'

'You're right about that.' Barry hung up.

The phone rang instantly. It was Detective Bill.

Foregoing their usual small banter, Barry asked: 'What did you find out?'

'There was a complaint in from the time of the incident but we didn't investigate. Too small. I guess these critters with the posters are doing a little do-it-yourself community enforcement.'

'They're a fucking menace to the drunken bus-rider constituency of which I am a proud part.'

'That's not why I called.' Detective Bill's voice did not attest to an appreciation of Barry's joking. 'We arrested one of your boys last night.'

'Aw shit.' Barry grabbed a pen. 'Name?'

'Wayne Stickner.'

'Fuck me.' Barry dropped the pen. 'Why?'

'Defacing bus shelters.'

'What?'

'He was going around with a bag of shit and an ice scraper and putting scratches in that Plexiglas material they use. The transit people post a reward to grab guys like this.'

'Fuck, Bill. He was working for me. Getting those goofy posters out of circulation.'

'Oh for chrissakes. How could you ever believe such a nut-plan had potential?'

'It was working fine until you guys interfered.'

'The boys love to roust fresh cons. They can't resist.'

'Well that's just great, but cut him loose right now, okay? Don't make this injustice any bigger than it already is.'

'I take it you're not going to suspend.'

'What the fuck does it sound like, Bill?'

'Are you sure? We got him on a by-law for sure but we could expand it into some kind of willful damage criminal code. It might look better for you.'

'How the hell would it look better for me?'

'I don't know. If you cut him loose it looks like you're favouring him.'

'I am favouring him because he hasn't done a goddamn thing wrong since he left the joint! Even if he hadn't been doing me a good turn I would have no reason to suspend him. We've got bigger fish to fricassee than some bullshit bus-stop vandalism rap.'

'I see. I was hoping this might make up for that grand screw-up we pulled on you the other night.'

'Hey, thanks for at least admitting to it, albeit unofficially, but that one's gone by and it'll never be something that can be squared. Meanwhile, we all have to just soldier on.'

'So we can just give this Stickner kid an appearance notice and send him on his way?'

'Yes, just do that.'

'Uhh . . . okay. We'll pull the stuff off the system.'

'You put him on the system?'

'I felt sure you'd want to nail this guy.'

'Shit! Now my sucky supervisor's going to find out about it. I guess I'm glad you told me. I'll have to think up something to explain.'

'Sorry boy. We haven't been much use to you this last little while.'

'Oh don't be so hard on yourself, Bill. The streets are still relatively safe. As long as you don't try shooting at the police or insulting hookers or scraping things off the bus-stop walls.'

'Ah there's that good old sarcasm coming through. Barry is back. Nobody can keep you down, eh boy?'

'I'll let you know after they've finished piling the file boxes on my chest. But please, in the meantime, don't try to help me unless you check with me first, okay? And let that kid go.'

'So we got nothin' on him, huh?'

'Not from my end.'

'Gotcha.'

Barry hung up almost reluctantly, because he had no idea about his next move. He'd likely be able to explain his action regarding Wayne in view of the insignificance of the charge. But cosmetically, the fact of the kid being arrested under suspicious circumstances at a time when a competency investigation was going on was just too ugly. If Myra looked even cursorily at the circumstances, Barry reasoned, she might easily ferret out the extraneous facts. Barry swivelled and gazed out the window for a few lost minutes.

The phone rang. He reached for it and then stopped. He could not take the chance of it being Myra. He had to think this thing through. He let voicemail pick up. Then, to make things even more authentic, he grabbed his coat and left. The paperwork, he mumbled to himself, would have to wait. In these hectic days Barry was not without awareness that he seldom got any real work done.

[22]

BARRY WAITED UNTIL the line was installed at his apartment before talking to Tanya. He borrowed a spare phone from the storage cabinet at work, opened a beer, settled on the futon and, with full knowledge that she possessed caller identification and used it, dialled the number.

'Hello.' Barry detected a deflating sigh.

'It's me.'

'Good of you to finally call.'

'You got my message?'

'Of course I got your fucking message.'

Barry hadn't heard her use this type of language in ages, such oath uttering was usually reserved for when she stubbed her toe or couldn't find a parking space. It shook him a little. He managed a tentative: 'Okay . . .'

'Nothing's okay and you know it.'

'Of course not . . .' He had prepared something to say but now forgot what it was, and his silence quickly warped into a guilty dissonance over the phone line. 'We should talk.'

'You sound awful. I don't know if I want to talk right now.'

'I wouldn't blame you. I really wouldn't.'

'Don't try to plead this whole thing away. Of course you feel guilty. You fucking well should.'

'This is getting off to a bad start . . .'

'This is getting off to the only start it's going to get. It's been nearly a week. What have you got to say for yourself?'

'Well I . . .' This was the thing he had dreaded and the reality of it left him dumb. 'I guess nothing.'

'Nothing.' She let it hang for a second. 'Is that it? Nothing? You're willing to throw away our life together over "nothing"?'

'That's not the way it is . . .' Though the air in the room was cool, Barry felt perspiration on his face. 'Nobody's throwing anything away. I don't know how to say it.'

'Oh wow. One of the rare occasions anyone has ever seen the gabby Barry Delta at a loss for words . . .'

In the pause Barry imagined her eyes narrowing.

'Are you drunk?'

'I don't think so.' Barry hoped that would settle it. Instantly he knew it wouldn't. 'I'm drinking though.'

'What else is new?'

'You know that's not our problem.'

'You mean it's not our only problem. It's problem enough all by itself but I agree with you, it's not our only problem.'

'It's not a problem at all and you know it.'

'Don't take that pissy tone with me. What the hell has been going on? Where are you?'

'I'm at home. I mean, I found a little place. It's not much but . . .'

'What? You just went out and set up house someplace else?'

'Yeah. What did you think, I'd live in a dumpster?'

'Yes.'

'Oh . . .' Barry snapped awake to a sense of how deeply he had hurt Tanya. 'Okay. I'm getting a sense of how you're thinking these days.'

'You're getting a sense for nothing. If you knew how I felt you wouldn't have stole away in the night like a sleaze. You wouldn't have left me hanging like a bimbo, which is what I think you think I am anyway . . .'

'What are you talking about?'

'Never mind.' She seemed about to say something, faltered, then: 'You listen to me . . .'

Barry intuited that Tanya might have herself been drinking. It lurched him a little. The depth of things, the seriousness and the pain, flooded through and created an unfamiliar sickness in him. 'We've got to talk in a constructive way.' He tried to be self-possessed but sounded to himself like he was choking. 'Don't let's get too emotional.'

'Barry, Barry . . . you don't even know what emotions are.'

'Uhh . . .' The comment hung. His mind clouded as he scrambled for any comeback. 'That's just ridiculous . . .'

'Yes . . .'

In the pause Barry was debating his response when Tanya uttered a simple: 'It is.'

Then she hung up the phone.

He stayed on the line, shocked, at first imagining that he'd only dreamt her withdrawal. In all their time together, the push and pull, the conflict and joy and ambiguity, she'd never done this to him. Hung up the phone. Just like that.

The only thing to do was call somebody else. Ignoring a spreading retch impulse he dialled the other number on his mind. Diane. Barry wasn't sure why he needed to speak to her. As near as he could figure it was simply a primal impulse just to hear her voice. Just to speak to her one more time.

'Hello?'

When she spoke Barry wondered if Tony, the hulking putative progenitor, whom he had never met but knew too much about, was somewhere lurking in her apartment. He decided to get that one out of the way forthwith. 'Diane it's Barry. Is Tony with you?'

'No.'

'Can you talk?'

'I guess so, but I don't know what about. Where have you been?'

'Changing things. Laying low and reorganizing. I got a new place.'

'I took a bus the other day and saw a picture that looked an awful lot like you.'

'Oh that. It's a long story.'

'So it was you.'

'Yeah but it's a complicated deal, not to mention quite funny.'

'What's funny about an assault on a bus? Honestly, sometimes I think you've been in that business too long. It's affecting your mind.'

'Well it has been a decent living.'

'Where are you?' Her mirth was just audible.

'On a bare mattress under a naked light bulb. It kind of fits my mood.'

'It sounds like you're living like a mental patient. This is worse than I thought.'

'Aw come on.'

'So you did hurt those people?'

'Of course I didn't. It was all a big mistake.'

'Mistakes are all you seem to be about these days.'

'Oh wake up, Diane.' He tried and failed to keep anger from his voice. 'Open your eyes.'

Diane gasped. 'I don't know what you mean. I thought I knew you. Despite what might have gone on recently, I still think you're a fine man. But I know now that you're not right for me.'

Barry was almost relieved to have hurt replace his anger. 'Oh.'

'That's right.'

'Fine.'

'I didn't mean for that to sound so ugly.'

'You don't have to say anything else. I know you care about me but there's no way of making goodbye feel good. You just have to say it and let it sound like it sounds.'

'Thank you, Barry. You haven't lost your understanding heart. That's what I liked best about you.'

'That's a lovely thing to say.'

'There are many lovely things about you. You know that.'

'I'm pretty sad these days.'

'It's bad times.'

'They're bound to get good someday.'

'I just know it.'

'So do I, I guess.'

She sighed heavily. 'Goodbye, Barry.'

'Goodbye, Diane.'

Later, curled in his sleeping bag, he turned toward the wall and watched passing car lights compose monochromatic imagery on the canvas of his world.

Barry knew as soon as his eyes registered the steady light of morning that he would not be getting up this day. He activated his cell phone only long enough to leave an out-for-the-day voicemail greeting and left the beeper off. Back to sleep he went, knowing that by the brightening day and the outside work-bound rumble he would dwell in that zone where dreams are their most intense. His waking, before noon, interrupted a folk concert. He caressed the hand of his old girlfriend Janis. With full consciousness the easy feelings corrupted into sorrow. There were tears.

As usual, knowing why was no help.

He was simply wracked with an astringent remorse, and he came to know despair as something of his life, as inseparable from his body as his liver and heart and brain, his pain elemental as air to water. His mind sizzled, his core a black hole of regret. The pity of it nearly made him retch, then it made him laugh.

He quaked, guffawing, rolled off the mattress and onto the floor. With his sleeping sack around him he thrashed, howling. After a time he had worked himself some distance and then decided to roll some more. He did a worm-like tour of the apartment, ending in the kitchen. From the floor he worked open the refrigerator door and reached from the warmth of his wrapping to get an apple. With increasing skill—creeping the bag on a gastropodal shine of the dusty floor—progress back to the mattress was quicker. He drew his knees to his chest and hunkered against the wall, facing outward. The apple was hard and reassuringly cold in his hand. He chewed each bite with deliberation, gazing with puzzled jaundice at the blue sky out the windows. Eventually, his eyes mucked with dried tears.

Before he fell asleep again Barry reached for the telephone to check his office voicemail. There were no messages of any import. He turned and drifted into another squirming sleep.

In the resulting nightmare Barry punched a bus-depot locker.

Awaking with a throbbing fist, he scowled, rubbing to get the circulation back. Dreams. Mental crap, he reflected acidly. His hand cramped but felt better after flexing it for a few minutes. He was encouraged that he could form thoughts, black ones even, and not become tearful. He lay considering the ceiling as going-home traffic raised the city-noise to noticeable levels. He imagined himself an art installation—Man-In-Sleeping-Bag Atop Futon—mounted on an austere, hardwood setting. The trace of gloom in his room graduated into dusky dim, on its way to darkness.

The phone rang.

His hand struck out to get it, then stopped. Barry let it hover. Despite the instinct to respond to the electronic warbling that was the dinner bell of his work, play, and love, he resisted. Why this was he was not certain but he was quite sure of his current comfortable, cozy reclusion. The phone rang and rang. He regretted not being able to afford the call answer service. He thought about how lonely he wanted to be.

The phone kept ringing.

Barry picked up.

'Barry? Is this the right number?'

He could hear the little ant voice from its transmission point an arm's length from his ear. He did not recognize it. He put the receiver to his ear.

'Can I speak to Barry Delta, please?'

Seconds passed before Barry had it. Rikki.

'Yeah . . .'

'Is there anybody there?'

'Uh . . . how did you find me?'

'Oh that is you, Barry. I just dialled information.'

'Aren't I unlisted?'

'I don't know. Are you?'

Barry stressed his ragged lobes to verify that he had remembered to exclude his number, as he'd had all his years in the crime business, from the phone book. He could not verify.

Rikki was speaking:

' . . . So I thought if it was cool with you we could finish that talk we were having. I mean, we could just keep going, if you want. I don't know. You're kind of nice. I didn't expect to see you again because I see a lot of guys in my work. Not that I take all of them home with me but it tends to nearly happen more than if I were a legal secretary or a bank teller or something like that. So . . .'

'Uh . . . yeah.' With his free hand Barry gripped and squeezed his cranium, clenching eyes and bearing down, trying for a mental foothold.

'Wait a minute. Forgive me. I've got to get back to this phone book business. You actually got my number from four-one-one?'

'Uh huh.'

Barry rubbed his head and concentrated on the set of facts just presented him. He had gone ahead and got himself a phone without insuring that his number, not to mention his address, would not become easily obtained public information. Such vulnerability was unheard of in the parole business. As any parolee knew, the worst thing in the world to be when involved in criminal justice—either side—was easily locatable. He struggled further to learn what this clear and ridiculously obvious lapse might indicate.

'Hmmm. Maybe I'm leaving the business, consciously or otherwise.'

'What was that?'

'Sorry. Thinking out loud. My listed number mistake, maybe it means that whether or not I make a decision soon I'm going to leave the business, like it or not.'

'Oh.' Rikki seemed to be having her own grappling session with the facts. 'Is that good?'

'I don't know.'

'Oh.'

Their silence gave Barry a chance to disengage himself from self-obsession. 'So. You want to get together?'

'That's what I was thinking. If you're not busy.'

'Well . . .' He nearly laughed. 'Busy is not what I'd call it.' He unhanded his skull and snapped to, eyes wide at the far wall. 'I am occupied, though. I don't know if I can actually move.'

'Lazybones. You can't be that tired. Did you have a bad day?'

'I didn't have any kind of a day.'

'Well then, things can only improve.'

'You don't understand, Rikki . . .' Barry coughed and cleared his throat, not used to the strain of talking. 'I'm stalled. Static. Out of it. Holed up, as they say. Since yesterday I haven't done anything except curl up in a ball. I haven't even gotten up to take a piss.'

'Oh. Well, okay. Actually, I was thinking about making dinner.'

'Dinner . . .' The simple mention of food weirdly energized him. 'Hmm . . . what an idea.'

'I think so. Would you like to eat with me?'

'I actually kinda would.'

'Should I come and get you?'

'Sure.' Barry rubbed his face. 'Why not?'

'That's fine. What's the address?'

'Fourteen-oh-six, west eleventh.'

'I like that neighbourhood.'

'Yeah, it's nice.' He peered once again out his windows. 'What I've seen of it.'

When he hung up Barry knew he had maybe thirty minutes to make the transition from cloistered rummy to presentable dinner date. He knew he could fight out of the malaise but he was not sure he wanted to. Life had been relatively fine in a zone of twilit indifference. It was fine not to be dressed. It felt damn good, actually. Barry struggled to develop enthusiasm at the notion of going out. In truth he did not want to go out with anyone, even a woman promising not only food, but also, more than likely, sex.

Barry put off getting ready, put off even stirring from his trap, to ponder the reason for his confinement, his ex-communication. There was a subject he had been keeping from himself. Sex? Yes. He thought hard, going headlong into it. After painful confrontations with his memory, he could clearly delineate the source of his main darkness; his plethoric history of wanton carnalities.

He thought about Rikki. She was perceptive and entertaining, but what else was she now but a random sexual encounter? A random sexual encounter that promised calamity on personal, professional, and marital fronts. This line of thought pushed Barry into self-anger and he shrugged it away, testily aware of the simple truth. Ultimately, if he looked himself firmly in the eye, he wasn't the least frightened by social/vocational/emotional disaster. He was vastly more transfixed by the prospect of boredom. Sex and boredom. They were melding dangerously.

He reflected, lying still. Sex. He'd had so much sex. So much he couldn't remember. Sex and more sex.

Barry shivered, let the mind-tracks go slack and closed his eyes against the truth, knowing Rikki was speeding near.

The knock came when he was still in the bathroom. He let her in with a towel around him. She was turned out more girlishly than at the bar; the look excited him in a surprising way. For the first time in two days Barry was at least aware he had a pulse.

Over food Rikki was talking about her work. Barry caught himself becoming less and less interested, putting it down to the usual loss of intrigue that befell subjects of interest when they became too familiar. He poured himself more wine and began to slug it down.

She stopped mid-phrase, looking at him.

He offered her a half-smile. 'I guess I'm in no mood . . .'

'I guess.'

'Good. That means things will be okay. As long as you pick up on that.'

'I do and I'm used to men being bitchy. It's an occupational thing . . .'

'Yeah, I know.' Barry cut her off. He did not want to know anything more about her jobsite.

'How about a nice walk to work off dinner?' She kept smiling, strong.

'Fine.' Barry drank some wine. 'But we should get something out of the way first.'

'Yes.' She clipped her voice so that Barry knew that she knew she had spoken too quickly.

'About the other morning . . .'

Rikki interrupted: 'I didn't go for the morning-after pill.'

'You . . . you didn't?'

'I react to that kind of stuff. Allergic. I mean, the pill. Generally.'

'Okay.'

'It mucks me up good. My periods don't come. I get infections. Everything.'

'That's rough.'

'I think we're pretty safe though. Pregnancy-wise.'

'That's good. How safe?'

'Within a few days.'

'That doesn't sound wildly safe.'

'Well I guess we'll see. I'm more afraid of disease.'

'I guess well you should. I am too. I was tested not long ago. Part of my ex's quest for procreation.'

'Well I know I'm clean. I got tested when my husband left. I suspected him of fooling around.'

'Hmmm . . . well, I guess that's that.' Barry drank the rest of his wine and stood up. 'How about that walk?'

They sat for a time on a bench at English Bay to watch boats and the lights of the city. Rikki did not speak as much as she had earlier. Eventually they strode back to her place, arm in arm. Barry had a brief curious sense of being her prisoner, but then, arriving at her bed, lost any sense of reticence in the warmth he was given.

In the early morning Barry half-woke to glass-breaking sounds. He snuggled the snoring Rikki and closed his eyes, but then found he could not fully return to dreamland. From a doze he realized he was listening to the *whoop-whoop-eee-aww* of a violated car. The sound went on. He picked out the odd refrain of someone singing along with the alarm tune, *eee-aww-doo-whop-whop waaaaaaaaa* . . . The clamour ceased and there was then only the clear, jaunty serenade—the voice of the thief, Barry understood—in the 4:00 a.m. stillness. He stirred slightly, cursing city noise and the comedic futility of spending money on protection sirens to make a city full of uncaring people know you were being victimized. Stupid. To think that citizens whose sleep was being summarily revoked were expected to help the supreme a-hole who had the inconsideration to install a noise pollution device to simply demark his own urban fear. Asinine! The idea would not fade. He chuckled to himself over the idiocy of spending tens of thousands of dollars on a fancy vehicle and expecting it not to be stolen. The anger woke him thoroughly. He loathed the mentality that girded these people, that force and defence and the expense of security services were better than attempting to mend the society they were at war with. Why not spend the money and time and care on creating a place where forlorn desperadoes found no need to steal cars in the night? Barry acknowledged an affinity with the thief, then turned aside and renewed his sleep.

He left the apartment an hour later knowing the first busses were running. He was eager to get back to work, if only to see what interesting new calamities awaited him. It was nearly light, a vague illumination spread over the heavily treed streetscape. He had a soreness in his lower back, a sleep-position related minor injury, he surmised.

The stillness of the hour made movement all the more noticeable. Even more noticeable to Barry-the-parole-officer-of-lifetime-standing was the furtive nature of the two scrofulants he saw walking with speed a little distance away. They spotted him in the silence and with certainty he knew they'd taken notice. They'd been walking near a rundown apartment building and froze still when they made eye contact. In an instant he sensed they had acquired him as a target. For Barry it was the same intuitive solidity as knowing a guy in a bar was going to fight, a drunk on the subway was going to barf, or a woman was thinking her way through your lies and was going to cry on you. He considered flight, then steadied—not liking the image of an awkward break into running. Instead, he opted to simply stride, reasoning that he might be wrong about their intentions. He felt strong despite the funny hurt in his pelvis.

In seconds the footfalls behind him demanded attention. He turned and their eyes were glazed and deadly. There was no need for conversation; to Barry's regret, no words at all. His flight instinct was so automatic he did not realize his speed until he turned to aim himself down the street. The air in his ears blocked any sound from behind and he almost thought they had given up when then he was flying forward and just got his hands out to break a fall face-ward to the sidewalk. One of the boys had, with athletic skill, kicked his feet out from below. Barry rolled and sprang standing. Before any other thought could occur there were hands at his face and pushing with hands everywhere. He fell backward, twisting. He managed to grab an arm of one of them on the way down and twisted as best he could, not having a clear plan, but instinctively accepting his impending travail, accepting inevitable bludgeon and pain, but knowing his only chance for retribution would be in injuring one of them enough in some way as to require medical attention.

To Barry it was certain within seconds that he himself would require such treatment. He tore at the eyes of one of them but got no purchase as a boot impacted his face. There were other boots. He let go and curled into a ball but that was not enough to cover the pummelling. He was being trodden. Trampled and bruised and damaged. Barry choked at the understanding that he had no repartee with which to observe the occasion, not even to himself—if he could talk—not to the concrete beneath him or the sky above. His mind began to empty. There remained just a scant hope for survival and no more impulse to fight back. Then there were cold memories of police accounts, of bodies found lifeless, autopsy photos with gooey details, bruised faces draining liquid, swellings in grotesque disproportion. And that was all. He was as alone as alone could be as the blows rained and he wished ever so tightly that his beaters would at least speak to him.

[23]

HE WAS SURE Tanya was there at one point. Diane too. Thankfully they chose separate times, though any possibility of rancour between them was as remote a dread for Barry as could be, his body was so broken. Someone from the correctional service came because he remembered being assured that his caseload would be tended to by a replacement parole officer. Rikki sat by him daily. He wasn't sure who else. Of those appearing for him—capitulating to guilt or wistfulness over leaving him too alone—only one in particular Barry remembered: John.

It was night. The place was as quiet as it got, lights at a minimum. Barry had been morphine-dozing and was not awake for the entire conversation in the hall. The fragment he got was:

'Sir, I asked you nicely. You are outside visiting hours. He's asleep, anyway.'

'Then what's the big deal?'

'The big deal is . . .'

Then Barry saw out of his only working eye a hulking senior enter the room. There was no conversation. John leaned over him in the dark for some time and then stood by the window, one foot on a low table, crouching with arms folded. Barry wondered what his own first gurgled word should be. He had attempted several by this time, moaned epithets, grunted gesturing indicators, and whines.

For minutes Barry struggled with an idea. Eventually he stared through his face-wrap up at the silhouette image and did not know what to try to say. John moved back, pausing, then to a corner of the room where there was a chair. Barry could not see the seated black blob but sensed his presence. Neither made a sound.

John stayed for a good hour. Though fading in and out, Barry guessed it was getting to be sometime after midnight, and took warmth from knowing this was the preferred roaming time of John's night. He had been endlessly told of nocturnal forays in whatever jalopy; ranging over town, checking on cabdriver buddies, having coffee in the greasy spoons, chatting with waitresses, checking the people-action, doing occasional deathwatch duty for an old friend. Barry put this last scenario out of his mind, but sensed the tired-moving form rise from the chair and saw it tribute a respectful gaze in his direction.

There was a hanging moment, a weighty pause that hurt.

Barry knew in seconds he would be alone again.

He revisited then the comfort he had always taken from the hovering presence; a great eagle, soundless and vigilant, a powerful and benevolent spirit. Barry spontaneously rejoiced in John's guidance and care and then fell, lying pained in his hospital bed, upon a tremendous need. He wondered if John were aware of the golden comfort his presence afforded him. In an instant Barry knew that he did, and loved the old man all the more. He rued the inevitability of his own solitary existence and winced at the certainty of John's eventual permanent passing from it and tried in that instant to actually say something through the gauze.

He could not, other than a sleep-sounding gurgle, and he knew this would not stop the receding figure as it quit the room. When in the next moment John was gone Barry could not stop a tear hot as tea from forcing itself from the slit of a swollen eye and searing the skin all the way down the lacerated cheek and into the cut by his ear. There was another tear and then a flow. Barry let himself make hot salt water for his face and hoped it would wash something away. Or wash what was there. Wash. Whatever it was that needed washing. He struggled to know what. In all the pain, anger and loneliness, he had not yet completed that thinking.

Days later Detective Bill came to see him.

'Whachs wis da uniform?' Barry hissed through a wired jaw. 'Makesh me feel like a con . . .'

'You got yourself a lickin' on my patrol rotation, geekboy.' The big cop looked him over. 'You gonna be permanently gimped?'

'I havven deeshided jet.'

'Well . . .' Bill took a seat. 'Dammit son. See what you can do.'

Barry smiled as wide as he could.

'So . . . since I'm the one here with a complete jaw, I'll do the talking.' The detective leaned close. 'We checked all the hospitals and walk-in clinics. If you hurt one or other of them, he didn't get help for it. We put the word out through the gang squad and the biker boys. Nothing. We checked the juvie group-homes in the area. They had nobody missing at that hour. We checked for stolen cars and B&E's to see if there might be any connected arrests. There were vehicle attacks but nobody pinched. We looked up your girlfriend's ex and he checked out clean. Seems like not such a bad guy, actually . . .' Bill looked at a notebook in his hand. 'Now is it possible it was somebody on your caseload or connected with somebody on your caseload?'

Barry wagged his head side to side.

'Then I guess we have to go with the obvious. They took your money. Threw your wallet in a garbage can down the block. Nice of them. You don't have to go re-collect all your IDs and stuff. Call it a robbery, I guess. Vintage-type mugging. More of a beating than we're used to in this town but not unheard of. Opportunistic little sons-abitches.' Detective Bill snorted. 'Musta thought you were dangerous. Musta thought you needed considerable pacification. Considerable overkill, I'd say.'

Barry grimaced.

After thirteen days they let him go to his apartment. There were bottles of pills, stitches to watch out for and strict instructions about no work and his future medical appointments. There were crutches. Talk of reconstructive surgery. Rikki helped him home and gave care.

Barry lay on his bed and watched television for two weeks. He was grateful Tanya had had some of his stuff delivered. He sat in a chair and drooled. There was the faintly disgusting presence of suture thread in his mouth. After days he was insane with teasing it with his tongue and fingers and trying to get it to dissolve sooner than it was designed to.

He did not mind the pain. The pain made him feel valid. While there was pain there was no blame.

As he began to feel better the darker thoughts advanced, eventually launching a frontal assault, turning Barry's denial mechanisms aside with little difficulty. As the shouts and explosions sounded in his brain, Barry found it desirable to step outside himself and hope that he learned a lesson by all this.

He tossed the crutches aside and struggled to his feet. All this pain could not be for no purpose other than to remind him that life was not always fair.

Hah!

Barry was startled by the sound of his own voice.

Fuck! He tried it again. Fuck, fuck, fuck fuck fuck fuck . . .

It came out more as 'puck'. Barry tried to fashion his lips closer to the phonetic function. *Fffffuuuukkkkk* . . .

He let the word echo in the apartment. Then he tried another one. Please. Thank you. Please. Thank you. Hello. How are you.

The drugs did not let him get any more sophisticated in his self-lesson than that. He fell to a moaning sleep.

It was six weeks from the day of the attack that he went back to work. The doctors were more worried about his mouth and vocal cords than any other physical aspect, though Barry had sustained broken ribs, bruised lungs, a fractured vertebra, deep cuts and contusions. His face had been deconstructed, with crumbled cheekbones, teeth missing, jaw fractured, nose displaced. His throat had swollen shut. His life was saved by a motorist who found him and flagged another car whose driver turned out to be an industrial first aid man on his way to work. He forced an oxygen tube directly through the ground-beef mass of Barry's mouth and turned the valve in time to revive suffocating brain cells. The paramedics yelped with alarm at the sight of him. The triage nurses and doctors hopped to their work with special urgency. Barry experienced all of these events—his heart stomping against his ribcage—because for the whole time he had never once passed completely from consciousness. Only when morphine prickled the top of his head and then swarmed downward, melting everything he knew, did the horror fade.

And that was another thing, morphine. He got used to it. Many times in the ensuing days and weeks he looked forward to the sweet onslaught, the excuse from life it gave, the exalted giddy freedom.

Morphine. Fruit of the pretty poppy. Distillate of transcendence. Ticket out.

Snapping to one day when the pain was no longer severe, Barry made a point of refusing it. He kept himself a few days in suspension, craving, but loathsome at the implications of giving in. Eventually he settled back, enduring his aches, having a beer when he felt like it, smiling whenever anyone asked how he was. But never again, he resolved, would Barry speak to a junky about addiction, recovery, abstinence and relapse prevention with the blasé ignorance he had once had. He was wryly unsure—recalling the buzz—whether this widening of perception was a good thing or bad.

The defining moment of his first day back at the office came via the call from downstairs that there was a bicycle courier looking for him. Barry held open the outer door.

'Mr. Delta?'

'Barry, please.'

'This is for you . . .'

The helmeted fellow handed him a thick envelope. Barry looked briefly at it and knew what it was. He turned to the sweating lad and said: 'So you're not just a bike courier you're a process server.'

'Yup.'

'Nice angle.'

'I hope you don't mind.'

'Oh gosh. It's close to my line of work. Why should I mind?'

'Some people get upset when you tell them it's a package and they're expecting a present or a sweater from Sears or something but it's a subpoena instead.'

Barry smiled at the wit.

The envelope was as official as he knew it would be and held the expected summons to an administrative tribunal examining events in connection with the murder charge laid against one Daisy Louise Smith, a.k.a. Misty Apres Cantaclere, a.k.a. Chantal Delicia DeAlbrecht. There was another document relating to the police shooting. Barry gave the papers only a glance before tossing them aside, hoping the phone wouldn't ring and the computer wouldn't message before he finished filling out the long-term medical leave application he was preparing. At lunchtime he trundled out of the building, lurching with his sore spine through the nicotinic entranceway, trying to make himself not care that people puffing on cigarettes would notice the purple splotches on his face. He headed steadily to the old part of town and the offices of his lawyer, sweetly secure in the knowledge that during all these weeks of suffering his case against condemnation had been arming up.

Though stumbly on his walk, Barry rejoiced. Summer had come full-on; trees lush, flowerboxes overflowing. The pollen-laden air energized him. There was possibility in every pained step. At Lance's office he barely had time to walk in before the attorney leapt up, a sheaf of documents in hand.

'Barry, before I tell you about our case, did you know that the most recent Auditor General's report frankly admits that the structure of the correctional service puts case worker personnel like yourself in a state of administrative impairment?'

'No, I didn't see the report . . .' He made much of his scowl. 'But I could have told them that for a fraction of whatever it cost.' Barry saw by Lance's flat expression that he was not interested in personal bias on this or, likely, any matter. He scorned himself for forgetting he was in the presence of someone trained in dispassion. 'It really says that?'

'And other things too. It's helpful to us in answering the general allegations of lack of due diligence. That's our most serious hurdle. It's a firing offence if they can prove it.'

'Can they?'

'Not likely.' Lance shook the papers in his hand. 'Not by what's in these documents and what you tell me.'

'Awright.'

'But I'm glad you've recovered . . .' Lance shone a clinical look to Barry's face. 'You are mending, aren't you?'

Barry straightened in his chair. 'I look worse than I am.'

'Good. I need your input about these details.' The lawyer gestured to a thick dossier on his desk and a cardboard box Barry assumed was full of paper. 'If what I think happened happened, they weren't even dealing with you by the statutory rules of their own making.'

'Doesn't surprise me.'

'Makes one wonder why anyone would work in such an environment so long.'

'I'm sure it does.' Barry smirked. 'By that logic they may have a case for mental incapacity.'

'Do you think so?'

Barry was startled to see that Lance seemed serious. 'Why do you ask?'

Lance took his glasses off and sat down. 'Are you stable? Mentally and emotionally?'

'Well I took a few terrific whacks but . . .'

'I'm not talking about that. Have you ever seen a psychiatrist?'

'Ah . . . no.'

'Don't be embarrassed. They'll likely ask you the same question.'

'Yeah? What's the right answer?'

'Excellent line of thought!' Lance laughed, breaking what was for Barry a mounting tautness. 'Those knocks in the head haven't dulled your insight. In fact the whole mental health issue is a landmine. It'll blow up for us whichever way you testify.'

'I figured. Crazy if I have. Crazy if I haven't. The old catch-22.'

'Right you are. We'll have to develop some kind of strength profile for you. It'll mean hiring an expert. It'll mean having you examined.'

'You mean, I finally will be going to a shrink?'

'An occupational health specialist. I'll arrange it.'

'Okay.' Barry was pensive. 'If you think it's necessary.'

'It's the only thing they might have on you. Some kind of negligence argument based on your not seeking mental/emotional help and taking yourself off the firing line when you knew you couldn't take it anymore. Something of that nature.'

'Alright.' Barry looked again at the stack of paper on Lance's desk. 'What else might they have?'

'Almost nothing. In fact, if the psychology part goes well I think we may have them on a case of harassment.'

'Oh? Jeez, that was true a long time back . . .' Barry flashed to years ago when his relationship with management was far worse. 'But since they inadvertently solved the problem with satellite offices and isolating us from regular contact with bosses I thought that part of our wonderful world was cleared up.'

'Maybe so, but this angle is perfect, Barry, if you're willing to draw blood. Your supervisor Myra is vulnerable. If we bring everything to the fore, given the directives, it will show that you at least did your part and that she was negligent.'

'Ummm . . .' Barry bridled at the shift of conversational gears. 'How might that play?'

'To start with, her position requires that she make sure the legal standards are applied in every case. You, the parole officer, must perform these tasks; but she, the case management supervisor, is ultimately responsible for them being done. If your caseload, which is administered by her, is too large or cumbersome for you to successfully perform these duties, and you duly report this fact . . .' Lance patted a file. 'As you have, then that is also her failing.'

'Well, you'd have her there.'

'And too, if they do emphasize your psychology problem . . .'

'If I have one.'

'That too could be shown to be a result of Myra's negligence. She is the authority who deals directly with you. One of her tasks . . .' Lance opened a large binder with government insignias on it and adjusted his glasses to read. 'To discern and determine the mental and emotional condition of operational employees and to counsel and refer to assistance services those affected employees as required in order to carry out the mission of the service.'

'Wow.'

Lance looked over his bifocals. 'Were you ever referred?'

'No. I never asked to be.'

'Immaterial. According to this, that's not your job.'

'That's terrific, Lance.' Barry shook his head, incredulous. 'You've done a helluva job.'

'Thank you.'

'But it will hurt Myra's career.'

'Potentially.' Lance shrugged. 'What is your point?'

'To be maligned in a public service tribunal as even vaguely incompetent, while maybe they can't fire her for it, it's a major curse that'll follow her forever. That's how it goes in this business, nobody ever forgets. Everybody else might be doing just as badly or worse, but they don't dare get caught. Right here with this case, Myra's definitely getting caught. And she's a woman. They'll jump on her extra hard.'

'That's unfortunate.' Lance took off his glasses. 'But as I see it, given the situation, you have little choice.'

'She's just a kid. I mean, a management suck, maybe, but she wasn't looking for this kind of trouble.'

Lance receded into his chair, his eyes went away.

'Somebody's got to do this work, Lance.' Barry pressed into his argument, tapping his fingers against the files on the lawyer's desk. 'Somebody. And during my convalescence this past month or so I've realized I can't anymore. Just can't. The thought of going back to it for good rattles me to my DNA. My hands shake, my eyes go blurry. But kids like Myra are willing to step up. I mean, the system sucks. They made her my supervisor when she still had a lot to learn and it pissed me off, but that's not her fault. If I hadn't been such a screw-up for so many years that might not have happened.'

'Barry . . .' Lance took a long moment. 'Let me understand this completely. You don't want to close in for the kill. You want to let her run over you. Even though you assert you deserve to be spared in this thing.'

'I'd like to keep my . . . reputation.' Barry gagged on his own words. 'But I guess I'm saying let's at least take it easy.'

Lance soured visibly. 'Your reputation.' For the first time since their collaborations Barry heard an echo of the courtroom authority Lance could muster into his voice. 'And what reputation might that be?'

The air in the room had petrified. Barry pulled heavily on it and tensed his abdominals. 'I guess I'd just like to go out as pro-person.'

'Pro-person?'

'Yeah.'

Barry was prepared for the period of silence ensuing, and even got casual about it, gazing out the window and swinging a leg from the arm of his chair.

'It sounds to me that here we have something I've always suspected, in the back of my heart, about people like you.' Lance put his glasses back on and joined Barry in looking out the window. 'People who work for the government.'

'What's that, Lance?'

'You lack . . . spirit.'

'Hmmm . . .' Barry held his glance across the desk. 'That's the kind of skanky thing a lawyer would say.'

Lance raised his eyebrows. 'Well. Tit for tat, I suppose.' He straightened. 'But whether or not we continue to trade slurs today I must counsel you against attenuating any aspect of the case I have prepared for you. According to my reading here . . .' He tapped the civil service binder. 'If they score any hits on you you will not keep a good reputation and you might not keep your job. In which case there will be little point in your being pro-person or pro anything. No?'

Lance's words penetrated—as they were meant to—but they did not change Barry's heart. With effort he turned in his chair and hand-assisted his legs to get him toward a standing position. 'Forget about the shrink. I'll stay screwed up.' Barry stood straight. 'I'll pay you for your work.'

'Will you still require me to represent you at the tribunal?'

'I'll think about it.'

[24]

THERE WERE THREATS of rain and also sunny periods the morning of Barry Delta's last day on the job.

Good weather and bad weather, depending on how you looked at it. If you wanted to go to the beach, you'd have to hold back and watch the sky. If you were a gardener, you might like what you got. If you were an office worker you didn't care. But on the sidewalk outside his soon-to-be-former workplace Barry felt like he cared, turning his face to the heavens. It felt good to care about something. Barry walked grinning into the building.

The commissionaire gazed at him quizzically. 'What's the meteorological assessment there, Mr. Delta?'

'Fair to moderate with middling outlook and prevailing normalcy.'

Barry made for the elevator, aware and ticklish that every move he made, every sight he saw, every quip—the sum of his moves and thoughts in this place today—were the last here and now. For this life, anyway.

This is it. He said it out loud. This is it.

The words had a sweet, yet slight stomach-achy flavour. Chocolate-coated poison.

Yes, the end.

For now at least.

Barry was not as sure about it as he wanted to be. He had conducted an exhaustive inner dialogue on the subject: It was an extended sick-leave to get over his beating, the breakup of his marriage, the blowup of his cases, the hassling of his superiors; to fight off the encroachment of final burnout. He had laboriously qualified everything he told himself.

Once free, Barry knew, he'd likely never come back. At the same time he knew himself just enough to know that after a few months of R&R he might be wistful about the old street-life he had once loved.

On the other hand, he also loved to be idle, and idle was something Barry was looking forward to. On that thought, as he opened the office for probably the last time and put down his coffee for likely the last time and turned on the computer, took off his jacket and flumped into his chair for hopefully the last time Barry wished for himself that the day might pass easily.

The phone rang during his first pull on the coffee.

'Yeah, Barry Delta.'

'Good morning, Barry.'

'Hi Myra.'

'Who else calls you before anybody else every day?'

'I guess you, for sure.'

'Don't sound so glum. This has to be a happy day for you.'

'Well, maybe. It's not the best of circumstances.'

'At least you're going. I've got two things . . . no, three things to let you in on today. One is that I'm going, too.'

'Going?'

'Yup. You heard right.'

'You mean leaving the job?'

'That's right.'

'Um. Nothing unfortunate I hope.'

'Unfortunate? What would be unfortunate?'

'I don't know . . .' Barry gulped, hoping against more than he had known he would hope that Lance had not released the sum of his work to the civil service commission. At least not just yet. 'Maybe your boyfriend dumped you or something. You're leaving town on a bad note. Or just leaving the job because you can't stand any more guff from the likes of me.'

'Oh heck no, Barry. They're kicking me upstairs. I'm taking a secondment to Ottawa.'

'Back east.'

'Yup.'

'To headquarters, I guess.'

'Yup. Correctional investigator's office. It's what I've been working toward.'

'Well, congratulations on hitting the big time. But to live in a Frigidaire like Ottawa when you've been spoiled by the west coast?'

'It rains too much here.'

'Spoken like a true Torontonian.'

'Oh Barry, don't spoil things on our last day.'

'Oh, I guess I could leave off.' Barry paused for the second required to indicate his sincerity. 'So there's two of us going away.'

'Yes, but before I forget, there's these other things to tell you. I just got off the phone with Mr. Seville, he's the—'

'The audit branch ghoul who snooped through my files and computer and desk drawers and wastebasket to see what I had for lunch. Yeah, I remember him.'

'Anyway, it looks like they're going to stand down on the allegations.'

'Huh?'

'You can throw those summonses in the trash.' Myra continued, exuberant, ignoring Barry. 'You're off the hook, Mr. Lucky.'

'Jeez . . . great.'

'Aren't you happy?'

'Well sure, I guess. But I have to say, I never took that crap seriously anyway.'

'I hope you didn't spend money on a lawyer. You don't need one now.'

'That's good news all by itself.'

'Yup, it's all over. You can go on sick leave and come back secure in the knowledge that your job is safe and your reputation is as lascivious as ever.'

'Ha ha. I'm not so sure I'm coming back.'

'No? You're too young to retire.'

'Let me be the judge of that.'

'Maybe we'll work together some time again. Maybe you'll get a posting to Ottawa too.'

Barry had to laugh aloud. 'Bye . . .' He almost had the phone hung up when he remembered. 'Hey, what was the third thing?'

Barry's voice must have just penetrated the space between Myra's ear and the descending telephone because an instant later her voice came back and said: 'What? Did you say something, Barry?'

'Yeah. You said there were three things. What was the third?'

'Oh . . .' She hesitated. Barry sensed she was angered by not having signed off successfully on such a personal high note. 'I guess it was just to wish you a happy convalescence.'

'Thanks.'

'I mean it.'

'You do?'

'Of course.'

'Well . . . thanks again.' Barry felt a fatigue rising. 'I guess this is so long, then.'

'In a strange way, though there has been conflict, I'm sad to say goodbye, Barry.'

'Hmmm . . . I guess I know what you mean. Maybe I will come out to Ottawa sometime . . .'

'Oh do!'

'As a tourist!'

The way Myra laughed told Barry she hadn't an inkling of how serious he was.

Later on, Barry saw to the few emails there were and then picked up the phone and dialled the new number he had received, by way of the relief PO's meticulous case records, for Wayne Stickner Jr.

'MacDougal and Jenkins. How may I help you?'

'Uh . . . Mr. Stickner, please. He's a new . . .'

'He's in the editorial department. One moment, sir.'

Barry waited twenty seconds and then young Wayne's voice came on the line.

'Barry!'

'Hey good, you seem happy to hear from me.'

'Of course I am. Why wouldn't I be?'

'I cost you a couple of nights in jail.'

'Hah. Ancient history. I've got a job now.'

'Yeah, I heard. What the hell're you doing at a publishing house?'

'Well I guess I didn't tell you about the rest of my plan. Along with going to school and going to Europe and all that.'

'I guess not.'

'Well I wrote up a lot of stuff in the joint. My opinions on things. Observations. Slightly modified essays from my degree work. I guess I had a vague idea I'd like to pile it all into a book.'

'Oh yeah? A penitentiary penman. Poignancies from prison. Lockup literature.'

'Yeah, you got it. Con writing. It's pretty hot these days.'

'Hmmm. I guess I'd know all about it if I ever read a fucking book once in a while.'

'Well, you gotta make the time.'

'You sure do.' There was a lull of reflection. Barry sensed Wayne's busyness on the other end of the line. 'Yeah, that's what I have to talk to you about. And I have to actually lay eyes on you. I see the other PO only saw you twice. The last time was two weeks ago?'

'More like three.'

'What's your address these days?'

'Eighty-five twenty Osler. The basement.'

'Whew. That's up in Shaughnessy, isn't it?'

'Yup.'

'Pretty toney address. You must be doing well.'

'I got lucky.'

'I'll say. So how about seven tonight?'

'Okay. You want some dinner?'

'Naw. I'll only stay a bit. They don't pay overtime in this biz.'

'Okay, seven. See you tonight.'

Barry was contemplating a trip down the street for another coffee when the phone interrupted him.

'Barry, Lance Pithorn.'

'Lance. I was just about to get off my ass and call you.'

'Funny you should use that term because I have news of your ass. It's salvation, specifically.'

'Oh, you must mean the public service commission deal. They're dropping everything, I'm told.'

'Who told you?'

'My soon-to-be-ex supervisor.'

'Oh.' Lance went quiet for a moment, allowing Barry to detect there was tension over the phone line.

'What's up, Lance?'

'I had to give them pretty much all we had, Barry. There wasn't any other route, the way it came down.'

'What are you talking about?'

'The call I got. From this Mr. Seville. I guess they thought they'd head things off at the pass.'

'They called you?'

'Yes. I assumed you told them you'd retained me.'

'Yeah.'

'So they called and requested a pre-tribunal conference. They wanted to share what we had. I saw no harm in cooperating. We did it all over the phone.'

'Alright. Did you spill the stuff about Myra?'

'Yes. It came to that. What they had on you. Apparent dereliction of duty on the jewellery store robber. The police would not back you up. And the miscalculation on the prostitute woman. That was at least a suspendable offence, given that you had knowledge of the inefficacy of the electronic monitoring program.'

'So you had to go up against Myra.'

'It made all the difference. Stopped them dead. Mr. Seville took it badly. He became quite heated because it sufficiently refracted his case against you to make all his audit work for naught. And as you feared, he started talking about rebuilding his information into a disciplinary action against your supervisor. It's too bad it worked out that way. Sorry.'

'Oh don't sweat it too much, Lance.' Barry was jovial. 'You might be a damn smart lawyer and I might be some kind of wimpy afraid-to-win civil servant, but there's a thing or three you don't know about government work.'

'What are you saying?'

'Don't worry about Myra, she's not losing her job. Quite the contrary. She's going to the top. She's been drafted to the show. She's gonna play in the big leagues. They're warming up the jet engines right now to fly her to Ottawa.'

'A promotion?'

'Right you are, counsellor.'

'Incredible.'

'Not at all. It's dynamic management in action. They get rid of her and she's somebody else's problem. I'm going away of my own volition, so I'm nobody's concern. And if anybody wants to know who pays for the slip-ups, the administration points to these "executive decisions" they've taken. Simple and effective. And there's nobody like me or Myra filing union grievances or lawsuits or any other troublesome thing like that. It's all over. So there you go.'

'Well . . .'

Barry pictured Lance doing something lawyerly like taking off his glasses and rubbing his eyes so as to see a complicated concept more clearly.

'Glad I could be of help.'

'Kidding aside, Lance, I am too.'

'Well . . .' Barry could sense Lance's mild mystification at the ease with which this supposedly heavy phone conversation was resolving itself. 'I suppose this is bye for now.'

'For now yes it is, Lance. Maybe we'll do lunch sometime.'

'Lunch? With you?'

'Who else? Of course me. Or don't you keep up with clients?'

The silence over the phone transmitted Barry's answer.

'Well anyway, Lance. Thanks.'

'You're welcome, Mr. Delta. But . . .'

'But what?'

Over the phone Barry could hear the rustle of paper. 'Your colleagues faxed me quite a collection of documents. Intake assessments, psychological results, performance reports, risk assessments, et cetera.'

'Uh huh.'

'And . . .' Lance paused and seemed to be choosing his words carefully. 'As I read it here, Barry, they have quite a reason to complain about you.'

'You don't say?'

'For example . . . did you know that Ms. DeAlbrecht was a lost child, that the last family she knew was as a small child in the home of her grandmother in the Yukon?'

'Yeah, I knew all that.'

'Did you read her eyewitness testimonial regarding the murder of her grandmother at the hands of her stepbrother? There is much detail here about her having observed the repeated rape of her guardian by various family members. There is also a sheaf of autobiographical writings she did for the psychology department outlining her repeated sexual exploitation from so young an age that she literally cannot remember when she was not the object of vaginal and anal rape by virtually all male family and some female. She apparently witnessed the butcher knife murder of a young girl cousin by the girl's mother, who was under the influence of alcohol and drugs at the time. Her mother was found frozen to death in a snow bank when Ms. DeAlbrecht was four years old. She has detailed accounts of foster home abuse, including forced prostitution from the age of eleven. When she was thirteen she was nearly killed by a half-sister in a knife fight. This brought an end to the social services attempts to keep the family together in foster care. At the age of fourteen she was found in the company of biker gang members who were suspected of running an internet sexual slavery ring . . .'

'Yeah yeah . . .' Barry fought to suppress anger. 'Welcome to krekshuns, Lance.'

'Barry, you made me well aware of your work conditions. But now I'm asking you straight out whether or not you were informed of the full presenting problems of this case.'

'I knew most of it.'

'Most of it?'

'And I imagined the rest.'

'That doesn't sound good to me.'

'Who cares? There's not going to be an inquiry.'

'Nevertheless. I have to say I'm appalled.'

'Well. Be appalled all you want. Outside of a courtroom, you won't ever have to deal with these people.'

'I'm concerned that those who do aren't practising due diligence.'

Barry stifled a bitter laugh.

'Did you know . . .' Lance further made paper noises over the phone. 'Did you know about the ritual abuse?'

'Hey . . .' Barry contemplated hanging up. 'I wouldn't be surprised at anything Chantal's family got up to.'

'I'm talking about your robbery offender. He was a ward of the Ontario child protection services at the age of seven. He spent a year in the Hospital for Sick Children recovering from various torture-related injuries, malnutrition and psychological disorders. Investigators found that he was the offspring of cult members who committed mass suicide before they could be prosecuted. When he was a teenager he spent several terms in juvenile detention for the mistreatment of animals. He skinned a dog alive and made a video of it . . .'

'Yeah yeah yeah, Lance, I know all about the atrocities. Is this going anywhere? Because if you knew anything about me you'd know I'm the last guy who needs to hear this.'

'There's more.'

'Grotesqueries? I've heard them all.'

'How about this? Three-and-a-half years clean.'

'What?'

'Your man received intensive therapy while incarcerated and responded well. He sought and maintained a relationship with a psychology professional after release and had only recently broken it off. He was gainfully employed and apparently thought he could handle life without his psychotropic medication. He was doing well, Barry, relatively well.'

Lance's last sentence had been delivered in a tone above and without the calm level the lawyer usually reserved for professional exchanges.

Barry was startled by it. 'Yeah.' He collected himself. 'Them's the breaks.'

'He could have been saved.'

'Oh yeah.' Barry hung up the phone. 'We can all be saved.'

[25]

STILL SMARTING FROM his exchange with Lance, Barry was lined up ordering coffee when his cell phone warbled. He saw by the readout that the number was a police local.

'Detective Bill. How are you?'

'The shits and so are you.'

'Thanks for the good wishes.'

'Nevermind the kibitz. Are you someplace you can talk?'

'I'm just paying for a coffee.' Barry shoved change in his pocket and grabbed his Colombian blend, cradling the phone on his shoulder. 'I'll go outside.'

'Keep walking when you get there. Come right to the station. We've got trouble with that crazy pair of yours from the bus.'

Barry was on the sidewalk. 'What?'

'They're down here threatening to bring in the TV cameras because we haven't made an arrest or acted on any of the tips their wacky posters scared up.'

'I thought those were all gone.'

'They are but they nevertheless got some people who think they recognize the picture or some such guff. The media is this close to jumping on it. Thus the chief is involved. He's now on our ass to get somebody and because I happen to know who it actually is I gotta ask you to get your particular ass over here right now.'

Barry stood, planted on the sidewalk, thinking feverishly. He rued the idea of re-calling Lance Pithorn. 'What if I take a pass on that?'

'Don't get me going, Barry. Just do as I fucking say to the fucking letter. If you get over here right now I think I can defuse the whole abortionate debacle once and for all.'

'You think so?'

'All the crazy bitch wants is an apology. She knows you wouldn't get badly nailed in court. She just wants to know somebody did something to somebody in a legal way and she gets her satisfaction and walks the hell away. Her and that numb-nuts boyfriend of hers.'

Barry let Bill's words go by, still trying to see the situation clearly.

'Are you listening to me?'

'Yeah I'm listening all right . . .' Barry switched the coffee from one stinging hand to the other, juggling the phone. 'This sounds like a job for super-lawyer. I just kissed off my legal pit-bull. I guess I'll have to call him right back.'

'Oh fuck Barry you haven't listened to a thing I've said. If you lawyer-up we'll have to nail your ass so hard it'll make your chest hairs fall out. We'll come at you so dirty you'll have to stand in a carwash for a week. We'll be the ones getting the TV cameras on you. We'll be painting you up as some kind of psycho-bureaucrat who not only beats people on busses but sabotages the parole system and lets out vicious killers and loonies who slash citizens and commit officer-assisted suicides. We'll tell them about the kid you had killed in prison by that parolee of yours, the one you gave the car to.'

Barry tried not to lurch at the completeness of Detective Bill's information.

'We'll leak it about your crazy go-round with those girl-cops a few years back. I think one of 'em's still in rehab. And that thing with your boss, dead in your car with a murdered hooker. Nobody ever asked you the hard questions about that. That should send the old police-parole official working relationship to hell nice and fast. When we get through with you your name will be shit.'

'Christ man, calm down . . .' Barry sipped coffee. He felt a burn from the only part of his lower lip not nerve-damaged. 'I'm coming, don't worry.'

'You better.'

Barry turned the phone off and took another drink of coffee, slow this time so as not to burn himself. He let the flow of pedestrians waft around him. As he levelled the cup and started moving he was aware of two black-clad presences hulking on either side. He looked to both of them, smiling. 'That was fast.'

'Thanks.' One of the cops stepped in front of him, sneering.

'Let me guess, the old cell phone receptor triangulation trick.'

The other cop put a huge hand on Barry's arm. 'That, plus the fact your office is just down the street.'

Barry looked around and saw a patrol car stopped in a bus zone. 'Oh well. At least I get to ride in comfort. Can I keep my coffee?'

'Sure.'

The ride was a flurry. In what seemed like seconds Barry was encouraged to exit the police car as it stood idling in the underground police parkade. He climbed the stairs to the reception level alone, pushed open the doors and was greeted by a red-faced, patrol-uniformed Detective Bill.

'Thanks for the lift.'

'Sorry I went so hard. The chief's got me crapping bricks.'

'Am I under arrest?'

'Aw for chrissakes, Barry . . .' The detective guided Barry to a bank of elevators. 'Just come up and apologize to this lady and we can go get some lunch.'

Because they were alone on the ascent Barry could not help himself: 'After we get this done, you can tell me why you fucked me on that surveillance thing. I nearly got nailed on that, you know.'

Bill's face turned slightly more crimson, but he said nothing. The elevator doors opened. 'I'll fill you in as soon as we piss on this particular fire.' He led Barry into a conference room.

Barry had met the chief of police on a couple of occasions, mostly Christmas parties and other schmoozeramas, but had no reason to believe that such a busy man might remember him. The two men nodded to each other when introduced.

Barry was not introduced to the bald-headed couple. Though more than four months had passed, he immediately recognized them from the bus incident.

The woman glanced at Barry, rolled her eyes in disgust, then turned to the police officers. 'And who is this supposed to be?'

Regardless of the time that had passed, and the relative brevity of their encounter, the shrillness of her voice and the placidity of her male companion during her speech were indelible on Barry's mind.

'Well . . .' Detective Bill cleared his throat. 'This is the man who was on the bus at the time of the incident you described.'

'Oh no he's not.'

Her ardent tone quieted the room.

'But . . .' Detective Bill stared at Barry. 'I thought you . . .'

Barry contemplated a retort, a growling guilty plea to express both the truth, his attitude toward the proceedings, and especially this woman. But then inspiration struck and he reasoned that it might be better not to help incriminate himself with a sampling of his voice. He opted instead for a puzzled shrug.

'Come on, Barry.' Detective Bill was irate.

'Bill.' The chief spoke quietly. 'Why is Mr. Delta gracing us with his presence this fine morning?' Barry noticed that the senior cop's smile was strained nearly to the point of reddish explosion.

'Well sir, he . . .' The detective twitched his gaze from Barry to the chief and back to Barry. His eyes hardened. He turned back to his boss. 'I have information to indicate that he is the particular individual who was involved in the alleged incident.'

'And what evidence do you have to suggest this?'

'He admitted it to me. Over the phone. At the time of the postering business. There was a picture of him. Remember, we arrested a guy who is on his caseload.'

The chief turned to Barry. 'Did you confess to this bus business, Mr. Delta?'

Barry issued the barest, mumbling "Nope" and shrugged again.

'Wait a minute.' Detective Bill's colour was even more acutely fire engine. He turned to the two complainants. 'Take a good look. Are you sure this isn't the man who attacked you?'

'Allegedly attacked.' The chief was quick with the lawsuit-averting qualification.

'I don't believe it.' The woman sniffed. 'What kind of dummies do you think we are?' She gazed again in Barry's direction. He felt her sweep his battered features, check out the purple-black bruise on the back of one hand. When he dared meet her eyes they expressed a softened, compassionate attenuation toward him. 'The thug who attacked us was straight looking and well kempt. Given his behaviour his look was deceptive. Like a family man or something, but full of frustration and sexism and hatred. This unfortunate soul is obviously some vaguely similar-looking street person you dressed up to put on this charade.'

Detective Bill threw up his hands. 'But there's a video you say looks like the man who attacked you. I happen to know that that man and this man . . .' Bill swung his arm widely to point a stiff-fingered accusation at Barry. 'This man here, are the same man.'

The woman sighed and looked to her companion. 'Arno, can you believe this?'

Arno had been peering at Barry. 'This ain't the guy, Sheri.'

'Who brutalized this man, anyway?' Sheri turned to the chief. 'What kind of deal has been made here? What has this . . . Mr. Delta, if that's a real name, got to gain? Is this some kind of perverted use of a police beating victim?'

The chief grimaced.

Detective Bill collapsed back in his chair and rolled his eyes ceilingward.

Barry smiled and shrugged still again, fighting a nearly irresistible impulse to quip something clever.

Seconds later he was being escorted down the elevator by his two cop kidnappers and Detective Bill. They crowded him, seeming to make sure he felt dwarfed and outweighed by a fatal margin. He recalled his parolees' stories of physical assault at the hands of jailers in police elevators. He glanced nervously at the deep dents in the walls of the car.

'Forget favours.' Bill had calmed down and de-reddened but his voice was diamond-hard. 'Forget lunches. Forget interdepartmental cooperation. If I ever see you even so much as do a U-turn, Delta, it's gonna be shoot-to-kill.'

'Good policy. Consistent.'

'None of your smart talk.'

The elevator doors opened. Barry glared back at the faces of the cops, then slipped past them and walked toward the street exit. He nearly bumped into a TV van unloading at the front. He turned reflexively and sped away.

Barry took a cab back to the office. He arrived just in time to pick up the phone.

'Barry Delta here.'

A second of silence unsettled him and then he knew who would speak.

'Barry . . .'

'Tanya. How are you?'

'Fine. Are you recovering?'

'Yeah, I guess. But not very fast. People still find it hard to recognize me.'

'Oh my god.'

'Don't sweat it. It's not so bad. I mean, it hurts some but there are advantages.'

'Advantages?'

'Yeah. It's subtle but . . . well, it's a drawn-out explanation. Perhaps better left.'

'I agree.'

'So . . . how're ya getting along?'

'Fine. I came to see you in the hospital. Do you remember?'

'I don't remember much of anything. I vaguely recall. I had a pretty bad brain bruise. I have trouble distinguishing things that happened from things that were a dream. And the drugs they give you in that place. Wow.'

'What happened?'

'I got beat up.'

'I know that much. Where were you? What were you doing?'

'Look ah . . .' Barry closed his eyes, concentrating. He knew what she was actually asking. 'The details aren't important.'

'I don't believe that. I'm starting not to believe anything you say.'

'That's good. You shouldn't. It'll be the first step on your road to recovery. For what it's worth, I don't believe you, either.'

'About what?'

'That you're fine. You say you're fine but nothing could be further from the truth.'

'How do you know?'

'I was married to you for ten years, remember? I know when you hurt.'

'Well . . .' Barry thought he heard a sob and hoped it was something else. There was uncomfortable silence. Then Tanya spoke: 'What are you going to do about it?'

It was Barry's turn to be silent. Finally: 'What am I going to do about it?' The question hung. Then he decided to let the floodgates part: 'How stupid is that?'

She did not reply.

'After all that's gone on. After all the talking we've done. It's pretty obvious things are finished, don't you think?'

'But we haven't even really tried.'

Barry stifled a laugh. 'Tanya. For crying out loud, woman . . .' He rued his developing state of tongue-rigour, and tried to loosen himself by coughing.

'Are you all right?'

Barry took this as a query on the state of his soul.

'Tanya, I'm so far from all right you have no idea.'

'Don't forget Barry. I was married to you for ten years too.'

'And you never knew about the girlfriends, did you?'

'Girlfriends?'

'My girlfriends. Lots of them. I had a regular stable.'

'You mean female friends you had. I know some of them.'

'Secret ones. Mistresses. Sex partners. Relationships of many aspects and depths. I can't believe you had no suspicion.'

Her weeping became audible.

But later on, trying to get paperwork done, Barry opted to answer the ring on the off chance it might be Rikki. Though he'd seldom used it, he rued now the government's decision not to install call-display on their inside phones.

'Barry Delta here.'

'Hiya Barry Delta there.'

'Jill!' Barry had the phone crooked in his shoulder, his fingers still typing. 'What the heck can I do for you?'

'Good question.'

'Why didn't you come and see my wrecked body in the hospital? I cried every night you weren't there.'

'I can't stand those places. Ever since my mother died.'

'Oh.' Barry stopped typing. 'I'm sorry.'

'It was years ago. I'm okay. I just don't like hospitals.'

'Well, we agree on that. Unless you're high on morphine, then you don't care.'

'So they beat you up bad, huh?'

'Somewhat. They messed up my face, darn 'em.'

'I hear you're pretty rugged-looking now.'

'You might say that.'

'Well . . .'

Barry detected a drawing in of breath.

'Well indeed.'

'So . . . what do you want to do now?' Jill's voice nearly jiggled into giggledom.

'Huh?' Barry was caught puzzled. 'I don't think we have any cases in common anymore. Besides I don't think I'm coming back . . .'

'Should we have lunch sometime?'

The question, as presented by the lovely Jill in a water-singing-on-stones-in-a-Japanese-garden type voice, lulled and welcomed Barry. In fact, it stirred his heart, cleared his most isolated blood vessels, made him more alive than he thought he would be this day. For a few seconds he allowed himself to buzz, fondly comparing the feeling to a morphine rush. But when he opened his eyes and made to form words in answer he got tough with himself and firmed his gut to say: 'Hey, thanks. But no.'

'Oh?'

Jill's surprise sounded to him as genuine as his own.

'I got a girl right now. Darn it.'

'Oh.' She let an intake of breath punctuate the emphatic pause. 'How sad for me.'

'Jeez Jill, you're a babe. And a sweetheart. It's too bad. Another time. Another place. Any other time or place . . .'

'Well . . .' Her voice descended. 'Maybe we can just talk about work.'

'Atta girl.'

'Let me see. Oh, I know, how would you say Chantal's case could have been better handled?'

'Huh? You want an assessment or something?'

'I don't know. I have this creepy feeling we did something wrong. Or not enough things right.'

'You're the second person today who's asked that kind of question. I just had some lawyer try to allege I didn't know what I was doing.'

'Really?'

'Yup. Wanted to know if I knew how bruised and abused she was.'

'Well, did you?'

'Let me put it this way. I read the file, but not all of it and what I did read I didn't read carefully. I might not have completely winged it, I've been around along enough to know the general score, but if I was younger and more eager and full of life I might have worked a bit harder on her.'

'Whew. You make it sound so futile. What value can we get from having participated in all this?'

'Heck, that's easy. Chantal taught us all the lesson not to be born poor and socially marginalized.'

'I know you're not that jaded, Barry. You're not really that brusque.'

'Thanks. I'm glad you know me. Besides, I think I have the definitive statement on Chantal. She was especially instructive to men.'

'How so?'

'She graphically illustrated the danger of being insolent to hookers.'

'You are so weird, Barry.'

'I'll take that as a compliment.'

Her sigh once again descended.

Barry noted the time showing on his computer clock. He calculated how late he would be getting to dinner at Rikki's.

When Jill spoke again her voice was as mellow as ever he had heard it. 'Are you sure about this . . . other person?'

'Yeah.' Barry shuddered, collecting all his strength. 'For now.'

'Okay.'

'Well, it's not exactly okay, Jill. But leave it at that.'

'Okay. Well. See you around.'

'I sure hope so.'

And then Barry didn't let himself think anymore but kept typing like the wind and the resultant mind-squeeze nearly shrunk his brain. His fingers quavered over the keyboard. He wondered if it was just that he was so eagerly exerting, or maybe it was a hangover from the injuries, but when he finally finished the last report he had to strive not to let his eyes get misty. He slowly locked up the office and carried out his belongings in a plastic shopping bag. There had been a shift change at the front and the new commissionaire did not know him. There was thus no farewell, and the smokers on the sidewalk paid him no notice. His pace on the way to the subway was slow.

But as he sat in the whizzing car as it emerged from the tunnel under downtown, and climbed like an airplane over False Creek, the sight of waterfront and moored sailboats began to ease the weight from his forehead. On the barrelling transit over the industrial lands and into the cool green of the railroad ravine he was feeling fine. He even rejoiced in the ruffling of greenery on the trees as the car sped by.

Prancing up Rikki's street Barry was elated. Dinner together was a twice-weekly affair, dependent on her nights off. Barry celebrated again his good fortune.

Tonight it would be blackened snapper with citrus. Sautéed asparagus. Garlic new potatoes. She had cooked for him too and was good at it. She seemed to like it just as well when Barry cooked, so things were going well as far as each were concerned.

He tended to the snapper as she pulled a bottle out of the fridge.

'Wine?'

'Naw . . .' Barry wielded a knife and measured the asparagus stems. 'I gotta go see a crook after dinner.'

'Just as well.' She replaced the bottle and found a screw-top bottle of mineral water half-full in the door. 'I'm going to have to lay off. Maybe for good.'

Barry twigged. 'Oh?'

She poured the fizzy water into two glasses. 'It's not abuse related.'

'I already know that much.'

Rikki picked up the glasses and offered one to Barry. 'A toast.'

Barry took the glass. 'How thoughtful.'

'To the end, maybe, of a long run at the parole service.'

'Here here.' They drank.

Rikki looked at him with not quite so beaming a smile as he expected. 'There's another thing.'

'What's that?'

'I'm pregnant.'

In his mind of minds Barry had known there would come a day in his life when this line was spoken to him. He had been determined not to react as if it were weighted with lead and fallen a great height. He made an effort not to fumble the knife in his hand.

'Uhh . . .'

'I'm sorry.'

'Wait a minute. Whoa . . .' Barry carefully laid the vegetable chopper on the cutting board. 'Are you sure?'

'Fairly. These home tester things are supposed to be pretty reliable. I go to my GP tomorrow.'

'Yeah.' Barry looked downward. 'Well. I guess our wild first time, that dream I had, the unprotected wham-bam . . .'

'Please, sweetie . . .' She went to him.

They hugged hard. He tried not to get moisture from his hands onto her blouse. They unclasped and Rikki looked at him squarely. 'We both did this.'

'Of course.'

Silence. Barry hoped he did not haunt her vision too grimly. He searched within himself to connect with the positive side of the situation and then took it. 'I never thought this would happen.'

Rikki shook her head slightly and stepped back to slip up onto a high stool. 'I don't know what I thought.'

'But look at you.' Barry stepped away and swept his arms wide. 'I'd know that glow anywhere.'

'Where have you seen it?'

'On pregnant women.'

Rikki's smile rewarded him. 'How do you distinguish a healthy rosiness from simple amusement at the sight of you?'

Barry made a show of wincing at her jab. 'I just do.'

'You lie so well, Barry.'

'And of course we share a sweet secret.'

'That's a cute way of saying it.'

'Better than saying you're preggers. Or knackered. Or up the stump.'

'Knocked right up. That's what I am.'

No elegance for you, Barry thought, referring to himself. Casually, ignoring how Rikki's candour chagrinned him, he further tried the positive route: 'There's supposed to be some joy here.' He conjured a goofy grin. 'I read about it.'

'Don't try to be funny.'

'I'm serious.'

'Well, try to be cool, or something. We have options.'

'Sure we do, but let's just sit down and consider here. Let's try to bottle this moment and put it on the table in front of us.' He joined her at the counter and perched atop the other stool. 'There's no rush.'

'No. Well . . . yes and no.'

'No. Definitely no.'

'Barry, do you know what you're talking about?'

'Likely not, but I'm going to pretend as much as I can. First things first. Do you think we should go ahead and have this kind of talk before you see your doctor?'

'We can have it any time we want. It doesn't make much difference.'

'Why doesn't it?'

'I can tell . . .' Rikki leaned forward and touched his forehead with hers. 'There's someone inside me.'

Barry had to think hard. 'I like you a lot.' Despite the stressed talk, he enjoyed the citrus-sweet scent of her hair.

She straightened. 'And I do you.'

'We could have a long-term thing.'

'Thank you for that much.' She cleared her throat. 'I could keep this baby, you know.'

'Uhhh . . . lemme think.'

'We'll both think, Barry.'

'Let's think more, and faster.'

They sipped water. Barry began to account in his head the amount of time that had passed. 'Let's see, you're what? Seven weeks or so?'

'We still have time.' Rikki's expression turned grave. 'Or none at all, depending on how you see things.'

'I don't know what that means.'

'I'm thirty-six. I may never have a child—'

'Look . . .' His interruption came off more harsh than he wanted but he could not help himself. 'I pledge to see you through this experience, either way.'

'Thank you, but I don't know for sure. Which way to go.' She shook her head. 'Anyway, I'm talking more about myself.'

'About yourself. Okay. Exactly how much thinking have you done about this?'

'Not all that much. But right now I don't want to do it.'

'It?'

'You know. A termination.'

'I've gotten too used to the word "abortion". Thanks for not using it.'

'Well, whatever. I don't want to.'

'I don't blame you. It must be a hell of a thing.'

'It's not the procedure. That's simple. I've had it done before.'

'Oh. I didn't know that.'

'Well, I have.'

'There's so much we don't know about each other.'

'Yes. Anyway . . .' Rikki spoke tentatively, as if waiting for Barry to contribute. 'I just right now decided I wanted to talk about not doing it.'

'Okay.' Barry looked out her kitchen window. 'We can talk about it.'

She reached to turn his face so that she could look him in the eyes. 'Are you afraid?'

'Of course. I'm afraid of everything. Scared spitless.'

'So am I.' She looked away.

Barry was relieved. He stared out the window again and after a time said: 'I've made so many mistakes.'

'Uh huh.'

He looked to her. 'You're not going to politely disagree with me?'

'Oh far be it . . .' Rikki bore into him with hardening eyes. 'I wouldn't want to contradict what a man obviously holds close to his heart. If you need to classify yourself as a screw-up and eternally whip yourself then go ahead. I don't want to try to change you or even help you. I don't know if I can. I'm considering having your child, though.'

'Sorry. I'll try to buck up.'

'You better.'

'God, I can't stand this.'

'I noticed, don't worry. Now say it straight and out loud what you think about parenthood. Have you even thought about it?'

'I've thought about it plenty.'

'Well then, maybe you've felt the same way as me.' Rikki's words were growing in volume and assurance. 'You're not so young anymore either.'

'True.'

'You may never have a child.'

'That's right.'

'You're sitting here with me and there's a baby inside me. Perhaps it's time to think again about parenthood.'

'Believe me, I have thought about it. Mostly, I was a parent of a group of adult children for almost twenty-five years. I fear fatigue, if you know what I mean. And what a pair we are. You're a waitress in a blues bar. I'm a broken-down social worker with no future. Between us all we have is rent bills, aching joints and a beat-up old car. You have an ex-husband and I have an ex-wife and all I can think about is how bad I want a drink of scotch.' Barry patted her middle and smiled acidly. 'Is this sounding anything like a pro-social birthright for our young'un here?'

'That's not all there is. I know what's what.'

'Sometimes you don't sound like it.'

'Sometimes you try to sound like a dead-eye drunk who pretends to be some kind of a noble loser but really just hasn't got the guts to live up to his potential.'

'Whoa, psychology!'

'You should talk.'

'Oh come on . . .' Barry gulped water in an effort not to snap back at her. He shifted his stool to be nearer. 'After all. This is the kind of thing that makes some people insanely happy.'

Rikki brightened. 'Yes.'

'So. Where are we?'

'Where are we?'

'Have we decided?'

'I don't know.'

Barry sighed. 'Man . . .'

Rikki had darkened back down. 'More than anything else, I'm just wondering.'

'What about?'

'When are you going back to her?'

'To who?' Barry winced and understood. 'Absolutely no way. Completely not. I talked to her today as a matter of fact. It was pathetic. She's still looking to me to make her feel better.'

'She's your wife. What's wrong with that?'

'She's my soon-to-be-ex-wife and better off without me. I mean, I didn't tell her this but, every day since I left her I've felt better. I really have. Maybe you haven't noticed because you didn't know me, other than as a bar waitress, through my dark years, but everything is opening up for me. I have a spring in my step. I'm crazy and loving it. And more and more every day.' Barry paused, uncertain, for the sake of decency, how exuberant he should be. 'Am I being cruel again?'

'Only to her.'

'And besides, she's supposed to be so smart. If she had half a brain she'd know I'm the last person in the world to make anybody feel better.'

Rikki smiled again. 'Oh, I don't know . . .'

'You would if you'd heard me telling her about my years of infidelity.'

'You really told her?'

'I did. In as cruel terms, I now realize, as I could. And I'm sorry.'

'It's not the sort of thing a person wants to hear at all. Cruel or not. It's all cruel.'

'Yes, it is. And I've got to stop living in it. I've got to stop being cruel.'

'Can you?'

'I think somebody asked me that recently. I've been thinking I'd sure like to try.'

'I hope so.'

They ate, the conversation dying down. Over cups of tea Barry enjoyed the golden hue of sundown visible through Rikki's kitchen window. He stretched to see the shadowy freighters in English Bay, their dark hulks evocative, for him, of a world beyond his own. He became aware of her staring at him. 'You know. It kind of makes you more attractive. The scars.'

'Nice to know.' Barry spoke easily, relieved.

'I'm serious. Lots of women go for rugged men. You're rugged now. Boy are you ever.'

'They're going to put that cheekbone back where it belongs. They promised. And the scars will recede. They say in about a year I might look like my old self.'

There was time before she spoke again. 'Are you going to be your old self?'

Barry took an equal amount of time to answer. 'I sure hope not.'

[26]

AFTER DINNER, BARRY aimed the car westward toward the posh district and noted the block numbers until he turned off into a quiet tree grove in Shaughnessy. He pulled up to a less-than-well-kempt mansion with a circular driveway and large, unused parking area. Ever the servant, Barry parked on the street and walked to the building. He found walkways at the side and followed one. When he knocked at the appointed door and a bespectacled Wayne Stickner Jr. opened it, he had nearly forgotten what had been haunting him.

'Hey, come on in.' Wayne stepped aside.

Barry peered at him, stepping past. 'You look all scholarly.'

'I was reading.'

'Nice neighbourhood.'

'I lucked out.' Wayne shut his door. 'Holy hell!' He peered at Barry's face.

'I know.'

'They did a number. Somebody was demonstrating something.'

'I'm lucky to be able to add two and two.'

'Could you before?'

Barry chuckled. 'Good point.'

'Did they get the guys?'

'Never will. It was random as the wind.'

'The way you look, you'd be right at home in the joint.'

'Hmmm, nice to know. I guess.' Barry sniffed the air. 'What's that smell?'

'Hey, that's an aroma, man.'

Barry followed his nose into the apartment, through the nearly empty living room and into the kitchen. 'Aha. Campfire stew.'

'Guess nobody can fool you.' Wayne took a wooden spoon from the sink and stirred the simmering mixture in its Dutch oven. 'Standard permanent rations for a writer.'

'And most cons, as I recall.'

'Well I'm trying to leave that part behind.'

'Sorry. I won't mention it again. 'Specially since I'm about to do the same thing.'

'So it's true what we hear.' Wayne swung a kitchen chair before Barry slung himself over another. 'You're hanging it up.'

'Yup. Pulling the pin . . .'

'Folding your tent.'

'Saying goodnight.'

'Burning the bridge.'

'Well . . .' Barry halted the game. 'I hope not that radical. But I'm thinking I'm not going back.'

'What's the plan?'

'Retirement, eventually. But first I gotta get over this beating I took.'

Wayne's expression went grim. 'They did a good job.'

'Yup.'

'The cops got any idea at all?'

'Just kids. Kicked me in the face a bunch of times. Took forty bucks. Lucky they left some of my brain behind.'

'The babes are gonna like your new tough-guy look, once you catch up with it.'

'Oh, man, I hope not. I've been in the damnedest trouble.'

'What? With women?'

'Uh huh.'

'Pussyhound, eh?'

'You could say that.'

'Well . . . we all got our vices.'

'Right you are.' Barry looked around. 'What's yours?'

'Right now it's my job. I totally lucked out.'

'Sounds like.'

'They even got me this apartment. The guy who runs the press knows the guy who owns the house. Got me a deal. I'm working off the first month's rent until I get a paycheque.'

'What exactly do you do around there?'

'Copy editing right now. They liked my prison manuscript and signed me to a contract. They liked it so much they let me work on it on-site. When the guy found out I didn't have a place to stay or a job he got some people in his office going and made a place for me at the company and got me the keys to this place. That day, for chrissakes. It was a miracle. I mean, I couldn't write it up straight and have anybody believe it. Talk about things falling into place.'

'Sounds like your life got charmed as soon as I was out of it. I never did find out how that business went of your getting popped for cleaning off those posters for me.'

'Oh the cops did their usual shit, trying to figure out what else they could get me on, but they chilled right out as soon as you talked to them.'

'Oh hell, that reminds me. Stay low, okay? I used up more than a few favours over this whole bus assault thing. My name is shit. The cops, at least one in particular, are pissed supreme at me. I wouldn't put it past them to lean on you, just to piss me off.'

'Message received.' Wayne looked grim. 'Gonna leave town?'

'I dunno. There's a lot of things I don't know. If you want, I'll keep you posted.'

'For sure. I need you to read my story. Dad's in it.'

'I can do that.'

'So are you.'

'God, how pathetic.'

Wayne appeared to ignore Barry's self-assessment and stood up to the stove to do more stirring. 'Hey, this stuff's ready. Want some?'

'Naw. Thanks. Just ate.'

Wayne scooped himself some dinner and sat at the table.

Barry watched him eat. 'Seriously though, I don't know what you could write about us guys that anybody would want to read.'

'Don't sweat it. It'll all make a terrific story when I collect it all up. The stuff about you and Dad particularly.'

'What stuff?'

'Oh hell it's slick stuff. The money, the fights, the barf in your car . . .'

'Oh man! Don't write all that stuff down. The parole service'll come after me for sure.'

'I'll disguise your identity.'

'How the hell would you do that?'

Wayne smiled with his mouth full. 'I don't know but I'll do it.'

'You fuckin' well better . . .'

Barry chuckled.

And it was perhaps this exchange or the whole of the exchanges Barry had had with Wayne and even with Wayne senior and perhaps, he considered, it was all of the exchanges he'd had with all the thousands of offenders over the decades that struck him as so funny because Barry's mirth or perhaps his hysteria infected itself inside him acutely and he guffawed along with Wayne Junior for many minutes and then he resumed a solo chortle that lasted a longer time. Perhaps, he mused, this was the ticket, the passage: Hilarity.

The element with which he was to survive the resumption of his life.

Barry sobered slightly and looked around Wayne's kitchen again and then back at Wayne, eating. 'You're pretty settled, aren't you?'

'Yup.' Wayne answered between bites.

'Anything at all you need?'

'Girlfriend.'

'Can't help you there. Good luck, though.'

'Thanks.'

'Anything else?'

'A little history.'

'You have a history. You told it to me yourself.'

'Not mine.' Wayne stopped shovelling stew and settled eyes on Barry. 'Yours.' He went back to spooning his dinner, but did not take his gaze away.

'My story?' Barry shifted in his chair. 'Hah.'

'Hah yourself.'

For Barry the short silence thereafter became instantly uncomfortable. 'I guess you want some kind of quid pro quo . . .'

'You could say that.'

'Some kind of symmetry.' Barry knew he sounded now like a man mumbling to himself.

'I think I need it to balance my own story.' Wayne said. 'I'd like it, anyway. I mean, of course there's no obligation, you're the boss. But I told you mine . . .'

'And you maybe might get some good from comparing?'

'Something like that.'

'Well I don't know if it would conform to any kind of formal psychology.'

'Who cares?' Wayne ate and smiled at Barry. 'We're near to our ending. I think it's time.'

Barry smiled. 'I guess you think you're going to need it for my unauthorized biography.'

'Maybe that too. But think about it . . .' Wayne put aside his emptied bowl. 'It might make you feel better.'

Barry tried not to let this comment show its effect on his face. By the look on Wayne's, he could see that whether he had or not, it would make no difference.

'Now?'

'Sure. We have time. Don't we?'

'I guess so.'

They sat quietly.

'Aw forget it.' Wayne lightened and threw up his hands. 'It's just me being a goof.'

'No no . . .' Though uncomfortable, Barry found that he was saddened by the notion that he might not do as Wayne was so bravely requesting. In fact he felt strangely anxious to do so. 'It's okay.' He waved a hand. 'I think it fits. It's entirely legit, in fact.' As an afterthought, Barry added: 'You're a damn good guy, Wayne. And a sit-down like this with a guy like you is something I can say with certainty has never happened in my career. In all those times, I never felt unperturbed like I do. Maybe it has something to do with the fact this is likely the last act I will do as a parole officer. So it deserves something special, I guess. Something unique.' He spoke this without looking at Wayne, but cleared his throat, considering a place to begin, settled his eyes to the floor and began, eager to interrupt the disquieting silence in the room. 'I've never told this, but it's pretty damn simple . . .' Barry's voice caught.

'I'm the son . . .' The utter weight of beginning a story he had never told twigged an ache in Barry's head not unlike a muscle spasm. It stopped him. He cleared his throat again, leaned forward and cradled his head in his hands. 'I'm the son of a guy who grew up in difficult times and felt hard done by. We could have grown up together . . .'

Barry stopped talking because he knew he would be tearful if he continued. For some reason, though he had just now revealed all that was in him to the last person he would ever have thought he would have, he did not wish to weep openly. He simply added: 'But we didn't.'

Wayne had slowly aimed his gaze toward the floor. He looked up. 'Yup.'

Neither man spoke for some minutes. Then Barry rose and buttoned the front of his sport jacket. Wordlessly they made for the door.

On Wayne's front step they shook hands, meeting solidly in the eyes. Barry knew this was as near to an appropriate time for a manly, reassuring hug as he would ever get with a parolee, but the seconds between them wavered and then the moment was gone. A missed opportunity for some kind of epiphany, perhaps. Given their respective histories, Barry was not surprised.

[27]

THREE DAYS LATER, Barry loaded Rikki's Honda with food for a daytrip and clothes for a possible overnight, gassed up, and checked the oil.

He pulled in front of Rikki's building. She was dutifully packed and collected at the sidewalk. The sight of her, efficient and grim, pushed Barry's heart. Though faintly sickened, with the last whiff of spirit left in him he powered up a smile and managed a wave to her through the windshield.

He got out of the car, gripped her bag and her at the same time. 'Ready to go, sweetheart?'

'With you, anywhere.' Rikki's voice was brave, but her eyes were edged by wrinkles he had not noticed before. 'With that smile, anytime.'

'Are you sure?' Barry stepped away from her, still holding her luggage.

'Uh huh.'

'Say, Yes.'

'Yes.'

'Say, Yes, Barry.'

'Yes, Barry, I'm sure.'

He swung her valise into the auto and headed them out, accelerating onto the Oak Street bridge, heading south.

'But I'm awfully sorry.' Rikki uttered the words as they settled to freeway speed toward the border.

'Sweetheart.' Barry spoke with his eyes directly ahead. 'Every phase of my life is smudged with dirt, even the good stuff.'

Rikki wanly watched scenery. 'I wish we didn't have to go out of town.'

'Me too, but I passed by the place again today. You should see it. Idiots wall to wall. I'd be on television again, for sure.'

'God, you've got a history.' She looked at him, then away. 'Why do I always end up with men with histories?'

'It's that fascination with pain and suffering. You're an angst junky. I'd have that looked at if I were you.'

'Well, I'm already having something looked at . . .'

They drove. Barry fought to come up with something to say to her—something comforting or at least compensatory—anything to relieve the tension about what they were doing. But he feared bringing her closer. Times like these brought people together. A strong instinct in him forbid such action. He almost swerved the car, fighting himself.

As they approached the border the sky ahead appeared intent on rain. There was moisture in the air as Barry rolled down his window to speak to the customs officer.

'Citizenship?'

'Canadian.'

'Purpose of the trip today, folks?'

'Uhh . . . tourism. Just down to see the sights.'

'What sights?'

'Seattle, I guess.'

'There's a lot more down there than Seattle.'

'The Space Needle. I've never seen it.' Rikki's voice held the cheery lilt of the perfectly carefree day-tripper.

'Yeah, I'm taking the wife down to see the Space Needle.'

'Well, have yourselves a time.'

'We will.'

As they pulled into America the rain started hitting the windshield. Barry looked to Rikki a few times but there was no further conversation until they were almost into Bellingham.

Finally she cleared her throat. 'I could keep this baby, you know.'

'Uhhh . . . I thought we resolved something about that.'

'Speak plainly please, Barry. I've been reconsidering.'

'Let's think about that.'

Barry steered the car off the freeway at the first city exit and found a drive-in restaurant. They ordered coffee. Barry glanced at the carhop's wristwatch as she roller-bladed away.

'I just right now decided . . .' Rikki spoke tentatively, as if waiting for Barry to contribute. 'I wanted to talk again about not doing it.'

'Okay.' Barry looked across the drive-in lot. 'We can talk again.'

'I know we already more or less decided and you took some time and got the money and we made the arrangements and all that. But this trip's got me thinking.'

'I guess I should have got you to do the driving.'

'Don't try to joke.'

'I didn't think I was . . .' Before Barry could consider what he was doing he gripped the door handle and pulled. He turned to Rikki. Her face hurt him with its fear.

'What are you doing?'

'I don't know.'

He stepped out of the car and pressed-closed the door gently and then leaned against the open sill of the window and looked in at her. At this angle his view was largely aimed at her thighs and heavily socked ankles. She eventually leaned down so that she could look him in the eyes.

'I just need some air.'

She looked ahead and away. 'The coffee's coming.'

Barry swung back into the car as the service came. Then they held paper cups close to their faces and sipped to silence amid the encompassing murmur of the interstate. Barry navigated his beaten face, touching a section of damaged lower lip to the steaming cup to see if there was nerve recovery. There was some sensation that hadn't been there before. He stared directly ahead and said: 'Let's just drive some more.'

'Good idea.'

Barry gulped the rest of his coffee and started the car. 'Where do you want to go?'

'To the fucking clinic. I'm getting an ache in my gut . . .'

They found the place with no trouble. Barry parked near the entrance.

Helping her from the car he held her arm and spoke distinctly: 'Okay, once and for all. Are we going to do it like we said we would?'

'Yes.'

'Okay.'

'Right.'

They strode together through the electric doors and entered a huge waiting area. There was a grove of office plants, low couches everywhere and reading material in racks. The familiarity of it lurched Barry. They reported to the desk and waited until a woman in medical wear appeared. It was at this moment Barry touched Rikki's arm. She twitched as if startled and looked intently into his eyes. The woman said something and she stood looking at Barry and Rikki.

It was a moment before Barry realized something had stalled. 'Pardon?'

'We take cash or credit card. In out-of-town cases, we need payment in advance.' She named a figure.

'I'll go get the cash.' Barry spoke to the woman, but held Rikki's arm and led her to a couch.

'I guess there is the matter of business.' He tried to sound self-possessed. 'I haven't got a card with any room on it. Have you?'

'No.'

'Okay. I just got paid. I'll hit an ATM and get cash.'

'You go. I'll wait here.'

'Are you sure?'

'You'll only be a minute.'

'Well, maybe a couple, but not much longer.'

'No big hurry.'

'Okay.'

When he was out the door, Barry stood with his heart beating hard. There was a hole in the air beside him. He felt it, but didn't know who should be standing there with him. He drove out of the parking lot and down the avenue toward a mall where he'd seen an ATM sign. He strolled in and stood in the short line. He had his bank card ready. There were funds in his account. Enough for an abortion south of the border. Desperado money.

Sad.

Barry snapped awake as someone a'hemmed him toward the unoccupied machine. He pulled money out in uniform US greenbacks and made back for the Honda. Whipping the key out, he looked across the street and saw what he'd seen on the drive in and had thought much about.

Greyhound. The Bellingham Bus Terminal.

Without a break in motion Barry swung his valise from the back seat, slid the key off his key chain and stuck it into the door lock. He slammed the car door. Then he stepped around the vehicle and marched with speed across the parking lot, over a short landscaped patch, onto the sidewalk and then across four lanes of traffic.

Inside the terminal he immediately spied the departures board and saw that most buses were leaving for eastern and southerly routes to the great centres of Montana, Idaho, Oregon and California.

He hadn't thought of where he might go, but since before his beating he'd been thinking of going.

Maybe east.

There was a departure for Spokane in twelve minutes. A mindless road-trip across fields and forests, meals in diners, a plain room in a budget hotel in an anonymous downtown. These images were to Barry in that instant the most paradisiacal manifestations of the mind that had ever enticed him. Then, with determination, he knew he would act.

With a fluttering stomach he bought a ticket and went to the men's room, looked in the mirror a long time, then washed his face.

His face.

The long examination, his deformities and artificial cragginess, was a thing to be suffered. Even two months after the fact, he was not used to the dire mash his face had become.

He looked like . . .

Barry struggled with an appropriate comparison.

A scuzz, a scroat, a street person. A criminal. A caseload type. He feared that the gnarled men coming and going from the washroom would think him dangerously strange. Then he understood that they did not. He concluded that his physical mutilation might be keeping him safe. Hmmm . . . is this face a saving grace? He nearly said the words aloud. Then he did.

'Is this face a saving grace?' Barry guiltily enjoyed the poetic metre. Then he tried hard to consolidate a meaning. There was one, somewhere, he was sure.

Other than this ponderation, Barry was successful for nine of the next ten minutes in not thinking. Then through the direness yanking at him he became aware of another agitation: odour. Barry stood back from the mirror. He was alone in the space by the basins and the mirrors, but by the sound and smell of things, some unseen someone in a far stall was having a terrible shit. The grunt-heavy yearning of it all and the searing stink transfixed him. Repulsed, Barry did not know what to do. Having taken guilty refuge, he felt it was too soon to leave the washroom just yet. But in the next instant a further sewerific wave fumigated Barry face-on and he knew that he could not remain there another second. He unbolted himself from the floor to blast out the swinging door.

Relief was only momentary. As he moved back into the terminal and toward the departure area and the ubiquitous benches and magazine racks he pictured Rikki. The clinic. Her patience. The waiting room. Her alone. Waiting.

He fingered the coin in his pocket he had intended for calling the receptionist to leave the location of the car. He pictured the abortion as he imagined it and had seen it pictured and he pictured much more. He staggered against the coin lockers, a hand extended to steady himself.

He imagined her tears tracking down.

He saw the wet stains on the faces of all of them, every one since it started and every one probably that he would know until someday somehow he would die. Tears, tears, and tears. How fearsome to be responsible for so much weeping. He closed his eyes, hearing the boarding announcement for his bus, fighting to keep his heart in his chest. There was a troubling swirl. His head vortexed, irreversible, sickening, powered—he knew—by a fate-force far beyond him. He squeezed his hands into the metal of the locker door and held on for dear memory. He thought: What do you want?

He quavered and shook, striking the locker with his head. If others around took notice he took none of theirs. He shook himself back and forth, slamming his forehead into the metal. With pain there was no enlightenment. Finally there was only a security guard, peering at him gravely from a few cautious paces away.

He knew he should be taking some kind of action, to go or not. But he could not give up on his struggle to understand. A terrible impact was forming itself, he could feel it, a meteor of understanding, plunging toward the hard vacuum inside him.

His legs trembled, so weak in an instant that he nearly stumbled, standing, at the thought of the encroaching loss. It made his hair stand stiff, his skin turn to frost.

And it struck. A something that penetrated each of his cells and all of his spirit with cold knowing. A something Barry realized he had been avoiding all his life, knew he'd have to embrace someday, wished it wasn't now, regretted it had taken him a half-century. Barry was hit with knowing that he would forsake the shit-smell of his fears and remove himself from this stream of transient humanity and do right by this woman and this approaching baby and himself. Until this moment of naked offence he had not understood just how right indeed he would be. It stopped him with its simplicity and its finality and then he knew he must immediately seek Rikki's warmth.

The lack of it enclosed him in hurt, in and out, on the edge of unbearable.

There were other announcements over the booming PA. Barry barely heard them, staggering ahead, out of the terminal, toward the car and then the clinic and to personhood perhaps, and possibly a chance of redeeming love; feasibly happy, on and on into eternal impulse.

ABOUT THE AUTHOR

Dennis E. Bolen was born in Courtenay, British Columbia, and spent most of his teenage years in the Port Alberni area. He obtained a degree in Creative Writing from the University of Victoria, and a MFA in Creative Writing from UBC.

An associate editor of *subTerrain* magazine from 1990 to 1999, Bolen also worked as a parole officer in Vancouver for more than twenty years. His first novel, about a world-weary, womanizing parole officer on Vancouver's eastside, *Stupid Crimes*, appeared in 1992. A follow-up novel, *Krekshuns*, was released in 1997, and a third novel, *Stand in Hell*, appeared in 1995. Bolen lives in Vancouver.